Cadence of Consequences

Part Two of The Chronicles of Xannia

M.J. Moores

Cadence of Consequences: The Chronicles of Xannia

Copyright © M.J. Moores, 2015

Published by Infinite Pathways Press 2015
P.O. Box 4, Caledon Village, ON Canada L7K 3L3

ISBN 978-1-988044-01-9 Paperback Edition

10 9 8 7 6 5 4 3

The Chronicles of Xannia

The Lost Chapters: Prequal

Time's Tempest

Cadence of Consequences

Rebels Rein

Forgotten Fallacy

Dedication

To you, for being there with Taya every step of the way.

Acknowledgements

This time around I have to thank my extremely supportive husband for allowing me to focus on writing full-time. Having that kind of support opens up not only doors for opportunities in the publishing industry but doors to the creative mind and soul... the place where the magic happens.

I'd also like to thank my two editors, Wendy Lawrance and Melissa Barker-Simpson. These two skilled women helped bring the pages of Cadence of Consequences to life.

Finally, I'd like to thank all of my colleagues both locally and online for your support and enthusiasm.

From the depths of our despair, hope and trust will give us today's truth and tomorrow's strength.

Thank you all.

Chapter One
The Nightmare of Existence

Taya

*T*he metallic darkness hangs thick like air in the bowls of summer. Faint echo-y whispers refract throughout the warehouse growing fainter, then louder – tick, tick tick, tick, tick – multiplying, then dying out altogether to be replaced by... silence? I pull against my restraints, my mind foggy, my thoughts distorted.

I have to concentrate. I yank the handcuffs against the pole; the clang of metal-on-metal ricochets. A quiet chuckle seeps its way into my head, steadily rising in volume forcing the rhythm of my heart and my breathing to match it.

I snap my restraints against the pole. His laughter swirls around me – in my head – through my heart. I hit the cuffs again: smashing, pulling, banging, yanking. The shriek of my scream joins the cacophony of laughter and the reverberation of clanking and crashing...

"No!"

I woke up just as my head smashed against the stone floor beside the couch. My feet tangled in the afghan Gerrund had given me as a house warming gift, five weeks earlier. Low static hummed from the closed-circuit radio on the coffee table. I tried to push myself up in the all too familiar darkness of my living room, but my arms shook and collapsed under me. Tears followed tracts of exhaustion due to dreams, and the avoidance of them. The wet dripped along my neck as I rolled on my back between the couch and the table.

Dez... why the Trinity aren't you here? At least if I'd had a warm body to wake up next to, I wouldn't mind going to sleep at night... would have someone to hold me until the fear dissipated.

I hate this!

Just over a month ago, when Gerrund had me released from the Underground Hospital, he'd anticipated the probability of nightmares – I'd nearly rammed the sleeping pills assigned me down his throat... and now –

I hit the front of the couch with my fist and banged the back of my head against the smooth rock of the floor. I kicked out and thrashed about, ridding my legs of their restraint. My shin smashed against the side of the table.

"Sister Zita—" I cursed.

Pain shot through my leg like liquid fire. I slammed the table with my foot and flipped it. The radio flew across the room. Something else crashed to the floor as the table connected with the bookcase. I let the anger fuel silent sobs as I writhed on the cold floor... alone.

At five in the morning, when the building's generator clicked on, I found myself staring into my bathroom mirror: water dripped from my forehead, nose, and eyelashes. The roots of my hair were beginning to show as the coppery strands of my once black mane hung lifeless around my face. The bleached tips framed a sharper than usual jaw and neck line, making my borrowed pale-pink features look washed out. Even the purple coliths Magda, the body stylist, had so painstakingly perfected five weeks ago looked dull from lack of sleep. The dark bags under my eyes appeared richer and deeper than the once black hue of my irises.

I splashed more water from the simple granite basin over my face, willing its chill to wake me to a point where I could function. Methodically, I rinsed my green contact lenses in their rejuvenating solution before slipping first one, and then the other, back over the last traces of who I used to be. I was no longer Taya Fyce, the now-shattered persona I'd grown up believing in; I couldn't bring myself to be recognised as Jadis Jutaya Doire, my birthright, or even J.J., Gerrund's pet name for me and a throwback to the childhood I had no memory of.

No, the woman with the pink skin, purple wavy coliths, green eyes and bronze hair was now all the world could see of me – Aelonia Trellice – but even she was compromised.

The timer on the coffee pot dinged while I dried my face on the towel near the sink. Folding it neatly, I set it in place before straightening a loose white blouse over my simple black flare-pants. A heady aroma of Insic and sweet-dray wafted in through the small door of the washroom. I let my nose lead me the short distance from the tiny room across the now pristine living space and into the adjoining open concept kitchen. The only delineation in the space was the island counter where two stools sat on the living room side.

The incessant chill of the Underground made me long for the suns above. But I was trapped down here against my wishes, and away from everything that mattered. Gerrund had seen fit to follow Dez's *concern* about my well-being top-side. He'd pressed his advantage with Gerrund to keep me out of harm's way, hidden where no one could find me. Not even Dez, apparently.

My stockinged feet made no sound as I slipped into the kitchen and poured the robust coffee into an equally dark mug. My gaze slid to the digital clock on the coffee maker. It didn't matter that I knew what time I'd set it to, it was the approaching time that I watched for.

Leaning back against the single sink in my small Underground apartment kitchenette, I took a sip of the strong steaming liquid and grimaced. *Still doesn't taste the way it smells.* I wasn't used to the blend they roasted down here. The Insic bean was coarser than coffee and the UG refinery attempted to use sweet-dray to cut the bitterness, but it didn't work. I wasn't about to start adding sweetener to my coffee though, fake or not. I didn't need it in my diet or eating away at my meagre budget.

Gerrund had sent a team of scouts back to my house a few weeks ago, but other than a couple of outfits, there was nothing to show for my years of hard work with the Contractor Training Facility, or the sizable bank account I'd amassed in order to buy my house… which was no longer mine but the bank's, since my mortgage had gone unpaid.

The world thinks I'm dead. But even that wasn't right. The Kronik *believed* I was still alive and that was the problem. That was why I couldn't resurface, even though I'd completely changed my appearance. I'd gone and saved Dez's life at the Rally the Kronik intended as his funeral.

I took another sip of the hot liquid. I would've done without the Underground's version of the caffeinated drink, but I'd decided to try it a couple of weeks ago to help keep me awake at night. The only problem was, the generators shut down at twilight, bathing the hidden subterranean tunnels in near darkness for six hours until true dawn. No power meant no hot, fake coffee and invariably I would drift off into the world of my nightmares.

I pushed back the silky lavender scarf covering the ancient clockwork watch on my wrist. No one in the Underground was permitted a watch-com; Gerrund was convinced the Kronik was tracking the signals and using them as GTDs, Global Tracking Devices. If that were true, having the outlawed tech where the dead lived, and the missing were never meant to be found, wouldn't be a great way of keeping a lid on Gerrund's Underground City.

I sat down on the couch, put the coffee on the table and wound the small dial on the side of the watch before replacing the scarf. I covered over the simple clock-face with the fabric to block out its incessant ticking – a sound I didn't need reminding of in my waking life, too.

Winding was a task I did automatically now, but perhaps more often than necessary – to keep the darn thing from running slow or stopping altogether. Dez had given me the antiquated piece the day he left. A day that had spelled disaster from the moment I'd woken up.

The thought made me grip the mug so tight I risked cracking it.

For three days, Dez had stayed with me at Gerrund's apartment after the Rally bombing. He *promised* he'd see me in a week and gave me the watch as a memento, and to keep track of the time till we saw each other again.

I felt the unmistakable grind of ceramic and forced myself to relinquish the mug to the table.

Pulling a calendar I'd made from under the lip of the coffee table, I slid the clipped pen from the bound pages and then found the current date. With enough force to rip through the page, I crossed off yesterday's square. Flipping back through the five weeks I'd already tracked, I found only one circle amidst the myriad of Xs, which didn't even correspond to Dez's promised week – or the promised life we would lead together *above* ground. I slammed the booklet on the table. The fake coffee sloshed.

"What were you thinking!" I yelled it to Dez, but the echo reminded me I was just as much at fault. I whipped the pen at the mostly empty book shelf. *I sacrificed everything for you.*

Instead of a future together, all I got was a reminder of the empty passage of time and the echo of abandonment. I tore at the knot binding the scarf to my wrist. My fingers fumbled repeatedly and I gave up. Instead, I threw myself back against the couch and stared at the smooth rock ceiling overhead... the rock walls... the equally rocky floors, and shuddered.

Leaning forward, I caught sight of today's date on the calendar. It had a large star drawn around a time. I had an appointment to keep. Snatching the pen off the floor I tucked it, and the calendar, back under the table. My gaze drifted to the deep purple cloak hanging from the rack by the door. Taking another sip of coffee, I scrunched my nose and slid my feet back and forth over the polished floor to try and warm them. As I downed the last of the offensive drink, I turned away from the cloak, and the door, to return to the kitchen and rinsed out my mug.

Today I had to go outside; my first 'daylight' venture since *the incident*. The day Dez left me down here.

Slipping on the shoes Gerrund gave me, after my time in the hospital, made me long for a sturdy pair of work boots. I grabbed the hated handbag dangling from a short strap on the coat rack, along with my ring of mini key-cards, and a couple of chocolates from a shallow dish sitting in a rounded void in the wall by the door.

I reached for the knob and stopped.

With a glance out the spy hole, a modification Gerrund willingly agreed to when I first moved in, I checked the hall. I couldn't see anyone. Nor did I hear anyone walking around. It was safe to leave.

I turned the knob, entered the hall, and locked up before dropping the candy into the mail basket screwed to the front of my door. There were only a few such baskets in existence. The others were for folks who had difficulty getting up and down the stairs.

I was supposed to go to the central mailboxes in the large front foyer. A week after the incident Etain, the landlord, paid me a visit to remind me to check my mail – apparently my box was full and the carrier complained. So, I'd walked down the front flight of stairs with Etain as he headed back to his flat, just off the main entrance.

There'd been a small crowd waiting to get mail. Before I had a chance to see the individual faces of my fellow residents, someone attacked me – someone who knew me. Not as Taya, J.J. or Aelonia, but as something else entirely… the half-breed who helped save a dying sun – a woman who caused an incident at the Chosen One's Underground Rally.

Etain had grabbed my arm and pulled me into his flat before more than a few patches of fabric were ripped from my jumpsuit. I'd sat in a chair in his living room for six hours before the hall cleared and the generators revved the one-hour warning before lights out. Since then, Etain had kindly brought my mail to my door and I'd gladly serviced his sweet tooth as payment. That moment only served to remind me how no one down here understood me. There was too much at risk being seen in public – down here or top-side.

I hurried along the hall past three other residences to the back stairwell carved from the surrounding dark brown rock. It led to a lower hallway inside the building, but more importantly it exited out a back door to the narrow alley, the apartment's side-cavern walkway. Most large dwellings extended down one side of a smaller offshoot from the main cave-system. Mine was a two-storey building, one of the smaller styles available, but there was still plenty of room to walk between the apartment and the far wall of the cave without feeling claustrophobic.

A random pedestrian jogged past the opening at the top of the alley. He looked at me. *Maybe I should've grabbed the cloak.* Then he looked away, never faltering in his pace. *No, I made the right choice. The cloak would only draw attention at this time of day.* I focused on keeping my strides steady as I turned to follow the early morning jogger, rubbing my wrist under the scarf where the old leather band of the antique tech chafed my skin. The rest of the street was blissfully empty. The main tunnel towered five storeys high, and nearly the same distance across, radiating fake sunlight.

I'd changed my appointment three times – not the day, but the time. Magda had originally set it for midday, when her usual clients knew she was on lunch. But after the incident, I changed it to her last appointment of the day. Then, after Etain saved me, I got to thinking that more people were likely to be walking or biking home from work at that time. So, I changed it again to early this morning.

The shops integrated into the side walls of the tunnel were just setting up for the day. Regular employees wouldn't be heading to work for another half an hour and the walk to Magda's salon was only twenty minutes. I forced my shoulders to relax even as my grip on the handbag tightened. I dug my nails into the stiff black cloth, hating that it wasn't a belt-pack, hating that I was dressed in someone else's clothes, in someone else's skin – hating that Dezmind had left me alone down here.

The whole reason I got the make-over was to hide-in-plain sight above ground – to work with Dez on the next phase of world enlightenment… so we could make a difference together. The fact he was on the surface, doing exactly that without me, made me wonder why I bothered to keep up the charade. *But there's always a chance. I might yet convince them enough time has passed. Maybe at the next meeting.*

The majority of the street lanterns flickered and shut down as their energy resources re-directed to the central day-lighting system. The integrated illumination globes made it appear as if the suns shone in this Underground world. Even the smaller three and four storey caverns linked into the central lighting system. Though I knew it was an illusion, walking under the diffused light somewhere other than my tiny apartment, gave my heart a robust rhythm that had been sorely lacking of late.

It had been several weeks since I'd been 'outside', but I didn't dawdle past the shops, stores, businesses, and homes that lined the street. The pittance of credit Gerrund gave me each month just managed my groceries and toiletries, but even then, I sometimes went without deodorant or toothpaste – I never saw anyone anyway, so really, what did it matter?

I reached a large tunnel extending to my right called Major Minor. This was one of only a couple of streets where the artisan of the Underground lived and worked. During my initial transformation in Magda's salon chair, she'd told me that this was the first major tunnel explored after the settling of Centre Street, the road I'd just turned from. At the time, it was considered a minor causeway in the grand scheme of the Underground's development, but due to its popularity with the exiled crafters, the nickname Major Minor stuck. Even though no other passages branched off from this street, it was one of the most frequented locales in the Underground.

Walking beneath a shop sign displaying two mirrored faces, I pushed down on the door handle of an elaborately decorated façade decked out with a technicolour awning and painted figures on the front display window. I opened the salon door and slipped in, unnoticed by the few people purposefully walking up and down the long street.

Magda's stylist shop was about the same size as my apartment, although currently only half of the actual space was visible due to small screened-dividers marking out a floor plan for her employee work spaces. The front was for daily appointments during work hours. The back, where I headed, was for special after-hours customers or important rush-jobs like I'd experienced during my last visit.

When Gerrund brought me here to help me resurface without being recognisable to those in the government looking for me, I had no idea what to expect. Nor had I realised that by saving Dez's life at the Spoken Truth Rally, I'd risk revealing my true identity to the Kronik.

The back door stood open. Magda puttered around in her office. I caught a flash of her hair as she skirted around the items in the cramped work space. Magda's hair, like that of my best friend – *ex-best friend* – Zaith, was a serious statement of fashion. Only, with Magda it was a billboard for her livelihood as well.

I leaned against the doorway waiting for her to notice me as I fought an impending yawn. Resting my head against the door frame, I took in the glory that was my body stylist. Her long hair glistened several different shades. It looked as if her entire head was highlighted using only the metallic hues. The base colour was a deep auburn verging on burgundy, then a hot rust-orange and the same coppery-bronze that she'd used on my hair shimmered as if the suns played over each strand. Lastly, with strategically placed strands, an iridescent pearl gave her an other-worldly appearance – absolutely stunning.

Nobody really knew Magda's heritage, as she apparently changed her skin tone and colith colour every year on the anniversary of her arrival. This year she was as golden as the Beta sun on a clear day with solid black coliths – the naturally occurring S-shaped markings that randomly appeared over all Xannian bodies. Hers was a combination that didn't biologically exist.

I inhaled her light wild-flower scent as she scooted past me for the third time. I finally felt the tension ease from my body. Abruptly, she turned to me.

"Well, come on, girl. I have to open up soon. Plant your rear on the swivel chair and let's get you started." She snapped on a pair of thin, white rubber gloves.

I sighed, loosely ran my fingers through my layered shoulder length hair and flopped onto the black salon chair. Magda turned me around with one hand as she shook a bottle of solution with the other.

"Did we get you up too early this morning?" she teased and tapped a finger to the side of one of my red-rimmed eyes.

"No, I've been up for a while actually." She gave me her "mother" look and I scrambled to clarify. The last thing I needed was to set off Magda's radar and have her innocently mention my lack of sleep to Gerrund. I didn't need him mothering me as well, nor did I want it getting out that something might be wrong with me. Things were bad enough without adding that titbit to the list.

"I have a lot on my mind. Mostly, I'm worried about Dezmind. It's not like him to miss sending a letter."

Magda worked on parting my hair and painting on the solution to cover up my exposed black roots. As much as I needed to watch what I said to Gerrund's close allies, I couldn't help but talk to Magda.

"I want to go home, you know?"

"Yes. We all do. But it's always hardest on new Undergrounders, like yourself."

"But it's different with me, Magda."

"Oh? Why's that?" One of her finely pencilled eyebrows lifted.

"You know my real parents gave me up when I was two?"

"Yes."

"Well, my foster parents – who I thought were my real parents – abandoned me when I was eight. I lived on the streets, fending for myself until I was old enough to apply to work in the mines.

I let them abuse my body for the sake of Zerillitite for five years."

"You worked the mines as a child? Whatever for Ali?"

The new name still felt foreign to my ears. "I didn't trust anyone else to take care of me. My track record wasn't exactly great up to that point." I still didn't trust anyone to take care of me, and yet that's exactly what Gerrund was doing on behalf of Dez.

The thought of it made my teeth ache.

Magda massaged more of the colour into my roots.

"But I was smart enough to know that if I could pay the entry fee for Contractor Training, I could make a good life for myself… and I did. When I graduated just after my eighteenth birthday, I bought my own house. And then I made it a home when I adopted my Lynx, Jadis. One year, Magda."

"One year what?"

"I was happy for one year, before I lost it all."

"Weren't you happy during your training?"

"I was too busy to be happy." The image of Jezetek, my almost first boyfriend from upper-level training, slipped into my thoughts. Then Dez's face superimposed over Tek's. I bit my lip. "I miss him, Magda. More than I thought I would." She set the bottle aside and gave my shoulder a squeeze. "I'm not supposed to be down here."

"None of us are, child… none of us are."

She didn't understand. I wasn't ignorant of the fact that everyone in the Underground was in exile because of what the Kronik thought of them. The difference was, I had allowed Magda to remove every trace of who I was in order to *return* to the surface – but I was still stuck down here *for my own good, for my own protection*… because the men in my life didn't trust me. But I couldn't explain any of that to Magda. She'd take their side.

I looked around her office in the following silence, but nothing was really different from the last time I was here – except maybe the soft leather shoulder bag sitting in the middle of her chair. I was about to divert the conversation and ask her what shop she'd picked it up from, when she spoke.

"How's your reflection behaving these days?"

It sounded odd, but I knew what she meant. Magda had a unique way of referring to the everyday to make it seem, somehow, controversial. Perhaps it was simply a part of her nature, or a bad habit she picked up as the mistress of a salon.

"I still feel like I'm wearing someone else's skin. I look in the mirror and I don't recognise myself." I held up my hands as if to look through the pink dye I'd been stained with, back to the bronze colouring I'd been born with – my mostly Matin heritage. Dropping them back into my lap, I absently rubbed at the raised scars on my palms. "Not to worry though, the colour is holding; there's no premature damage due to my early re-entry after the initial treatment."

"That's good. You shouldn't need to visit me again for several more months."

"Months?" I asked. "But you said once my roots start showing, my hair will be over the shock and grow faster."

"Don't you worry now. Gerrund told me all about the incident. I'll send along the supplies you'll need to be able to tend to your hair yourself – or Dezmind could do it for you when he's in town."

"That's a rarity." *Damn. Did I just say that out loud?*

"What do you mean?"

I had to tread lightly here. "Oh, he's usually tied up with meetings and Rally-walks and visits with important people behind the scenes. I'll take care of it myself."

"All right now." Magda twirled me around to face her. "You need to let this set for half an hour. Sit tight and read the paper. I have to finish setting up before my staff arrives." She patted me on the shoulder after disposing of her now-copper-coloured gloves, then hurried into the main shop.

Forty minutes later, after I'd been rinsed, washed, re-rinsed, blow-dried and gossiped to death, I stood just inside Magda's office waiting for the other five patrons to be thoroughly engrossed in their styling affairs before speed-walking through the main salon.

I managed a quick wave to Magda, who was busy with a customer, and received a blown kiss just as her client's eyes widened and looked from my hand to my face. Not good. I rushed past the window and down the street.

As I walked, I pulled a collapsible wide-brimmed hat from my clutch bag, shook it into shape, and then stuffed as much of my hair as possible under it while matching pace with the few remaining commuters walking to work.

I couldn't help but shake my head at the absurdity of it all. I didn't look like me and yet because of a Rally Dez held down here the day he returned to the surface, everyone knew the role I played in saving the Gamma sun, or Zerameteth as the Trinity Guardians and Followers of Light called it.

When no one so much as glanced at me over the next few minutes, I rolled my shoulders and breathed steady, controlled breaths to allow my muscles to loosen up. I let my arms fall to my sides and swing with the rhythm of my steps, calm and natural.

Magda would be sending one of her girls by my apartment with the supplies I'd need for my hair. She was supposed to arrive just after lunch with the package. I inhaled deeply, filling my chest, and slowly letting out the breath.

I was okay. It felt good being out of my self-induced confinement. I allowed myself a small smile. *Maybe I overreacted. Maybe they've forgotten about me. It's been nearly three weeks since the last mobbing. Maybe I don't need to hide anymore.*

But even though I managed to walk un-accosted, the innate cold of the Underground seeped under my skin. A few couples walked hand-in-hand along the wide road as others bartered or paid for merchandise in the small shops. Other than Magda, I'd spoken with no one in a week, not even the grocery runner Gerrund sent to the apartment. The high ceilings of the caverns and faux shop façades only made me feel more like a puppet, or doll in a very large playhouse. The smile I'd managed just moments before dropped flat.

Crossing Centre Street, just down the road from my building, I dug in my bag to retrieve the key-cards to the apartment. The front and back entrances required one, the mailbox, and the interior lower stairwells another. A bio-chip reader stored my DNA in its memory. It was meant to allow only residents access to the apartment building: old, repurposed tech Gerrund and his cronies were able to amass without suspicion, became useful in this world of exiles, rock, and replicated sunlight.

A woman with pale blue skin and gold coliths sitting at an outdoor café, reminded me of the poet, Merik, I'd once travelled the Deserts with. Leaving her half-eaten breakfast, the woman looked from something in her hand to me and back again several times. I gripped my bag and continued the half-block to my building. *I shouldn't have made eye contact.*

"Zimi," the woman said, weaving her way around the other patio tables.

"Zimi!" she called louder. I walked faster. I didn't want to run and risk drawing even more attention. I didn't know if she was an FOL, Follower of Light, or survivor of the incident. My heart bruised my chest as it tried to break free and force its way up into my throat.

No. Not again. Please Zola.

Other bystanders and pedestrians took notice of the woman following me, their heads turning or looking up from broken conversations. I risked a glance behind me. The woman waved something in the air above her head as she ran through the crowd. Suddenly, my hat was snatched by a stranger. I raised my hands to grab it back. The Nirian man holding it stared at the starburst-shaped scars covering my palms.

"Emvaso-al," he whispered. *Child of the Sun*. It felt like my blood drained from my head into my legs, making it harder to move, to run.

The woman's chants turned to desperate pleas, "Emvaso-al! Emvaso-al, please!"

People closed in around me. I tried to push through and break free, find an opening somewhere. But the closer I got to any one person, the more hands reached out for me. They grabbed my clothing, took my watch-scarf away, stroked my face, my hair. The air filled with an onslaught of voices and cries for help.

"Emvaso-al, please! Just touch them. Touch their faces. They need you Emvaso-al," said the woman from the cafe.

"Child of the Sun, I'm in need of your guidance—" an old woman begged, pulling at the hem of my shirt.

Tick tick, tick tick, tick...

"Zimi, please touch my child's cheek. Zimi—" said the man who'd grabbed my hat.

"Child of the Light, say a prayer for my daughter," came another voice.

"My children are dying, give them peace, give them warmth, daughter of Zerameteth."

Tick tick, tick tick, tick... The voice of the old watch ricocheted in my head with the absence of my wrist scarf. My sensitive half-Talian hearing magnified the sound and brought with it echoes of more than just my nightmares.

"Here, he's right here." The man dropped my hat, picked up his son and held the young child before me. "Let your spirit protect him."

"Zimi, give me grace for long life. I have much yet to live for, my own children to protect," crooned the older woman.

"And I," chimed in an equally old man. "My family are lost to me. Guide my heart to find them before the Kronik—"

The father and the boy, the café woman, sick children, worried adults, all shifting places and changing faces – touching, grabbing, pleading, begging for me to do something I couldn't.

Tick tick, tick tick, tick...

They demanded I be their saviour; that I help them when I couldn't even help myself.

My knees trembled. My body shook with a scream trapped in my throat. I couldn't hurt these people in order to save myself, not again. But I had to get out of there. I turned one way, then another. A new face, a new plea, a new sorrow crashed over me.

Another shift in the crowd. A void in the mass of bodies. My building became a beacon, waiting for me. Seizing my chance, I sprang forward and burst through the assembled masses. Like wildfire, I consumed the distance between me and promised solitude.

Crashing through the main doors a nano-second after the biorecognition sequence unlocked my sanctuary, I didn't look back. I raced down the hall of the main level to the central staircase. Using another mini key-card I yanked the stairwell door open, ran up to the second floor, and careened down the hall to my apartment. Jamming the third mini-card against the bio reader above my mail basket, I wrenched the knob, slipped in, and slammed the door.

Tick tick, tick tick, tick...

Chapter Two
Letters & Words

Taya

Falling back against the door's solid mass, I inhaled a shaky breath as my sleep deprived body sank to the floor. I pulled up my knees and rested my head on my arms.

I sucked in great gulps of air. My body convulsed as both my brain and my heart ricocheted in their chambers. Quiet, unwanted sobs threaded past my lips as the last ounce of my sanity, my self-control, disappeared.

At least I didn't hurt anyone.

I sat there for a while. My face and hands were wet with the previously unshed tears of Dezmind's leaving, the incident, the self-confinement, the face I saw in the mirror, Jadis, and Dez's missing letter. That's what hurt the most, really, being abandoned in the Underground when I should've been on the surface protecting him... and him protecting me; it damaged me more than those damned nightmares. This wasn't the forever I thought I'd signed up for with that kiss.

Tick, tick, tick, tick... The contradiction strapped to my wrist challenged my sanity. Grabbing the bottom of the cloak hanging beside me, I wrapped the hem around Dez's token of remembrance.

I pushed my fists into my eyes, trying to force the pain to leave my chest. *I should be up there with him. Curse Gerrund! Who says I'd be recognised? My stature, my walk, my vocal cadence can change.* But he didn't agree; said I was too entrenched in my ways – something the CTF did to all its employees. So, what did the future hold for me now?

The soft pad of footsteps in leather-soled slippers wisped slowly down the hall. I rested the back of my head against the door and listened to their progress. Even as my emotions lay scattered over the floor, I knew I was safe now and needn't fear the man walking in those slippers. My dulled senses focused on the rhythmic steps, if only for something to do.

The padded feet stopped just on the other side of my door. I hoped they would. A gentle rustling of papers followed a barely audible humming. I felt the thump of something drop into the basket on the other side of the door. The crinkle of cellophane ripped through the fragile quiet but managed to bring a faint smile to my lips.

At least I know the kids down the hall haven't been helping themselves to the chocolate.

I sat a little more at ease as my landlord gradually made his way back down the hall to the front stairwell. My hand twitched in anticipation of what could be on the other side of my door. But I refused to scramble up and let my emotions rule my actions. I had to rein them in, take back control. So, I purposefully paced my movements: unwrapping my wrist; standing; straightening my blouse; smoothing my hair, and *then* opening the door.

A small pile of mail waited, bundled neatly together at the bottom of the basket. I removed the letters and papers from their nest with one hand as the other held the door ajar — just wide enough to reach through. I dropped a couple more chocolates in for good measure, in case I really was supplying the kids, too, and then retreated.

Walking over to the breakfast bar between the living room and kitchen, I shuffled through the mail. My heart fluttered at the sight of the broad, angular writing on two of the three envelopes. Tossing the Local Inquisitor and a few pieces of junk mail onto the counter, I tucked the letters under my arm and, more light of step, popped into my room for another wrist-scarf.

Back in the living room, I bounced down onto the small couch, dropped the envelopes beside me and wrapped my watch in gold fabric. Shifting the pile of letters from the cushion to my lap, I smiled as I examined the special date stamps of the UG for *post received* and *delivery date*. I tore into the one with the oldest 'received' date; sometimes letters made it to retrieval points but missed standard dispersal runs. This was the first time it had happened to me. Even though a few thousand tons of dirt separated us, Dez had always managed to send a letter every second day. This letter was dated five days ago.

Dearest Ali,

I despise how brief these past few messages have been and hate even more that it can't be helped. Jadis is settling in well to her new home and has recently taken to resting her head on my knee every time she sees me sit down with a piece of paper at the kitchen table. I'm certain she senses how close you are for these brief moments. Perhaps that explains why I try to write as often as I do – to be that much closer to you.

I miss your biting sarcasm, the flash in your eyes when you're about to verbally knock me off my feet, and your insatiable smile that catches me off guard.

I continue to count the days till we are together again.

DL

I read and re-read his letter half a dozen times before I felt as though I could put it aside and open the next one. This one was even shorter than the last. No excuses, no code, no intelligence update, just six simple words.

Ali,
Dying to be with you.
DL

I gripped that one to my chest. Sighing, I thought back to the few hours we'd been able to spend together *alone* before his return to the surface...

"I'm tired of being cooped up," I said.

"Gerrund's arranging an apartment for you. It should be ready in a few days."

"I notice you said the apartment was for *me* – why not *us*?"

"I guess it could be. I just didn't want to get your hopes up again. You know I'll be living in the apartment above The Chalklin Pond."

"What is it about that restaurant?"

"I like the smell of roast ganoo." He smiled and tapped my nose. "Besides, they feed me." I turned and pulled him up from Gerrund's couch. The man's voice drifted out of his study into the living room where Dez and I sat.

"Let's go for a walk."

"It's nearly twilight."

"So?"

He laughed and followed me out the door. The apartments in Gerrund's complex were more like townhouses: each had its own entry way to the side tunnel where the building was situated and no internal connecting hallway.

The lighting above slowly dimmed into nothingness as we walked arm-in-arm under the growing pools of street lights. But even they were positioned few and far between, leaving us in a dim world of shadows. The sharp gnawing feeling at the back of my stomach returned, reminding me that Dez would be leaving tomorrow – without me.

I didn't want to think about it or start another long argument about being left behind. Bunking at Gerrund's place was like being trapped at a sleep-over party that never ended. The forced happiness at my rescue from the government warehouse, and anticipation of moving forward with the next stage of the coup, only supplied mixed emotions and a feeling of ensnarement. Pushing those thoughts aside, I buried them deep.

Dez gave my hand a squeeze, as if he knew where my thoughts lingered. He hadn't linked with me telepathically; he hadn't needed to. Wrapping a warm, solid arm around my shoulders, he leaned over and kissed my forehead, shattering the last of the negative thoughts…

There was still so much we didn't know about each other. We were practically strangers. And yet, from the moment he kissed me as we lay hidden under the dirty public transport, caked as we were in my blood after that disaster of a Rally, I knew we had a future together. Something deep inside clicked into place that day, and there was no denying it.

Reading news of Jadis, my lynx, always helped calm my nerves. Knowing she was safe and healthy, if not a little homesick for my lap, brought me a measure of peace. I wanted to be with her just as much as I wanted to be top-side with Dezmind, but there was absolutely no way I would condemn my last friend to this sunless purgatory. If these walls felt like a prison to me, then Jadis would go stir-crazy long before I did. Still, knowing my home, the house I'd bought with my own wages, the place where I was supposed to be rooted, remained abandoned left me angry and empty inside.

Carefully, I folded the short note into a small square and put it in my pocket. I rubbed my face with my hands in an attempt to force life into the muscles. Opening the small drawer in the coffee table, I took out my writing notepad and pencil in an effort to connect with my last remaining link to sanity, and the life I'd left behind. Reclining back into the couch, I raised one knee and rested the pad on it. I crossed out the words I'd written last night before going to bed.

Dear Dez,

Nights are the worst without you. It seems no matter what thoughts of you I fall asleep to, I wake up screaming and wondering why you're not here.

I hadn't realised how much I depend on hearing from you until your letter arrived late in the mail. Every day I wonder if life would've been easier if we'd only had a chance to say a proper goodbye. My world has shrunk to four walls since you left. In a place where no one is supposed to know who I am, I dread walking outside here more than I ever did there.

I left a smattering of dots over the page as I tapped my pen and thought about just how much I should reveal in a letter – one that could get intercepted. Suddenly, knowing that Dez might not be the one to read my words, made me look at them again for clues as to who I was or more importantly *where* I was. But I couldn't concentrate anymore. Thinking of spies only brought back more painful memories.

I tossed the stationary back into the drawer and shut it. Maybe I'd feel like writing later. Instead, I grabbed the last envelope resting on the couch beside me. This one had a typed label and was post marked as of this morning. The tell-tale purple infinity loop immediately told me this letter had to have come from the Underground system.

The only ones down here who knew where I lived, other than Magda, were Mardel and Gerrund, and Gerrund was the only Cause member who wrote to me anyway. I slipped a long, bony finger along the top crease of the envelope and gingerly pulled out its contents. This message was also short, but typed and all business –

JJ,
   *11^*
GK

Well, at least I'll have something to help keep me awake tonight. I still couldn't fathom why Gerrund felt he had to keep up appearances with Dez gone. Once a week, the same invitation arrived, asking me to attend the Consolidating Meeting, where the major players for the Cause locked themselves in a room together to hash out plans for the following week. They talked about long-term plots, on-going schemes for the coup, and addressed any relative concerns weighing on the UGC's, Underground Citizens', minds.

I was supposed to add my two-drezeks worth whenever I felt issues fell within one of the various areas of my expertise, but really, my presence was little more than a farce – a bandage slapped over an irritation. Clearly Gerrund was just trying to appease Dez by keeping me in the loop so that I wouldn't go complaining about my situation down here and become a distraction.

I didn't appreciate being patronised, but it did help break up the long weeks on my own... which were mostly Gerrund's fault in the first place. If he'd only backed off and let Dez help me when the crowd swarmed after the UGC Rally, I might've been able to hold it together.

Suddenly the couch seemed too big and the walls too close for comfort. I stood up, but really, where was I to go? Not to sleep. So, I paced, holding that joke of a life-line in my hand.

I usually said little to nothing during those meetings and felt more like a figure-head than someone who would actually be taken seriously. If they really valued my input, respected my commitment to Dezmind and the Cause, then just maybe I might've considered my position *adjacent* to the Board a little more valuable.

As it was, Gerrund knew Dez was committed to me and vice versa. He knew I'd write to Dez if I *felt* I wasn't being treated with respect – and that's the only reason Gerrund bothered with me at all. He was a nice guy, but egocentric and single-minded once you got to know him. I was the extra baggage he watched over while an important asset was away.

For the last five weeks I played my part and let him and the others think I felt included, but the ruse, mixed with the sleepless nights and being stuck in my prison of an apartment day in and day out, wore thin.

Following protocol, I went to the kitchen, grabbed a pot, shredded and then burned the note from Gerrund – not because I agreed with the caution, but on the off chance that there ever was a spy in attendance, I wouldn't be the one to blame. That occupied me for all of three minutes.

Maybe I'll wash the walls today and then polish all of the fixtures. By the time I'm done, I should be weary enough to fall into an exhausted sleep for a few hours before the meeting. I undertook the cleaning task once a week in order to keep the natural moisture of the rock out of my apartment. The special sealant they used for the interiors of living quarters only needed to be applied sparingly once a month – this would be my fourth application in as many week… boredom did that to me.

I leaned forward and turned on the slightly dented radio, checked the time, sighed deeply and resigned myself the laborsome, and unnecessary task of cleaning.

I jolted awake to the alarm blaring and hit the off button. The digital clock on my bedside table flashed half past ten at night. Falling back onto my pillow I stared at the ceiling. My head pounded in time to the shrill beeping, now silent, but still ringing in my ears. I'd managed another three hours of sleep but my body screamed after the punishment of washing the apartment.

I'm not that out of shape. It's only been just over a month.

The point had been to wear myself out, but this felt like the aftermath of the cliff-climb from the reservoir of verrin during my time in the Deserts. No. I wasn't out of shape, I just needed more sleep. I also needed to get out of bed.

With only half an hour to effectively reawaken, look refreshed, and make an appearance at the meeting ten minutes down the road, I still couldn't convince my legs to move or my feet to support me. So, I threw myself out of bed, landing on my ass on the floor.

This did not improve either my headache or my disposition, but the anger managed to motivate me.

Pushing my back against a now perfectly spotless wall, I wobbled up to standing and dragged myself into the washroom.

Yet again, I found a bleary-eyed stranger staring back at me, slightly damp from the dunking I'd just given my head in the sink. Since I was still dressed from earlier, all I really had to concentrate on was finding my way to a coffee mug, and then the meeting. Luckily, it was just down the road in an office space, tucked into the back of the second floor of the Local Inquisitor.

By the time I'd finished my last mouthful of the hot, bitter liquid, my joints had loosened up and the fog in my mind cleared somewhat. The headache remained, but that would persist – a dull reminder of my new life.

After draping the long, dark-purple cloak around my shoulders, I checked the hour, the peep-hole, and my insecurities at the door. I didn't have a problem getting around at night, though it only happened infrequently. Flipping my hood up to cover my hair and shadow my face, I left my apartment for the second time that day.

The length of the cloak muffled any residual sound my footsteps made as I moved through the corridor, down the stairwell, and out onto the street. The overhead lights had dimmed, and the street lamps glowed in anticipation of twilight.

Although it was still a couple of hours off, the inky blackness that bathed the streets with only vague spots of luminescence would thankfully wash over me on my way back from the secret meeting. But tonight, the weight of the silent streets made each step twice as difficult to take. *Why do I bother? I should just go back.* But even then, it would take too much effort to slow my momentum, turn around, and stop all the pretending.

Slipping into the shadows of the nearly invisible side street, used as an emergency exit for the offices of the newspaper, I let the only palm reader in the Underground scan my hand. The lock disengaged and I disappeared inside.

Skeletal shelving units held antiquated technology, reams of paper, and general office supplies, towering up to the ceiling where they were bolted in place. My eyes adjusted to the near darkness with annoying slowness. On the far side of the room, a faint light filtered in through a window in the door.

Sweeping around the large obstacles, my cloak rasped against the metal as I rounded shelves through the labyrinth. I peeked out first one side of the window and then the other before pushing open the heavy door and slipping into the lower offices. Weaving my way through dozens of desks and banks of printing equipment, I found the spiral iron stairs leading to the second floor. Now that I was here, the prospect of actually seeing a friend stripped away the gloom of the Underground.

There was no one at the top. A clear view across the expansive unused space to the room at the back, made placing a sentry here irrational. Just to the left of the office door, with the brightly lit window, the black of the wall took on an angular depth.

Keeping to the outer walls in the cavernous space fed by that single light source, I slid through the air monitoring the black-on-black shape. A breath away from the dark figure, I leaned close to an exposed ear and whispered.

"Dew-nuts."

Mardel jumped. I swore I could see his silver coliths drop to the floor.

"Zola, have mercy," he grabbed his chest as if holding it would keep his heart from jumping out. "J.J. you've got to find some other hobby." He was still one of the few people who referred to me by the nickname my real parents had called me down here. But that was another bruise I didn't like touching. Mardel reached into the air where I'd been a nano-second before, then turned and caught the folds of my cloak as I tried to sneak behind him.

"I gotta stay sharp somehow. No place to train down here." *And nothing for a washed-up CTF Agent to do.*

He chuckled and opened the door for me, tugging off my hood as I passed.

"You're worse than my kid sister." I looked over my shoulder and stuck my tongue out at him as I walked down the short hall to the room of chiselled rock. Mardel was one of the few of the UGC who made me feel welcome right from the beginning, like I was family – a distant but much-loved cousin who needed to visit more often. But he was the only one in the Cause who ever acknowledged me with anything beyond a sense of duty.

The other four regulars, excluding Gerrund, were very business minded, almost so with blinders on. Perhaps, it had something to do with the fact Mardel was the only other one, besides me, who didn't have an ancestor shipped off as part of the Nine Seas Massacre by the very institution that was developed to "protect the people".

The core of the Cause was about more than just revealing the truth – Dez's original mandate. It was about returning balance to a corrupt government. The Resistance had been about revolution and rebellion, for which the highest price was paid. The Cause, which grew from the ashes of the Resistance, foresaw a subtler approach – a coup.

Pushing though the doorway at the end of the hall, it was obvious this room wasn't supposed to be here. The ragged opening supporting the rough-framed door forced me to duck as I walked through. I knew there was enough headroom, but the two-foot difference compared to all the other openings down here made me second-guess myself every time.

Hanging up my cloak on a wall-hook behind the door, I could see the uneven hack-marks made by excavation tools. The room was covered in them. The space stood just large enough to hold the oversized oval table in the centre. I ran my fingers over the low ceiling on my way to the stool in the back corner – my official observational post.

Gerrund had initially invited me to join the others around the table, but I wasn't a fool. The subtle looks of contempt I endured and the more than obvious way the conversation travelled around me as I sat there, said volumes. So, I'd found a nice cushioned stool down in the storage room, brought it up before my second meeting, and stuffed it into the corner – bowing-out from *their space*.

Listening from that vantage point, the others more often than not forgot I was there, which allowed me to gather more intelligence than I might have otherwise. Then, if I absolutely deemed it necessary to bring to the fore something that hadn't been considered or might've been overlooked, I could catch them off guard and actually get them to consider my words.

At first, Gerrund seemed genuinely interested in what I had to say at these times, but lately his patience for my intrusions ran thin. I saw the scowls, the pursed lips, and the narrowed eyes in response to my probing questions… something drew his trust away from me, closing him off from *outsiders*. I could only wonder if it had to do with the aftermath of the incident.

We were each given a slightly different designated time of arrival. Mardel always showed up first, for obvious reasons being head of security and training, and I was more often than not second. Gerrund realised I caused less of a distraction if I was already here when the others arrived. Everyone else received a random time to ensure they came alone – without witnesses.

Next to arrive tonight was Thenticia, granddaughter of Neldek (*Tony*) Denton, master of crops, man of his word, and devoted Kronik hater – so says the legacy from Ticia's point of view.

She blustered in, pretending not to see me. But as I was the only witness to her show of self-importance, she continued to *ignore* me as she moved about the room setting a sheet of notes before each chair. Her rich fuchsia business suit made her purple coliths stand out and her grey skin-tone wash almost to white. She dressed in training gear all day and made up for it at these meetings.

She stood behind her chair reviewing her update as Hevex burst in. The massive wooden door hit my cloak and not the wall, muffling his grand entrance. A slight wrinkle creased his brow, right above his nose, as he surveyed the room.

Mardel had mentioned once that he could tell who approached the meeting site simply by the echo of their feet in the empty antechamber. Hevex and Ticia were the hardest to discern, simply because they both tromped about like a herd of richtors.

Negative waves radiated from Hevex. He not only lost his father in the battle against the Kronik's soldiers, but his mother was sentenced to travel the Nine Seas with Magistrate Delenon.

Gerrund and Randek arrived in tandem of each other. While each wore his "serious" face inside this room, it was not uncommon to hear them bicker good-naturedly on the way out.

Gerrund stood at the head of the oval table in front of a large wall map; Randek followed immediately to his right. The two had grown up together in the early days of the Resistance, of which their families had been key supporters. When Randek lost his older brother in the Resistance, or the Cause as it became known after the Nine Seas Massacre, Gerrund and his younger sister had been taken in by Ran's family. Mardel had told me as much when he walked me back to my apartment after my first meeting.

Gerrund set his notes in front of Ran who scooped them up off the table and handed them out, making an unimportant task seem all the more grand as he was now the only one moving in the small room. It was clear from the start that he worshiped the ground Gerrund walked on. *It's that kind of blind devotion that'll get him killed one day.*

The silence had yet to be broken. No one tended to speak until the meeting was officially called to order. As usual, the last to arrive was Dias Betauni. Although *Dias* was commonly used as a term of reverence for citizens over the age of one-hundred and thirty. Being the oldest surviving member of the Resistance after The Collection, gave her certain privileges – this included the use of the honorific at the age of seventy-one. She was not a woman to trifle with – I liked her.

Mardel slipped into the room after The Dias, and took his place across the table from Gerrund, closest to my corner of the room.

The ritual began.

Dias Betauni joined the others standing around the table. She nodded to the group and sat down. Everyone followed suit, except Gerrund, who remained standing.

"Welcome, my brothers and sisters of the Cause. May the hands of our forefathers of the dawning of the Age of Migration guide our hearts this night." He gathered together the notes before him. "Let the Consolidating Body acknowledge Aelonia Trellice."

"Here," they said as one voice. This was the sum total of recognition I could expect for the rest of the evening.

These meetings ran like a well-maintained rider, so now that I was considered official, I could resume my weekly reading of the Tunnelling Map behind Gerrund and still appear attentive. The extensive veins of caverns and passages must have been hollowed out by underground lakes centuries ago… or maybe even the sea at one time. There were no confirmed lines leading to the cliffs by the Compound, but that didn't mean they weren't there. The cliffs often drew my thoughts because of the story Dezmind shared with the Kahn-lea in the Deserts; the story of the Lost Lady Lynnia… my real mother. As far as I knew, she was still a prisoner on her family's estate there.

"First item of business: progress on the tunnels." I ignored him, thinking of the potential reach of this Underground City all the way out to the coast. Wondering if there was a way to get there from here.

Gerrund and his crew, and the crew before them, had been exploring these subterranean tunnels since their discovery; Gerrund knew more about tracking and boring, stalactites and stalagmites than anyone else. I spent much of my time at the meetings decoding the growing map on my own. It was pretty basic but without an actual legend to refer to, I had to listen well enough during these updates to learn how to read the map.

It was easy enough to identify the existing housing/business tunnels and the generators connected to each. The sheer amount of power this place used boggled my mind at the best of times. Prior to the perfection of the hydrogen fuel cell and electrolysis, existence in the Underground during the Resistance would've been dismal and risky. Luckily the New Renaissance sprouted immediately after the Nine Seas Massacre and paved the way for growth, especially in new technologies.

There were current exploration routes, unexplored portions of the system, underground lakes of water and verrin, breaches to the surface called Junction Points, compromised routes to the surface, and danger zones: rock slides, weak rock, mineral beds, cave-ins and noxious gases. The Junctions were monitored constantly but there were relatively few throughout the cave system.

I refocused on the update as Mardel concluded his report on the Compromised Zones. Randek spoke next.

"The flyer campaign for The Awareness of the Cause and the Spoken Truth is showing vast improvement compared to initial numbers. Between the success of Dezmind's *Walks* and the increase of upper citizenry subscribing to the Inquisitor, our production and delivery of flyers is a positive sign that we're reaching the average citizen."

A spot on my face near my eyebrow twitched. The Dias coughed. I took a deep breath and exhaled slowly. She would address this the right way.

"What evidence do we have that people are reading the flyers and not just recycling them as common junk mail?"

Randek's face lost a marked amount of enthusiasm.

"Well, we don't know for sure, but we can infer from the increase in Inquisitor subscriptions that people are interested in what we have to say. Even if the flyers are being discarded, there's the initial visual cue that the title gives." He paused. "This is a positive outcome."

"I'm not denying that, Ran," The Dias leaned forward. "Your next step should be to devise a way of tracking this progress. Timing is everything, and the culmination of our plans means nothing if the average citizen is deaf to the Cause. We can't let their ignorance and indifference continue. It's our duty to help them open their eyes."

I leaned against the wall, crossed my arms and nodded my head. Whenever my hope and trust in this process failed me, The Dias said exactly what I needed to hear. Apparently, I wasn't the only one. Several heads echoed my approval. Ran sat a bit taller after The Dias' clarification.

Ran had mentioned Dez's *Walks*; I wanted to ask how the Roving Rallies directly contributed to the Cause, but that would just be selfish. Dezmind wasn't able to give me much information in our letters. The best we managed was a casual code just in case one fell into the wrong hands, but it didn't seem right for me to bring it up here – it was redundant information; I was the only one in ignorance.

My shoulders drooped and I let my elbows fall to my knees as I rested my head on my hands. The raised scars on my palms felt intrusive against my cheeks.

I shouldn't have come.

"What intel are we getting from the Network on Dezmind?" Gerrund asked. *When did he learn to read minds?* It wasn't what I'd been hoping for – it was better.

"As long as he remains in the public eye, they can't touch him," Hevex said.

My chest constricted. I slowly blinked to calm my rising blood pressure.

That's it? We already know that!

I sat up straight. The warmth at the back of my neck travelled up to my ears and across my cheeks.

"It's clear from our sources that his ability to cause serious doubt in the minds of the general public as to the *real* origin of the second super-quake, has the Kronik busy doing damage control. They're not going to risk a backlash by trying to take him out again. The same goes for a private assassination. Enough citizens have heard him speak that even those currently not convinced would believe in him if he suddenly wound up dead."

Finally, we're getting somewhere.

"The Kronik's aim is not only to publicly discredit him, but highlight the supposed positive developments the government has made in the recent past. It's an all-out media war. This is the most coverage we've ever achieved. Because the Wire Networks are fighting for footage of Dezmind and the Kronik, places Dezmind and the Local Inquisitor have never been are aware, to some degree, of what's going on." He paused. "As Dias Betauni pointed out, we need to find a way to closely monitor what effect this publicity is having on the general populous."

"Good. What about Aelonia?" Gerrund asked.

Hevex narrowed his eyes and tugged at his collar. "The Kronik still believes she is alive."

Silence permeated the small room. I stared ahead at nothing in particular. This wasn't helping Gerrund's reasoning for keeping me down here… for convincing Dez not to bring me back top-side with him. If the Kronik only *believed* I was alive, there was no solid proof I remained a threat, that I was the woman who helped Dez escape the bombing masked as a super-quake.

"And—" Gerrund prompted, trying to force the man to come up with answers that supported his claims. *Maybe he needs to keep me away from Dez for some reason…*

"And we've been focusing our efforts on more current matters."

Clearly, I'm not a priority up there and there's no reason for me to be stuck down here.

Gerrund's gaze darkened. "I expect a full report at Consolidating Meetings on *all* matters, whether you deem them current or not. Thenticia, the recruits," he snapped.

Ticia leaned forward and clasped her hands before resting them on the table. "We've nearly maxed out our resources. Currently, I have scouts in the farthest caverns of the system. I'm not expecting much. Most of the UGC in the outlying areas are there because they don't want to be involved."

"Is my sister giving you any trouble?" Gerrund asked.

"She's reminded me that they chose seclusion to make a point. Otherwise, no, we've been able to speak with anyone willing to listen. What we need to do is send sensory scouts above for reinforcements." Her eyes met and held each of the others' in turn, settling on Gerrund.

His gaze flashed at her bold statement. Ticia's mouth quivered in silent retort. His nostrils flared. Everyone waited. Taking word of the impending coup top-side was tantamount to suicide. But she had a point... we might just need the numbers to hold the breach when it happened. That's why the Resistance failed. I leaned forward, curious to see how this would play out.

The Dias spoke, "The surface is our last resort. Finish what you've successfully started down here—" Ticia opened her mouth to retort. The Dias raised her hand. "Develop a plausible tactic for recruiting on the surface. When our resources down here are exhausted, we'll revisit your proposal."

Gerrund's shoulders relaxed. Ticia's mouth tightened but she nodded in agreement. The Dias had smoothed that one over for now, but it was an interesting predicament – what would we do if there weren't enough volunteers?

"What about the training?" Gerrund asked. I shifted and crossed my legs in the opposite direction. Absentmindedly, I closed my eyes and rubbed my temple. The headache I'd woken up with had been an incessant throb most of the night, but chose this moment to flare up. It wasn't surprising though. I was tired of listening to her backward understanding of military training.

Ticia cleared her throat. "Mardel and I have agreed to continue basic training with the current recruits until the last of the volunteers have arrived from the outer-reaches. We've compiled lists according to prowess in each division. When our lists are complete, we will separate the volunteers and continue training accordingly."

Nobody said a word.

I looked at Mardel to see if he would add anything – no. Gerrund seemed satisfied, and The Dias completely dropped the ball on this one.

"What does your basic training regimen consist of?" I asked.

All eyes shifted to me. My heart crashed into my ribcage. My skull throbbed in maddening waves.

"That's need-to-know information, and you don't need to know," Thenticia's voice froze the room. I quirked an eyebrow. It was Ticia's turn for her face to flush.

"I wouldn't have asked if I didn't need to know," I said.

"Ticia," Gerrund spoke calmly.

A purple colith twitched beside her eye. "Running various drills." Gerrund's stare didn't waver. She reluctantly continued, "That consist of physical endurance, mobility, duck-and-cover tactics, working with a weapon, target practice – do I really need to go on?"

I frowned. "What's the schedule?"

Ticia looked down, scowling. She shuffled her papers around.

"Do I have to tattoo my body with the Contractor Emblem for you get it?" I said, louder and harsher than I intended. When it came to Ticia, my self-control evaporated. "Or have you been living down here so long that your ignorance of my status is preventing you from realising my intelligence? Perhaps you're prejudiced, huh? No? Racist then? You seem to like Dezmind well—"

"Enough, Aelonia," Gerrund boomed. He usually called me J.J. "Make your point."

My head buzzed, my vision blurred from the growing migraine, and my patience with this place and these people disintegrated. I fallen back on the very arrogance that nearly cost me my place as a Contractor... I knew all of this in some small part of my mind, but the anger and fury overrode that logic.

"Ticia," I lowered my voice, took a breath and rubbed my forehead, "the schedule?"

"Half a day for each pack."

"Do you not have the resources for smaller packs and more frequent training stints?"

"Our resources are limited but sufficient for our needs."

"Many volunteers are being housed with host families, right?"
"Yes. What of it?"

I was quiet a moment, struggling to assess the situation as my humour went from bad to worse. "I – I don't even know where to begin." I sighed and let my arms fall as I stood up. "You need to begin eliminating their familial ties. Choose an unused cavern or tunnel. Set up additional barracks—"

"That's insane! We don't have the time to waste on ridiculous CTF policies that have no business being in the Underground."

"What? Do you think I'm here for the good of my health? Do you think I'm a spy for the Kronik because I worked for the Contractor Training Facility, or because I'm half-Talian? You don't know me."

I slammed my hands down on the table. "I'm a valuable resource." Bright red and white spots flashed in front of my eyes, just as the pain in my head reached a crescendo.

I looked around the table. My gaze settled on Gerrund. "If you'd bothered to recognise that, and had invited me to daily meetings from the beginning, you wouldn't need to rely on physical numbers for your elaborate plans. The volunteers you have now can be effective soldiers in whatever capacity, as long as they know how to think."

I pushed away from the table. "I'm wasting my time here." I stalked across the room, whipped my cloak off its peg and, with a sweep of deep-purple fabric, I left.

Chapter Three
Aches & Pains

Taya

I float under a clear lid, in a sealed grey metal box filled with red-tinged water. Holding my breath, I want desperately to feel the pain of my marks release, but my gills refuse to open. I heave my body around in circles as the metallic cuffs rip into the tender flesh of my wrists and ankles. A thick, muffled, tick-tick-tick ebbs through the water. I try kicking out with my bound feet to free myself. My heart pounds in my ears, even as the ticking echoes through my brain. My lungs burn.

A faint pin-point of light flashes somewhere above me. Help me! *I scream in my mind. My neck goes limp; my chin drifts to my chest.* Help me – Four *bubbles of air escape from my nose. The light disappears as the metal walls push in toward me…*

Gasping for air, I jerked backwards. The island stool fell away and I smacked my head on the edge of the breakfast bar as I crashed to the floor, cracking my hip against the stone.

I opened my eyes, but they refused to adjust; the room remained black. Grasping at the smooth floor, I pulled myself forward on my stomach until the glow from the timer on the coffee pot became visible through the pulsating ache above my right eye. My chest constricted against my lungs before I managed another gasp, taking in oceans of air. Great sobs wracked my over-taxed body. In the pool of dim light illuminating the kitchen floor, I curled into a ball and wept.

That feeling of helplessness and confinement clung to my skin like cobwebs. The nightmares were evolving and coming more often now. What hurt even more was the reminder of Gerrund's words after leaving me alone in my new apartment for the first time: *They found you once, they'll find you again. No amount of body art is going to change that. They know you.*

He'd claimed that the Kronik's Special Agents evolved from the CTF just as I had. That my employer's knowledge of my actions, reactions, body language and vocal patterns made me easy prey in the wrong company.

Being abducted and tortured in the Warehouse showed that I wasn't invincible after all… that maybe Gerrund and Dez had a point about it being safer for me to remain Underground – but the only things this cage reinforced were failure and susceptibility to the whims of others. The truth serum had been in my veins… *if Gerrund's team hadn't saved me, could I have held out against it?*

Sitting on the cold floor, against the half-wall of the kitchen island, I leaned my head back as the last remnants of tears dried in salty streaks along my cheeks. I sat there, in the dark, afraid to move and ignite an electric shock-wave in my head. My arms hung limp beside me, my legs at odd angles on the floor, as my breath came in shallow, uneven wisps.

I had no idea how long I'd been there. It was obviously still twilight, so I hadn't slept for long – *just long enough.* The more time that passed, the steadier my breathing became. The longer I waited, the clearer my mind got; until a plan formed.

As my brain eagerly welcomed the onslaught of budding thoughts, the feeling slowly returned to my fingers and toes. This was what I was trained to do: identify the situation, analyse it, deconstruct it, and plan for the offensive.

I had to stop the dreams. If I didn't, they'd kill me. I couldn't go on like this. *It's time to get mobile again — gain some semblance of control.* Reaching forward, I rested on my hands and knees before crawling into my bedroom.

I sat beside the nightstand with my back against the bed. Yanking the drawer out, I spilled the contents on the floor in front of me. My eyes finally adjusted to the dark. This simple function took three times longer than usual, and had never really worked since the nightmares started. My special half-Talian abilities were rendered useless.

I sifted through the mess on the floor: pens, paper, a book, some loose hair clips, and a couple of small plastic containers... until my wrist bumped the empty bottle I searched for.

*   *   *

Taya

Stumbling through the darkened streets of the Underground, I pulled the hood of my cloak further over my head. I kept to the shadows, the lanterns casting faint auras around their bulbs. I couldn't see anyone else around, but that didn't mean they weren't there. The main generators were synchronized to turn on in a few minutes as dawn neared its breaking point on the surface.

I knew of a Pharmacy nearby that opened with *sun up*. Oh, how my body ached to feel the true warmth of the Alpha sun caress my body in the early morning hours. Doire's exile to the Deserts seemed far preferable to the games and redundancy of life in these cold rocky caverns. I still couldn't readily connect the Desert Explorer to being my real father, and let the faint connection slip away.

The plan was really quite simple — it had to be. My brain couldn't process complex thought any more. I had one renewal on the bottle of sleeping pills Gerrund had given me that day at the hospital — it was time for a refill.

I should've done it sooner, but I couldn't bring myself to believe I needed them. After telling Gerrund they weren't necessary, I'd stuffed them at the back of the nightstand drawer and forgotten about them – for a week. Then, just as Gerrund had predicted, the dreams started. Dez was gone, and I was on my own avoiding another incident; living out one mundane day after another.

Three days later, I gave in. Half a tablet to get me through the night. Then I went back to rationing my sleep to three hours. But every few days the nightmares returned and I'd need a full tablet. Last week I ran out.

My original aversion to medication set in as I turned the corner of a smaller connecting tunnel housing only small shops. *No. I can't go through another week like this.* Gerrund likely had the refill flagged so he could monitor my progress, but that didn't matter now. I palmed the empty bottle deep in my pocket, my fingers memorising its contours. *I'll find a way to get past this before I finish the next bottle.*

The sign turned to "open" on the Pharmacy door. I slipped in.

"Good morning. How may I help you?" The male pharmacist asked, overly pleasant. I winced as the interior lights brightened with the dawning of the day, reflecting off his pink Glaaon skin and wavy silver coliths.

"If you could just refill this prescription for me, I'll be on my way." I passed him the bottle and my ID card over the main counter. Getting used to carrying print identification was more than a little annoying, but the Kronik would notice if any large shipments of palm or DNA scanners went unaccounted for.

"Sure thing, young lady. This'll only take a moment." He hurried to the back shelves behind a low processing counter, deeper into the shop. He didn't make any more small talk.

I wandered around the public portion of the Pharmacy, looking at the displays of non-prescription medicine, magazines, and breath mints. He was as good as his word and had me settled in under five minutes. I paid him with the few dakors and drezeks I had left from groceries this week.

Pulling my hood closer around my face, I paced my steps back to the door. There was no sense in alarming him by rushing, if there hadn't been a flag on the medicine.

It's first thing in the morning. No one else should be wandering the streets anyway. People are washing their faces and eating their breakfasts. I inhaled a calming breath and pushed open the door.

Stepping through, I walked right into someone. He grabbed my arm to help steady me.

"So sorry. Thanks for your help." I didn't even look at him. I turned to leave, but he didn't let go. I swung back around to see a shock of blue hair – *Gerrund.* My heart stopped and then started again.

"J.J.? I thought you would've made it home hours ago." He leaned against the outside of the closed Pharmacy door and released my arm.

"I did go home, after a short walk to clear my head."

Concern flashed across his face. "Are you all right? You looked a little out-of-sorts at the meeting, and with your abrupt exit –"

"I *am* sorry about that. I've had a raging headache. It just got the better of me. The walk didn't help and neither did the silence at home."

"You didn't have anything for a headache at the apartment? Are you out of sleeping pills? They would've helped." He was fishing; I could hear it in the tonal change of his voice. My mind chugged to keep up with the conversation.

"No – I mean, yes. Yes, the pills are still there. I just forgot about them – stuffed them in a drawer and haven't bothered about them." That sounded strained even to my ears.

"Can I see what Penik gave you?" He was pushing. I hated that I wasn't on the top of my game. I pulled a white plastic bottle out of my cloak pocket and placed it in his waiting hand. He studied the label intently then returned it to me. "Yup, they're good and strong; they should take care of it."

He turned to go inside, then seemed to think better of it.

Scanning the area, he confirmed we were alone.

"By the way, as grossly out of order as you were last night, you were still right. You *are* a valuable asset. Dezmind asked me to watch over you. I guess I should've considered you'd get bored down here without something to do."

"It's not entirely your fault—"

"Let's avoid the blame game. Look, as much as the team is threatened by you – don't look so astonished, they're well aware of your background as you so deftly pointed out. Anyway, they finally came to an agreement. They're willing to let you help. We want you to start attending daily meetings."

I didn't know what to say. All I could do was stare at him and wait for my mouth to catch up to my brain, which had fallen behind in the conversation again.

"I take it you'll come?" he prompted.

"Yes," I found my voice. "Yes, of course."

"Just be aware that you're there for *intelligence* purposes. We need to know what you know. Your personal insight will be a fresh way of looking at things. Get some rest." He clapped me on the shoulder. "We meet mid-morning."

I nodded.

He smiled. "I need a little something for my head, too. It was a disaster trying to mediate after you left. We only finished up a few minutes ago." He ran a dark-grey hand over his face and rubbed a spot on the side of his head over a small jade-green colith. "You really know how to put a wrench in things. I'll see you later, J.J." He closed his eyes briefly, as if to reprimand himself, "I mean, *Aelonia*."

"Goodnight – um – good morning, Gerrund."

He walked into the store as I dropped the white bottle back into my pocket. It came to rest beside the other bottle sitting snugly in the crook of the fabric. Some unconscious part of my brain was to thank for grabbing the headache medicine along with my prescription. Was it simply luck that I'd pulled out the right one to show him?

Chapter Four
Augitmein

Zaith

The Alpha sun awakened to the new day as I slipped through the dense bushes into the Goddess' canopy. Immediately I registered the change in temperature. I could have been floating through the heavy mist shrouding the tall grasses the way my shins disappeared.

Breathing deeply, I stood with my eyes closed. The Memorial Pipes filtered the breeze with a gentle melody. Exhaling, I opened my eyes and then sat beneath the dark limbs of the Tree Goddess.

This was my morning sanctuary. The only place the others avoided, except when they were on Generator duty. It was here I most often thought of Taya and Dezmind; it was here we'd fought so hard to get to, and it was here where my certainty in Taya's evolving belief in the Spoken Truth finally solidified.

I knew the bond I shared with my best friend had shattered, but there were times, before she left, when it almost felt as though my betrayal hadn't happened. The worst times were when she looked at me with a mixture of surprise and pity; it always came after one of our closer moments. I hoped to get the chance to repair some of the damage one day… maybe if Dezmind brings his vision of the future to fruition… then again, maybe not.

I reached up an ebony hand and caressed a tendril of blue moss, draped over a bough near my head. My breath shimmered white in the air. *Six weeks. Six weeks and we've heard nothing.* I let my arm fall. *If only things had turned out the way they were supposed to…*

The cracking and snapping of branches broke into my reverie. I stared across the alien Memorial Grounds to the source of the disturbance.

Raylan and Syvis breached my sanctuary.

I sighed and ran my fingers through dull, lifeless black hair. The only sign that I wasn't a walking shadow were my jade-green coliths. *What I wouldn't give for a simple bottle of peroxide to streak this mane.* I watched them approach.

Raylan's wavy gold coliths glistened with moisture as his dark-green figure blended with the surrounding trees. Syvis' tanned and finely-toned body followed close on Ray's heels. *This can't be good.*

"Zaith," Syvis said before Ray could open his mouth. "We need to talk."

"And you couldn't wait until I joined the group for breakfast?" I'd stressed the importance of Community and made sure everyone started the day sharing a meal and their plans.

"I thought it best to bring this up in private," Syvis said.

"He was afraid I'd make a scene," Ray clarified, crossing his arms and causing his colith markings to ripple like snakes.

"About what?"

"A few things, but mainly food," Syvis said.

"We have plenty of food." I looked at Ray, even though Syvis spoke.

"Sure, plenty of the same stuff all the time. I want to put a party together and return to the lower forest, then the plateau. We can gather some spiky fruit and the root vegetables that grow out that way – see if anyone is coming in from the Deserts while we're there," Ray said.

"I'd like to replenish the medical supplies as well. I think it's a good idea," Syvis added.

I considered the request for a moment, weighing the positives and negatives of the trip. It was true; we hadn't left the City since arriving, and Ray wasn't the only one getting restless these days, but the man's volatile nature and the false hope such a trip might bring... *Ah, the heck with it. We all need a break.*

"We'll make it an over-nighter," I said. "We can camp at the boulder, gather our supplies and then return tomorrow. Ray, bring it up at breakfast and we'll get organised to leave shortly afterwards." He nodded and they both left.

I looked up at the brightening sky through the large circle in the branches above. *Now, who to bring?*

With the gear packed and Syvis holding onto my travel cart, strapped with several empty packs, Deltek and Ray discussed what they planned to gather as we waited for Lutrice, Deltek's wife, to return. Of the eight of us who'd crossed the Deserts in search of the Chronicles, five of us would return to the lower forest and cliff's edge; the other three members of the Kahn-lea, Jantice, Tamaine and Merik, would keep the camp and the Generator running in our absence.

Lutrice jogged over from her dwelling across the Common. Merik met her half-way. She handed him four metal books and a small sculpture for his growing collection.

Over the past five weeks, Merik, our resident poet, had taken it upon himself to set up a library-museum in Dezmind's former dwelling. Without any encouragement, the Kahn-lea had taken to his cause and, whenever they came across an interesting artefact or piece of literature, they sent it Merik's way. It was common for him to return from scavenging to find a pile or two stacked by either his dwelling or Dez's. Using Taya's notes, he was slowly identifying and translating the resources collected.

"Okay, I'm ready," Lutrice said as she hauled her pack over her shoulders.

"Good. Let's head out then," I said.

The hike to the lower forest took the better part of the day. I remembered the way and managed to convince everyone not to rush.

It stayed quiet during the first part of our walk. Everyone was glad of the change and enjoyed the physical activity. As we neared the Great Black Gate, I noticed how much farther the Kahn-lea had opened the only operational wing – twice what Taya and I had managed when we first arrived in the south lands. It'd been a bugger for the two of us to budge far enough to pull Dez through on the supply cart. *Well, there were more of them. I suppose it's only natural they'd open it as far as they could.*

While the others had come down this way from time to time to fish at the base of the falls and to bathe, I kept mainly to the small stream we'd found on the far side of the City. It never felt right for me to leave the alien City – too much to do and too many people to keep organised.

I never asked for this – I look out for number one and now I don't even rank in the top ten. Even with Taya and Dez's absence, they placed higher in the pecking order than any of us. Dezmind was supposed to save the world and Taya was supposed to save these people, not me.

Lutrice slowed her pace to match mine. I smiled a hello. She and Deltek were as dark as me, but being pure Jeridan both she and her husband sported bold yellow coliths that beckoned sunlight and bred warmth. Were it not for my jade coliths, we could pass for sisters, with matching high cheekbones and strong noses. Deltek was altogether more round, with a heavier jaw line.

"Hey," she said. "I was just thinking. We should start taming the small gardens in the City suburbs, like Jutaya suggested. I can supervise the teens and show them what to keep and what to weed out. I want to bring back several bunches of plants while we're out here and see if they'll grow in the City."

"Good, yeah. I think that'll help minimise the number of major outings we'll need to make. Remember to leave the roots of the healing flower as full as possible – they wilt so fast if they're cut short."

"Of course, don't worry. I'll handle the medical garden myself. At least at first."

I grinned at her, "Doctor Lutrice at your service."

She laughed, "It's about time I took on a new profession." Then she winked. "We might be here for a while."

We continued to talk, even as we moved single file through the dense bushes and trees that lined the natural path down the side of the falls. It was agreed this morning that we'd take lunch here and enjoy the water.

After a simple meal of dried game, white-root, and a dense round fruit that grew throughout the City, I dangled my feet in the pool at the base of the waterfalls while the others went swimming. My thoughts turned serious as they splashed about and caught fresh fish for dinner.

The verrin crystal Taya had left us was almost gone. I agreed with Taya's dislike of the back-up chemical version everyone had brought along – *only use it if you need to*. I'd been alternating the fake stuff with thin slices from the box of crystals, but lately I'd had to reduce the number of flakes I included with our meals. I only gave it with drinking water when someone looked considerably weaker than usual, but it wasn't going the distance.

This was a simple fact of our existence – we couldn't live without verrin and yet there were no natural sources of it this far south. I was going to have to bring someone with me into the Deserts, and soon. This wasn't a trip that could be made when the effects of verrin loss became more pronounced. It was also not a journey I wanted to make.

I dried off my legs and signalled to the others to pack up. I focused my mind on the hike ahead of us, and pushed the thoughts of verrin from my mind.

Eating an early dinner as we walked up through the dense forest, we crossed the stream where the healing flowers grew with plenty of daylight remaining. It wasn't long after we reached the boulder clearing and set up camp.

"Ray, you said you wanted to collect the spiky fruit, right?" I asked.

"Yeah."

"I'll go with you and show you where the biggest patch is."

He scrunched his nose at a passing thought but grunted an affirmative.

"Lutrice and I will gather the healing flowers," Deltek said. "I saw a hardy patch down by the stream."

"Right. I guess I'll collect root vegetables and leaves after I show Ray where to go. Syvis?"

"I'll scout out the Plateau at the cliff and then help you with the tubers."

"Good. Let's meet back before Beta sets and organise our findings." The group dispersed. I walked over to Ray, who seemed to be both ignoring me and waiting for me at the same time. *He is a strange one.*

"I want to make regular trips out here *without* your supervision," he said with a gruff voice.

"I understand."

"What do you mean *you understand?*" This obviously wasn't the response he expected.

He forced his way through a thick bush ahead of me, even though I was still the one leading the way. Several small branches whipped back at me. I caught them before they smacked me in the face. The heady aroma of sun-baked leaves forced me to breathe through my mouth.

I wanted to shout at him for being a big baby, or remind him that Taya and Dez left a pretty big void to fill. But I was still responsible for *everyone*, and this wasn't the office and he wasn't a pain-in-the-ass newbie reporter I had to deal with. He'd find a way to use it against me. He always did. Taya had rightly passed-on her distrust of him.

"Let's see how this trip goes first. Then we can talk about plans for the future, okay?" He had that set look on his face. I knew it well.

He weighed my words, waging an inner war; battling with himself about saying what he wanted to, or saying what he ought to. In the end, he didn't say anything at all. I wasn't sure if I should be relieved or concerned.

I hadn't intended to make regular trips out here. I totally understood why he wanted to: we were trapped — caged animals needing to sniff around in the hopes of finding our way to freedom. Our freedom lay north beyond the Plateau of boulders; well, theirs did anyway.

Even if we became self-sufficient and were able to cultivate many of the plants here back at the City, I supposed we'd need a scouting party to watch for Taya's return — even if it never happened. *She's probably dead. I told her not to go back.* Still, as much as we wanted the same thing, everyone had to be careful with Raylan.

As we passed through a dense patch of tall, spindly saplings, I caught sight of the spiky fruit a moment before Ray took off at a jog toward the bushes.

"I'll see you back at camp!" I called, and turned to look for the tubers in the lower forest.

A light misting rain stayed with us most of the evening. Deltek and Lutrice had been the first to return to camp. They relocated our supplies farther back into the trees surrounding the boulder clearing, to help protect the gear from further saturation. I swung back into camp just as the couple finished the move.

I checked in with the guys when they returned separately a short while later. My simple travelling cart now bulged with supplies in the starlight. The trees kept us dry as the rain increased to a drizzle, continuing on through the night.

The deep sighs and low snores assured me I was the last to fall asleep. The pattering sound of water on leaves soothed my tired soul and calmed my now constantly racing mind. It was bad enough Taya had left me in charge; I didn't have the same kind of training she did. Espionage and spy-craft don't go hand-in-hand with gardening and community building. I could take care of myself out here, with Doire's notes of course, but dealing with the masses without a View-lens between us, pushed my patience and my sanity on a daily basis.

What if I'd never accepted the Kronik's offer? Where would I be now? Home? On assignment? At Dezmind and Taya's funerals? My fingernails were constantly filled with dirt, my hair never stayed contained in the braids I wove it into, and I desperately wanted a cheeseburger. I'd lost fifteen pounds since coming out here – I hated the feel of my skin sliding over bone, but I could only eat so much fish and fruit. *Red meat or even a saucy roasted ganoo…* I rolled over and stared at my jagged nails, devoid of hot pink, burnt orange or bullooberry passion. *I don't belong here.*

The instinct to want to *know*, to be a part of the *action* still prickled the nape of my neck and made my brain twitch with anticipation – but I couldn't pry into these people's lives and not expect a backlash. More than once I started writing our story: mine, the Kahn-lea's, and most especially Taya's. But that wasn't newsworthy anymore – where our next meal came from, how certain plants react together, and living in a city built by aliens, far outweighed any of that. If I ever did get around to reporting again, at least I'd have a dedicated constituency; one thing I somehow managed to get right out here – keeping the lines of communication open.

I fell asleep dreaming of hair dye and curling irons… and Touf kissing me – his hot breath on the back of my neck… but his blue face shifted to bronze and the arms of an entirely different man encircled my dreams.

The wind lashed rain against my face, startling me awake. I raised my arms as a shield. The sky was dark, the weather harsh and unyielding. As I turned to wake the others, undignified shrieks and grunts whipped across the spent fire.

"Come on!" I yelled. "We have to get to the upper forest – there's more protection there!" Bodies scrambled to wrap sleeping mats and gather backpacks. Deltek and Raylan grabbed onto the contoured cart handle and pushed it toward the stream. Lutrice jogged beside me as Syvis raced ahead to find the clearest path.

A vicious crack echoed above, ricocheting across the blackened morning sky. My heart jumped into my throat. *Was that a tree or the sky?*

"Keep moving!" I shouted, and glanced at Lutrice. Her eyes were wide, and her face flushed. I grabbed her hand to reassure her – of what I don't know, but we ran that way for what felt like an hour.

The wind whipped thin bullets of rain at us. It stung as if it pierced skin. The howl echoing through the older trees deafened and numbed my senses, younger trees bent nearly to the ground with the force of the gale.

The sky cracked again.

Great streaks of light sizzled across heavens absent of any one of the Sun Guardians. Weather this nasty never happened in Darzeth Prime.

At the stream, the water rose fast and fierce. The three men lifted the cart above their heads as we all waded through water chest deep. My feet kept getting pulled out from beneath me.

Lutrice and I went under.

I opened my eyes to churning bubbles and a black arm. I grabbed it, tried to force my body to sink; then I pushed hard with my feet against the rocky bottom. Lutrice came with me but slipped again. I dug the fingers of one hand into the moist loam of the bank. The fingers of the other hand dug into her tender skin as I pulled her torso up out of the water.

She coughed and gasped for air. Firm bronzed hands hooked me under my arms and separated us.

Regardless of the close call, Lutrice and I scrambled to our feet and pushed the men back to the cart. Our saturated clothes restricted our ability to run. My teeth chattered incessantly; I couldn't stop shivering.

CRACK!

A giant tree crashed to the ground across our path. I pushed wet hair from my mouth and eyes. The trunk was too large to go over, so we steered around the jagged end.

An eternity passed as we struggled against the raging storm. *My eyes are useless. Where are you when I need you Taya!* I had to find us shelter. There was no sign of a cave, or hollow anywhere and things were only getting worse.

At the waterfall, Syvis stopped and gathered us together in a huddle.

"We should see if there's any natural shelter in the area."

"We don't have time," I said. "The storm's getting worse, not better. Let's hide the cart in those bushes and keep going. We're almost back."

"But the supplies," Deltek said.

"They'll be fine. We'll return for them." Breaking free of the huddle, I slammed my body into the handle of the cart to get it moving. Syvis helped me secure it in the midst of the brush, where the wind couldn't push anything over. We scrambled up the slippery path beside the falls, but the wind changed direction – broad-siding us.

We're not moving fast enough! My foot shot out from under me. I fell and slammed my chin against the rough stair.

"Zaith!" Lutrice panicked.

Those same strong arms from the stream picked me up. Syvis held me tight against his body, supporting my weight. For a nanosecond I let my head rest against his taut biceps.

"Keep going!" he shouted to the others.

His yell jolted my head up. Last night's stars appeared behind my eyes. This wasn't good. Sliding one of my arms over his broad back, Syvis held me even closer, if that were possible, and we scrambled up the path behind the others. The jolting motion of climbing the stone stairs made my head pound, and my teeth ache.

Maybe Taya was right; there was just too much Thyafeen running through my veins. But a woman has needs, and it had been too long since a man held me in his arms.

The tingling jolt to my lack of sensibilities actually helped clear my head – that or we'd actually reached the top of the falls and my head had stopped bouncing. We fell behind, but Syvis kept our pace steady until we reached The Black Gates and the others.

I looked from one side to the other too fast, making my head pound again. Deltek and Lutrice strained to pull the wing open again, but the wind wouldn't allow it.

"We'll go around," Syvis shouted. Lutrice stopped yanking at the bars, resting against Deltek as she alternately heaved and then gulped great mouthfuls of wet air. A gale blasted through the clearing. It blew me off my feet and brought Syvis to his knees. The gate clanged shut the few inches it had been reopened. The others were flattened against the thin spires.

"Okay!" Deltek yelled in agreement to the plan. Everyone pushed forward to help me and Syvis up. We went left, Raylan in the lead.

"It's getting worse," I said in Syvis' ear. "We won't make it back." Though I was steadier on my feet now, he still held me close as we sloshed through the rain.

By the time we could straddle the tapered end of the gate's arm, the road was nowhere in sight. Ray led us on an angular trajectory back through the trees, hoping to regain the road farther ahead. It was risky but necessary. Heading straight back to the gate we'd lose time, but we travelled into unknown territory between here and there… wherever *there* happened to be.

Our pace slowed by half. The trees here offered no break as they were too far apart and too young to resist the blast of elements. Time lost meaning, and even the shared body heat between Syvis and I dwindled as the cold took purchase.

Another volley of rain-whipping wind knocked us to the ground. I landed flat on my stomach and didn't have the strength to fight back, to get up. Salty tears mixed readily with the streaming spray assaulting my cheeks. My lungs burned from trying to run against this invisible barrier. There was nothing I could do to stop the nightmare.

Rolling onto my back, closer to Syvis' side, I shielded my eyes with my hands and looked up. Clouds swirled and funnelled above, as the rain thrashed at us from all angles. *What the Guardians is this!*

"I found something!" Ray's voice barely registered.

Syvis grabbed both of my hands and hauled me up. Just inside the denser tree line, a metallic domed building glistened among the trees. Ray ran to the door. I knew it wouldn't budge, but he didn't let that stop him. Grabbing a large rock, he raised it above his head...

"No!" I screamed, flying out of Syvis' grasp and across the twenty yards between us. "No– Don't!"

"What! Are you mad?" Ray shook me off his arm. "We can't stay out here." He gripped the stone with both hands above his head. I lost feeling in my legs and collapsed. Lutrice ran over.

"Ray!" She yelled. "We can't go in there. You know that!"

He heaved the rock anyway. The window smashed. He picked up another one and knocked the loose shards out of the frame; then he dove in.

It's sealed for a reason – Dezmind's voice echoed in my head.

It's sealed for a reason – Taya's voice echoed the echo.

I grabbed Lutrice's shoulders, bringing her face to mine, "It's a death trap!"

She nodded and hugged me tight. Deltek grabbed both of us, shivering and shaking. I followed, numb to everything around us but the gaping hole in the side of the small dwelling.

"Some trees have fallen over a ditch on the other side of those bushes," he said. "Come on." Deltek pried Lutrice out of my arms, just as Syvis wrapped his around me, leading me from the alien house... the one harbouring the promise of death.

"What do we do about Ray?" he asked, his hot breath partially thawing my earlobe.

"We leave him."

Chapter Five
Back to Basics

Taya

This time I was prepared. I wouldn't be caught off guard again, which meant I wouldn't place anyone at risk either. The swarm of bodies that had overpowered me after Dez's Underground Rally had rattled more than just my nerves... that panic, coupled with Dez being whisked away from me, back to the surface, without a proper goodbye, made something snap – a something I now had to keep in check. The best way to do that was to avoid any and all contact with the Followers of Light – and since they could be anyone, I had to avoid everyone.

I walked down the streets of the Underground with a forced confidence. I'd carefully wrapped my hair up around the crown of my head, and put on a white luma – a soft contoured, front-brimmed hat that Guardians of the Trinity wore when they were observing rites. Sure, it was more than a little blasphemous, seeing as I only believed in Zola, Zita, and Zerameteth when it was convenient. Gerrund's errand girl, Trina, had come by early this morning for my grocery list. I decided to list the hat instead of starches – I could live off protein and root vegetables for a week.

Trina offered me her anti-glare shades. I wanted them, sure, but not if it meant she'd go without. She needed them for work. I only accepted them when she told me she had a backup pair at home. The hazelnut glasses were more evidence of adapted old-tech, but they were a common accessory for anyone who worked outside – well, out in the tunnels anyway. They covered my finer features, while still allowing passers-by to see my eyes.

The getup was perfect; I couldn't be recognised outright from a distance, and I wouldn't draw curious stares up close. I think what helped the most was smearing a tinted moisturising cream over my face, neck, hands and arms, which gave my pink skin a noticeably bluish hue. Thank Zola, Magda's runner also came by the apartment this morning. It was like she'd read my mind – that woman's intuition was uncanny.

Double checking Gerrund's directions, delivered by Trina, I ventured down a street I'd never been to before. Breathing deep and slow, I could finally take in and enjoy, the wonders of the Underground without the threat of being mobbed. After getting home this morning I took a quarter sleeping pill to help me rest for a few hours; I didn't want to be dozy for my first Daily with Gerrund.

Four hours of uninterrupted sleep invigorated me. No feverish sweat, no nausea, and still lying in the comfort of my own bed – now that was the right way to greet the day. If only Dez were there, then it'd be perfect. I buried the thought, or at least I tried to. It was far easier to ignore the fuzziness at the back of my mind and push through the lethargy of my strides knowing that today was a fresh start. I couldn't believe Gerrund had actually taken me seriously during my headache-induced rage.

While I meant what I said, I hadn't raised my concerns in the best way… in fact I'd probably alienated Ticia. I couldn't help wondering how hard Gerrund had worked to convince the others to include me after pulling a stunt like that.

But was this just part of the ruse? After all, if I'm not happy then Dez is not happy. I'd have to keep an open mind. Gerrund made it perfectly clear my involvement was for intelligence purposes only – but anything was better than nothing at this point.

Allowing myself the pleasure of looking around, I noticed several large-scale shops in the area dealing in furniture, bicycles, sporting goods and slider repairs. I hadn't seen many sliders whizzing around, but then not getting out much meant I missed a lot. I'd never owned one top-side due to the necessity of travelling greater distances for work. Down here, the light modular frame, and small electric motor, made it a handy way to move quickly through the Underground. Each unit was compact enough for one person to stand on, with a briefcase or pack-purchase within the back raised portion.

Turning off the main road I followed a narrower side tunnel leading to the larger cavern, where I'd join today's Daily. A fragmented glint in an old shop window caught my eye as I passed. Slowing my strides, I walked toward the small shop and peered inside.

From the layers of dust and the hodgepodge of items scattered around the room, it had been turned into a storage shed and forgotten about. I caught sight of the item that glinted – it was a solar cell. A small grouping of them actually. They were propped up against a box whose dust cover had slipped off. I scanned the rest of the room, my brain trying to piece the beginnings of an idea together.

A bicycle bell rang out behind me. I spun around as the bike and its passenger sped past. The bell had been a warning for me not to step back into his path. He disappeared into the cavern at the end of the tunnel. I slipped the turquoise scarf back from the face of my watch to check the time, and started off again before I was late.

The tunnel opened into a mammoth cavern with no obvious exit. The scattered shops around the perimeter were clearly run specifically for the Cause Training Ground: a cobbler, several tailors and cafés. In addition to those were a pair of solid metal doors marked "Authorised Personal Only". The rest of the space was devoted to barracks.

Nearly two hundred volunteers drilled in the open common space in the centre of the expansive cavern; some with weapons, and some manoeuvring around basic obstacles. A command post squatted like a miniature helio landing pad in the middle. As I made my way toward the group gathered there, the cyclist from before sped back toward me. I stopped as he neared, but he flew past without taking notice.

Then it dawned on me. *This* is *the only road in or out of here.*

I smiled, watching Gerrund as he kept one eye on his conversant, and one eye on me as I approached. He likely suspected who I was, but a giddy elation bubbled inside knowing my simple disguise worked on several levels. *If I can fool Gerrund, maybe he'll let me go top-side to work with Dez.*

Gerrund nodded to Hevex, who promptly took his leave; likely working on the latest batch of statistics. Gerrund met me as I approached the octagonal ring of small tables on a raised wooden platform. He, too, was smiling, but the expression didn't reach his eyes. He was all business.

"J.J., you're just in time." Even though he'd given me a new name, he rarely remembered to use it. "The volunteers will break for breakfast in a minute. Then I can get you, Thenticia, and Mardel together."

My excitement plummeted to the bottom of my stomach. I nodded, removing the glasses and hat. "What gave me away?"

This time, the smile did reach his eyes, "I've told you before, J.J., anyone who *knows* you would never be fooled. But then, that wasn't your goal, was it? You're trying to fool strangers."

"You're avoiding my question."

He reached out and thumbed the tip of my nose. "You don't walk like a Sun Guardian observing her religious rites. I know every last Guardian down here personally; *and* you have that set look on your face – it's been a while since I last saw it. That, and your overall personal bearing – nothing I haven't said before." He paused and tilted his head, "What's on your mind?"

I ordered the words in my head before speaking; I still wasn't as prepared as I'd hoped to be, but this idea would test his sincerity about keeping me involved.

"I appreciate being included in this *undertaking*."

"There's a *but* in there somewhere." He cocked his head to one side, waiting. I felt that determined set align my features again.

"I'm concerned about the Kahn-lea." He nodded. "I want to further our efforts in reaching them safely and swiftly. There's no verrin out there – they desperately need more supplies."

"And..." he prompted.

"And I have a plan. I want to build another Desert Vehicle – a small one this time." The idea invigorated me, pushing the words out faster. "This is a worthwhile task that no one else is focused on – a task I can throw all of my energy and knowledge into. I just need some help."

"What? Manpower?"

"Not exactly."

"You have that much faith in your new disguise that you'd risk multiple appearances in public to gather supplies? And just where do you propose to construct this Desert Vehicle?" He glanced at his digital watch.

Ooo, I need one of those. I fingered the leather strap of the mechanical watch beneath my wrist scarf. *But Dez gave me this – he didn't know... didn't know how the ticking would affect me.* I was running out of time to pitch this idea.

"That's just it – what gave me the idea in the first place are the contents of a storage unit just down the tunnel there." I waved to the main thoroughfare behind me.

"What makes you think I can help you?" He was being awfully approachable today – maybe it had something to do with the promise of boosting the efficiency of the recruits. Whatever it was, I needed to take advantage of it before his mood turned and I suddenly became a liability again.

I flashed him my version of Zaith's "aren't I charming" smile.

"It has the Cause's insignia in the lower left corner of the shop window."

Gerrund rubbed his chin. He squinted slightly as he mulled over my idea. His eyes peeled away the layers of makeup on my face; they pierced and analysed. Then he looked me straight in the eye. I flinched. *Smarten up. Stand your ground, Taya!*

"You don't look well. At the last couple of Consolidating Meetings you haven't been yourself. Is everything all right?"

The switch in conversation set off alarm bells in my brain. It took me a moment longer than usual to recover – not a good sign.

"I've– I'm fine. I'm just tired of feeling like a rat in a cage. I need this, Gerrund. And it's important."

He studied me a moment longer. "I'll tell you what." He squinted at me. "You meet with a friend of mine and I'll see about making that old shop *yours*, along with whatever other resources you'll need. This'll be a long-term project that you can launch *after* the coup."

The "so what do you think?" was left floating, silent, in the space between us. Not only did I not know when the coup would happen, which left Zaith and the Kahn-lea surviving on a huge question mark, but the last time I'd agreed to meet with a *friend* of his I'd lost my identity. What kind of game was he playing?

"Gerrund!" Thenticia called.

"Come on," he said, and escorted me over to one of the lower command posts to get down to work.

"That's it!" I tossed my pen at the middle of the table. "I'm done." I turned and walked away from the command post, ending the madness of that morning's Daily. Three hours and seven demonstrations later, I couldn't take it anymore. If it wasn't for Mardel, and the entire platoon of volunteers, I would've severely incapacitated Ticia.

From now on, if Gerrund insists on another one of these sessions as part of the Daily, I'll only speak with Mardel – then he can deal with Ms. Obsessive.

She blocked every suggestion I had, her logic was riddled with holes, and she tried to find a way to show me up at every opportunity. The woman was more stubborn than I was, with half the intelligence... well maybe not half, but we were supposed to be improving the training regime, not verbally sparing over every minute detail.

Gerrund had left immediately after the daily update. At the time, he was satisfied with my input and information regarding Facility trained troops. I didn't know firsthand how the Kronik operated, but the best of the Facility's *anything* was always absorbed by the upper echelon.

I wasn't watching where I was going, and nearly got run over by another mail carrier on a bike. But my fury at Ticia's blatant disregard for my intel overrode logic, and the need to focus on where I was walking. Because of an insider they'd been liaising with, an informant from the depths of the Kronik's Secret Agency, Ticia had refused to entertain the notion that I might know something about the situation.

Leaders can't afford ignorance.

She was working with tunnel vision, and Mardel didn't hold enough sway to get her to see reason. They were dealing with nearly two hundred innocent lives here, volunteers who saw only hope for the future. The grim reality of warfare, and reminders of the Nine Seas Massacre, were not being heeded because Ticia chose to place her trust in someone claiming to be on our side— just as Zaith and Werks had claimed loyalty to the Spoken Truth... *to me*. If my best friend could lie convincingly to me, if a grandfatherly gentleman who worked as head chef at The Chalklin Pond Restaurant could be a sleeper assassin, then no one claiming to be on our side from inside the government should be given such absolute trust.

But they refused to listen to me. *She* refused to listen.

My skin crawled. I tightened my grip on the glasses and hat; in my haste to leave I'd forgotten to put them back on. A shadow of movement flickered to my left. It was one of the Cobbler's workers, a Danieth woman who stood visiting one of the volunteers. She looked at me.

She can't know who I am, can she? I glanced at my reflection passing a storefront window. *The blue's gone...*

"Moisturiser," I cursed. *And my hair is trailing down the nape of my neck.* "Oh, no," I groaned. And then there were my hands... I clenched my other fist. My cover was broken. My skin had absorbed the cream, and Ticia made me pull at my hair more than once. *I have to lose this woman before she draws a crowd.*

Luckily, there was no foot traffic down the connecting tunnel back to the main road. I picked up my pace gradually, glancing at my watch to hide my true intensions.

It took several minutes to walk the length of the side tunnel. In that time, the orange-skinned woman nearly halved the distance between us. Not a good sign. Making a wide arc at the end of the of the tunnel mouth, I tried to make it look like I was crossing the road at the intersection.

I swung back around to the opposite side of the street when I was out of visual range. Hiding in a small niche in the cave wall between two shops, I blended into obscurity as a bustling crowd thrived along the walkway.

I watched as the woman looked down the road where she'd last glimpsed me, and then peer into several shops and cafés. Finally, she gave up and slouched her black coliths back where she came from. I stood there for twenty minutes before, I too, back-tracked down the empty tunnel. Only this time the training cavern wasn't my destination.

Gingerly, I made my way through the shadows, pausing in the occasional crevice or hollow, until I settled in a nook almost directly across from the abandoned shop. Not three months ago I was an elite Contractor at the threshold of my career, and now I was forced to hide in the shadows and slink around like a thief or rodent, stripped of everything. I made a fist and slammed it into the rock behind me – the pain of the impact reminded me why I'd come back here.

What'll it be? Gerrund's voice echoed in my mind. Was he honestly concerned for my health, or was this just a way to monitor me indirectly? I didn't know who to trust anymore. I didn't want to end up a pawn in someone else's game.

"What'll it be?" I mused.

"Researching the neighbourhood?" A soft, male voice whispered from the adjoining cranny.

My heart slammed into my throat.

The unbidden memory of dozens of bodies suffocating me… asking me to be something I wasn't, calling me the names of their chosen one… standing between me and the man I was supposed to spend the rest of my life with… and then the blood…slammed into me.

I coughed. *This is ridiculous! No wonder Gerrund's people don't take me seriously; even when I'm hiding people find me.*

I spoke through clenched teeth, "I'm not Emvaso-al, Child of the Sun or Zimi, Life Giver. My name is *not* Aelonia, Jadis or J.J.! You've got the wrong person," I growled.

He chuckled softly. It wasn't menacing or taunting, just… joyful? It didn't make any sense. He cleared his throat.

"I don't respond to any of those names either." Even though he was hidden by the thin band of rock between us, I could tell he was smiling. My muscles relaxed and my breathing evened out. "So, tell me," he continued. "If you're interested in this unit, why are you avoiding your neighbours?"

Of course! He didn't sneak up on me – he was here the whole time. He saw everything. Who in Zita's name is he?

"Who says I'm interested in the shop?"

"You mean, other than the fact you just ditched someone following you, only to double-back discretely and stand in the shadows to stare determinedly at the place? Oh, I don't know, maybe I'm just a keen observer."

I snorted.

He chuckled again.

There was something so honest and unassuming about that sound... and yet–

"My interest in that shop is none of your business."

A card-key dangled in front of my face, from a disembodied hand reaching around the rock between us.

"On the contrary." He stepped gracefully from the shadows. I caught a quick flash of his smile, a streak of pale blue skin, and watched a shock of dirty-blonde hair turn and walk across the street to the shop door.

I didn't move.

The lock on the door clicked, and the tall Balanis-cross with the gentle laugh, loped into the unit. The door stayed open. *Gerrund must have sent him.*

I squared my shoulders, hazarded a glance to either side of the now quiet thoroughfare, and followed him.

I shut the door behind me. His caramel coloured tunic stretched across a broad back and solid shoulders as he cleared off a junk-strewn corner of the main counter. He sat down and looked at me.

I locked the door. Leaning back against it, I crossed my arms in front of my chest and stared at him.

"I know why you're here," I said. His eyebrows rose. A flash of jade by his ear registered somewhere in the back of my mind. "And you can tell Gerrund that I haven't made up my mind yet." Then muttered to myself, "I don't even know who this person is he wants me to meet."

"A therapist."

"He told you? Is it you?" My voice cut through the dust motes like a throwing blade. "He didn't even–"

"No," he spoke over me. "I'm Gelden, Gerrund's nephew." I glared at him anyway. He pulled a package out of the pack at his side and motioned toward me with it. "Hungry?"

There was something about his simple, easy nature that was completely disarming. I let it draw me over, but sat across from him on an old crate. He passed me half the sandwich and a flat flaky pastry.

"I guess I should introduce myself – I mean," I faltered. What could I say? *Who am I – really?*

He noticed the hesitation. "Well, I clearly know who you're not." He gave me a smile and winked.

I sighed, giving him a half-hearted smile in return. I couldn't ask him to call me Taya – she was dead – the woman I *had* been, the Facility Contractor/Desert Guide no longer existed. My life top-side had been erased along with my face. The person I used to be might as well be dead.

"Dalla," he said, around a particularly full mouth.

"Excuse me?"

"I'll call you Dalla. It's short for Dallaal"

"And I'm supposed to know what that means?"

He laughed, covering his mouth to stop from spraying his food at me.

"No, I guess you wouldn't. It's a term that developed in the Underground which reflects the state we seem to perpetually find ourselves in. It refers to flux, a conundrum or contradiction."

I nodded, savouring the sweet pastry he'd given me. *It fits.* As I'd probably never see him again, or rarely at that, what did it matter if he gave me yet another name? This one at least described who I was now, instead of who I used to be or who everyone wanted me to be.

"State your terms," I demanded, bringing things back around to business – something I was more comfortable with.

"Terms?" I'd lost him.

"Yes, terms. You were sent here because Gerrund knew I'd listen to you. You have a certain quality, a gift as it were, and he's using you to get to me."

He rubbed his hands on his deep red slacks and linked his fingers around one knee.

"You're right. He did ask me to come."

"Why? You don't know me…" Actually, he and everyone else down here probably knew more about me than even I could keep track of, but then again, that was *Jadis Doire* the child of Matheson and the Talian Lynnia who broke all the rules… who got me into this mess in the first place. So much had happened since then.

"I agree with you," he said.

"About what?"

"About needing to make the Kahn-lea a priority. About finding a reliable way to cross the Deserts. If the Kahn-lea don't want to stay in the Great City, we need to let them know they have a home here – or a temporary one at any rate – and that means having a backup plan for keeping the Generator operational."

I leaned forward. There was passion in his words, a sincere concern with my issues – he might even have sway with Gerrund…

"I'm listening."

He leaned forward as well.

"I can help you. I can get you anything you'll need to make this happen: materials, research, labour – you name it. I'd like you to accept the position of Mentor on my behalf."

What?

"Working with you would not only allow me to complete my training, but I believe it'll help make a difference."

I had no idea what training he was referring to, or what being a Mentor entailed, but the spark in his eyes and his straight-faced honesty spoke volumes.

I sighed.

The glint faded.

I gave him a wan smile. "What's the deal with this therapist?" The sparkle returned briefly, before a serious set came over his face.

"Gerry thinks you're having Night Tremors."

I burst out laughing. Gelden tilted his head and gave me a funny look. I held my side and gasped for air, as a tiny trickle of moisture dripped from the corner of my eye.

"Gerry!" I wiped the laugh-tear away with the back of my hand. "You can't sit there and expect me to keep a straight face when you call the Leader of the Cause, the Overseer of the Underground – *Uncle Gerry.*"

He cracked a smile and ran a hand through his thick straight hair. Though it was cropped relatively short, it had that loose, wild look Zaith would've drooled over. *Well that was a buzz-kill.* I pushed her name and her memory back into the dark, back to wherever it'd dredged itself up from.

"Bajak's been helping victims of the Kronik's wrath for years – since I was a kid anyway."

I didn't like the sound of *victim.* I'd been trapped in that Agency Warehouse, but I'd fought with every ounce of my being. The term *victim* was for the helpless, the defenceless–

Is that really the way they see me? Is that what I've become? I guess I couldn't blame them. I never went outside during the day, and when I did, I avoided interacting with others just in case the FOL recognised me – I was hiding in a hidden world... and it didn't help that those closest to me paid me little to no mind.

Gelden collected the remnants of our lunch. I knew he couldn't tell what I was thinking, but he did recognise he'd said something wrong.

"Look, Dalla, Bajak's someone to talk to at the very least, and maybe that's all Gerrund wants you to do – tell someone what happened." He unlocked and then opened the shop door, before turning and tossing me the key. "Think about it," he said and shut the door behind him.

Think about it.

I looked closely at the small shop. Layers of dust-covered counters, boxes, tables and fixtures. They sat there waiting for me to decide. The small bit of solar panelling winked at me.

Chapter Six
Above

Dezmind

I sat down at the desk where we'd once haggled over stupid bits of contract prattle, knowing even then there was a chance she was *the one*. Those nine days in the Desert seemed a life-time ago. While I didn't want the uncertainty they'd brought at the time, I did want her back.

After the assassination attempt at the last Rally, as we lay together under a public transport to avoid detection, I'd taken it for granted that we'd be together during this phase of the Cause.

Absently, I ran a hand through my hair, picked up the pen and wrote down a name… just not the right one.

Aelonia,

Last night I dreamt of the Deserts. I relived the attacks: both human and animal; the suffocating effects of the sand, and the near-drowning in pure verrin; the immobilising dehydration that put me to fever and delirium. Yet, all of the fear was gone. It was as though I observed from a distance. I knew what was happening, and yet I was calm.

I realise now that after every bone-jarring moment, you were there. You were there to save me – to save us all.

On some level I know I understood this from the start, but that dream brought everything crashing back. You've never asked me, but I've seen it in your eyes – you wonder about the real reason I requested you for the contract, why I wouldn't release you from it… why it had to be you.

I see the worry, the dread you mask with bravado. I see you second-guessing yourself, and I see that silent question.

It's true I had my suspicions about you at that first Rally – about who you might be, but that's only where it all began. It was your convictions; it was your strengths as well as your weaknesses – the few that managed to squeak out; your belief in natural chaos and the chaos waging at your very core; it was knowing that you would risk everything – your life even – if it meant you could save one soul.

That's what calmed me and turned a nightmare into a revelation… I miss you, Ali.

I miss your abrasive pinioning, your brutal honesty, your selflessness – but most of all, I miss your smile. And yet, that isn't what I remember most about you as I lay down to sleep at night. It's the terror entrenched on your face, etched into your features after the Underground Rally that turned into an incident. Yes, I heard about that. I can't help but wonder if things would've worked out differently had I been able to stay just a few moments longer.

I hate that I wasn't there when you needed me most, and in some ways I curse what it is we've dedicated ourselves to, for it only seems to be tearing us apart.

Here, I'm leading constantly. It's so isolating at times. Yes, I'm forever surrounded by people, but I lack connection – it's gone from being a mission to a job I don't remember signing up for.

I miss us working together. Even as I mentally scoffed at the insistence of it, all those weeks ago, I knew you spoke the truth.

I wish you were here.

I miss your keen eye, your wit, and most of all your friendship. I promise I'll visit as soon as I can.

DL

I leaned back in my office chair, the smell of ganoo slow-roasting on the spit in the next room invaded my senses. Gamma swooped low as twilight neared. I whispered a prayer for the Kahn-lea, wondering how they fared after my abrupt departure. It was a choice I'd had to make.

I'd known Taya and Zaith were planning to keep me in the alien City, and I couldn't let that happen. I should've known, too, that Taya would come after me. I guess part of me did know, had hoped she'd catch up with me in the Expanse. I never fathomed the Kronik wanted her dead – they were supposed to be after me.

My hand shook as I grabbed an envelope and encoded Taya's address on the front. I'd make the drop in the morning before the next Rally walk.

I closed my eyes, still holding the letter, and reached out with my mind – stretching in vain to make a telepathic connection I knew was impossible at this distance. Still, if she was thinking of me too…

Chapter Seven
The Situation

Zaith

Once Raylan went in, he never came back out. I massaged my forehead as I walked the long road out to the edge of the Great City. But Raylan wasn't the type to submit quietly. After the storm broke, Deltek and Lutrice had raced back to the Common for supplies. As the rain and the winds abated, Ray made his first attempt. I didn't want to make the call, but in light of the situation, we had to keep him there without putting ourselves at further risk.

Pulling a canvas mask out of my backpack, I tied it snug across my nose and mouth. Jantice had fashioned six of them from her pack. Having volunteered at the local Health Habitat, she knew the tighter the weave the less likely airborne germs and contaminants would spread.

The small domed house materialised amidst a coppice of trees. The board Syvis and Deltek affixed to the broken window screamed of my failures, of my inadequacies. I stopped and closed my eyes as the memory assaulted me...

"Syvis! Don't let him leave!" I shouted.

"How? You won't let me get any closer!"

Ray's head and shoulders pushed beyond the small window opening. I searched the ground, shoving away soaked debris and scraping my nails through the mud. My chest ached, my head throbbed. My hand closed over a large stone. I snatched it from the moist ground and hurled it through the air. It cracked against Ray's cheek bone. He slipped and fell against the frame. I threw another rock and another. Syvis followed suit until we beat Ray back into the alien structure...

I shook off the grip of the memory. He'd left me no choice. Shielding my eyes, I leaned close and peered through an undisturbed window. Ray completed his morning exercise routine – the same work out every day for the last three days. His faint voice counted the reps of his wall push-ups. He broke into a fit of coughing.

I leaned away and walked over to the boarded-up window. Deltek had sealed the opening a couple of days ago with an old metal trunk-hatch using a mixture of mud, dry grasses, and strips of canvas. So far, there were no visible cracks in the thick seam, but he vowed to return every other day for another application just in case.

I fingered the latch. Syvis had cut the metal support bracings from around a trunk lid, using several different metalworking tools from the table in the Common. He beat the excess metal around the lid to round it out, enough to conform to the slope of the alien house. There was no seal to keep the lid air-tight, but no matter how stupid Ray had been, we couldn't starve him to death.

I knocked twice on the wall with a nearby rock. He struggled to contain his cough. Releasing the catch, I let the lid fall open and dropped in three packages made of leaves: meat, tubers, fruit – enough for another two days – plus an extra cloth packet. I closed the hatch as I suspended a thin piece of cloth, one of Lutrice's extra T-shirts, across the opening. Pushing harder than usual, I got the latch to close. Jantice had suggested it might help keep the cracks around the hatch sealed a bit tighter.

"Ray?"

Silence.

"Ray, I've included a sachet of dried healing herbs. Dissolve them in some water twice a day." I sighed. He refused to talk to me anymore. "I'll do everything possible to find a way to get you out of this."

I knew everyone was anxiously waiting for me to get back for breakfast. Tami and Jan were on kitchen duty this week. I watched as they jumped into action after catching sight of me walking toward the Common on my way back from the edge of the forest. By the time I sat with the others around the dining table, just inside the ring of tables that made up the utility stations around the central fountain, I was the last one served – no time wasted. They were restless and eager, but this was not a morning meeting I wanted to hold. I ate my prerequisite mouthful of food, their rule not mine. Apparently, I didn't eat enough in a day.

"It's possible—"

"Zaith, don't try to spare our feelings here." Syvis caught me with his eyes, telling me he'd already guessed the outcome.

"I'm not. It's still too early to know for sure. He's developed a wracking cough, but whether it's due to dust allergies, a cold from the storm, or the dormant Virus, I can't tell. He's still quite strong and, other than the cough, he seems okay. I'll look in on him every day, but I don't want any of you risking exposure. The system isn't perfect, but it's all we've got." I turned to Merik. "Have you found anything in your collections that could help?"

"No. There are a few journals, but they only relate to the suffering their writers were forced to endure. No new symptoms to add to the list." He paused for a breath. "You know, it took over a year to decimate the entire population; so even if Ray doesn't show signs in the next ten days, that doesn't mean he's not infected, or even a carrier."

"So, what are we going to do?" Tami asked quietly. "He doesn't deserve to stay locked up forever."

"We can't risk him infecting the rest of us. You know that, Tamaine," Lutrice chastised in her motherly way. Jan patted Tami on the back.

"Zaith, how can you be so sure this is even a problem? We might be torturing Ray for no reason," Jan said.

"I can't take the chance. Both Dezmind and Taya believed in not disturbing those sealed houses. I would rather Ray be thoroughly outraged with me after a bout of the flu, than dead." I nibbled a piece of fruit from my plate. I had to be proactive about this or risk fracturing our community.

"We should take turns scouting the City. Syvis, keep mapping out the unexplored areas, but don't search in-depth anywhere, it'll only slow you down. Divide the known areas into four quadrants, we can head out in pairs and focus our morning searches for anything that might give us a clue as to what we're potentially dealing with. Merik, you and Deltek work on translating any findings in the afternoons, and Lu, you can tend the herb garden."

"Jan and I found some machinery we're certain makes cloth. We're going to keep looking for natural elements we might be able to use to run them. Zola knows, our clothes are already wearing thin, and we need lighter fabric more suited to this humidity."

"Excellent, Tami. The sooner we're self-sufficient the better."

Syvis inhaled his food, keeping his eyes on me the entire time. I tried to smile, but flirting was the farthest thing from my mind. Immediately after breakfast, he started organising search paths and teams. Lu helped put together travel food for everyone's packs.

We're gonna beat this thing — we have to.

Chapter Eight
Risk

Taya

"Welcome, my brothers and sisters of the Cause. May the hands of our forefathers of the dawning of the Age of Migration guide our hearts this night. And so, our numbers rise as Aelonia Trellice joins ranks and breaks bread at the table of the Consolidating Body." Gerrund nodded at me.

Leaving my stool in the corner, I joined the others at the table. Poised to sit across from the door, I observed the silent twist of the handle behind the Dias. My eyes flickered to Mardel and back to the door as every nerve in my body sizzled on high alert. But Gerrund nodded toward the door in expectation.

"Let the Consolidating Body acknowledge Dezmind Lisle."

"Here," the others said in unison. I watched, frozen in disbelief, as Dez entered and stood to the left of Gerrund; Randek, as always, was to his right. As everyone else sat, Mardel pulled me down, elbowing me.

"Unfortunately, my time here is limited, but the news I bring could come safely no other way." Dez made eye contact with each representative as he walked in and joined the meeting. I tried to make a telepathic connection.

Dez!

Taya—A distant inner voice and then nothing.

Outwardly, he gave me nothing more than polite acknowledgment.

From the beginning of my involvement in the Underground and the Cause all those weeks ago, he'd warned me about "polite detachment" when conducting business – but we'd always had time together before the formalities, so it hadn't mattered. The invisible barrier I'd built to protect myself while living down here fizzled out. A chill crawled across my skin. I shuddered.

I focused on Dez as he laced his fingers together and rested the sides of his hands on the table. "The fiancée of one of the Kahn-lea is at risk."

"Bazdin," I said, thinking of Tamaine. Her tale of how the two of them met had entranced the Kahn-lea the one night in the Deserts we'd been able to share our stories. If I remembered correctly, they were supposed to be married sometime this month. Then it struck me just how similar our situations were: he and Tamaine were separated because her return might cost her life.

"Yes. His exposure to the Kronik is increasing daily. He's been to see me several times, but insists that I'm lying about the Kahn-lea's safety just to pacify him. He's blinded by love and relentless in his search for answers. I've explained to him everything I can, without making him more of a potential target. But if he continues digging around and asking questions of the wrong people, he could send up a signal to the Kronik's spies, of that I have no doubt.

"The man's life is on the line. As he knows little about the Cause and nothing of our motives. He's likely to be tortured to death – as past experience warns us."

My escape from the Warehouse flashed through my brain...

Drugged and nearly out of my mind... the flashes of light coming from the ventilation shaft above... dislocating my shoulder to climb the metal post I was cuffed to...

The ghost of a trickle of blood made me rub my wrist.

Dez flattened his hands on the table top with a sharp smack, bringing me back to the present.

"We need to make contact and find a way to remove him from the Kronik's radar before we suffer another civilian tragedy – before it comes to the point where he'll need all of the services the Underground has to offer."

"I agree," the Dias weighed in. "The Kronik could *entice* him to say certain things about you and the Cause. If he believed his life might be spared, he'd think nothing of revealing what little he does know, or make up what they want to hear to avoid being tortured. We cannot afford the Kronik this *luxury*."

"I'll meet with him." All gazes turned on me.

"I'm the best person for the job. Other than Dezmind, I'm the only one who knows his fiancée. I can relate to him on a personal level. Dezmind obviously doesn't have the time to commit to this, nor does he want the potential negative attention at such a critical juncture. Final alliances are being gathered top-side."

I leaned back in my chair. *This* was my chance to make a move and gain leverage to return to the Prime – my chance to break free of this subterranean prison and be of help above.

"Who am I? I'm nobody top-side. I can contact him subtly, and set up a meet at a safe location."

"Ali, the whole reason you're down here is that you *are* somebody, even if you don't look the same as you did. The average person might not know you, but the Kronik's Agents are trained to detect anomalies… like a clandestine Contractor trying to hide her true identity. It's too risky," Dez said.

Shards of anger sliced through my veins. It was the same thing he and Gerrund had been saying since he abandoned me down here weeks ago.

"It's been over a month." I tried to keep a calm head and even tone.

"The government is still looking for you. Think about it.

They're aware an unknown woman helped me escape the explosion at the Rally, even if they don't know it's you specifically."

"Hevex," Gerrund said. "What intel do we have on the Kronik's views of *Jutaya Fyce*?"

"As I suspected, she's not a major target on their agenda right now," he said, watching me closely. Even he was aware of just how much weighed in the balance between my staying down here and returning to the surface... and he didn't want to contradict his General.

Gerrund raised his eyebrows.

Hevex tried to ingratiate himself again, "But that doesn't mean they're convinced that she's dead, either. There could be an ongoing search we're unaware of. Unsubstantiated rumour puts her as having returned to the Deserts – some say to rejoin the Kahn-lea, and others say to find Matheson Doire."

A surprising pain shot beyond the anger and pierced my heart at the mention of my *real* father, silencing some of the bitterness.

"Because of this general belief," Hevex continued, "and her sudden *extended* disappearance, she's low on the Kronik's priority, but she's still in danger."

"But I *am* unrecognisable..." I reminded Gerrund of what he did to me, refusing to back down or chance a look at Dez. I knew he was staring at me with those sharp grey eyes I couldn't say no to. "Except to those who know me well," I added to silence Gerrund's next comment – but the look of concentration on his face told me he hadn't made up his mind yet.

I pressed my point. "The Kronik know what I represent, but only my close friends might recognise a trace of who I was, and I'm not planning on making any social calls top-side. I won't draw attention to myself. I won't wear boots or a cap and belt pack walking around like I'm queen." I pointed a finger at Gerrund. "Don't think I don't know my pride. But being down here *has* changed me. I won't be so easily discovered, especially when people won't think to look for me in this situation."

Gerrund nodded.

Is he really reconsidering? Holy Trinity – maybe I was wrong about him.

"All those in favour of Aelonia meeting with Bazdin?"

Five fists pounded the table; two, other than mine, did not – I wasn't allowed a vote.

"It's done. Aelonia, have a detailed plan ready for tomorrow's daily; this needs to be taken care of immediately. Moving on to the next bit of business," Gerrund said.

My heart attempted to kiss my cheeks. *I can show them this can be permanent! Dez and I could eventually –*

Dezmind rose. "Unfortunately, I have to leave."

My elation plummeted to my feet, taking my heart along with it. I tried to reach out to him with my thoughts, but the haze in my brain blocked the connection.

"I think I was followed to the Junction Point. If I don't appear when my rider is ready, it'll draw attention." He gave a curt nod to the group and left.

I didn't even have time to register what had happened before Gerrund continued without pause. I closed my eyes, trying to reach out to Dez again… and got nothing but airy static and an impending migraine. The one thought-word that he spoke earlier echoed in my brain – *Taya…* until *it,* too, was gone.

"Mardel, what progress is there with the volunteers?"

"The last have arrived from the periphery. Following Ali's advice, we've set up additional tent-barracks in the adjoining passage to the main ground. The café owner has been well compensated for the use of the access tunnel through his shop. Donated material arrives daily for the production of the remainder of the tents. The last of the volunteers being hosted by locals should be in temporary barracks by midweek. We're working on improving meal rations by gathering weekly donations of credit or perishables from supportive citizens." He paused and glanced at Ticia. His knee briefly touched mine under the table.

The next report would be difficult at best. I massaged the dull throb in my temple.

He cleared his throat; I watched as the silver tip of a colith bobbed on his tan neck. "Unfortunately, there's been little consensus on which direction to take furthering the skill-base and tactical training of the sub-divided volunteers. We are at an impasse and require direction from the Consolidating Body."

"State your concerns," Gerrund prompted.

"Two possible courses could be taken. The first is to maintain the current squadron training rotation of half-a-day, and instruct each dominant skill-base toward mastery. Down-time would be spent equally between morale building and personal leisure. The second course involves the same half-day skill mastery, but emphasises the second-half be spent on simulated tactics both theoretical and practical – with no leisure time."

The silence drew on. No one made eye contact with anyone else. The Dias took control. She placed her deep black hands into a pyramid in front of her chest.

"Perhaps if we hear a brief summation of the benefits for and against each option, we'll have a sound knowledge base from which to make our decision." Nods of agreement and encouraging sounds echoed the Dias' request. I sat forward, focused and ready to fight, to throw all my frustrations with Dezmind and this ridiculous situation into my side of the debate.

"Mardel?" Dias intoned.

Ticia sat back forcefully, folding her arms against her chest.

I bit my tongue to keep from speaking out. The alternate source of pain temporarily drew my mind away from my headache, and my heartache.

Relief coated Mardel's voice, "Of course, Dias. The theory for leisure time is based on the maintenance of essential bonds between the volunteers and the average citizens of the Underground. It is thought that this familiarity reminds the recruits of why they're helping us fight. The draw-back is that they may become reluctant to place themselves in danger and begin to let fear rule their countenance. This potential fear makes for weaker soldiers.

"The theory for extended training via practical and theoretical tactics is that a continued bond develops between the volunteers as they learn skills to further their survival beyond the level of novice and into mastery. It would give them an edge to be able to plan, organise and carry out segments of missions on their own – not be autonomous but self-reliant. The drawback is disconnection from the lives they've come to know down here in the tunnels. Many already feel homesick and might drop-out without regular contact with friends and loved ones."

Again, silence filled the room like water in a tank. I blinked away remnants of my last nightmare, and tapped the top of my foot against the back of the opposite calf; Thenticia's chair creaked as she shifted from one side to the other and back again; the Dias coughed and leaned forward.

"Perhaps there is a third option? As both training theories have equal positives and negatives, a combination of both – a compromise – might pose as the most plausible course of action for this particular situation."

Gerrund leaned forward. I grounded my feet, and Ticia stilled. The Dias continued, "In both theories it is agreed that half-day skill mastery is essential. So be it. The next quarter of the day could be dedicated to advanced tactical planning, and the final quarter to leisure time. Setting a curfew would provide the necessary boundaries, and only those volunteers who need to maintain constant contact with their loved ones may be afforded that opportunity. Random down-time or casual wandering will be deterred, and this will subtly encourage the recruits to stay focused."

"I second the motion," Gerrund said. "It's now on the table along with the other options. Let's vote. All those in favour of option one?" Silence.

"All those in favour of option two?" Silence.

"All those in favour of option three?" Five fists pounded the table top.

"It's settled then. I want a detailed plan put in place and followed through in two days' time, if not sooner. On the subject of volunteers – Thenticia, do you have a solution to our surface recruiting dilemma?

"Yes. Mardel and I believe we've discovered a way to track potential volunteers without being overt or attracting undue attention. Then, if the Body are in need of recruits from the surface, we'll have an expanding resource from which to draw."

"What's the plan?" Dias asked.

"We've developed a series of questions," she said and passed around a copy to everyone, including me. "To allow known sympathisers in businesses above, and at Junction Points, to use as a basis of casual enquiry for citizens they feel might support the Cause. I've spoken with several Point Reps about their ability to accurately read people, and estimates for potential supporters. On both accounts, results were favourable.

"Mardel and I could easily test the Reps' abilities under various circumstances to be certain we can trust them with such an important, covert task. As you'll notice, there are certain auditory and visual cues they'll need to master before putting the questions into play, but we feel there's great potential with these allies and this would open up another front on which to operate – if so desired."

Gerrund sat back and tented his fingers under his chin and nose. He seconded the proposed use of the questions; the Body voted and it was deemed an acceptable risk. The Dias hid a smile behind two fingers resting on her lips. Somehow, I knew she had inadvertently assisted Ticia in finding this solution.

"Any new business?" Gerrund asked, tidying up and making as if to adjourn the meeting.

"Yes."

He lowered his half-raised body and settled back onto the edge of his chair.

"Aelonia, you have the floor."

"It's been over a month since we've been in contact with the Kahn-lea. They need to know that we haven't forgotten or forsaken them. We need to find a way to maintain regular contact in order to ensure their safety, get them much needed supplies, and monitor the continued running of the Generator."

I didn't have to look around the table to know what each Body member was thinking. The palpable weight of their silence and Gerrund's raised eyebrows told me loud and clear that this was still *not* a priority. He'd given me leave to build the new Desert Vehicle, but had no intent on formalising its existence with the Consolidating Body. *How can he not see the importance of this?*

After dismissing my business, as an afterthought Gerrund called on Randek for an update on tracking the flyer distribution and the Cause's media exposure. Twice more Gerrund looked ready to call it a night when various other Body members remembered older items they wanted looked at before having them completely dismissed. The mundane attention to detail drew my mind back to my task with Bazdin, *and* the one person who kept disappearing on me.

Chapter Nine

Surfacing

Taya

"Honestly, J.J., it's noted. You left Zaith in charge. You have to trust that she'll know what to do to keep everyone alive. Right now, you need to be more concerned with what's on your own plate. Have you made a decision?"

With those five simple words he conveniently redirected the focus back to his priority: would I agree to see a therapist and mentor his nephew in order to get what I wanted... the old shop and a chance to build a new Desert Vehicle.

Gerrund glanced at his digital watch. Mardel was already out working with Ticia and the volunteers.

The Daily ended five minutes ago, but I knew I had to press the issue of making the Kahn-lea a priority. The contradictions of last night's meeting made me wary – why agree to send me topside to deal with Bazdin, but not acknowledge the importance of helping the Kahn-lea? Why make me jump through hoops? They were vulnerable out there... and I'd made them a promise – one I wasn't about to forget.

He was trying to side-line me by making reference to the shop, dangling it in front of me like my only option for furthering contact would be to relent – to give in to what he wanted. He knew his question was underhanded.

Gerrund obviously wanted to stay focused on the lives directly in front of him, the only ones that mattered in his grand scheme. I still couldn't figure him out. One minute he's the nice guy who gave me the tour of the Underground, and the next it feels like saving me was simply a strategic move to ensure Dez's cooperation in the coup. I didn't like not knowing the rules of this very deadly game.

I narrowed my eyes at him and pursed my lips. I raised my hand – he flinched – I straightened my white sun hat and turned away with a flash of copper.

"Gelden's Mentoring begins now." I walked off before he could respond. I didn't turn back and hoped he got the message. This issue was settled, but apprehension still clawed at my throat about *the deal.*

Passing the hundreds of volunteer troops out running drills made me feel even more alone. The CTF had worked in conjunction with the Kronik to dispose of me by placing that ridiculous ultimatum over my head right when they knew Dez had requested me for the suicide mission into the Deserts. My years of loyalty, my commitment to the Facility, and everything it stood for meant nothing in the end. Niless, Professor Gellik, all my fellow trainees, now only saw me through the tainted lens of the Kronik's lies. I hugged my arms around my chest and walked as a lone figure in a sea of nameless bodies.

Up the street, Gelden leaned against the shop door waiting for me. He stood tall when I got near, and gave an overly obvious appraisal of my appearance with his eyes. My sun hat cast a shadow over my face, and my copper-coloured hair twisted into a loose four-sectioned braid, giving me an elongated neckline.

His eyes quickly trailed down the length of my matching white sundress. It accentuated my figure with a modicum of modesty to the over-cut and layering of the skirt. He echoed Gerrund's eyebrow quirk from last night's meeting, only his action broke through my mood and made me smile. His return smile lit up his whole face.

"So, this is what you wear to clean up a dusty old shop? Should I be concerned?"

I tossed him the key-card and inclined my head for him to follow me. He matched steps as we walked toward the main tunnel.

"I have an errand to run on the surface." His steps faltered. I cut off his silent retort, "Later. I expect a lot to be accomplished today. Walk with me to my Junction Point." I didn't say please but hoped it was implied.

"Of course. What's on your mind? Should I be taking notes?"

"It's not an exhaustive list only *exhausting*. Since I'm Mistress of the Old Storage Shed now, on your way back to the shop get a spare key made. There'll be times when I'm running late with the Dailies and you'll need access." The deal with Gerrund was done, so I planned on making the best of it. We had an important project to plan for, and build, even if Gelden and I were the only ones to see it that way.

"Done."

I looked at him sideways.

"I mean, good as done. Don't worry," he chuckled.

"I'd like the existing door and window removed and replaced with double-wide doors instead. We're going to need to move the D.V. easily in and out of the shop for test runs."

"That's a tall order. It may take a few days to put something together. And D.V.? Is that what you're calling the project?"

"It's short for Desert Vehicle. Not very creative, I know, but it'll have to do. We're also going to need shelving and storage containers to organise what's in there, and what we'll accumulate during the project. I'd like to start cleaning and re-organising as soon as possible. Don't forget about a drafting table —" I stopped walking, folded my arms and stared at him.

"What?"

"Is all this even possible? Is it within our means?"

"Do you mean is Gerrund actually taking you seriously?"

I nodded.

He smiled again. "Don't worry." He took my arm in his and kept me walking. "Although we work mainly on the barter system down here, I'm sure we can arrange to obtain certain hard-to-get items purchased through the Network. We've been given access to the *what if* fund Gerrund put together for Cause activities. As long as we don't get overly extravagant, we should have more than enough to get a prototype up and running. After that, it'll be a matter of priority of funds to mass produce the D.V."

"More like a priority of politics, but we'll make them see. Look, I want to start working with you this afternoon, but I don't know how long I'll be top-side. I never imagined leaving you with all the grunt work."

"Don't worry, Dalla. That's what Mentors do. I know you'd rather be doing this alone–"

"No." We stopped in front of a clothing shop. Unhooking my arm from his, I turned to face him. "I really appreciate being able to work with someone on this project. It's true, at first I just wanted something to focus on by myself, but I get the feeling that the D.V. wouldn't have gotten off the ground without your interest to spur on both Gerrund and me. You've helped me gain focus. I was grasping at straws to be a part of something – to be useful again. Anyway, once I've dealt with business top-side, I'll meet you at the shop."

Gelden tapped the brim of my hat. "You might want to change first."

"Ha, ha – get to work, lackey."

He gave me a two-finger solute off the nose as he walked backwards. I shook my head at his innate playful nature, then turned and entered the shop. At the side counter I took a purple envelope out of my white purse and slid it over to the Nirian attendant. Her grey skin looked rippled like scar-waves, but she didn't look old enough to have lived through the Resistance. Something else had happened to this girl.

She scanned the note and nodded to a heavy blue drape at the back of the narrow store. Gerrund had explained the procedure to me at the Daily. The shop, although functional, was a cover for a Junction Point, making the shopkeeper top-side an undercover agent working for the Cause.

My hand shook as I reached out to pull the curtain aside. As much as I belonged above, working with Dezmind, part of me knew his and Gerrund's worries weren't for nothing. The Kronik wanted something from me... maybe they already got it, I don't know. Regardless, if they found me I wouldn't be alive for long.

But you're not you – isn't that the point?

At least, it was the point I'd been trying to make since the night before Dez left, but was it true? Until last night, no one else had thought so.

I passed beyond the curtain and squeezed behind a tower of crates to an arched entryway. Ascending the steep curving staircase, my bare pink arms brushed against cool, slightly moist walls. I kept one hand out to steady myself as there were no lights to guide me back to the surface.

I moderated my walk, hunched my shoulders slightly, and attempted to loosen the tense muscles in my neck. I would beat my CTF training and show them that there was no longer a trace of the woman I used to be... that I could blend in top-side as an Executive Assistant to Dez and... *and what? Turn around and become his bodyguard two seconds later? His wife? Isn't that the point? Being that close is all the tip-off the Kronik needs – what other woman would do that?*

I shook off the second-guessing, the flawed logic that Dez and I were meant to be together but had to remain apart. We just weren't looking at things from the right perspective yet.

At the top, I stood before the sliding wall Gerrund had described. It led into another storage area. Placing my hands on the portal back to the real world, where I would feel the suns on my face and the breeze against my skin, I shuddered – the feeling was akin to being reborn.

Not all of the staff are sympathisers. His words echoed in my thoughts, bringing my mind back to focus on the assignment. Silently, I stood with one ear against the wall; pushing aside all my ridiculous doubts. The scuffling of feet and shifting of packaged goods reached me. I slid back the door during the noise, and then looked for the person on the other side. Another stack of crates blocked my view.

I waited for five, and then another ten, minutes to be sure the room was clear. Grabbing the two parallel handles nearly an arm's span apart, I slid the wall back into place behind me.

Pulling out a small mirror from the white pouch dangling from my waist, I angled it to see around the crates and into the room. The feeling of doing what I was meant to do, trained to do, calmed me at first – then not. My breath rasped as I realised just how easily I'd slipped back into being *Taya*. If Aelonia wasn't a second-skin, who I believed I was, then I wasn't going to convince anyone of anything – not up here and not when I got back.

The room was clear.

Crossing its length, I slipped into the public washroom just down the hall from the storeroom. My heart beat in my chest, surrounded by invisible chains, as I ran cold water over my hands. I stared at myself in the mirror above the sink. *Get a hold of yourself! Stay focused.*

The pale-skinned, purple colithed, copper haired, green-eyed woman stared back at me, uncertain. I pushed away from the sink and dried my hands. Closing my eyes, I pictured the dark-haired, dark-eyed, tanned skinned and red colithed woman who'd had the gall to fire a Clinex at a Talian in public. *I can't recreate myself in one day.* The pounding of my heart evened out. I licked my lips and walked out the door.

A murmur of voices blanketed the café. Bright natural sunlight shone warmly through the window. I sauntered with casual-purpose, if such a thing existed, focusing on that "I belong here" pace that both exudes confidence and familiarity – I'd been practicing it all morning. Making my way through the bustle of patrons and attendants, Taya and Ali waged an inner war that left my stomach in knots.

Not a single head turned. No one glanced up from their meal, and no one approached me. I left the building in a waft of morning coffee and fresh baked bread, leaving no trace of my existence.

It was a relatively short walk to Bazdin's neighbourhood. At this time of the day he was usually getting ready for work, or so Gerrund's intelligence group had informed me. They'd been keeping track of his movements since he'd first approached Dezmind. Bazdin had taken time off recently to search for news of Tamaine, but he was supposed to return to work today. He lived with his parents, so I had to make sure they didn't get the message meant for him.

I slipped the turquoise silk scarf back from the face of my watch and checked the time. He was expected to leave in fifteen minutes.

I spotted his dark-green older-model rider parked in the driveway. It was a quiet street with little white fences and long, lush green lawns – the normalcy of it gave me the shivers. While it wasn't likely that spies watched the house at that very moment, Gerrund, and my time surrounding the Deserts, had instilled trepidation in me – something I didn't fully understand.

I removed the small, red envelope from the purse-pouch at my waist and slid it under the windshield wiper in one swift motion before walking on down the street. I had written one word on the face of the envelope, certain he would see it as he sat down in his rider: *Tamaine*. I had to be sure he'd open it and take the message seriously.

I walked for another five minutes before entering a small café on a side street, which saw few customers at this early hour. I'd been informed that the owner, and sole operator, was a Cause sympathiser; he welcomed me graciously.

One older Matin-Nirian man sat at the window bench, watching the street as he sipped a hot beverage and nibbled on what looked like a sugar scone. The service counter ran the length of the café, displaying various finger-treats and eats.

I leaned against the toffee-coloured counter and scanned the drink menu.

"A small verrin-berry punch, please."

"Fourteen drezeks," the owner said cheerily, and turned to blend the drink for me. I pulled off my short white gloves, opened my pouch, and placed a small red, rectangular card on the counter beneath my borrowed drezeks. I stuffed the gloves into the pouch as he passed me the punch and nodded to the back table. He slid the payment off the counter.

The systems in place for inconspicuous liaisons and Underground Agents working top-side boggled my mind. Gerrund had obviously been building this network of supporters and informants for many years. His nervous behaviour of late and willingness to take a chance with me on this mission, clearly showed he was unsettled about something – probably the recruits. He'd need a dominating force to be able to take down the Kronik and, from what I saw working with Mardel and Ticia, the troops weren't ready yet.

I sat down at the little white-topped table, took a sip of my drink, and set up the space. A small radio sat on each of the tables by the wall opposite the counter. I tuned into a random music station and set the volume to level three – loud enough to mask conversation, but soft enough not to bother other customers. I removed another red card from my pouch, folded it in half, and stood it peak-up on the table.

The door opened.

A young man with pale blue skin, black coliths, and dark tussled hair walked in. He glanced at the old man, the shop keeper, and then me.

He focused on the red card.

I'd warned him in the note to purchase something before making contact. Distractedly, he ordered a mug of black coffee, house blend, paid and then tipped the owner – I smiled inside. My sensitive hearing had returned since I'd been sleeping better. I rubbed a thumb over the star-shaped scar on the palm of my left hand to help ease the tension creeping back into my body.

He approached me with caution. I took another sip of my punch and nodded for him to join me. He sat down with his back to the door.

I set my glass on the red card, flattening it into a coaster before linking my fingers together on the table and leaning forward.

"Have you made arrangements?"

"Yes. The office thinks I'm having rider troubles."

"Good." I still hadn't settled in my mind how to start this conversation. I looked at him carefully. His eyes were naturally dark, but clearly troubled.

"Tamaine is safe, Bazdin. Dezmind did not lie to you." His shoulders relaxed slightly, but his eyes pierced mine. "You cannot repeat anything we speak of. Do you understand?" I said.

"Yes."

"Do – you – under – stand?"

The flash of something hard flickered across his face.

He sighed, "Yes."

"I realise that you're worried about your fiancée, but second-guessing Dezmind's intentions won't bring her home any faster. Look, I was the guide who led the Kahn-lea into the Deserts. I worked closely with all of the members, and left them *unharmed* with a very important job to do."

"Run the Generator."

"Do you *believe*, Bazdin?" I couldn't help but wonder that those words came from my mouth.

"Not at first. But after listening to Dezmind speak, and knowing Tamaine's convictions – well…"

"I understand. You've made a leap of faith I couldn't. I had to see the Chronicles with my own eyes. Work with the Generator using my own hands, to truly understand what my eyes and ears were telling me. Just remember…" I placed my hand over his clenched double fists. "Jantice is with her. Tamaine is strong and capable and loves you dearly."

If she wasn't, she wouldn't have survived the Deserts in the first place.

A long moment passed between us. "Any questions or concerns you have, I will address – only once. After our meeting, you'll never see me again and you will, effectively, drop off the radar and go back to your life."

"What do you mean? I can't just pretend that Tami's not out there. That she'll *stay* safe. It's been what? Six or seven weeks since you last saw her? How do you know things haven't changed? How do you know she's not in trouble?"

"Oh, but she *is* in trouble and so are you."

"I don't understand."

"The Kahn-lea cannot return until things around here have settled down."

"Why?"

"Firstly, if the Kronik finds them, he will destroy them. The council has scouts and secret agents watching Dezmind, the Deserts, and anyone who they suspect might know more than they're letting on – like *you* or Tamaine's parents, her school friends… We're a part of something so much bigger than we ever expected." Bazdin blanched at the thought.

"The government's media campaign is a mask, a front. It's trying to give the impression that everything is under control and that Dezmind is the one causing a disturbance. The Kronik *is* working on the environmental problems, I can attest to that, but it's going about it the wrong way. There are secrets, things both the man and the council don't want revealed, and that's blinding them to Dezmind's Cause and everything he represents."

The metal room, being cuffed to a pole, the Grey man and *the Voice* flashed through my mind. I swallowed hard. The Warehouse had almost consumed me. His fiancée and the others wouldn't stand a chance against *the interrogator* if we couldn't get them home without being detected. Even then, I was sure that at least one member of the group would refuse to hide in the Underground if Gerrund could even get them to a Junction Point before being discovered.

"Tamaine and the others can't return right now because they won't survive if the government catches them." I ran my fingers up the side of my glass, collecting droplets of condensation. I rubbed the water over my left wrist. Pink makeup dissolved onto my fingertips as jagged, colourless scars sat like bracelets surrounding my exposed skin. This flesh would not take Magda's colour treatments.

"I was tied up for six days before my rescue. What you see is the result of rope burn and bladed metal handcuffs. I have matching scars on my ankles as well." I took a shaky breath, forcing myself to revisit that place in my waking conscience so he would understand.

"I won't describe the horror they, the Kronik's Agents, put me through but know this – I am not what I seem. My hair, the colour of my skin, even my coliths disguise who, and what, I used to be. I wouldn't wish this torture on anyone, not even my enemies," I whispered. "So, you must trust me when I say she *is* safe and you must to keep a low profile from now on to keep her that way."

We sat there drinking for a short time. It was as though we traded sips: first him then me. I removed a small container of tinted moisturiser from my purse and reapplied it to my wrist. I could feel him watching me dip a finger into the small, round jar and methodically rub layer upon layer over the truth until it was gone again.

"Does Tami want to come home?"

"Yes, very much so. But she also understands that it's not possible right now – that she and the others are vital to keeping the

Generator operational and Xannia from regressing back to the super-quakes – or worse."

"Is it true that Dezmind is the son of an advisor to the Kronik?"

"Yes. Has he been telling the public about his background?"

"He's made inferences – I just pieced together what I could. Where does all this," he waved his hands around, "the Rallies about the Spoken Truth, the flyers hinting at terrible lies and cover-ups by the Kronik – where does it all lead? When *can* Tamaine come home?"

I bit my lower lip. *How much can I –* should I *reveal of our plans?*

"Our hope is to make a big enough impact to incite a catalyst for change in the way the two societies are currently being run. Ultimately, Dezmind envisions a restructuring of the Kronik to reunite the people – to allow for centuries of hurt and division to be healed. He and some very important supporters believe the Talians have abused their power and that we need to be represented by all of Xannia's people, not just one sect of society.

"His dreams are grand and, knowing that, I can't say when he'll be able to achieve them. He and his supporters don't want to make the same mistakes their forefathers did twenty-two years ago."

Bazdin nodded as if I'd just confirmed what he already suspected – the Cause was another Resistance.

"Then you have to take me to her."

My hand twitched. The glass clattered, overturning on the table. I pushed my chair back to avoid having the pink juice stain my white dress. The owner scurried around from behind the counter to wipe up the mess and retrieve the offending glass.

"Thank you for your help, sir."

"Do you need anything else, miss?"

"No, thank you. I'll just sit with my friend until he's finished his coffee."

The owner held my gaze a nano-second longer until he was certain the situation was under control, then he gave the table one last wipe with a dry cloth and returned to the counter. I sat down again and confronted Bazdin.

"Are you insane?"

"The way you're talking, if things don't go the way your friends are planning, the love of my life might *never* come home again – so I'll go to her. Look, we were only together for a few months before she left to follow a prophet into the Deserts looking for answers no one seemed to have. We're supposed to be married in a week. I'm not going to lose her. Do you understand?"

I sat back and worried the star-burst scar on my right palm with my thumb.

"No. It's an unacceptable risk."

"If you won't help me, then I'll find someone else who will."

"Right now, Dezmind is the only other person who could take you – and he won't. Trust me; he's got bigger fish to fry."

The thought of going back into the Deserts so soon made my mouth go dry. As much as we needed to reconnect with the Kahn-lea, part of me had been glad when Gerrund hadn't been in a rush – a very small, insecure part I usually managed to silence.

"If you and the Kahn-lea did it, I'm sure I could hire someone – maybe even a Contractor. There are plenty of people out there willing to verify Dezmind's claims."

Alarm bells clanged in my head. Not only would he be making himself a bigger target, but the Kronik could plant another spy and possibly destroy the good that the Kahn-lea was doing, *and* decimate the entire encampment in the Great City.

I can't let him do this.

He must have sensed a change in me.

We both leaned forward at the same time.

I had to make a call here. If I left this man to his own devices he'd risk everything: the Coup, the Generator, innocent lives… he couldn't see past his own pain.

"If we do this, you'll have to *disappear*. You'll need to make arrangements at work for extended leave and set up a system where, if you haven't returned by a designated time, it will explain your continued absence."

I rubbed my forehead with a finger and thumb as my other hand tapped out standard code while my mind reeled.

You don't have the authority for this, Taya!

"You'll need to arrange things with your parents and Tamaine's so that if a Kronik Agent arrives on their doorstep looking for you, he won't be suspicious. This *must* look natural, be conspicuous and long-term.

"Are you honestly prepared to do this? You should remain here and build a life for the both of you. Eventually, whatever happens, I'm sure the Kronik will stop watching the boarders and—"

"No! I'll do anything to be with her again."

"Fine. I'll give you a couple of days to make arrangements and we'll—"

"No. Just a few hours. I've got a contingency plan; I just need a bit of time to tweak it. ChemTrak's training program is really flexible, and they already know I might go looking for Tami… quietly."

ChemTrak? Tamaine had mentioned he'd gone to school for business administration – maybe the job has something to do with his minor in Chemistry.

"I'll meet you this afternoon," he said.

"You do realise that we're not going to leave for the Deserts tonight, right? My people need time to make arrangements, gather supplies, duplicate maps – we've only just started talking about the possibility of returning to the Great City – nothing's been arranged yet. It doesn't make sense for you to meet me this afternoon. I'll come to you—"

"Miss, I don't care if it takes a week or a month. As long as I know we're working toward something tangible, that I'm finally making progress, I'll feel a hundred times better. Now, where can I meet you?"

Oh Zola. Gerrund isn't going to like this… not one bit.

Chapter Ten
A Daylight Haunting

Taya

For the tenth time that morning, I ran through the conversation with Bazdin in my head. He'd trapped me; cornered me with no way to get word to Gerrund without risking my cover.

The Alpha and Beta suns shone prominent, bisecting the central median in the skies above. It neared mid-day, but my rendezvous with Bazdin wasn't for another two hours.

I made another random turn down another perfect street. Large deciduous trees ran the length of the boulevard. The yard-grasses brushed the middle of my shins as my feet led me places I'd never been before – a perfect illusion of uniform velvety rectangles. I breathed in the nearly forgotten sweet scent of freshly trimmed lawn, then bit my lip to keep from breaking down.

I shouldn't be here, on this mission. I should be at my house with Jadis, considering a new Contract and laughing with Zaith over her love exploits. Had I only been able to convince Dez not to travel the Deserts, the status-quo would still remain. I'd be living the life I'd chosen, and not the one a man I hardly knew had dragged me into – but really it wasn't Dez's fault... he hadn't known of the CTF's ultimatum, about my job being on the line... but he suspected who I was in the grand scheme of things – a secret the Kronik wanted to bury along with me.

This was supposed to be a simple top-side mission to calm a man down and I'd blown it. I tried to scare Bazdin into backing down, and boy was he afraid... afraid of losing the love of his life. Now I'd gone and made a deal I didn't have the authority to make – *I've lost my chance to show that I can work up here and not cause a sandstorm.*

Suddenly, it seemed as if I didn't belong anywhere. Dez didn't want me top-side, and Gerrund didn't want to deal with me period. Any casual friends up here would think what the Kronik wanted them to – that I was MIA in the Deserts, and those few tentative acquaintances below had their own lives to contend with.

I looked up to the sister suns blazing above, then over to where little Gamma would soon rise, and thought of all the Dakturians had accomplished. *If transport off Xannia existed, that's the only place I'd be welcome – in outer space.*

Several people emerged from the front door of a house across the street. Led by an enthusiastic Glaaon woman with big hair and a clipboard who, with a sweep of her pink arm, drew the small crowd's attention to the façade of the building. A blue SALE sign sat in the middle of a flower bed in the front of the yard.

Having nothing better to do, I walked over and joined the group. *Maybe it'll take my mind off things.* I stood behind a Danieth couple holding hands, looking up at the second story.

Then again, maybe not.

I superimposed Dezmind's tall frame and broad shoulders over the image of the man before me, and a bronze-skinned, long black-haired version of the woman I was when I followed Dez back home across the Deserts all those weeks ago.

"—freshly waxed to bring out the subtle tonal quality imbued within the siding. The colour was changed only two years ago to update the street appeal. As I'm sure you're well aware, this product is weather proof and any damage attained—"

I tuned her out. I blinked my eyes and erased the vision of Dez and I before focusing my attention on the house. It wasn't like mine in the older part of the Prime. This house was practically identical to the rest that lined this street. The only noticeable difference was the new siding, the decorative shutters and the mullioned windows.

Whoever currently lived here clearly had a passion for gardening. There were as many flowerbeds as open lawns – it was all a bit dizzying. My house had multi-hued brick instead of all-weather siding, and sat just over an arm's length away from my neighbour's place. It was smaller than this one, but it fit me and Jadis exactly right… that home wasn't mine anymore.

The agent herded everyone into the backyard. As I passed the woman, she gave me a double look before flipping through several pages attached to her clipboard.

I guess drop-ins aren't welcome.

I slipped around the corner and out of sight, along the opposite side of the house. Several remarks floated past about the lovely fresh-water pond at the back of the property before the agent launched into her next speech.

I was forgotten.

I returned to the sidewalk running along the opposite side of the street. A sign posted against a tall fence caught my eye:

THE KRONIK SPEAKS
Personal Appearance
14.20 pm
Pokks Park – Gethersday

What! I have to tell –
"Lija!" A deep voiced called from the other side of the fence.
"Lija, bring out the salads now. Lunch is ready."
I froze.

"Sure thing," came the familiar musical voice. I held my breath. "Blain, honey, come and help me with this."

"Be right there, Mamma."

No! Not possible! This can't be...

Something orange soared over the fence and fell to the sidewalk beside me. I took two steps away from the posting. A body swung around the edge of the fence and bashed into me, knocking me off my feet and onto my white-linened ass. I shook my head, cradling it with one hand as I looked up.

"Oh! I'm so sorry, miss. Are you all right?"

"Blain! Hurry up now."

"Just a minute, Mamma," he yelled at the fence.

I couldn't take my eyes off him. *Lija – Blain. Blain – Lija. Mamma?*

He held out a young, teenaged, bronze-toned hand toward me, his red coliths wrapping around solid forearms. I raised my hand – my pink arm with purple coliths. Not Matin – not the same anymore. My hand twitched just before he took hold of it.

"Th- Thank you." I sputtered.

He lifted me to my feet, a task I normally would've done before anyone noticed I'd fallen – especially in a dress. Then he swooped down and picked up the Wiz Disk that had sailed over the fence moments before.

"I wasn't expecting anyone to be standing here," he said.

I pointed to the poster, my brain finally re-engaging. "I was inspecting the house for sale across the street and thought I'd walk around the neighbourhood. I was reading just before we collided."

"That damn thing. I wish we could rip it off the fence." I turned to scan it a second time.

"Oh, great. I've ruined your dress. Come on, we're having a family lunch –"

"What? Why? I don't understand." My brain gave up on me. Nothing made sense. *Family lunch? He knows who I am?*

Blain pointed to the skirt of my dress, mid-thigh. I looked down. Some dirt smudged the pristine whiteness.

"Oh. No, you needn't—"

"I insist. Mamma has a great home-made treatment for spot cleaning. It's the least I can do for smacking into you like that."

He led me by the hand, around the far side of the fence and through an open gate into my ex-foster parents' backyard.

He had no idea who I was.

He'd looked into my eyes – he held my hand – spoke with me… and nothing. But what could I expect? He wasn't quite four the last time he saw me.

A large yard, with tall grass and neatly trimmed shrubs lined the interior of the fence. A family-sized picnic table sat at the edge of a natural stone patio. My father, or at least the only man I knew as *father*, stood there tall and imposing but with a contented smile, cooking meat over an outdoor grill. His dark hair showed slips of silvery-grey, but his jawline held that familiar, determined set, only this time it was directed at the slabs of radder and not me.

"Daba, where's Mamma?" Blain asked, but I didn't hear his deep masculine voice – I heard his little three-year-old self saying those same words that last time as I lay on a cold floor listening to them through the ductwork as they left me behind. But instead of saying "in the rider" as he had then, his words brought me back to the present.

"In the house getting the salads you're supposed to be helping with. Who's this?"

"Maybe a new neighbour. I ran into her when I went to get the Wiz Disk. I might've ruined her dress."

Daba set the plate of radder on the table. "For Zita's sake, Blain, you're sixteen years old – you should know better than to go careening around a blind corner." But laughter edged his voice. He was trying to keep from smiling as he appraised my dress and allowed his eyes to linger a little longer on my face. My heart beat faster. Then he looked from Blain to me and back again.

"Ah, Miss…?" *Miss what? Oh!*

"A-Aelonia. Aelonia Trellice."

"Miss Trellice, my wife will be out in a moment. We'll have you cleaned up and on your way in no time. Please, have a seat." He motioned to the bench across from him as he sat down. I whisked around to the other side, not wanting to disappoint – old habits die hard.

A clink from the back door drew my eyes to its source. Mamma floated outside, holding a plastic bowl of salad in each hand while cradling a variety of fixings between her left arm and her side.

"Sorry, Mamma. Let me help."

"I've got it now, Blain. Help Jutaya."

"H-help me... what?" I whispered.

A dark-haired girl, maybe three or four years younger than Blain, with tanned skin and red coliths, came teetering out the door with a clear bowl of fruit stacked on top of a bowl of buns with a plate in between them, and a bowl of forks and knives stacked on top of the rest of the plastic plates. It was a tower of food and cutlery. Blain lifted two of the bowls from her and carried them to the table.

"What did you say, young lady?" Daba was talking to me – Taya – Aelonia...

I couldn't speak. The imposter, my doppelganger, looked up. We locked eyes. I scrambled to stand and staggered backwards. *This isn't happening!*

"Aelonia, are you all right?" Blain asked. He reached for me. I turned and ran.

"Aelonia, wait!" he called from his back fence as I ran down the street.

With my hands over my ears to block out their voices, I ran and ran until my chest heaved and my lungs burned.

I collapsed a few blocks away in the soft white sand of Pokks Park. Tears bathed my cheeks. I pulled at my ears, ripped off my hat, and tore at the hair on my head.

My mind reeled on perma-repeat, showing me again and again the impossibility of it all. One image after another flashed behind my eyelids...

The Fyces abandoning me – fighting Zaith on the plateau – training at the CTF – the Underground hospital – living on the streets – Dezmind leaving me – my death sentence...

I threw my head back and shrieked. The wail echoed inside the tube-slide and off the close-knit trees surrounding the play park.

Bazdin arrived promptly, two shops down from the Junction. I gave no indication that I saw him coming. I spoke at him, but not to him – he looked confused by my icy behaviour.

He had nothing with him but the clothes on his back and the basics: ID and a supply of dakors, stored in various pockets about his body – the average person wouldn't have noticed, but I did. I could tell he was ready for a fight – a verbal brawl – but I was well aware of his *promise* to look for help elsewhere, so I had no interest in fighting a losing battle.

I had outlined the plan before we parted earlier, speaking plainly and simply; had said nothing of where we were going, only that it was a *secret* and if he ever thought about revealing how to get there, he wouldn't live to see his fiancée. I was in no mood to be reminded of yet another failure, and by focusing on the plan I could pretend to be keeping myself together.

I entered the café first. I forced my body to relax by deepening my breathing and clearing my mind of everything but who my character was, and focused on why she was here. But I wasn't hungry and what was left of this morning's punch sloshed around in my stomach, making me queasy. Still, I had to order something – that was the rule. I walked up to the counter, scanned the main menu and then the dessert bar.

Nerves or no, I might as well get something I like.

"Two chocolate peppers, please." I paid and sat down at the back of the shop.

They weren't really peppers. The dessert was a spicy, crème filled chocolate drop, the size of a large oval nut. They were expensive. The crème filling was a guarded recipe. The confection had to travel from a central location in Darzeth Prime, and only a few were delivered each week to selected merchants. Dezmind had introduced the confection to me during our few days together Underground...

After having my palms tended to at the lower clinic housed in the same building as the hospital, Dez had wrapped my arm in his and led me along the strange subterranean street to a tiny shop tucked into the curve of a tunnel just off the main road. Inside, he'd asked for four chocolate peppers and the shop keeper had raised both eyebrows... few people knew of this treasure in the Underground, and even fewer purchased so many at once.

Back outside the shop, Dez had taunted me with the bag – drawing it closer and then farther away from my nose. It smelled sumptuous. Then, without warning, he drew me up next to him in the crevice of a cavern wall, let the tip of his nose hover next to mine as our bodies pressed against each other, and slipped the treat between my lips...

My body ached at the memory. We – no, *he* didn't have time for such frivolous things any more.

I popped one into my mouth, cradled it with my tongue, and let it slowly melt with the heat of my mouth. I closed my eyes, sat back, and prayed my stomach would behave.

The hinges of the door creaked open, shortly followed by a soft bump as it swung shut again. *Bazdin.* Steady footsteps walked to the counter and paused. I'd warned him not to buy anything that would take too long to eat or drink, but to make sure that what he chose was filling. I had no idea when his next meal would be. Who knew, maybe I'd be in the same situation too once Gerrund found out about this arrangement.

The last of the chocolate pooled on my tongue as the roof of my mouth collapsed the spicy filling, pushing it to every corner and activating all of my taste buds. I sighed and opened my eyes.

Without actually looking at him, I tracked Bazdin's movements through the café. He chose a table near the front of the shop, strategically by an aisle leading to the back. He shovelled forkfuls of demak, a kind of mishmash of fried leftovers, into his mouth. His gaze remained on the window at the front of the shop. A serving girl brought him a glass of verrin, and then returned to wiping down the tables.

I popped the second chocolate pepper into my mouth, performing the same ritual. Surprisingly, my stomach did not disagree with what I'd chosen to feed it. Actually, the tension I'd been holding in released a little more. I still didn't want to think about what had happened – the failure of this mission, the loss of Dezmind to the Cause, or stumbling into my foster family who'd clearly moved on *without* regret. Emptying my mind, I eased further into my chair and listened.

A glass clinked down a little too heavily; a fork clattered to rest on a plate; that plate was pushed away from the patron; a chair scraped back – recognisable footsteps walked steadily past me toward the back of the café. The washroom door whisked open, then shut. I sat forward and opened my eyes, busying myself with tidying up the table before heading back to the ladies' room.

I entered the short hallway, looking lost. Noticing the absence of other bodies, I dropped the act, slipped into the store room, and hid behind the wall of crates. Bazdin entered the back room cautiously. I hadn't given the warning signal, so he knew the room was clear. He eyed the stack of crates and hurried behind to meet me.

I didn't waste any time double-checking the space before finding the catch with my fingers, and pushing the wall forward to reveal the door. I slid through the opening with Bazdin close behind. The wall clicked shut. I removed my cloth belt and slid off the pouch, before tucking it between my legs.

"Come here." I doubled up the length of cloth.

"What? I don't understand. I've already seen how to get here –"

"That was just the front door. You're *not* supposed to be here.

From now on you have to be blindfolded." He didn't move.

He didn't speak.

"This is the only way," I said.

He stepped in front of me on the small platform and I fastened the strip of the cloth around his head. Grabbing my pouch, I linked arms with the man and led him forward.

"We're going down. Watch your step," I said.

Instinctively, he put out his free arm and slid his hand along the wall as we descended the narrow staircase.

Chapter Eleven

News

I sat on a small boulder just inside the tree line, cradling my head in my hands. Patterns flickered over and around me as light filtered down through the canopy above. A sheen of sweat moistened my face and neck. The scattering of stones and the steady crunch of pebbles broke the strained silence.

I didn't move.

I was expecting him.

The footsteps paused and then changed direction.

"Zaith? You're still here?"

I raised hazy eyes, likely rimmed with red. "He refuses to talk to me, to let me see him. Deltek, I—" I sighed in resignation. "I need to know how bad it is. Can you…?" I couldn't finish the thought, but he understood.

He stirred the mud-paste with a thick paint brush he'd made. I slipped behind a nearby tree as Deltek called out before raising his facemask.

"Ho, there! How's it goin', Ray?" Dipping his brush into the metal bowl, he applied a fresh layer to the seal around the broken window.

The pane of glass in the door and the window on this side of the dome were too dark to see through at this distance, but I caught sight of a shadow of movement.

I need Taya's eyes! She'd have no problem seeing Ray from here. Deltek's voice lowered with his closer proximity to the house. I strained to hear at least one side of the conversation. *Curse these ears – I'm useless!* I leaned into the tree, boring imaginary holes into Deltek's back as he worked, catching only the inflections of his voice as he spoke with Ray.

Yesterday, Ray stopped speaking to me altogether. He just lay on his bed with his back to me, blankets pulled up over his ears even in this heat – a personal boycott. I suppose it was my own fault for telling him he had to stay isolated, even if his cold got better. He just couldn't see the risk. He'd become a carrier, even if he was somehow immune, which he wasn't.

I was certain he was displaying the earliest stage of the Virus and only deluded himself. I told him we were making progress searching the City, and had discovered some promising medical data. But he still wouldn't talk to me.

Deltek flicked his brush clean against the bowl and headed back to the Common. I followed, still hidden by the trees just in case Ray was checking up on me. I joined Deltek once I cleared the sightlines from the small alien dwelling.

"Well?"

"It's bad. I think he's well into the second phase."

All of the fight and drive left me… drained from every muscle like water through a pipe. I felt fifty years older. Deltek noticed the change immediately but chose not to say anything.

"His breathing is ragged and the cough more frequent. He wouldn't admit to having a fever, but he was sweating and had very little clothing on. What concerns me the most is his constant scratching. Occasionally he'd restrain himself, but the moment I refocused on maintaining the seal, I'd catch him doing it in my peripheral vision."

"It could be the sweat making him itchy. A fever from the cold?"

"If it was an isolated incident I might believe it. Zaith, hope is one thing, but don't allow it to blind you. You were right. He knew the risk, whether he wanted to believe it or not. He was well-warned, along with the rest of us." He stopped and placed a dark hand on my shoulder. "This isn't your fault. You know that, don't you?"

I stepped out from under his strong, consoling grasp and kept walking.

"Believe what you must, Deltek. Taya charged me with protecting the Kahn-lea. I can't blame anyone but myself. I *am* responsible." A hard edge crept into my voice.

I had let Taya down once, I couldn't afford to do that again. If anyone could've outsmarted the Kronik, it was her. Still, if they had found her and these people were the last of her legacy, I had to keep them alive – *all* of them. Deltek slowed his pace and let me walk on alone.

I didn't join the others for breakfast.

I didn't return to the Common.

I already knew that Tami and Jan were experimenting with various plant fibres to use in the textile machine they'd found. Merik had helped them with a translation from a book on tanning hides as well. Several experiments ensued, using the pelts from the small game Syvis and Deltek were catching. The girls had yet to master the curing process, and chose instead to work on separating fibres from Pod Plants in a nearby grove.

Lutrice was confident the majority of plants transplanted into her medicinal garden had taken to the new location. She too was experimenting with several new plants, which Merik had discovered were used by the Dakturians for healing purposes. This work was especially important since much of the information came from a series of texts located in what was likely a lab or hospital at one time. Tami and Jan were helping locate these new specimens during their fibre finding missions.

Syvis continued mapping the city, but he was only finding pockets of villages now. He suspected a large water source near his current location, but he hadn't reached it yet.

The system I employed for this microcosm of society worked as intended. So much depended on it staying that way, and yet, so much more was now at stake.

I stood before a sprawling complex of integrated domes in what Syvis dubbed the Scientists' Quarter. It was this clinic where Jan found a series of metal notebooks describing all known healing agents, and how they were being used to combat the Virus.

I had flipped to the end of the last book and read, *"We are so close to a solution. Working with Neema and her daughters has convinced us that this is more than just a Virus. Dorion and I agree that we need to directly infect ourselves and observe the changes on a cellular level."*

I had a hunch; there was one more book to finish the series. In it would be the answer to this crisis. Klabec and Dorion were the only scientists still alive at the end and, with Neema and her family too far along, they were willing to sacrifice themselves and take the chance that the nine travellers who left the City might have a home to come back to one day.

I knew that hadn't happened, but that didn't mean progress wasn't made. It just meant that Ketic, Ballen and Mira never learned of the results when they came back to check on the Generator years later after finding the Ancient City.

I walked into the clinic, passing through several domed segments. I by-passed various rooms until I reached a sealed door etched with the alien word for *Lab*. All available hands had searched the open corridors and rooms three times yesterday. This was the only door they wouldn't open.

Placing my hand on the tinted window, set in the centre of the door, I peered inside. Several shelves of books lined the curved walls, but the one I looked for wouldn't be tucked away on some shelf. No, the one I wanted lay there, on the floor – open – beside the metal frame of a cot at the back of the lab.

As I shifted back from the window, I caught sight of my hand against the black metal frame. My skin was darker and richer than the cold metal. The door was a charcoal-black and glinted in the diffused light from a skylight above.

But my hand was no longer smooth. It was covered in the expected calluses, along with several welts, scratches and flaking skin. Altogether these things were merely proof of hard labour on a hand only meant to hold a View-X or microphone... maybe even a steering wheel, but not what these past long weeks had brought.

The welts and flaking skin extended from the crook of my thumb and scaled randomly under my long-sleeved shirt, up my arm to my elbow and on to the crown of my shoulder. They appeared at random four days after I started bringing care packages to Ray.

With all of our precautions: the mud, the masks, the confinement... *it* still got out. Deltek didn't appear to be showing symptoms and neither were the rest of the Kahn-lea, but the Virus was no longer dormant. My close proximity to Ray and my mandated daily breakfast meetings meant only one thing... *we've all been exposed now.*

With no cure in sight, I had doomed them all.

I picked up a long, cylindrical device from one of the tables lining the wall. Heaving it, I smashed the last barrier between me and a hunch.

Chapter Twelve
Consequences

Taya

"Could be considered a breach! Honestly J.J. what were you thinking? We have protocols in place for a reason—"

I stared vacantly at a spot just over his shoulder. I'd sent out an Emergency Message for Gerrund the second Bazdin and I entered the lower shop. I'd kept him in the stairwell behind the curtain, still blindfolded, sitting on the bottom step and constantly observed for the twenty minutes it had taken Gerrund and Mardel to arrive at the lower Junction.

I'd also closed the store on my way out to wait for them. The manager took her job seriously and kept a sharp eye on Bazdin.

What I hadn't been able to do was say two words in the last ten minutes, so I gave up trying. He wasn't telling me anything I hadn't anticipated. I'd just hoped he'd be willing to listen to why.

"—to say for yourself, J.J.?"

I snapped back into focus. "He threatened to hire a Contractor to bring him to the Great City unless we helped him. *Sir.*" My tone froze the words as they left my lips. I hadn't intended to sound that way, but the tension I held onto constricted everything – especially my vocal cords. Both men stood still, waiting for more.

I didn't know how to dig myself out now.

Mardel broke the silence.

"I'm assuming he expected immediate action? That's why you brought him here?"

I nodded, still staring at Gerrund who glared at Mardel, who focused on me. Mardel prompted again.

"He doesn't know where he is, right?"

"Of course not. I didn't give him any specifics on who we are, what we're doing, or where *here* is. All he knows is that he's in a hidden location organised by Dezmind's supporters. I think he believes in the Cause. He *can* be trusted. It doesn't make sense that the Kronik would have convinced him to infiltrate us – that's not their M.O. Still, he's here on a need-to-know basis.

"His main concern is his fiancée and her safety. He's willing to wait until we're ready to make contact with the Kahn-lea, but he's impatient to feel like he's making progress, and he refused to let me leave him behind – to wait until we were ready to do this in our own time."

Gerrund's eyes said it all. They flashed first with anger and then disappointment. *He thinks I'm doing this on purpose – to make contact with the Kahn-lea sooner than planned – to have things my way and not his.*

In that moment, the jaunty, proud man who called himself *friend* to my real parents was gone. He was suspicious of me, and there wasn't a damn thing I could say to change his mind. My skin prickled. Sweat beaded my upper lip as my heart struggled to beat against a clenched cavity. The man before me was completely unrecognisable.

The workshop lay dark. I slid my key into the reader and opened the door. Gelden had been busy today. The layers of dust were now only a vague memory. Boxes were organised and neatly lined the lower walls. But best of all was the new drafting table set up on the far side of the room. On it sat a paper bag and a note.

Dalla,

I didn't figure you would be back in time to clean. Didn't even have time to change, did you?

(I fingered my skirt)

At least have a bite to eat before you break in the new table.

Gel

I dropped down into the chair with a sigh and opened the bag: half a sandwich and a flaky pastry. I gave a tired smile. Without warning, the tears came. There were no great wracking sobs, just a steady stream down my face and neck. I hadn't needed a nightmare to lose control this time – it only took a simple act of kindness.

I pushed the food away, wiped my face on the hem of my skirt next to the smudge of dirt, pulled a sheaf of papers over, and picked up a pencil. I neatly printed *The Aerial Caves* at the top of a clean sheet, allowing the complex map to take over my mind. I needed something challenging to pull all of my focus, to drive every other intrusive thought far away... something to block the pain and the betrayal.

*   *   *

Gelden

I set a stack of boxes on the ground and reached to unlock the shop door, but it was already open. Noticing the light on, I figured Dalla must have gone home after the generators powered down and forgot to turn it off. I propped the door open, picked up my cargo and shimmied inside.

The counter was strewn with pages and pages of Desert maps and the Alien Forest. Setting my burden down at the base of the counter, I picked up one of the larger maps. The attention to detail, the information charted out, and the colour spoke to me as if I'd been there myself.

The box where I'd collected the old broken bits of coloured chalk and tinted pencils lay on its side with half the contents strewn about the floor. One box even wore her white sun hat. Wondering what else she'd been up to, I turned to check out the drafting table.

Dalla's body slumped over the desk as one arm cradled her head and the other draped across the workspace still clutching a pencil. I walked over to her. Her chest rose and fell evenly, but her eyes moved rapidly beneath their lids. Wisps of bronze hair, tipped in white, feathered across her pink cheek and chin, just barely hiding the deep purple colith slipping up the side of her neck to touch her jaw.

I glanced at the project she'd been working on – the D.V. After who knows how many hours of work on the maps, she still had time to focus on the main scope of our project.

Gerrund said she had special abilities – being half-Talian – something about enhanced natural attributes. I wonder if she can see in the dark? It's the only way she could've accomplished all this after I left yesterday.

I placed a hand on her shoulder.

"Dalla."

I gave her nudge.

"Dalla."

She jolted awake. "Wha–? Who? Gelden? I don't understand." She plastered the palms of her hands to her eyes trying to wipe away the lingering sleep.

"You're not the only one – although, I think I have more of a clue than you do at the moment." She looked at me with the haze of heavy sleep, but there was something else, too… thinly veiled panic.

"I guess you never went home last night. Got a lot of work done, too."

Her eyes followed the sweep of my arm around the room. She sprang to her feet, gathering up her maps. But no amount of forced wakefulness could hide the dark circles under her eyes. The white linen of yesterday's dress clung to her legs and looked permawrinkled where she'd been sitting on it. I wasn't sure if I should say anything, in case it made her self-conscious.

"I'm late." She shifted a turquoise scarf wrapping her wrist to reveal an old mechanical watch, then she neatly rolled up her oversized pages. "Or I will be if I don't get out of here *now*."

I plunked her matching sun hat on her head as she backed into the door to open it. In the space of a nano-second, we made eye contact before she disappeared down the tunnel for her Daily with Gerrund. She'd probably go straight home after the meeting, and I figured she might want everything she came with – especially her hat, since she was going out into the public. But that glance didn't hold the playful appreciation I'd anticipated. No. Those dark, piercing eyes looked haunted.

In the fraction of an instant, everything she'd been holding back, clinging to, was left raw and open – pieces of a shattered soul. It had been too much; I couldn't hold onto that look long enough to understand it all… not even long enough to show her the compassion she so desperately needed.

*   *   *

Taya

I raced to the Daily as though chased by the Desert Spike Beast. I struggled to hide being winded as Gerrund made me wait at the base of the platform while he finished speaking with two messengers. I'd always been good at code, but right then he was sending me a message my fogged mind struggled to process – at the very least, I knew he was still mad.

As the runners left to complete their next errands, I approached. Leaning against the back of a chair, I caught sight of a piece of polished metal lying amidst a sheaf of papers on the tables. I balked at my reflection. *If this doesn't prove my commitment…*

"Aelonia," he interrupted my thoughts. "Take a seat." He pulled a backless stool out from under the table, and motioned to the chair I leaned against. His voice matched his jaw – hard and rigid.

"Thank you for setting aside the extra time for this. I realise—"

He held up a hand and cut me short. I gave him the maps and then sat down. We'd spoken at length after yesterday's debacle, or rather *he* spoke and I listened. If we were going to get Bazdin out of here with all expedience, the project needed to be launched into high-gear as of this morning – hence the maps.

He'd also revealed that he'd been thinking about dedicating a recruit to act as Lead Guide, once the information chain started between the Great City and the Underground. That was all well and good, especially since I didn't want to be the one making those regular trips, but we couldn't just let someone blindly enter the Deserts.

As he methodically reviewed the maps, I pressed my case again about the need to train this person properly.

"I'll need time with the other Guide to go over these maps in detail. I've only included basic information, the general vegetation and dangers associated with each Desert. I need a solid block of time to communicate everything, and make sure she can relay it back to me flawlessly. I need to be absolutely certain that we can–"

"I'll make sure you have enough time. Those *volunteers* adept at tracking and thinking on their feet will be redirected to this. It's a problem we'll turn to our advantage."

"Exactly how many people are you thinking?"

"Seven, including Bazdin."

"Why so many? The D.V. won't hold that many at once. With all those people it'll take too long. In fact, it took us nine days to reach the Great City, with severely depleted supplies. If Dezmind hadn't insisted the Kahn-lea come, it would've only been the two of us and far more practical."

"I'm also *insisting*. Bazdin will reach his destination – eventually. If we're going to do this, then I want it done methodically. That means everyone gets hands-on training the first trip out. And I don't take kindly to threats, you know."

This is ridiculous. Why is he blocking me?

"I'm not threatening you, Gerrund. It's a guarantee. Every extra day spent in the Deserts is one day closer to your own mortality. This isn't a simple hike in the country. There are people's lives hanging in the balance. Look—" I paused to gather the right words.

"Dezmind would agree. If he had to do it again, he would've gone alone. Give me time to realise the Desert Vehicle. It'll accommodate *two* people. Dez and I made it back on our own in four and a half days, mostly on foot. The D.V. will cut that time by a third. That's three days in the Deserts, tops. It's far safer and more practical than offering up another Kahn-lea to the creatures inhabiting that death trap."

"We're on the verge of war, J.J. Do you get that? Any opportunity I can use to my advantage, I will. Besides, weren't you the one who pointed out that our troops need better training? What better training is there than taking on the Deserts and everything between us and the Great City? I need these people ready to understand the sacrifices that have occurred to bring us to this point in time. This moment in history."

"Yes, but have you given yourself time to think beyond today? You're the leader of the Underground. The citizens who reside here know they're safe because of you. Know they have a chance at a future because they are safe. Gerrund, not *all* of your people want this fight. Ticia even said that not everyone wanted to get involved, especially those in the outlying tunnels."

It was time to hit close to home. "What about your sister? She just wants to live in peace." He narrowed his eyes even more but I had his attention.

"*You* set the timelines – I'm asking you to send the Guides in waves of two in order to save lives. I've said it before, the Great City is in dire need of a people to care for it, and if we mess this up it's a huge opportunity wasted.

"The Kahn-lea only signed up for a one-week trip. It's been nearly two months since this fiasco started, and they can't come home because of what they know. Their risk is probably greater than my own at this point. The Kronik don't want Dez's version of the truth confirmed, and the Generator has to keep running. The super-quakes have stopped– Gamma's solar membrane is clearly regenerating, but slowly.

"We need to protect this asset. Some of your people won't want to be ruled by *any* formal government. Neither can they be expected to stay down here forever. The Great City will offer them a place to live, with the suns overhead and a grand mission to uphold and give them purpose.

"What you're planning is a suicide mission. I barely kept the first Kahn-lea alive long enough to reach the Powder Sands Desert and, while nothing big lies beyond it, they could have run into the small stuff – if Syvis hadn't agreed to keep everyone in line.

"Don't you see? The fewer people crossing, the better. We can make a trip there and back in one week with the D.V. and maintain a constant flow of information week-by-week. If we can establish that link and build up a reputation for *safe* crossings, it will open up so many possibilities to the people living down here. Gerrund, sometimes you have to take off the General's Badge and walk among the people."

Electricity ignited and rippled behind his eyes. I didn't look away. His anger with me, his passion for the UGC, and his fervour for truth oozed from every pore. I kept what I hoped was a cool, calm gaze to help his storm pass, doing my best to channel the woman I used to be. I may have my weaknesses, my fears, but logic always kept me sane, clearheaded and forthright.

But Gerrund was not going to be bullied into a decision. I rose, never breaking eye contact. Reaching out, I gave his shoulder a squeeze, nodded my respect, then turned and left. I knew he'd sit there for a long time, and he didn't need my face reminding him why we suddenly found ourselves in this mess.

The walk home was blissfully uneventful. A surprising amount of mail waited in the basket. I opened the door, grabbed the envelopes and tossed some chocolate in their place.

What is all this?

I flipped through the majority of the pile: there were no return addresses – it was all internal mail. I didn't see any letters from Dez, but then, the sheer volume of other letters made it difficult to see everything that had come. Dropping the load on the island, I picked one out of the heap and opened it.

Emvaso-al,

After hearing the words of The One when you first returned from the Deserts, it became clear to me the important and crucial role you played.

You were the conduit through which Zerameteth, youngest of the three, led The One to fulfil his great destiny.

As protector of the young, guiding light of Zerameteth, bearer of the mark, I beseech you pardon with my forward nature, but I have nowhere else to turn.

My youngest grandchild is ailing and the Underground's hospital can only do so much to help. Her diagnosis is unknown and we cannot risk bringing her to the surface.

Please, Zimi, think on her with your suns light and pray for her during this dark time.

Your humble servant,

Deznita Viat

An address was listed below. I tossed the letter and the envelope back onto the table and opened another, and another, and another from the large pile.

Child of Zerameteth,
Saviour of The One who bound Destiny's fate –

Zimi, I would not dream to be so forward but dire circumstances —
— in desperate need of your help —
— my daughter —
— my son —
— my sister —
— my neighbour's child —
— nowhere else to turn —

One after the other I read snatches of letters sent by desperate citizens of the Underground. One after the other I threw them back on the countertop.

Half. I read only half of what had come; their content freezing my blood and numbing my mind. The incident at Dez's UGC Rally invaded my synapses and brought me back...

"This is the truth. Aelonia found the Chronicles. She deciphered them and together we found the Great City and learned of the source of our changing environment — the cause of the super quakes, the rise in temperature, and most especially the decrease in verrin.

"United as a team, she and I brought the ancient Generator to life to start Gamma's healing process. And now, our fellow journeymen, the Kahn-lea, are dedicating themselves to this truth. I must now return to the surface to spread the word and unveil the Kronik's lies for what they are. May the Trinity watch over you as their rays warm the earth."

Dez jumped down from the small make-shift podium by the street lamp. But just as he turned to take my hand, the masses enveloped us, pulling him one way and me the other.

Gerrund, Mardel, and their crew disappeared from sight as hands touched me, stole strands of my hair, brought my hands to their lips, and reached for my face.

The bodies squeezed closer and closer.

I looked everywhere for Dez.

I could just make out his voice calling my name... my real name.

I pushed against the mob and lost my footing. Hands hoisted me bodily into the air above their heads. Farther up the tunnel I watched us grow farther apart as I bobbed and dipped on strange hands. Dez reached out past Gerrund and three other soldiers toward me.

Then Gerrund lowered Dez's arm, turning him around, and the man I'd bound myself to all those weeks ago for the sake of a Contract, the man I'd fallen in love with, ran away from me instead of toward me.

Back to the surface.

An internal scream shattered my remaining self-control...

"I'm not who you think I am," I whispered and shuddered. Abruptly, I turned my back on the messages both opened and unopened. No longer in the mood to write a letter to Dez, I went to my room and got changed for work in the shop.

Chapter Thirteen
A Forge Needs Heat

Dezmind

*D*earest Ali,
I miss seeing your scrawled letters dance across the page. It feels

like a year since you last wrote, though I know it's only been just over a week.

I'm sorry we had so little time together during my last visit. I'm sure you see it as having no time at all, but everything was arranged last minute – and you know how important it is for our friend to uphold ceremony.

I'm in the middle of important talks right now and any extended absence would be noticed. I can't deny the disappointment in your eyes, your set stature and white nails. I bet you thought I hadn't noticed, but honestly Ali, when I'm in a room with you my heart demands to be with you.

I tried to tell you, but those old mental walls were back. I couldn't reach you.

The ache in my heart speared my lungs when you offered yourself as a conduit for change. Just be careful not to channel your sorrow and disappointment into impulsive decisions, no matter how logical they may seem at the time.

I've been told of your growing involvement and the passion you hold for the plight of the Kahn-lea. You've brought alive the voice and presence I wish I had the time to make a commitment to. But the distance and the growing response to the Spoken Truth throughout the greater communities of Xannia, chain me to my duties here.

I promise we will have time together once the building blocks have been lain. All is well,

DL

I slipped the letter into an envelope, addressed and sealed it. Brushing aside the crimson velvet curtain, I handed my words to the scrawny waiter by the door. The boy disappeared into the kitchen, just as the voice of the new chef echoed back through the opposite swinging of the door.

Even though the letter was gone, thoughts of Taya lingered... The shadow of circles under her eyes and her slumped posture spoke of a weariness I hadn't seen in her a few weeks ago, when I'd stolen nearly thirty hours to be with her – granted I was weeks late in keeping my promise...

Not wanting the UGC to follow us around during my visit, we'd stayed inside during the day, and taken a stroll at twilight when everyone else was asleep. She hadn't brought up returning to the surface, but I knew it was constantly on her mind. I heard echoes of it in her thoughts, and felt it lurking behind every emotion.

The look on her face when the crowd separated us after the Rally wrapped around every synapse of my mind. I'd reached out to her, and intended to go back to her had it not been for Gerrund. The grip he'd placed on my arm made it go numb – the bruise that lingered days later a perfect shadow of his fingers and thumb.

If you don't leave now, you'll miss the meet with our insider. What's more important: that you say goodbye, or you make the Oracle's words a reality?

He had done so much to get me, us, the Cause to this point, I knew I couldn't sacrifice that for anything... not even my soul mate. It wasn't supposed to turn out like this. I'd envisioned her beside me, not hidden away in the bowels of the earth. But fear makes us do stupid things.

I sighed. She was caged, just as her lynx was. Jadis refused to go on walks with me and moped around my tiny apartment constantly sniffing… looking for Taya. I wiped my face with a hand as if to clear away the thoughts that never truly left me. There was work to be done.

Since my return I continued to reach out to the Sector Delegates. Convincing them all to meet with me, at the same time, outside of a Session. It had been a political nightmare. Still, I managed to persuade them they needed to hear my point of view personally before they condemned or revered me for their own agendas.

Walking into the main dining area, the noticeable lack of bodies in the restaurant set me at odds with the twelve individuals sitting around a table at the back. Standing at the head of the long table, I pressed the buzzer beneath the decorative edge. It sounded faintly in the kitchen. Two waiters bustled in carrying trays of food.

"Welcome, Delegates, to the Chalklin Pond."

The waiters placed four platters of formal appetisers, replete with mini-forks and spread-knives, along the centre of the table before disappearing back into the kitchen.

I sat down. I saw the uncomfortable glares at the food, brought my plate forward, took a sandwich corner and a piece of cheese. Only then did several of the others follow suit.

"Thank you again for agreeing to meet with me. I'd like this to be an open forum. I'm sure we'll manage without an official mediator. We're all professionals after all." I smiled, and made eye contact with each attendee. Concerned, serious faces did not smile back. I shouldn't have expected anything more, but I'd hoped there would be some sympathisers present.

"Let's begin then, shall we?"

At first no one spoke. I folded my hands before me on the table as I rolled my cheese around in my mouth letting it dissolve.

Sector Nine's Delegate, Sir Enay from Vrazeth opened, "As you know, not all of us have had an opportunity to hear you speak, and our knowledge is second-hand at best. Could you start with how you knew to look for the Chronicles?"

"Yes, of course. I'll do my best to be brief. As a young man, I became disenchanted with the *system*, so to speak. I started looking beyond what I was being taught and that led to questions the Kronik didn't want answered. I found that the further I looked into our past, the more challenging the questions became. It felt as if, not only my past, but an entire piece of *our* history was missing, buried deep and forgotten." I tapped my sandwich on my plate as I considered my next words.

"During my early days outside the Compound walls, I learned a lot about the realities the average citizen faced and the discrepancies between what I was taught and what the public was aware of. Like other followers of the Spoken Truth, I turned to the only clue I had – fragmented stories of our past. I actively searched out any and all texts relating to the time of the Great Migration, which led me to the legend of the Chronicles. The last piece of the puzzle – where to find the lost Chronicles – was held in the writings of the Ancient Tablets, located in a small museum within your own sector, Sir Enay. I knew, felt it deep in my being, the Chronicles would finally hold the answers I was searching for." Glassy eyes and vague inattentiveness told me I was losing them. I had to give them more.

"You see, the questions I was asking started out simply enough: Who am I? How did we get here? And the more I learned from the old texts about the way things *were* compared to what we're living through now – quakes, a changing environment, and an antiquated governing system – I knew the answers weren't going to be found here, in the new land. These were not just my answers I searched for any more, they were answers we all needed. But I digress.

"With the aid of my Contracted Guide we mapped out and traversed the Deserts with a Kahn-lea. Eventually, we found the Chronicles and an equally ancient journal. Together, these two items filled in the missing pieces and explained, not only why our environment is in a state of flux, but how to fix it." The number of crossed arms and sceptical faces surrounding the table was not reassuring. I pushed my plate forward to lean my arms on the table.

"How many of you have heard me speak of this first hand?" I asked.

The Delegates looked back and forth from one to another saying nothing. No one wanted to reveal more than their neighbour.

"How many of you are certain of what I am about to say next?"

Five hands rose slightly.

"I see now how important it is that you all joined me today." I sat back and took a breath, gathering my thoughts, though I'm sure many of them felt I was being melodramatic.

"Two-thousand years ago, there lived an alien race, the Dakturians, who resided in a Great City on our planet's southern hemisphere – on the other side of the Deserts. A thousand years before that, when they first arrived, the available, habitable land on Xannia was minimal.

"Much of what we know now as the Deserts was broad lakes of verrin, thriving with life. Many of our early ancestors, as the scientist Dr. Nadian referred to in his works, evolved from those lakes and, likely at that time, our species as a whole spent more time in the verrin than out of it." Sector Four and Sector Seven's Delegates looked ready to contradict me. I clasped my hands together and hurried on with my explanation.

"To make the planet more hospitable for their people, the Dakturian's devised and launched a solar orb – what we know of as our smallest sun, Gamma – and placed it in orbit around the equator. This orb has an active nuclear device contained within a state-of-the-art resilient metallic memory sheath, to protect the planet from the negative components of radiation."

Sector Four's Delegate, Sir Hetrick hit the table. "That's ridiculous. You have no proof, and that hack scientist's findings are still being debated. I knew you were just going to fill our heads with stories. I'm leaving." He slid his chair back.

"Please." I said, also standing.

I couldn't let him leave. Others would follow and I'd lose them all.

"As difficult as it is for you to hear what I have to say, wouldn't you rather stay, hear everything and then know exactly what people are talking about, so that you're able to refute it on an equal footing?"

Sector One's Delegate, Sir Plithis from Darzeth Prime interjected, "This is where most of us become sceptical at best, Dezmind. Why should we believe you? Why doesn't the Kronik know about this? An alien race – Hetrick's right. What *proof* is there?" Plithis turned to Hetrick and nodded. I wasn't sure if it meant he agreed with the man or was inviting him to sit down. Either way, Hetrick sat and folded his arms across his chest again. I nodded a thank you to Hetrick as well.

"But the Kronik does know – to a degree. My father is one of the twelve Council Advisors. This put me in the unique position to learn more than the average Talian, and considerably more than the average citizen living beyond the walls. That's why it's necessary to acknowledge that my positioning has given me a significant amount of insight."

I hadn't anticipated needing to defend myself quite like this. I hadn't prepared for the necessity of it. I tried to settle my rapid heartbeat by taking a few deep breaths before continuing. "In my youth I overheard several conversations that confused me to no end – conversations that became clear once I learned of the Dakturians." I'd gone over *this* part in my mind again and again in the last few days, trying to be ready; to explain it in just the right way.

"You see, they've known for some time that Gamma is not like Alpha and Beta. You've seen evidence of it in the news and in specials shown on the wire. They've had the ability to launch probes and satellites for a lot longer than they've let on.

"They learned about Gamma's orbital pattern, its low light and heat emissions, and its increasing fluctuations, well before it was ever released to the open community. In fact, they've been trying to learn more about it since they also believe it's at least a contributing factor to our environmental problems." The use of widely accepted facts helped lower a few pairs of raised shoulders.

"From what I've pieced together of their theories, they honestly believe Gamma is a rogue star that was pulled into our gravitational field and is slowly destabilising. The Kronik has chosen to ignore and block out a very important part of our history… why the Great Migration happened in the first place.

"You see, when the Dakturians launched Gamma into orbit, it dried up the surface lakes around our equator and made rich, farmable land for our burgeoning ancestors. But, by the time the aliens fled from their Great City to elude a deadly Virus, they found our Ancient City on the verge of destruction from the growing Deserts.

"They advised our ancestors to migrate north. During this time, the two species learned more about each other and the Virus. This was important because Gamma had to be, umm, recharged shall we say, with a photon generator on a regular basis." I don't know how many times I'd said the words out loud since coming home, but for the first time they didn't sound real, even to my ears.

Sector Five's Delegate, Madam Wekker asked, "So, where are they? Where are the Chronicles?" She looked around the room as if expecting to see them lying under a sheet, ready to be revealed.

"Unfortunately, I was unable to bring them home with me. They are quite large and cumbersome for a single person to carry. Know, though, that they contain detailed instructions for how to find the alien city, and how to locate the generator. However, I did return with *this*."

I reached into the inner pocket of my jacket and held up Ketic's metal journal. I slid it across the table to Madam Wekker, who eagerly flipped through it with Sir Plithis.

"That journal tells the story of the Dakturians. If tested, the age of the metal will show you that I'm not making this up. The problem is, I can't just walk into a government-run lab and ask them to do an age test. If what I'm saying is true about the

Kronik's hidden agenda, the results would be falsified. I need an independent group or someone with the knowhow, that others trust… and that can only begin with people higher up, like you, who are willing to take a chance and believe me.

"For now, you'll find pages of translated text between the thin metal sheets to decipher the alien writing for you. When the Kahnlea eventually return from the Great City, they'll bring with them, not only the Chronicles, but artefacts and stories of their time away. Right now, their mission is two-fold: keep the Generator operational, and stay alive. The Kronik has already tried to assassinate me, and tortured my Contractor upon her return. I would not wish for them to arrive until this dispute is resolved."

The journal passed from hand to hand, each Delegate eager to hold it and see it for themselves.

Sector Eleven's Delegate, Sir Renwin from Outer-Zanneketh said, "This artefact and your tale are intriguing. But I'm still confused. Why is the Kronik not working with you on this? How is it they remain in the dark about the Deserts and our southern hemisphere? They say you're spreading lies and rumours. That you're a rogue Talian who doesn't speak for the Kronik and, most importantly, that you're delusional."

"I know many of you had reservations about coming here today, and have even questioned my motives for not inviting the three Magistrates." I took a deep breath. It was always going to be my word against the Kronik's, but it was time to tell the *truth*.

"First of all, because of the target I've become, I didn't want the Magistrates here to deter you from expressing your true thoughts and concerns. As they report directly to the Kronik's Advisors, you might have been at risk because of something you said or did here today. Sir Hetrick, I especially thank you for remaining. Had you left, none of you would have the first-hand knowledge you need to either refute or support me.

"You see, I'm not so deluded to believe that after you hear me out, you'll all side with me immediately. When you leave this afternoon, it will be your choice to vocalise your support or not. But know this, the louder you are, the more attention will be brought to you. The more attention, the more your personal danger increases and thus the need for today's discretion." Head nods accentuated pursed lips and furrowed brows. I knew this would be a sore spot.

"It is not my intent to put you in harm's way – just to let you decide for yourselves what might actually be going on here. Know also that I fully intend to speak with the Magistrates *individually*, but I'm finding it difficult to contact them directly."

I struggled to keep my hands away from my face. I wanted to rub my eyebrows, or run my fingers through my hair to channel my frustrations. But simple, everyday actions like that could make or break belief… they come across as signs of weakness, indecision, or as accentuating untruths. Instead, I sat tall and flattened my hands against the deep wood of the table.

"At this point, all I can say in my defence is this: You've all now heard me speak and tell my story. You can decide for yourselves if I'm a raving lunatic, or just a man passionate about saving the people of Xannia. Know also that there've been two failed attempts on my life: Once in the Deserts when the Kronik sent an undercover agent to assassinate me, and another, one week after my return at the Rally in Darius' Square. That was not a super quake which devastated the park, and claimed all those innocent lives. There were six explosive charges set off underground – all in succession. Ask anyone who was there and they'll all describe the same thing. I'm confident in my assumption that the Kronik was behind it.

"They've recently changed their tactics – I'm too well-known now, too well-protected by those who *do* believe, for them to directly threaten my life again. They've had to get creative, they've had to go public with their message in order to discredit me."

Sector Three's Delegate, Madam Quellen spoke out, "So you claim. Again, it comes down to your word against the Kronik. You *say* you were attacked, that Secret Agents – the ravings of the tabloids – are real, and yet there's still no evidence." This was a woman who'd heard me speak in public. But again, it came down to proof. Several others echoed her demand.

"Yes, how do we know you're not just saying all this to scare us in to believing you?" Plithis demanded.

I stood up, loosened my tie and unbuttoned my shirt.

"Good Zola, man. What are you doing?" Renwin shouted. I was making a scene, but it had to be done. "Madam, Sir, the only thing you'll see with *this* proof is the aftermath." I pulled the shirt away to reveal the round purple marks left along my collar bone.

"Great Zita, was that from the Pergle Hold?" Sir Enay gasped. I sat back down and re-dressed before I lost them completely.

"Let me ask you this: When has the Kronik last been seen so often on the wire? When has he ever given a public appearance outside the Compound Walls? What is it that has our government so frightened of a single man and what he has to say in order to go to these extremes to silence him? If I'm talking nonsense, why are they trying so hard to make you believe that?" I had to show them how the Kronik was scrambling, changing its way of dealing with a problem, and using those actions as evidence, as *proof*.

"Previously, when groups of citizens have spoken out against the Kronik, they've simply *disappeared*. The Resistance, twenty-two years ago, was silenced by the Massacre. By gathering those opposed and sailing them off with the best Magistrate that ever spoke for the twelve sectors.

"Why is it we now have three Magistrates instead of only one? You know why: Svelik Delenon became too powerful, and anyone deemed too powerful is instantly considered a threat." At the mention of Delenon, the once Great Magistrate cursed with the burden of the Nine Seas on Massacre Day, heads nodded.

An assembly of eyes were focused on me and what I had to say. No one was checking watch-coms for cancelled appointments, missed calls or the time.

"One of the reasons the Kronik is keeping Talians separated from the masses, is that he truly believes Talians are a superior race.

I guarantee that each and every one of you has thought this was the case at some point in your lives, in your careers – that the Kronik, Talians, were far too full of themselves. Well, it's true. Why? Because we have *special* abilities. Abilities that are genetically linked to *Dakturian* DNA."

I supplied the links, but I could tell by stiff postures, the tilt of a head or a nervous twitch that, for some, I could have spoken about the origins of a mythical creature for all it mattered. They refused to believe, to take my word as truth... they were too much like Taya.

"Don't you see? They've been keeping these secrets for so long now, they've forgotten who they are and what they're supposed to represent. They publicly claim that Gamma isn't the source of our problems because, if they were to release that information and not explain how they know, especially without a resolution readily available, they'd be seen as weak."

Every man and woman present knew I spoke the truth on these matters – a truth left to whispers and shadows for too long. As to whether or not this could be construed in their minds as the proof they needed, was another matter entirely.

"We're all familiar with this. We've all kept secrets as we've waited for pieces of the puzzle to fall into place. Their secrets are just so big now, that this is what they need to resort to in order to maintain control," I finished.

The Delegates muttered quietly to one another. I'd ranted more than I'd planned to, but the pitiful excuse the Kronik claimed was governing the people pissed me off.

Sir Plithis spoke: "You've given us much to consider, Dezmind. There's just one piece to this puzzle I haven't seen yet."

"Yes, of course. Ask me anything."

"Where will all of this lead? What's your agenda? You've given us all of this knowledge – what do you expect us to do with it?

The table hushed. *What do I want them to do? Oh, so much more than I can say.*

"Support me, if you can. Believe me and believe *in* me. Tell your constituents, tell your families and friends, and let them decide what they believe. Right now, that's all I ask. As for my *agenda*? Let's just say I have hopes for the future. I want to see a change in the Kronik and, ultimately, how Xannia is governed." More than one intake of breath rang out at that little titbit of treason.

"I want to see our people united – no more walls between us. I want those who are being persecuted for self-expression to be able to come out of hiding and live free again. I'm not talking about hardened criminals here, just those loved ones who've had to disappear because they believed in a better world, too.

"I'm certain each and every one of you has a friend, family member, or neighbour who suddenly and inexplicably vanished under unusual circumstances. Maybe they were Resistance supporters, or simply in the wrong place at the wrong time. Now, I can't promise you they're all alive. But, I can promise that you will, one day, know their story, and maybe even see them again if you truly believe my story... my truth."

Chapter Fourteen
Progress

Gelden

She raced down the tunnel from one of the crevices lining the connecting street, skidding to a stop just outside the shop. I watched through the window as Dalla yanked on the handle and the door swung out. Leaping across the threshold, she pulled the door shut, collapsing against the rock wall beside it.

Gulping in a deep lungful of air, Dalla looked over at me. My forearms rested on the edges of a box of parts. I'd installed a new shelving system yesterday, and was just as eager as her to get things organised.

"You know they haven't followed you down here since your first Daily. I think they get that the work you're doing is important."

"Yeah, but I still don't want to walk here with a crowd of delusional people pushing all around me, either. Besides, it's been a while since I've worked out like this. Keeps my heart strong and my head clear." She walked over to see what goodies I'd brought today.

"Excellent! I can start working on the solar panel."

She looked over at the simple bike frame leaning against the wall by the drafting table. A deep crease furrowed her forehead.

It appeared so often, it was a wonder it didn't remain permanent.

"That frame… those thin tires…" She sighed.

I flashed her a smile. "I thought the same thing last night."

A knock rattled the door. She jumped. One of Gerrund's errand boys walked in.

"Miss Trellice?"

She stepped forward. He nodded a greeting and held out a purple envelope.

"Message for you."

She accepted the letter. As he disappeared back out into the tunnel, she flicked open the fold with a handy wall screw. She slid out the letter and read it to herself. The lack of dark circles under her eyes said she was sleeping better these days, or simply getting more rest. That first day we met she'd looked so frail… of course, her verbal attack made me smile at her spunk. She seemed to have a reservoir of go-juice. I wasn't sure if I should be envious or scared.

"He's busy this morning." We both knew who she referred to. "No Daily." Her eyes scanned the rest of the page. I could see the corners of her mouth twitch, but somehow she managed not to smile. She lit the note on fire with a lighter she'd taken to carrying around, and tossed the page into the metal wastebasket by the counter. I'd seen Gerry and Randex do it before but, watching Dalla perform the same ritual, felt less routine and more animalistic.

"We've got a week to get the D.V. operational. Gerrund wants Bazdin out of here. He doesn't trust the man, no matter what I say. I need to meet with the Guides the day before the journey." The way she lost the edge to her voice, and let that carefully hidden vulnerability slip out, meant there was a lot more to that letter than she was telling me.

"Who'll be going?"

She gave a small smile. "Just Bazdin and one other – whoever *I* think is strongest of the bunch."

She let out a long sigh, finally showing signs of relaxing. This was likely part of what had kept her tense and on edge since the project started.

"Gerrund doesn't want me to go – something about continuing to liaise with Mardel and Ticia on the progress of the troops, and making use of my experience with the CTF."

She collapsed onto the chair by the drafting table.

"I'm just glad he gave himself time to think this through and agreed to my plan. I– I wouldn't have been able to let a larger group go without my supervision... and... I– I just–"

Leaning against the table, she rubbed her forehead.

"I don't think, as important and vital as opening up communication and supplies between us and the Kahn-lea is, that I'm ready to do that again... go back out there."

I walked over and gave her shoulders a quick squeeze. I wouldn't usually have been so forward, but something about her sudden sensitivity made it feel like the right decision.

"Hey, this is a good thing. And you know what else?" I backtracked around the counter and rolled out a large, three wheel, cross-framed electric rover. "I was able to convince the tunnel excavation crew to sell this old chassis to me instead of trading it for scrap metal."

She laughed – big and full so that it bounced off the walls of our little shop. I couldn't help but smile. Her moods were infectious.

"Brilliant, Gelden. We just might be able to make our deadline after all. It's perfect. Thank you."

She knelt down next to it and ran her hands over the hollow, metal frame studying every inch of it. For a nano-second, I found myself jealous of the chassis.

"How wide can we get the wheels?" she asked.

"It's built for sixteen inches, but I can customise some rims and rework the frame to accommodate twenty to twenty-four-inch tires from our surface supplier. I'll have to put that order in this afternoon, though, to get them in five days."

"Yes, do that. Two twenty-fours for the back and a twenty for the front. I'd like a deep tread, but the lighter the better."

"Right. No problem." I shouldn't have said that. This was old tech, but I felt I could promise her anything.

"What size battery will be light enough... or do you think we should use a fuel cell and scrap the array? There's not a lot of time, but it would be more reliable than a battery. But, unless we had a sealed enclosure for the fuel cell, the sand might damage the components, and then we'd need an extra supply of water..."

"Dalla, work on the construction of the solar panel, and the basic energy converter. I'm sure you'll figure it all out while you're distracted with another task."

"I just don't want to commit to building something if we're not going to use it."

"Look at it as a test for yourself. It won't take long to sort things out once your brain is kept busy with other things."

"You're right. I get so far ahead of myself sometimes."

She collected the solar cells and several other components, sat on a stool at the rounded end of the counter, and began assembling the array. I took several measurements of the chassis, and then sat at the table to draft the alterations needed for the D.V.'s frame.

As we worked, I tried to focus on the modification and not watch Dalla. She caught me looking at her.

"Do you know what you're doin' over there?" I asked, trying to sound casual and keep things light.

"I've never built anything solar powered before, but I did study it at the CTF and worked with several devices during my time with Professor Denali. I can already foresee glitches and problems, especially installing the charge controller between the array and the battery."

"So, you've decided on your energy source."

"Yeah, but not the fuel cell. It'll actually be more efficient to use a battery. That way I don't have to find, or attempt to build an electrolyser – you know, the device used to breakdown water to utilise the electricity from the separation of the hydrogen and the oxygen. There just isn't enough time."

I nodded and smiled like I could follow what she was saying but, honestly, I didn't know the first thing about fuel cells.

When the main portion of the array was built, Dalla slipped over to study the new frame as I marked out expansion joints and reinforcement piping – altering my sketches and numbers as I went. She leaned over my shoulder to look at both the drafted modifications on the ground, and the marks I'd made on the frame.

I felt her breath drift across the nape of my neck as she assessed the rear of the vehicle. I forced myself to focus on the drawings. If I transferred the information incorrectly, we'd lose precious time.

* * *

Taya

I worked for the better part of the morning figuring out the placement of my photovoltaic array and the maximum amount of wattage the cells could convert, as well as the storage capacity of the various batteries at my disposal. By the early afternoon I had an operational prototype, just as Gelden finalised the design modifications. He marked the basic layout onto the existing structure.

"This is maddening." He pushed his rolling stool away from the frame and ran both hands through his hair. "The crew for the door was supposed to be here this morning. I can't continue with the fabrication until the new one's installed."

"Did you want me to talk to your contacts this afternoon? We need those tires too."

"They're top-side. Gerry doesn't want you up there for a while." He gave me the "nice try" look. "I'll have to go and see what's holding them up."

"Well, I– have somewhere I'm expected anyway." I pushed the navy-blue scarf up from the face of my watch. "Actually, I'm running late."

He tilted his head to one side as if to ask a question. I just stared at him openly, giving nothing away as I cleaned up my work station.

"I don't know if I'll be back later or not. If the doors are being installed then send someone to find me. Gotta run."

Gelden raised a hand in a half-wave as he tidied the drafting table and dragged the frame back behind the counter, away from prying eyes.

With a moderated glance from the door, I slipped out and headed for the main connecting tunnel. There was one other item Gerrund had mentioned in his message that morning. Something for my eyes only.

It was time to meet my therapist.

The location was new to me, down a side tunnel I hadn't been yet.

I should have swallowed my pride and asked Gelden to walk with me. Alone I'll be followed for sure.

Without realising it I found myself at a jog, and then running flat out by the time I rounded the corner of the shop's connecting tunnel. Even if there'd been a group waiting for me, they'd never have been able to keep up – that and I wasn't going my usual route.

I directed my feet to bring me down a series of smaller tunnels where buildings were situated only on one side – making for a narrower street path. I walked up to the door of a very long, low building with no name, only a picture painted on a sign. It wasn't elaborately detailed the way the wall frescoes were, not even stencilled like Magda's salon Twin Faces. What looked like rain swirling over a sun with bright rays brought to mind a child's drawing, more than something an artesian was capable of.

All Seasons – in a place where no seasons rule. Another contradiction, another satirical comment on this hidden, underground world.

I slipped into the dim, windowless expanse. My eyes adjusted fairly quickly and, by the time the door closed behind me, I could see clearly. My recent ability to sleep had improved my vision.

Small, round wooden tables littered the wide space, with a bar and service window opposite the entrance. Around the perimeter of the room private booths could seat up to six patrons. Smack in the middle of everything sat gaming tables of skill and chance. Three burly guys slowly patrolled the interior, while a fourth monitored the bar and grill. There were less than thirty people in the room, but only one looked right at me.

He or she wore a short-brimmed, soft crowned cap made of felt or wool, and a patchwork jacket or cloak, clearly fashioned that way.

I ordered a frosted verrin from the bar and wound my way amongst the gamers. They ignored me, just as I did them. In a way we were invisible to each other, outside the scope of importance. I slipped into the booth with the stranger, took a sip of my verrin, and stared back at the blue skinned person with the rainbow coliths.

"You're not what I expected." I surprised myself by speaking first. "This place isn't what I expected." I took another sip. "Who are you?"

"I am the one you seek." The voice was even, steady, without masculine or feminine tags.

"Really? No office? No couch? Is this standard practice?" I wasn't just going to go along with this charade.

"In a manner of speaking, yes. And yes, I do have an office with a particularly comfortable couch – but you didn't strike me as the type to *feel* comfortable there. Am I right?"

"And you think here is better?"

He smiled. "Better than anywhere else down here, if you know what I mean. Our resources are limited. This is one of only a few places not built for *necessity*. I didn't figure we could talk adequately while exercising, or viewing art."

"Are you *in character* right now, too? Or is this…" I waved at his general attire, "really who you are?"

"This is one of my many *sides*, shall we say. I'm a bit overdressed for the occasion, but I'd prefer my guests build their own impression of me rather than come into every situation the same. If we met and

I was wearing a crisp suit and tie you would immediately react to that stereotype. And yet, in my office with the couch, I often wear a jacket and tie.

"This way I've caught your interest, haven't I? You've dropped your guard, and we've already begun a conversation. In the other scenario, you would've sat, or stood, waiting for something I said to be, well, miraculous. But it doesn't work that way."

During the course of our conversation, his voice gradually lowered and his jaw line became more pronounced – *or had he simply removed it from the collar of his cloak-jacket enough for me to see?*

"Your characteristics have changed. Why? More moulding to the role?"

"Yes. Your tone of voice and general nature led me to believe you think I'm male, so I obliged and revealed part of my identity. If you would've felt more at ease talking to a woman, I would have highlighted my more feminine features. Gerrund suspected you would feel more at ease with my male persona, anyway, even considering your recent history. Still, I like to let my guests decide for themselves."

"Will I ever see the real you, or will you always play a role?"

"Try not to get confused with what I do, or don't, look like – with what's considered the *real* me. We all hide things about ourselves we don't want others to see. We all act differently around certain people than others we're more familiar with. You'll probably never see the *real* me, since I don't tend to walk around naked – either emotionally or physically. And neither do you."

He waited. People did that when they wanted you to think about what they'd said, or were hesitating before revealing something they felt was incredibly important. Dez taught me that. Not outright of course, just by being himself. I played the game, and waited for my turn to speak.

"I trust it is the real you in front of me, but only as much of that person as you're willing to show," he said. "If I'm not mistaken, Gerrund also mentioned you dabbled for a while with costume to hide yourself – to be unrecognisable, and yet it was still you under all that makeup and material. Is it still you who sits before me in body-art and borrowed clothes... or not?"

A sharp blade pierced my heart in rapid succession.

"What's your name?" he asked.

My name? His words echoed, just as someone else's had once before in a metal Warehouse I was never supposed to get out of alive. I mentally pushed past it.

"Call me—"

"No," he said evenly.

"Excuse me?"

"No. I'd like your name. Who *you* are. Not something you've adopted for the sake of knowing if someone is speaking to you, or about you."

"I—" nothing came out. My eyes clouded, a haze shrouded my brain as a male voice echoed off metallic grey walls saying very much the same thing. Then my foster mother's voice calling me Taya... Gerrunds's voice calling me J.J... Dezmind's voice asking me about the name Jadis... Gelden calling me...

"My name is Bajak, Jak for short," he said, snapping me back to the present. "This was a good start. Meet me here again in two days. We'll make it a bit later? Say half-past five, so you can focus on your project for Gerrund?"

I nodded.

He stood up and leaned over the table toward me. "Next time, though, I'd like for you to introduce yourself. Good luck with your Deserts project." With that, he blended in to the small crowd and disappeared. No one paid him any mind, and no one saw me sitting there nursing the last few sips of now warm verrin.

"Zimi!" called a female voice.

"Child of the Stars!" another woman yelled.

"Protector of the Young!" called out a man.

I'd left the All Seasons, distracted and unconcerned about being seen. I had, after all, just been in a room full of people of whom no one took notice. By the time I passed Major Minor, though, I'd been spotted by followers of the Trinity.

Their bodies coalesced around me, shrinking any avenue of escape. The sheer number of people slowed my walk to a shuffle. Flashes of *the incident* confused and distracted me: the suffocating closeness of strangers, the hands grabbing at me, being lifted bodily into the air, seeing Dez's arm fall away from reaching out to me. My body shuddered, almost as it had while being held aloft. I tried to suck in even breaths, but the air was filled with the exhales of so many other people.

I refused to look anyone in the eyes, keeping my hands over my ears and my elbows straight out to either side. It afforded some personal space, but not much. I was just down the street from my apartment, but I might as well have been a hundred miles away.

Then it started again.

Hands snatched at my clothing and hair. Pictures and keepsakes being thrust at my face. The din of voices clawed at my patience.

I trembled a second time. Unwanted tears bathed my hot cheeks.

"Emvaso-al!"

"Zimi—"

"Child of the Sun!"

They're innocent – They're innocent – They're innocent. But the chant drowned in the storm of voices ricocheting and clattering around me.

I swung my arms out. The starburst scars on my palms glowed red from agitation – to them it was a sign. Several gasps silenced the excessive prattling. Leaving my arms extended, I whipped around in a frenzy with my eyes closed. The crowd quieted, backing away. I opened my eyes to a hush.

Darting through a gap, I broke free and ran to my building. Slamming my body into first one door, and then next, I struggled and stumbled up the inner stairwell.

Jutaya – Jadis – Aleonia – Dalla – Orphan – Daughter – Contractor – Friend – Lover?

I snatched the pile of mail from the door basket, jammed my key-card in the slot, and fell into my apartment. Turning the lock, I then walked, quaking, through the black apartment. I ditched the mail on the breakfast bar on top of the other pile, without bothering to look at it, and carried on past the kitchen to my bedroom.

Yanking the top from the bottle, I dry-swallowed a pill, capped the container, and threw myself on the bed.

Who am I? Who am I?

Burying my head under the pillow I screamed.

*   *   *

~~Dear Dez,~~

~~Nights are the worst without you. It seems no matter what thoughts of you I fall asleep to I wake up screaming and wondering why you're not here.~~

~~I didn't realise how much I depend on hearing from you until your second last letter arrived late in the mail. Every day I wonder if life would've been easier if we'd had a chance to say goodbye. My world seems to have shrunk to these four walls. In a place where no one is supposed to know who I am, I dread walking outside here more than I ever did there.~~

Dez,

You have to stop the madness. Find a way to bring me home, or I'll find my own way out.

~~*Ali*~~

~~*Jutaya*~~

~~*Jadis*~~

--

Chapter Fifteen
Things Left Unsaid

Merik

Pulling my desk chair over to stand on, I shelved three more small metallic books. Our alien library grew larger every day with everyone scouring new sections of the city in the mornings.

Though Ray was never spoken of directly, except during the breakfast meetings, he remained foremost in our thoughts as the Virus continued to destroy him from the inside out.

I stepped down, returned the chair to my desk, then walked over to the doorway to look back and see the amassed knowledge held within the space. Not so surprisingly, I'd caught on to the Dakturian cataloguing system with relative ease. Blocks of red, green, blue... every colour of the rainbow, tinted the metallic bindings of their books. Each subject had its own hue, and even though personal journals remained the natural deep grey of the metal, mixed as they were amongst the more official texts, they refracted the colouring of their neighbours.

"What do you mean you can't say?" Syvis' raised voice sliced across the Common.

"One of the scientist's journals looks promising. I'm following up on a few leads. I don't know where I've been until I've been there.

That's why I can't tell you where I'm going to be today." Zaith said, with that ever-present edge to her voice. The others thought it was determination. It sounded like fear to me.

I stepped out of view of the door and leaned against the frame. I wasn't spying per-se. I was just curious. Zaith hadn't been acting like herself since she found that last journal... the one that promised a cure.

"You of all people know it's not safe to wander off on your own – it's *your* rule. I'm worried about you." Syvis stepped closer to her, eliminating what remained of the space between them. He leaned toward her, his head hovering over hers even though she was a tall woman. Equally, the invisible gravity of their masses pulled her toward him, and yet neither actually touched the other.

Zaith closed her eyes. I could actually see Syvis breathe in her scent. I'd suspected something growing between them since the incident with Ray, and yet neither seemed to want to admit the fact.

She tilted her chin up as if to kiss him, but said, "I can take care of myself." Stepping back, she opened her eyes, then grabbed her pack, and walked off in the opposite direction. Syvis shook his head, then ran his hand through a rather shaggy head of hair.

I stepped out into the Common, but before I could say anything he gave me curt nod.

"Merik," he said by way of greeting, and then walked off with his own pack.

I'd wanted to speak with him about Zaith. Obviously, he did not. I was certain though, that of everyone here, he'd have noticed the same things I had: the way she wore long-sleeved shirts, even in the worst heat of the day; pulled her hair constantly around the right side of her neck; kept her hands out of sight whenever she wasn't avoiding eating.

But then, maybe love really was blind.

Chapter Sixteen
Looking Ahead

Taya

I glanced behind me. The crowd had dispersed. No one followed me down the connecting tunnel to the training cavern. Jogging past the shop, the new wider door winked at me as the lights inside flickered on. Gelden had arrived earlier than usual the past two days, trying to get caught up on the necessary welding the D.V.'s frame needed.

He wasn't the only one putting in extra hours. I'd been arriving earlier, too. It tended to throw off the crowd if I shifted my departure times. Now, only a handful of regulars bothered to track me down for our *morning exercise.*

At yesterday's meeting, Gerrund had given me free-reign to check in for Dailies any time between five and seven in the morning. After that, he'd be making his rounds.

I was still cautious about pushing our uneasy truce. As the pressures of his job mounted, so were its effects on his personality. But really, I couldn't complain. He had, after all, granted me more responsibility in the last two weeks than he had in the previous month.

"Morning, Gerrund." I tossed an envelope with an out-going address in the mail tray, before using the edge of the closest table on the platform to balance myself. I raised a heel behind me. Grabbing my ankle, I stretched out my thigh muscles one at a time. He glanced up from a sheaf of papers.

"I suppose." He gave them a shake. "We're not making the kind of progress I want to see exploring several of the new tunnels. It's disheartening to say the least."

"Well, I have some good news for you then."

He raised his eyebrows.

I smiled at him for the first time in several days. Whatever tension was between us might simply be stress on his part, and a figment of my imagination. Today we'd start fresh.

"Gelden and I are ahead of schedule. We've both put in some overtime and, if we stay on track, we'll be ready in another two days."

"Excellent. I need you to meet with the Guides this afternoon. Obviously, you won't be able to go over the functionality of the D.V. until it's done, but I'd like them to get as close to first-hand knowledge about their mission as possible. They've been studying your maps, along with the basic survival tips and information you included, but you should put them through their paces – test them mentally and physically. Help them realise exactly what it's like out there so we don't lose anyone to shock or whatever. Can you do that?"

"This afternoon?"

"Yes."

"I have another *appointment* just after five, and I'd like to spend a good chunk of time with the Guides… it'll be tight, but I think I can work it out."

I'll just have to come back to the shop after my session with Jak.

"Good. I'll see you tomorrow. Meet them here later, and then take them wherever you need to." As he shuffled through his pages again, his scowl deepened. I left before it was aimed at me.

Today would be brutal. The array was producing as expected,

and the battery easily took and retained a charge, but I also wanted the battery to accept a charge at night. Gamma wasn't bright enough for the photovoltaic cells to register its faint light, so the pedals Gelden installed yesterday would perform two jobs: charging the battery when solar energy wasn't available, and moving the D.V. when magnetic interference cropped up.

The wiring of the frame had to be well-thought out and organised to reduce any future problems. *With having to prep the Guides this afternoon, my early enthusiasm might just turn around and bite me in the ass.*

Gelden was out front, angled over the frame taking measurements and making sketches. He had one foot on the ground, and the other in mid-air for balance. Stretching over the centre of the D.V., he contemplated something upside down, on the other side. His sketch pad and measuring tape were within reach on the ground.

"Rehearsing for your day job? I bet your act is the hit of the show."

"Welcome to the Big Top, where every day we complete stunning feats of the most impossible and bizarre. Front row seat today, Dalla?" Still draped over the D.V., he sketched frantically.

"What are you doing?"

"I'm trying to design an aerodynamic, lightweight housing for this monster of a creation. And... it takes... some... creative manipulation... on... my part to get all... of the... angles down." He stood up with several drawings clasped in one hand.

"I'll make a note of that," I said, then mimicked a recording. "Note to self, experienced acrobat required for design fabrication – end note."

Gelden manoeuvred the D.V. back into the shop. I pulled the new double-wide door shut behind us.

"The wire you wanted arrived. It's under the counter." He sat down at the drafting table and pulled over a calculator. I lifted the indicated box onto the counter.

"You've got to be kidding." I pulled out a giant clump of tangled strands. "Where did you get this? Will it even work?"

"My surface contact was recently compromised. That's all I could get my hands on. It's recycled, but still good."

"How was your surface contact compromised?"

"It's nothing. Don't worry about it."

A few days ago he'd been having similar trouble arranging for the new shop door, and now a different contact had actually fallen through on a promise.

"No, it's not nothing. What's going on?"

He tried to sound nonchalant, but I saw his shoulders stiffen. "Let's just say that not everyone is feeling the love when it comes to Gerry's plans. Rumours can be vicious sometimes."

He clearly didn't want to talk about it. I hoped it was a temporary issue. "You seem to have quite the variety of contacts. How do you manage? It's like a prison down here."

He turned the swivel chair to face me. Obviously glad of the deviation in the subject, he readily responded, "Dalla, it's only as bad as you make it. I've lived down here my entire life. You learn to adapt."

I didn't look at him. Instead I struggled to untangle the wire.

"Yes, and I've lived on the surface my whole life. Your movement is restricted up there, just as mine is down here." *Probably more so.*

"True, but you have a choice. You can let these *followers* of yours keep you from living your life—"

"The life I want to live has nothing to with down here... can't you see that? I've been my own keeper since I was eight. All of a sudden I have all these restrictions placed on me, simply because I said I'd help out a friend." *A friend I see and hear from less and less all the time.* "Even working for the CTF I didn't feel this chained."

"What then? Do you want to quit? You can leave whenever you want to, but without our help you're still a fugitive. You'll never have the life you once did. Don't you see? That's why we're all down here.

We believe in the Cause… the idea that someday we might have a chance at our former lives, or at the very least live as we were meant to – without persecution."

"You sound like your uncle. You just told me your life is down here. Why should *up there* have anything to do with you?"

"Are you listening to yourself?"

I glared at him.

He sighed. "Dalla, the Underground grows every year. We get new castaways and fugitives every month. And just as often these days, people are finding comfort in each other and starting families… but everyone holds tight to the hope that they will, one day, be given a chance to return to the surface without persecution."

Somehow, I got the feeling that Gerrund's sister was the exception, but I kept my mouth shut.

"What will become of the Underground when the Cause has *won*?"

"No one's ever thought that far ahead. I know Gerrund and Dezmind are working toward a goal date for the coup, but it's been tried before. The Kronik stopped the Resistance, so why not the Cause? The UGC remain hopeful but realistic. He might just fail again and, in that case, we still need to construct apartments and shops for the sake of those new lives down here."

Portions of the wire gradually worked loose under the manipulation of my fingers. What he said made sense, and yet I'd seen little evidence of it.

"I have Dez's stories, I have Gerrund's remembrances, and now I have your tales. I even have some convoluted fiction from the therapist who, by the way, hasn't even asked me about my dreams yet. What do you do Gelden? What *life* is to be had down here when you're waiting to be set free from oppression? Other than some old frescoes, and the odd UGC propaganda in the Local Inquisitor, what exists other than the Cause's mission?"

"Would you believe more stories, Dalla?"

I let the now stringy mass of wire fall to my lap. "Gel, the stories are the woulda, coulda, shouldas of hopes and dreams. What is *real* down here?"

He locked eyes with me. It was one of those intense stares that dared me not to look away.

"Come. I'll show you."

I itched to find out. I looked behind me, thought of the rock of the cavern in my mind's eye to the network of caves I knew. But then, I saw myself running... people surrounding me...

"No." I knew the *followers* bothered me less when I was with someone, but I didn't want that crutch. "Just tell me. Please."

He nodded. The daring light that sparkled in his eyes extinguished.

"It's true that we don't have the comforts of the surface. No Solar Plex, no chain of community centres, or game rooms. What we do have are the necessities, and that keeps us busy enough. For instance, twice a week I help the Development Planners by building new housing and shops for those saved. Since I don't have the time available to explore tunnels or excavate approved sites, I volunteer with a construction crew – as do many UGCs."

"What can't you do, Gel?"

"The Mentor program was put in place to provide a wide range of skills for those living down here. As you can see, it works pretty well."

"Patting yourself on the back now? You'll really be insufferable when we get this project operational, won't you?"

He smiled. "I help out where I can, when I can, on various stages of construction, anywhere from the ground up. Most of our resources come from whatever cave is currently being excavated. What tends to determine the size of a structure are the *extra* materials available to us – namely whatever we can scrounge from the surface.

"Usually any lumber or lighting comes sporadically from a source near the Expanse. It takes a while to get it here, where it's more central, or even to our expanded tunnels sites. You see, we occasionally need wooden or steel beams, mortar set or what have you. We do our best to use natural resources to reduce our dependency – but that's not always possible.

"I also like to join a group called The Tall Tales when I can spare an evening. They travel in a small nomadic group throughout the populated underground sharing stories, songs, poems and news.

Often, they meet when the overhead lamps dim and the street lights begin to glow. Most times they sit right in the middle of the street, but there's the occasional building large enough to accommodate both them and their listeners.

"And then, once a month, I help out the Food Corp. We get a bulk shipment in from the surface the same time, same place. Sometimes I help transport the goods to different sorting locations, either by bike, or hauling a wagon with other volunteers, or I help sort and distribute the goods to local stores and cafés.

"I really wish you'd join me. If you could just experience it for yourself, I'm sure you wouldn't feel so... trapped."

I methodically coiled the wire around my elbow and the crook of my thumb. There was more going on than I'd expected. I slid back the scarf on my watch. *Is that the time?*

"I've got to prep for a meeting with the Desert Guides, and make it to an appointment right after that." I dropped the coiled wire back into the box. "I'll be back later to wire up the D.V."

After storing the box under the counter, I retied my loose hair on my way to the door. "Gerrund sprang this meeting on me last minute. I have to find Mardel – get some supplies. I'll see ya later."

Gelden nodded and returned to his calculations.

I stopped, hand on the door. He worked with his back to me. Something pulled at my insides prompting me to say more... but what? I shook it off, pushed open the smaller inner door on the larger slider, and headed for the Training Grounds.

Chapter Seventeen
Trial by Fire

Taya

Seven men and women, including me, trekked through an unexcavated tunnel. Mardel had already given me a map of this explored, undeveloped cavern system, as well as a few specified training devices and a couple of recruits with strengths in espionage to help with the set up earlier.

I held up my arm. The procession stopped and I turned to face them, setting the scene.

"You are now exiting the Valley of the Dunes and entering the Powder Sands. You," I pointed to a male Guide who looked slightly stunned, "are in the Deserts." He stood rooted to the spot. I grabbed the front of his light-grey robes and yanked him out of the tunnel and into the cavern.

"Provide us with an open commentary as you cross these treacherous lands."

He glanced over his shoulder at his comrades. Blank faces stared back. They'd been warned that I was *different*... that I was recently an active Contractor associated with the Kronik – that I was also the infamous Quake Queller. But the young man, not much older than me, still hadn't made up his mind about me, and he definitely wasn't sure what I expected of him.

The cavern was mostly undisturbed territory. Giant stalactites and stalagmites riddled the expanse, giving the grotto a claustrophobic feel. Some walls and pillars glistened a shining rainbow of colours, and every surface appeared shaped or weathered somehow.

He took a step forward.

"Why did you make that choice?"

Startled murmurs petered out behind him.

"I thought you wanted me to go forward?"

"Not blindly, you idiot! Use your training. Examine your surroundings and then make an informed decision. Never assume that straight ahead is the best course of action."

I stared at him and he shuddered under my scrutiny. I did not look out at the *course* for two reasons: One, I didn't want to inadvertently give clues to where things were hidden; and two, I couldn't critique his progress if I wasn't looking at him.

He glanced from one side of the cavern to the other. "Th– There's a natural path slightly to my right with no obvious obstructions. I'm heading that way."

He took several tentative steps forward. Nothing happened. He walked more assuredly toward the gravel-strewn trail between several large stalagmites.

I glanced down.

He strode into the midst of the formations.

A claw cage flew up from under the gravel. It slammed into his body, trapping him flat on his back. Several yells and screams echoed through the expanse. I cringed. *Where's their backbone?* The Guide lay still but unhurt. Nothing I'd arranged would harm them, but I wasn't about to baby them either.

"Enough with the belly-aching and act like the soldiers you are." My voice silenced them, but echoed throughout the cavern on the emphasised word *soldiers*. "Let's deconstruct."

"But Laiviis…" a girl said.

"What about Laiviis? He can participate from where he is."

Silence.

I sighed. *This isn't going well.* "What was Laiviis' first mistake?" I'd learned, on that long trek through the Deserts, that familiarising myself with the names and general aptitudes of Dezmind's followers helped moderate my propensity to be abrupt. The group finally looked at each other, and then their hands as the gears in their minds whirred into action. Finally, a girl at the back raised her hand.

"Yes–?"

"Robin Leigh."

"Yes, Robin?"

"Laiviis forgot to make an assessment of the new terrain before entering the area with the rock formations, sir."

"Indeed. He did forget, but that wasn't his first mistake."

Silence.

This time they refused to make eye contact with me at all.

"Okay. Let's try this another way. Why did he go *alone* into the Deserts?"

"Because you told him to – uh, sir."

I glared at the young woman addressing me.

"Name?"

"Vitina."

"Vitina, think carefully now. Did I actually tell him to go by himself, or was that merely the impression you got?"

"Umm, well, sir – to be honest I don't remember exactly what you said, but, from the demanding tone you used, and the way you pulled him to the edge of the cavern, it appeared that way."

"Laiviis!" I turned to invite him into the conversation. "Now that you're not under any pressure to perform, what would you – should you – have done differently?"

He looked at us upside down from the flat of his back.

"Brought help."

"Thank you, Laiviis." I turned my attention back to the Guides. "You will need to be able to make life or death decisions under pressure out there. Rule number one: never go anywhere alone. You may think you're invincible but you're not. I'm a Contractor and the risks *I've* taken have not always panned out. You can be damn sure that my training far exceeds your own. Based on what we've covered so far, what do you think rule number two is?"

A Matin male raised his hand and spoke, "Detrius, sir. We should never make assumptions?"

"Correct. Always *be prepared*. Do your research, be organised, make ready your supplies, anticipate what you might be faced with on any given trek through the Deserts and, above all, know your strengths and those of the people you travel with. All of this falls under the umbrella of be prepared." I stared at them. *These are supposed to be the best trainees for the mission?* If things didn't improve fast, I'd have a choice word or two for Gerrund.

"Now, pair up. Take turns leading each other across this *Desert*. Use the resources available to you and provide a running commentary of your decision making. If you get into trouble, it's just as much your fault as your partner's."

I swept my arms wide and turned as if to embrace the space. "The cavern has every conceivable trial you might face that has been discovered in the Deserts, so far, just on a smaller scale. Once everyone makes it across, we'll discuss what the last three rules are. Get to it."

They paired off. No one entered into the cavern without first consulting their partner or checking what resources were readily available to them. A few Guides picked up rocks, some removed the belts from their robes and attached them together, while others discarded their loose robes for greater range of movement. *I'll have to make sure they're aware of the cons of that decision during the debrief.*

I followed Laiviis' exact footsteps to the cage, lifted it off him then reset the mechanism. I didn't bother to cover it over again. I offered him a hand up. Surprisingly he took it without hesitation. I liked that.

"Join Robin. She doesn't have a partner yet, but let her lead first. When your turn comes, I don't want to see you caught unaware again."

He nodded.

"Now, follow my exact steps back."

For the next hour, the Guides put to practice the theory they'd been studying, and integrated the practical lessons they'd learned from Basic Training to successfully cross the cavern. Although the course was only a half-mile long, and a couple-hundred yards wide, it took a great deal of time and patience for them to make their way through the gauntlet.

Each pair faced the harrows of at least one failed assessment, but Laiviis was not among the fallen. They were bright and they learned fast. I could finally see why they'd been chosen for this task.

The debrief lasted another hour and a half after everyone crossed. I made sure they analysed everything. I even set off a few undisturbed traps just to discuss what-if scenarios. If this was my only time with the Guides, other than training them on the use of the D.V., I had to be thorough.

Having left checkpoints on the way to the training cavern, I knew I could assign them the task of cleaning up and returning all the borrowed equipment to Mardel. I now had another appointment to keep.

I sat in the same back booth I'd found myself in two days ago. I sipped some kind of warm chocolate peppermint drink – sipped because it likely had alcohol in the mix. Something I'd failed to inquire about.

The din of the gamblers washed over me. Muscle by minute muscle, the tension eased from my body. *The alcohol must be working.*

Overall, I was pleased with the progress the Guides made. They had eventually warmed up to me as they got used to my instructional style. Some lessons were better learned by doing and assessing – the first-hand experience would be etched into their minds and become another tool to rely on.

I'd given them homework, too. They each had to develop a plausible Desert Creature that could be either passive or aggressive, and outline a scenario where that creature might be encountered in the Deserts. They would then take turns deconstructing the encounters. I had to get them used to thinking ahead – rule number two might just save their lives.

I breathed in the warm steam of the coco and stared at my hands as they held the large brown mug. I still hadn't come up with a satisfactory answer for Jak. Sure, I had a smart response, but he'd make me dig deeper. I knew that.

A flash of movement caught my eye. A hooded, grey cloaked figure wound its way through the central gaming area toward my table. I glimpsed the colourful patchwork lining. *I wonder if it's reversible?*

Jak sat down across from me, and produced a small glass of verrin from the interior of his large sleeve.

"You're here early. Looking forward to our appointment?" He grinned, pushing his hood back onto his shoulders.

I glared at him. "Hardly. I had a few minutes to spare after my instructional session, and I wanted to unwind."

He sat back and let an arm drape over the cushioned bench. "So, tell me then. Who are you?"

That's fast. "I am me. My mother's daughter. My father's joy. A healthy body with a healthy mind." *Maybe that's stretching it a bit.*

"A *healthy* mind? I would be interested to learn what your definition of a healthy mind is, but not today." He sat and stared at me. After an impossible minute he leaned forward and whispered, "By what name does your conscience refer to you?"

I am inquiring into the name or names which identify you for the person you are… The cold metallic voice ricocheted through my head. I watched as a small pool rippled from the centre of my mug to its rim. My eyes hazed over and lost focus. The man before me, the building around me, disappeared as I found myself back in that concrete cell.

Tick – Tick Tick – Tick – Tick Your formal birth identification…

NO! Not that. Not the same thing.

Your conscience – your conscience – by what name does your conscience refer to you?

I blinked. The mug of coco returned. My lips twitched. I wiped the wet from my cheek. That had been happening far too often lately.

"Taya."

"Nice to meet you, Taya. How are you feeling?"

It was a fairly standard question for a therapist to ask, and yet there was more weight in that one question than any other he could have asked after the first.

I sighed and closed my eyes, looking for that inner strength that had abandoned me not so long ago. *These sessions really aren't going to be helpful unless I open up… but he's hiding something from me.*

"Betrayed."

Jak nodded.

"For a number of reasons and most recently by *you*."

"Me? Whatever for?" he leaned forward, perplexed.

I didn't smile. "Something just happened to me. Now, being the astute therapist you are, I've no doubt in my mind you noticed. But you purposefully decided not to talk to me about it. You kept your words casual and asked a probing question instead. You've got to be honest with me before you can expect me to trust you. If you can't do that, then this will be our last session."

He shifted to the edge of the bench and folded his hands together on the table top. He looked right at me.

"I believe you. But I have to tell you that I can't be completely honest with you. And that's the truth."

I released my mug and pushed my body back in order to slide out of the booth.

"Wait. Hear me out."

I folded my arms high across my chest and narrowed my eyes at him.

"I agree that a better question or a confirming statement, acknowledging what just happened, would've been better. But I can't tell you everything I'm thinking. I'm building a picture of you, and what's happened to you, every moment we share company. You would recoil from the analyses vying for a diagnosis in my brain. However, I can treat you like a friend, rather than a client. You have to admit there are some things even friends don't share."

I glared at him. Every nerve in my body screamed at me to jump up and leave. My training chided my childishness. Regardless, I held his stare – looked right back at him, searching for his soul. I peeled away layer after layer of his cloak-and-dagger act, his training, his words, all in an attempt to reveal what lay beneath.

"All right." I didn't relax, but I didn't leave either.

"Okay. Let's try that again. What I just asked you, about your name, it bothered you. When we spoke of names last time you were confused, but not aggressive or agitated. Today, just now, clearly something triggered."

I dropped stiff arms, as my hands rested in my lap. But I couldn't sit still. I raised them to the mug, the mug to my lips, and drank deeply.

"By saying this out loud," I said, hesitating as I lowered the mug back to the table, "I'll be admitting to a weakness – to being defective, or having an unhealthy mind. But I realise now that I can't beat this thing on my own. Don't– you can't– Gerrund…"

"I understand. All I have to do is let him know that you're making an effort. That's it. He knows my program works, but what he also knows is he's not always right about these things. He will never know if you're struggling with something from your time in the Warehouse, or something else from your past. After four sessions, I don't even need to tell him if we're still meeting. He believes that if there's an underlying problem, I'll be able to pick up on it by then."

The muscles in my face slowly released the tension, the worry and anticipation. I slid back to the middle of the booth.

"That's what *He* wanted to know, too – the man who had me tortured. He desperately wanted to know who I was. You startled me the first time you asked, but having a prepared second way of asking... well... so did *He*. I don't know if you're working on a hunch with limited information about me, or if this is a generic structure you do with all your clients but – you hit it straight on – punched me in the gut with it. *Who am I really?*" I shook my head. Admitting this out loud to another person was like admitting every failure in my life.

Jak nodded. "I wish I could say we'll find a way to fix this – to unravel the mystery and everything will be okay again. The truth is, nothing will ever be the same. From the start, from your very birth, a series of events was set in motion that was beyond your control. What I can tell you is there are several things you can work on, and forgiving those who are closest to you is one of the biggest. Now, that's far headier than I wanted to get today. However, I'm not letting you leave without homework."

"Homework?"

Jak grinned. "Yes. I want you to record, in the manner of your choice, everyone and everything that has influenced your life up to now."

"And you thought today's session was heady? You do realise I'm not going to have a lot of time in the next couple of days, right? I'm working overtime to get this Desert Vehicle launched, and I need to instruct the new Guides on how to use it – likely hours before launching our first mission out?"

"Four days. We'll meet here again, say... an hour earlier? We'll keep our visits as irregular as possible." He gave me a knowing wink – but how could he know unless someone was keeping tabs on me?

No, Taya. Likely everyone of some import or another has heard of the incident by now and, in any case, Gerrund knows why I've been trying to disguise my new appearance. Stop trying to read so far into things.

"Yeah, that'll be a big help."

He finished off the last of his verrin and left the glass empty, except for a couple of ice cubes. Winding his way back through the dim club, he disappeared in the crowd.

Chapter Eighteen
Buried in Work

Taya

As I walked to the shop the next day, my skin pricked with cold-bumps. The hair on the nape of my neck lifted as if from an electrical current.

Something wasn't right.

I slowed my pace to a walk, and looked over my shoulder. *No one there. No one following me that is.*

I glanced from side to side. Few people were on the street at this early hour to begin with, but those who were, ignored me. *They wouldn't have given up this fast.* I neared the straightaway before the turn to the workshop's tunnel.

My heart slipped into my stomach. I rested a hand to steady myself against the nearest storefront. Blinking rapidly, I inhaled a shaky breath.

All of them... here?

It was bad enough small groups of them followed me around when I wasn't working, and they sent me batches of unwanted letters. Now, fifty or so bodies blocked the tunnel access. The last time there'd been so many was at the incident.

I felt naked. I hadn't worn a disguise in nearly a week, but now I couldn't out-run them and, if I hid, I'd be late for work.

A vein in my neck pulsed faster and faster. I forced one foot in front of the other as if wading through mud.

I should be moving faster.

No!

Let them spread out and come for me.

Yes...

Need to create pockets of space... need to—

A few bystanders broke from the main crowd. I pretended not to notice – pretended I was deep in thought. Two-thirds of the pack shifted, moving toward me instead of standing still. Those who remained were widely dispersed.

Not yet...

Not yet...

Wait for it...

Wait...

Now!

Launching myself forward, I raced past surprised faces, deked around small groups, and moved faster than I had in months. It seemed that all week I'd been training for this moment.

A small child stumbled before me – thrust into my path by a desperate parent. I lunged deeply and sprang over the pale, little girl before diving into a controlled tumble on the ground behind her. Climbing out of the roll and up into a fast stride, I sprinted the remaining yards to the shop.

Wrenching the door open, I then spun inside and slammed it behind me – locking it for good measure. My legs shuddered and turned to jelly. I collapsed to the floor. Taking in great gulps of air, I tried to feed my body much needed oxygen.

Gelden dropped the roll of tape he held, and rushed over.

Crouching down, he rested his hands on my knees.

"Dalla, are you all right?"

My eyes settled on his, seconds before I dropped my head back against the door. I felt him tense up. I don't know what he saw in that look, but it wasn't good.

The walls were down.

I shuddered.

It echoed through him.

I guess he never quite realised how completely the Underground depleted me. He reached for my shoulders and pulled me into a hug.

"Shhh… It's all right. Everything'll be all right."

I was crying. Not on the outside – but my body sobbed in his arms.

Do these people not realise what I'm capable of? The image of blood, splattered across my blouse as I sat in Gerrund's bath tub being doused in shower water by Mardel, plastered itself over every inch of my brain. *There can't be another incident.*

"And you're sure this will dry in an hour?" I asked Gelden. I looked at one of the cans of brown spray paint, as he continued masking off the controls of the D.V.

"Yes, it will. And no, you won't find it printed on the can. This panel was missed. Can you sand it for me while I finish up here?"

I grabbed the one-hundred and fifty grit sandpaper from the counter, and rubbed the light-weight sheathing encasing the wires that ran from the controls back to the array. I wiped it down with a dry rag, and stood back to look at the vehicle.

"Maybe we should take it for another run down the tunnel – you know – before we paint it?"

Gelden stood up and threw the tape at me. "It works. Stop fretting and stop wasting time." I quirked an eyebrow at him. "Now, if you want to be useful, grab that can and tilt it like this." He demonstrated the technique. "And keep it about a foot away from the housing. I'll start. When I'm on the other side, you go over what I've done to even it out."

He shook his can like a maniac, making brief crazy-faces at me. I finally laughed. He'd been trying to break the tension all morning.

Methodically, he sprayed the sheathing and frame with even strokes. As he worked, I shook my own can. Even though we didn't need to fuss about the end product – *as long as it works* Gerrund had said. This machine had been created with care and diligence from the very beginning. It felt wrong to rush the simple things.

I angled my can as instructed, and sprayed a light second coat. My movements weren't as graceful or as fluid as Gelden's, but the paint still applied evenly. We coated it four times before the cans started to sputter.

Thanks to the heat lamps, at the end of an hour we'd have an element-resistant D.V. The trick, apparently, was to remove the masking before it completely hardened… that timing was left entirely up to Gelden.

We stood on either side of the Desert Vehicle. The transformation from that simple three-wheel, light-duty hauler to the streamlined masterpiece of ingenuity before us, in less than a week, was truly inspiring.

I sighed. "I guess we'd better clean up the shop and take inventory." I tossed the empty can at Gelden, brushed my hands on my pants, and went back inside. The crowd from earlier had dispersed in less than twenty minutes. Now that I was working, they kept their distance and stayed out of sight. It helped that Gerrund's patrollers came by every so often to make sure we weren't being disturbed.

Gelden entered behind me and dropped the cans into the recycling bin by the door. I reached for a notebook and pencil on the drafting table. Flipping to the back, I looked over the list I'd compiled of required parts for making the D.V. It detailed what, how many, dimensions, and resilience factors. The last column in the chart was for items in stock. Since this was bound to change with every D.V. made, I added a new column for the next build in order to start fresh with the inventory.

A loud *pop* reverberated in the small room. I swung around, ready to strike out. In his hands, Gelden held a green bottle, fizzing at the opening, and two stemmed glasses.

"What...?"

He flashed me one his disarming, rakish smiles. "A celebration is in order." He poured. "Here." He passed me a glass. "To the D.V.!" I smiled back. We never did come up with a better name for it.

"To teamwork." I clinked my glass to his, and drank deeply.

It was a fruity verrin-based drink with a mild aftertaste. I spied the alcohol content on the side of the bottle, and decided to drink slowly after that. Leaning against the counter, I watched Gelden kneel by an open box to check its contents.

"There are a couple dozen solar cells and some circuitry here, but not enough for a complete array."

I jotted the note on my chart. He shifted to the box beside it.

"This one has two small batteries, a couple yards of wire, seven hexagonal screw bolts..."

The hour went by faster than I thought possible. As I rifled through the last box, Gelden turned off the heaters and coiled up the electrical cords. I slid the box back into place on the shelf, and sat down at the drafting table. I couldn't help but frown as I flipped through the tracking chart.

Are we that low on everything? I bit my bottom lip and tapped the end of the pencil on the table. When we started this project, Gel had said the money would last, but we'd used so much already and... he'd lost some important surface contacts this week. He never fully explained why, but his hints had not been reassuring.

I glanced at the final tally again. We had half the parts necessary for building another D.V., and no frame. To fabricate one from scratch would take a week or more just by itself, *if* we had the right metal and acetylene needed.

The pencil dropped to the table. I pushed my hands through the hair by my scalp.

"There's nothing more I can do."

I slumped back in the chair, and watched Gelden through the open double-door as he walked around our creation.

"It's done then." I stood up and went out to circle the D.V. with him.

The silence was amiable. We couldn't have asked for a better end product for all our hard work. It was perfect: sleek, manoeuvrable, lightweight, self-sufficient, and well-crafted.

"The project is yours now, Gel."

"What?" He turned to face me. "I don't understand?"

I looked at the D.V. "There's nothing more I can do here. We've got limited supplies and no frame for a second unit. It'll take weeks to build up the necessary supplies to start over again." I finally looked at him, and handed him my builder's guide.

"This has everything you'll need. I've taken all your notes and sketches and drawn everything to scale, noted the practical applications, and listed the supply chart at the back."

The unasked questions and his look of open abandonment threw me.

"Don't look at me like that. Just call it phase-two of the mentoring program – flying solo." I smiled, but had no muster behind it. "Look, you've exhausted your resources and connections and, if you can't get access to another frame, you'll have to fabricate one from scratch. I'm not telling you anything you don't already know. Besides," I gripped his shoulder and gave it a squeeze, "I'm tired…" *of running*. "After the instructional session with the Guides tomorrow morning, this project has effectively outgrown me." I let my arm flop down to my side. I glanced over my shoulder.

"The cave is clear. I'm going home." The image of the house I'd shared with my lynx, Jadis, flashed through my mind. I squashed it, and replaced it with the cold simplicity of the cavern apartment.

He still didn't say anything. Perhaps his brain froze. He glanced down at the manual in his hands. I took a half-step back, then turned and jogged away.

Since it was just after lunch – we'd worked through yet another one – there was no one waiting to follow me. I kept on alert, but slowed my pace to a fast walk. I didn't want to think about tomorrow yet… or the next day for that matter. Maybe I'd curl up on the couch with a digital book, or have a hot shower to work the tension from my muscles.

Sleeping was easy again, now that I had the pills; it was the late nights and stress over the D.V. that brought on the tension. And being followed. I could only hope that things with Jak progressed faster, or I'd be looking at a reoccurrence of the short temper and sleepless nights.

I slid my key-card on the reader by the front door of my building, and entered. Waving to Etain, who'd popped his head out his apartment door, I then plodded along to the central staircase and up to my apartment. From down the hall, the pile of mail overflowing the basket jolted me to a stop. *Can't I get any peace!*

I unlocked the door, then made a basket with the bottom of my shirt and stacked the mail from my hips to my lower ribs. *I'll have to leave Etain a handful of chocolates for lugging up this disaster.*

I shimmied through the door, and closed it with my heel. Dropping the load on the breakfast bar with all of the other scattered envelopes, my arms suddenly felt heavier than they had carrying those simple, folded pieces of paper.

Why can't they just leave me alone? Why aren't these Dez's letters?

I shuffled over to the bowl by the door to get Etain's chocolates. Four feet away, the doorknob turned. My heart jumped into my throat. *Dez?*

"Dalla." Gelden pushed it open and came in. "We need to talk."

Anger, fear, surprise and a numbness of the senses, flashed back and forth across my nerve endings as I stared at the man closing my door. Anger won – telling my body to beat him senseless.

With a single raised fist, a valve in my chest released and all those feelings puddled out onto the floor between us. My arm dropped, but not before he'd seen that flash in my eyes and the rise of colour to my cheeks. I staggered to a stool by the bar and fell onto it.

"What are you doing here?" I asked.

"Worrying about you – and rightly so, I see." He sat down on the other low-backed stool. "What's all this? Aren't you reading your letters?"

"Ha." I burst out. "I don't need to go through them. I already know what they say." I got up and walked over to the couch. He tugged an open letter out from the bottom of the pile.

"Emvaso-al..." He quickly scanned the rest of the letter. "How long have you been receiving these?"

"Ehh – maybe a few days, since they followed me home one night. Look. Just ignore it. I haven't had time to sort through it all, and Gerrund's letters have a tell-tale purple infinity symbol in the upper left corner, if the whole damn envelope isn't purple to begin with. They're easy to spot after I've dumped the load on the counter." I kicked off my shoes and stretched out on the couch.

"Don't worry, Gel. I know how to take care of myself. Go home." Instead, he tugged a couple more letters out and read them.

"Dalla, you have a real opportunity here. Don't let it pass."

"Opportunity!" I jolted upright, and looked over the back of the couch at him. "Have you lost your mind? I'm not who those people think I am. They're obsessed with a figment of their imagination. I'm not responding to those letters."

"I'm not talking about writing back to each person individually. You could put a notice or a response in the Inquisitor. Maybe... yeah. Maybe even start your own column. Not every writer here is requesting the same thing."

"Perhaps not, but they are all asking something of me I can't give."

"No?"

I glared at him, the hot flush rising to my cheeks again. He smiled at my ire.

"Dalla, the fact that so many people follow you around, write you letters, make up strange ideas about you, it shows that they're grateful for what you've done – what you're a part of. And, quite frankly, you've never spoken to them to set them straight."

He dropped the letters onto the pile.

"Let me help you. We can sort through this mess, and I can get in touch with the editor of the Inquisitor. He'd be insane not to snatch this up. You'd have a direct conduit to the people – to tell them *your* story, set them straight, whatever."

"No. I won't feed into this fantasy they've created. Now, this isn't why you so rudely burst into my apartment. If all you wanted was tell me you were worried – you've done that – well noted. Thank you and good day." I collapsed back onto the couch and closed my eyes.

It stayed quiet for a long moment, although I heard him rise and cross the room. I opened my eyes, sat up, and stared at him. He stood there looking at me with such intensity it made my skin crawl.

"Come with me tomorrow, after the morning launch. I'll be joining the building crew out that way, constructing a new row of shops. We could use the help."

I just stared back. I didn't want to make plans and yet...

"I'll think about it."

He gave a curt nod and left.

"But not right now."

I got up and slipped a handful of chocolates into the mail basket, and then locked the door behind him. The D.V. was done – it was time for a celebratory bath before the meeting tonight.

Chapter Nineteen
Covert Mission

Zaith

I coughed into my bandana to stifle the sound. Leaning my back along the curvature of the large dome building that once housed Dezmind, I considered how it now contained the most vital library on the planet. With it being mid-afternoon, no one lingered in the Common. I waited a few more minutes to be sure. At least Merik was where he was supposed to be, as I heard the delicate clink of thin metallic Dakturian pages.

I glanced in the open window to be certain he was alone, then slid my aching body forward and around the corner.

I stumbled in.

He glanced up.

"Jeeze." He jumped a little, from where he sat behind a large metal table. "I didn't expect you, yet." His hands fell, palm-down, onto the book he'd been reading. Standing up, he leaned forward and squinted at me. The light from the suns bathed my back, but I still felt cold. I coughed again.

"Here." I crouched in the middle of the room, and removed the items I'd found. "This is the niccori root, the yellow marin leaves –

I didn't extract the syrup, you'll have to do that. Here's the ina bark – I haven't peeled the soft inner layer out yet."

"How far along are you?" he asked.

"What do mean?" The bandana hid the aggravated and flaking skin on my face and neck, the gloves I'd pieced together for touching prickly plants and rough bark covered my forearms, and my shirt and pants hid the rest. I was no glamour girl, but I'd found a way to cover up. He walked around the desk, crossing the invisible barrier between infected and clean air.

I stood up. Spots flashed behind my eyes. I wavered, searching for my balance. Merik took my elbow and guided me back to a crouch.

"I may be an artist, but I'm not an idiot. I know you didn't just *find* that journal you left with me. Holy Trinity, Zaith – why did you do it?"

I shook his hand off my arm. "Do what?"

He sat down on the floor with one knee up, and a wrist casually draped over it. "I checked the building, you know."

"I told you not to," I snapped.

"If it's out, then you know as well as I do that it's only a matter of time…" He didn't need to say the rest. He moved that carefree arm out to hold my chin. I shifted back and sat down, just out of his reach.

"How's Ray doing?" I asked, taking the rest of the specimens I'd collected out of the pack.

"'Bout the same as you. Guess that means you've had it all along?"

"Someone had to make sure he didn't starve."

"Syvis has been demanding to know where you are."

"What did you say?"

"Exactly what you told me to. He knows Ray's supplies need to be brought today."

"I already took him the last of what I had in my pack."

"If I tell Syvis that, he'll know you were here – to see me. He'll know I've been lying to him. We need to tell them, Zaith."

"Not until we have everything we need for the cure."

"This isn't all of it?" he counted each of the ingredients I'd lain out on the ground between us.

"I can't find the marrow-weed. I'm going back out."

"You need to stay and rest. Taxing yourself only makes it worse. Let us help."

"If they don't string me up for lying to them, and for cursing them with this alien Virus–"

"Ray did that, not you."

"Semantics. If we at least have the ingredients, it will give them hope."

He rubbed a hand over his blue face. It wasn't until then, that I noticed the darkening of his gold coliths, the circles under his eyes, and the way his lashes sat on lowered lids.

"I can't figure out the equations… the medical jargon. I'm a man of the arts, not science… none of us are. I asked Jan, but her time volunteering with the Health Habitat had nothing to do with science or chemistry. What kind of hope comes with the knowledge that we have what we need for a cure, but we don't know how to develop it?"

Footsteps scuffed the dry earth outside. I grabbed my pack, launched myself around the desk, avoiding the orb which rested on a chair by the window, and kept myself out of sight. I swallowed the sudden desire to vomit. Peering between the metal slats fronting the desk, I watched as a tall, muscular, bronzed heartache blocked the light streaming in the door. I shook my head; I couldn't help it.

Had the circumstances been different…

"Good afternoon, Syvis." Merik said from the floor.

"Merik." He cocked his head sideways. "What've you got there?"

"Presents. I guess."

"Who left them?"

"Who do you think?"

He crouched down where I'd sat only a moment before.

"She was here? You saw her? What's going on?"

Merik held up his hands in surrender. "She left a message in the dirt."

"What did it say?"

"I fed him."

"I fed him? That's it? What's going on Merik?"

"I think she's on some kind of mission. She blames herself for Ray." He held up a hand to stop the very words he'd said to me earlier. "I think she found the last journal."

"What? The last journal? Why wouldn't she just tell us?"

Merik clasped his hands together and tapped his thumbs. I couldn't see the expression on his face, but I could see Syvis. It was as I feared –

"She's sick? Zola, help us. How bad?" He was more concerned about me than the bigger picture. I refrained from shaking my head in case I bumped the desk.

"I don't know."

"How long ago did this stuff show up?"

"Not long. Maybe ten minutes or so. I was just sitting down to look at it when you came in."

"So, she might be nearby." He stood up and took off out of the library. I heard his feet scramble over the ground outside, and send a cascade of rocks scattering down a side street. Merik stood up, grabbed his own pack, and went out to the supply tables surrounding the central fountain. I stayed under the desk as I listened to him bite into a piece of fruit, slosh water over the edge of a canteen, and walk to the far side where Lutrice's healing herbs were hung to dry.

I emerged from under the table, pulled my pack open, and met him just as he came back to the door.

Half the width of Syvis, Merik did his best to block any unsuspecting eyes from seeing inside the building. He transferred the food and supplies to my pack, and I gave him my canteen in exchange for his – because, in the end, he was right. If I was infected, so were they all and it didn't matter if he drank from the same canteen or not.

"Maybe Deltek or Lutrice studied science," I suggested.

"Social science. Not the same thing, I'm afraid."

I clapped him on the shoulder, slid behind the large orb of the Chronicles, and scouted for others out the side window.

"Ask them anyway. I'm going to find that last ingredient." I slipped out the door on the other side of him, and turned in the opposite direction from Syvis. I didn't say when I'd check in next. Regardless, Ray needed food in another two days.

I kept to the narrower side streets in areas already well searched and mapped by the Kahn-lea. Voices in the Merchant district pulled me toward them. Tami and Jan had been working on a special project. I hadn't had time to ask Merik for a colony update – but I was curious… and some part of me needed the company of women – even from a distance.

Through a large pair of windows, unique to this building, likely for air flow, I watched the two teens work. They first pulled free fine silky fibres from large plant pods littered around their feet. After spreading a quantity out in a thin layer over a wire rack of sorts, they worked together to push the holder back and forth into the weaving machine. I couldn't see what the end product looked like, but the thread would probably make soft, strong, yet light fabric perfect for the humid weather down here.

The acrid scent of a dye bath whisked past my nose as the breeze shifted. I inhaled too fast, and choked on the smell. Both girls startled. I dropped below the window's sightline, trying to stifle the cough. I knew better than to risk staying – everyone was likely on the lookout for me.

Now was not the time to get caught.

No. I had a promise to fulfil.

Chapter Twenty
Other People's Plans

Taya

"How can we be sure this thig will work? Thenticia interrupted my explanation to the Consolidating Body as we sat around the oval table. The muscle beside my right eye twitched.

"Tomorrow – uh – evening, Aleonia?" Gerrund checked with me.

I gave a short sharp nod. He'd changed the time, but I wasn't about to complain – it wasn't the time or the place. I didn't have to be petty. Actually, I didn't have anything better to do, so really what did it matter?

Gerrund took a moment to connect with each person around the table. "Prior to the Deserts Mission, Ali will thoroughly demonstrate the D.V.'s capabilities to the Guides. Laiviis will take point on this run, as the others observe. This will afford all of us an opportunity to see the D.V. in action. The Expanse will provide plenty of secluded space for prep. And send off. Have I missed anything, Ali?"

"Gelden and I will both be present for the launch. After the overview Gerrund outlined, Laiviis will instruct Bazdin, teach him the basics of the D.V. and Desert survival as they travel together. Tomorrow needs to reinforce Laiviis' and the other Guides' understanding of the machine."

I'd chosen him over the others because of his rapid progress after being ensnared in my fake Desert obstacle. Between that and his *what if* scenario regarding a possible new Desert creature, I knew he could handle himself out there.

"Their first stop will be the Temple in the Ancient City. From there, Laiviis will locate the first marker point and re-calibrate his position according to the suns. The second marker is at the base of the Ariel Caves, where they will rest before the third day of travels. It is at this point the D.V. will have to be abandoned. The Kahn-lea left the hauler in an alcove along the base of the cliff. The D.V. can be stored beneath the hauler. From there, only essential supplies will be brought to the Great City. It's a treacherous climb, but not impossible.

"By the third evening, they'll have reached the central Compound. Laiviis can relay our message to Zaith regarding our intent to make regular trips out, help with restocking the verrin, bringing messages to and from family members, and readying the City for their eventual replacements. After a rest and restock for a night or two, he should be back just outside of a week. This would also allow him time to speak with the Kahn-lea, and learn the sequence of the Generator.

"As you know, it's imperative we keep that piece of alien technology operational. Word of mouth understanding about the nature of their mission is as equally important as bringing Bazdin to his fiancée. We may not be able to invite them all home yet, but they need to know that we're working on a solution no matter the outcome of the coup."

I took a deep breath before continuing, "Also, to further Dezmind's work, I'd like to request that a camera be taken along, and Laiviis be permitted to return with the Chronicles. If he's going to be travelling alone, he'll have the space to mind them on the trip back."

Gerrund nodded. "Is there a second to Ali's motion of re-con and collection?"

Both Mardel and the Dias responded.

"All those in favour?"

Every fist pounded its support. I released a breath I hadn't realised I'd been holding.

Gerrund moved on with the rest of the night's business. "Mardel, update on the volunteers."

"Progressing better than anticipated. The revised solution to last week's hiccup in the training schedule is proving to be an excellent balance."

"Yes." Ticia shuffled her stack of pages. "I'm hopeful at this stage the recruits we have are sufficient for the coup. However, I don't want to discontinue the outreach program we've started topside. Tactically, the larger the number of supporters we have, either directly or indirectly involved with the Cause, will strengthen support after the takeover. We don't want to make the same mistakes as the failed Resistance."

"Excellent," Gerrund noted. "Do we have a time frame for training completion yet?"

Mardel responded, "Surprisingly, sir, course completion and scenario dispatch reinforcement should commence in approximately two weeks."

Appreciative murmurs broke the usual formality of the Consolidating Meeting. Even Gerrund's eyes shone bright with the news.

"Randek."

"Yes, Gerrund?"

"Intelligence update."

"We get less information from our informant each week, and it often contradicts what the moles are telling us."

I whispered to Mardel, "Moles?"

"The collective term for the group who rescued you from the Warehouse."

I nodded.

"—most recently, and yet our informant assures us that the Kronik is working on several different levels to defeat the uprising it senses is coming. The government is pulling in more agents all the time, and not just Contractors. They don't know what our numbers are, but they are assuming it's a larger force than twenty-two years ago. They're still in the dark about our target, but they're attempting to prepare for a volley of strikes in different locales."

"So, the Kronik's troops will be spread out in pockets around the Compound?"

"Not just the Compound, Gerry, the surrounding civilian towns as well. It gives us a tactical advantage to have them spread thin, but it also reduces our ability to move unimpeded on the surface."

Gerrund slammed the table. "Hevex. News on the tunnels?"

"We won't have access in two weeks, I can tell you that."

"When?"

"Unknown, sir. Maybe four weeks or so."

"Why?"

"We're down on manpower. Perhaps when the troops have completed their training, we can utilise their efforts in exploring the tunnels, but right now we're nowhere close to the Compound. We have, however, identified several new secluded portals to the surface. Crews are working extra shifts to make them manageable for a surface assault—"

"Unacceptable. You heard Randek. We need the element of surprise both physically and mentally. We can't wait another month on this!"

"I have a proposal, General." All eyes focused on Dias Betauni.

"Use the girl." She inclined her head toward me but didn't make eye contact. Strange. "She has *gifts* and an innate sense of direction. She wouldn't need a team either—"

"Dias, that's unheard of." Mardel recoiled physically, and grasped my shoulder. I didn't understand the suggestion and tried not to show my ignorance.

Mardel squeezed my shoulder. "It might as well be a death sentence. Without the protection of a team, a single miss-step could mean her life. Those unexplored caves—"

"Are like a playground to her, Mardel. Your concern is noted." The Dias faced Gerrund again. "Among other things, I believe she has the capacity to see in the dark, and we know her strength and agility have superseded that of anyone else's down here." Now, she smiled demurely at me. The yellow of her sleek coliths glinted in the half-light of the room.

"Surely, Aleonia, you feel comfortable working alone and using your physical skills to achieve a means to an end? Your D.V. project is complete now, correct? You mentioned that Gelden would need several weeks to gather enough supplies to begin another unit. Could you not then use this *free time* to help further the Cause, and aid what's happening down *here* as much as you have helped the Kahn-lea out *there*?"

"Dias," Gerrund broke in. "You know what Dezmind would—"

"Dezmind's not here. Isn't that right, Aleonia?"

I still wasn't following what was happening. Ticia smiled and nodded along with the Dias, and yet Gerrund and Mardel were overly concerned about the endeavour – for different reasons – but concerned nonetheless. I didn't have all of the information and, as much as I tended to side with the Dias, I had the feeling I was being played.

"What exactly are you proposing? And Mardel, why are you so concerned?" I asked outright.

"Ali," Dias paced her words. "Our goal is to locate a tunnel that'll lead beneath the Compound. That way we don't have to break in, so to speak, from the surface. However, the current rules state that a team of three or more must explore new tunnels – for safety reasons. Those precautions were set in place by this very Committee, but honestly, they have little to do with you. Could you list for us your known abilities – both gifted to you at birth being half-Talian, and those gained from your time with the Contractors?"

It was a straight forward request and nothing I hadn't told Gerrund or Mardel before. I decided to play along.

"The CTF taught me to explore options and use my intelligence to solve problems before resorting to brute force, or relying solely on my strength. My analytical skills have aided me in the past, as you mentioned, with the Deserts journey, and whatever natural strength I possess was enhanced through rigorous training."

"And your gifts?"

I frowned. "Yes, I have the ability to see in the dark, but not in the same way I see with light. I can also hear better than most people, a fact that saved Dezmind from his first assassination attempt."

"You see, Gerrund? She has supreme survival skills that the others do not – which would afford her the luxury of staying in the field longer, thus searching the tunnels and caverns over a greater period of time. And you've seen her mapping skills. It's not like the girl can't draw."

"Even with her skills, and *gifts* as you call them," Mardel spoke up, "there are still major risks Ali would have to take. Risks that may leave her trapped or in mortal peril."

He turned to face me. "Ali, explorers have slipped on slick rock, they've been crushed by falling stalactites, and have gotten themselves into small areas unable to back out again. The perpetual dark is staved off only with rechargeable lights, because there is no sun to manage standard light-tubes. It's exceedingly cold, and any extra clothing would only slow you down. These are not situations you can ignore or take lightly." He looked pointedly at the Dias.

The silence stretched for several minutes. It was true, I'd even said as much to the Desert Guides, never enter the Deserts alone. I hated the fact that Laiviis would be returning solo, but both Dez and

I had done it, so he could too under the circumstances. But, should I ignore my own rule and take the Dias seriously?

Each member looked at the other, their faces showed both concern and curiosity. Gerrund remained sitting at the head of the table. His eyes transitioned from bright to cloudy so many times, I nearly laughed at the absurdity of it. Obviously, he didn't want to see me hurt, but he was a general running a campaign in which I could play a vital role. Whether or not his loyalty to Dezmind weighed in, I had no idea.

Regardless of everyone else's expectations and reservations, a glimmer of hope kindled deep in the recesses of my mind... something I could use to help me put the pieces of my life back together.

"Okay. I'll do it."

But I'd never tell them why.

Chapter Twenty-one
The UGC Effort

Taya

What?" I muttered. The pounding on my door made me crack an eye at the bedside clock.

"Who's bothering me at this hour?" A hard edge crystallised in my voice.

Wrapping myself into a robe, I wiped the sleep from my eyes and finger combed my hair as I walked from my bedroom, through the living room, and over to the apartment door.

Three more bangs startled me. I looked out the spy-hole.

"Oh, no. He didn't get the message." I opened the door just wide enough to stick my head out. "Gelden, the launch was moved to dusk. I sent a message. I know it was late, but…"

He flashed an eager smile and pushed the door open the rest of the way.

"That's not why I'm here, Dalla."

I crossed my arms. "It's six in the morning. The streets are only just fading for sunrise. What do you want?"

"We start work in an hour. I thought you might want to wake up a bit before I hauled you outa here."

I shook my head. "Work? What are you—?"

"I'll put the coffee on. You get dressed." He turned me around by the shoulders, and walked me back across the living room.

I briefly imagined grabbing one of those hands and activating the pressure point between the base of his thumb and the next knuckle... he deserved it.

The corner of my mouth twitched. In my mind's eye I saw him on his knees begging me to – but no. I wouldn't do that to Gelden. He didn't need to see that side of me.

I ducked down under his arms and turned out of his light grip. Slipping out of range, I put the couch between us.

"Oh, come on," he said. "I'm helping the construction team today, and I want you to come along."

"I only got to bed four hours ago!"

"I know you can function on less sleep than—"

"But I *wanted* to sleep in, Gel. Today is supposed to be my day off. No commitments... at least none until this evening. Go without me."

"You wanted to know what it was like down here. No more stories, Dalla. So, hurry up and get dressed." He turned and walked into the kitchen, and rummaged around for coffee fixings.

"Twice now you've entered my apartment without being invited. Under any normal circumstance I would have kicked you out with one foot still hovering over the threshold."

"But you didn't. And do you know why?" I glared at him. "Because it keeps you on your toes. If you really wanted me to leave, I'd already be gone."

I sprang over the couch and caught the cuff of his sleeve over the island of mail. With a single jerk, I had his arm plastered behind his back while I walked him back toward the door. I stopped two feet before smacking his head into the solid mass.

He balked, speechless.

"And don't you forget it, Gel. You're lucky I value our friendship." I dropped his arm, stuck out my tongue at him, and went to get changed.

I took my time about it, too. My morning routine lasted all of eight minutes on average, but I tacked on an extra ten just sitting on the bed wondering why I kept letting him into my sanctuary. The way he got under my skin reminded me of Dez when we were in the Deserts.

Something happened between the Great City and the Kronik's assassination attempt at the Rally in Darius' Square. All at once, Dez had become both overprotective and extremely distant.

I never saw him anymore, his letters had stopped, and yet, I kept being told this Underground prison was for my own good. I stared at the knotted star-shaped scars on my hands, and felt Dez's firm but gentle grasp wrapping them with gauze. The walls of my chest ached – it hurt to love him. Now I only felt like a check mark on his long list of *things to do:* find the Chronicles, save the world, find my soul mate, overthrow the government…

Slamming my fists on the mattress, I beat my anger, confusion, and frustrations into the forgiving material. It helped drain me, but it didn't solve anything.

I stood up and joined Gel in the kitchen.

I refused to talk to him again until after I had my coffee… and I didn't gulp it like usual. He'd given me an hour, or thereabouts, after all.

Finally, I set my mug down by the sink. "So, where are we going?"

"To the site I told you about with the shops. I brought bikes so we can get there faster. It's about an hour's walk from here – south-ish. We can bike it in half the time and then meet the others at the Expanse later. I got Gerrund to send me the meeting locale and time."

"Hmm. Give me a minute then. I need to grab a few things…" I let my voice trail off as I walked back to my room. Gelden followed. I nearly walked into him on my way back out. He scanned the items I held, and plucked the cream from my hands.

"Blue skin cream? A hat and glasses? No." He tossed the cream on the bed. "No disguises."

"Who are you to tell me how to dress?"

"Dalla, it's early. No one's up yet. Besides, once you start working you'll sweat, and the cream will wear off."

"Then I'll apply more and re-apply as necessary. *This* disguise works. No one will know—"

"No. You'll be self-conscious the whole time – and unreliable. The hat will reduce your peripheral vision. Look, the team will give us safety gear, including helmets, when we get there." He gingerly pulled the life-line out of my hands, walked around me, and placed the rest of the items on my bed next to the cream. Then, he guided me by the elbow to the front door.

Part of me willingly followed him, but the other, larger part, waged an internal war making me numb. He even had to grab my keys for me.

We biked in silence to Gelden's construction site. He'd been right – only a handful of citizens were waiting for me and, since they hadn't anticipated bikes, they were left far behind. Gelden brought me down streets I'd never taken before, so it was also unlikely that anyone would be waiting to mob me along the way.

It was so stupid.

I'd gone to all the trouble of erasing every physical trace of who I was: skin colour, colith colour, hair colour, eye colour and yet, because of one simple Underground Rally and Dez's thoughtless announcement that *I* was vital in helping restore Gamma and Xannia's celestial balance, followers of the Trinity decided to turn me into a conduit for their pain and suffering. If he'd just left me out of it, I might've actually stomached living down here.

My ire and earlier frustrations bubbled up again. I forced myself to focus on my surroundings instead of my thoughts.

The streets were quiet as most shops only just opened for the day. The longer we rode, the more sparse the dwellings and shops became.

Either Gel had a poor sense of timing, or he lied to me about how far we needed to travel. It was clearly an hour's ride to the site, not an hour's walk. *I wonder if Gelden's Aunt lives out this way. Gerrund never mentioned where his little sister lived but she never came around either.*

"Here we are." Gel hopped off his bike and steered it around the corner to the adjoining street. A rack set along the side of the cave held nearly twenty bikes already. I found a free space and set the kick-stand.

"Why is the tunnel sealed off with that tarp?" I pointed to the behemoth of cloth blocking our way.

"Don't want dust and particles being filtered into the other tunnels. Depending on the day, the air can get fairly thick. Come on. We need to check in over here."

A tent-like portal sat between the two sides of the tunnel. We entered the flap. Gelden spoke with the only attendant there.

"Hello, Naina. I have a guest volunteer with me today."

"Pretty thing. This isn't exactly the best place to bring a date, Gelden."

I could only assume he blushed, since his back was to me. His stature stiffened.

"Aelonia is a colleague of mine from another project. Don't be spreading gossip now."

The woman jotted down both our names. She winked at me as Gel and I walked past the desk and through to the other side.

Anticipating a blaze of activity, I was disappointed by the relative silence. Several completed apartments lined the left side of the tunnel – empty and lifeless. Gelden guided me towards an array of scaffolding farther up the road.

"A couple of landscape artists will stop by later in the week to sketch out the wall mural, and take stock of required supplies. I'll bring you back when I find out what day they'll be here. The transformation from rock-face to village is truly inspiring."

Muffled voices and the grunts of labour reached my ears. I turned to enter the nearest partially-constructed building. Gelden grabbed my arm.

"Not so fast, Dalla. We need to gear up. The safety table's over here."

I grabbed one of the smallest protective helmets and plunked it on my head. "Do we need the safety goggles?"

"Not sure. I think we're forming walls today, but if you wind up not needing them, just stash them in a pocket."

I also nabbed a pair of work gloves and tucked a large square of green cloth into my back pocket. Gelden inclined his head, showing me which way to go. I followed him into the structure.

Here was the flurry of bodies belonging to the rest of the parked bikes out front.

"Gelden! We need an extra hand." A faceless voice drew away my only life-line in this strange place. He smiled, clapped me on the shoulder, and disappeared among the bodies and the growing construction.

"Hey you – miss." I turned to the other end of the site to see who called. "Those sacks of Crete aren't going to move themselves."

I glanced down at the pile of large stiff bags at my feet.

"Where should I take them?"

Using his thumb, he pointed to a mixer behind him.

I nodded. Pulling a bag up into my arms, I nearly ended up in the pile as I staggered under the weight. I set the sack back down. A puff of fine dust flashed up into my face. Swallowing a cough, I pulled the green cloth from my pocket and tied it around my neck. I pulled the front over my nose just as I noticed an available wheelbarrow.

I loaded the basin with a couple of Crete bags and then pushed them over to the mixer. My body easily fell into the routine as I relished the muscle-taxing labour, and good-natured volunteers.

Each trip over to the mixer taught me a little more about the process the crew used in order to make the shop walls.

"What do you keep staring at?" The man with the dark-green skin and black coliths croaked out from a parched throat, as he shovelled two more spadefuls of Crete into the mixer, and lightly sprayed it with water.

"Just curious."

"'Bout what?"

"Oh, where do I begin?"

He chuckled.

"Does all the material for the mix come from the surface?"

"Nah, only the Crete. It's a bonding agent to prevent the walls from crumbling. It's usually used on basements top-side."

"Do you just dig anywhere to get the stone?"

"I suppose we could, but we generate plenty of rubble when we scrape down the caves to make them habitable."

"Scrape down the caves?" I looked from side to side at the back wall. "Whatever for?"

The Jeridan-Danieth man laughed. "For a few reasons, girl. They're hollowed out, so-to-speak, with a few mechanical devices we designed and built, but mostly by manpower. The loose rock, stalagmites and stalactites are chipped away, and any natural fungus or other parasitic plant or creature is scraped down and washed away. Then, a thin layer of sealant is sprayed on the walls and ceiling to harden the surface, just enough to push the bulk of the natural moisture back into the rock and, theoretically, down further beneath us." He stopped. "You with me so far?"

I nodded and broke open another sack of the Crete for him.

"We take the rubble and grind it down to pebbles and dust — both of which you see here," he pointed to two large piles near the mixer. "Now, some of the oldest tunnels down here have little to no sealant, and no Crete-set to keep the walls from crumbling with age. They need constant drainage, repair and attention."

A woman arrived with an empty wheelbarrow, and my lesson was cut short. The man dumped his load of concrete from the mixer into her waiting basin.

"Are you the only one mixing?" I asked him, as the woman made her way up a series of ramps back inside the building.

"Bless the Suns, no – we'd never get anywhere if that were the case. There are four mixers available. Depending on the size of the job is how many of 'em we use. All four are going today. We want to have a good stretch of wall poured."

"How long does it take to form-up?"

"Well, the Crete-set helps speed up the process, as do the heaters we use overnight, but it'll take a couple of days before we can remove the forms holdin' it all together."

I pictured the length of the tunnel outside the construction zone – Gelden had said this was one of the smaller sites, too.

"A project like this must take months to complete!"

"Almost a third of a year from clearing to inhabiting." He smiled slyly. "It's a good thing we're growin' none too fast. We've got the time to take the necessary care."

"Do you think this will be the last tunnel turned into a street?"

A shadow flitted across his dark face. "I'd rather not think that far ahead, miss. I just come when the hands are needed for the work."

He turned his focus to setting up the next batch of Crete, water and stone. I nodded my head in thanks, and searched out Gelden as I pulled the bandana down to my neck. He was a way off, helping shore-up forms for more walls. I walked over, grabbed a hammer, and placed it in his reaching palm.

He looked up and smiled.

I smiled back, grabbed a spare hammer from a workbench near the back wall, strapped a nail bag around my waist, and joined the group as they struggled to stay two sections ahead of the pourers.

I floated among the three jobs for the rest of the day: helping the mixer, pouring the Crete, and forming the walls. Resources tapped out as the shift wound down, and site cleanup took prominence.

As Gelden and I washed up, a group set up the large heating fans.

"Do we have much farther to travel?" I asked Gelden.

"About the same distance again should bring us to the Junction at the Transpoint we're after – then on to the Expanse from there.

We exited the tent-check, claimed our bikes, and rode down more unfamiliar tunnels. After beating the dust from my clothes I almost couldn't tell I'd been working all day. The gentle heat in my muscles felt good, even though I was tired. Luckily, the tunnel was fairly flat.

It didn't take long for the few people and living areas to dwindle into obscurity. Even the main area we travelled became more of a service tunnel than a habitable space. It was well-worn and gave off a different hue when the lights above hit the stone.

"This tunnel feels different somehow."

"It's unfinished. No sealant. We only use this one for trafficking supplies from various Junctions along this run."

"You post guards out here every day?"

Gelden chuckled. "No, Dalla. Most of the guards over here are on the surface. A rotating watch team rides through every eight hours – that's how long it takes to go from base camp to the Expanse and back on a bike."

"Why don't they just use the all-terrain vehicles or sliders? They could make the run in less than half the time."

"Fuel is at a premium down here. We have access to a bunch of old fossil-fuel models for the ATVs, but getting our hands on oil and gas draws a lot of attention from the surface. The batteries on the sliders don't last long enough."

"You could retro-fit our shop to convert the older machines to hydrogen, while waiting for the D.V. parts from the surface to arrive – maybe even take on a team to help with the project."

"If Gerrund's plans don't pan out, then yeah – we could really get a business going."

I sighed.

He glanced over his shoulder at me. "What did I say?"

I gave him a weak smile. "I don't do well staying in one place for extended periods of time. With the CTF my longest fulfilled assignment was just over one month – five and a half weeks. The reason I agreed to a placement that long was I got to chauffeur around big-name clients and, well, looked into a few of them for someone I knew. If I was stuck behind a desk or in the same location, I never would've accepted it. You see?"

"Better all the time. No wonder this place freaks you out so much. But you didn't move around a lot, did you?"

"No. My training at the Facility moved me from one level to the next, learning a new tactic, concept or move nearly every day. The job kept me active enough, and it often took me away from home for days at a time. I had a very understanding neighbour who liked Jadis."

"Who's Jadis?"

"Oh! I haven't told you? I guess it never really came up... She's my lynx. Dez is watching her for me." My voice trailed off. We rode in silence for a while.

Nothing had turned out as I'd imagined – not that I'd really thought that far ahead. Keeping Dez safe had been the only thing that made sense at the time. It never once occurred to me that I'd have to go into hiding. All I had to do was sell the house, move in with Dez somewhere downtown, and become his personal assistant. Why would anyone assume a Glaaon-Balanis cross was the same woman he contracted to cross the Deserts with?

There was so much happening when the ground gave way at the Rally – people running about, focusing only on staying alive. Besides, Dez and I were careful to wait for twilight before he brought us to the closest Junction down to the Underground. I never agreed to give up my freedom... but then, it's not like I asked to be the only living half-Talian – the embodiment of the very secret the Kronik wanted to keep buried.

Maybe I was just fooling myself… maybe whatever Dez did to my sensibilities, knocked me into La La Land and I've been paying for it ever since. How was it possible to both love and hate someone at the same time?

The diameter of the tunnel expanded and contracted the more we travelled, but overall it shrank in size and grew rougher in texture. The lighting faded the farther away we got from the Central Underground.

"I can see why we won't be going the whole way down here." Gelden saw me looking up.

"Gerrund only turns the generator up to full capacity when we're expecting a shipment. With the minimal number of people joining us tonight, travelling down here just didn't make sense. Gerry isn't one to waste resources.

"So, I've noticed." I grinned and shook my head, glad for the distraction from my thoughts. "Gerry." Clearing my throat of a threatening chuckle, I asked, "Exactly how many people are we expecting then?"

"I didn't get an exact number. A group of three will be escorting Bazdin – that'll include Gerry. Mardel is bringing the Guides – all of them and, other than us, I believe Dias Betauni will be coming with an escort for posterity's sake."

I did a quick calculation. "That's around fourteen, not including the lidez driver who'll take us the rest of the way out to the Expanse, and – are we going public or private transit?"

"Private."

"Okay. Say fifteen bodies. Huh, this is going to draw a lot of attention. Maybe Gerrund should have wasted a bit of energy on us down here."

"It's late. We're all getting on at different locations along the route, with us as the farthest pickup. No one will be anywhere near

Vitexid's Lakes, and we're following a known lidez route. It won't be as obvious as you think. The Junction is just up ahead."

"I don't see anything."

"That's surprising. I thought you might with your ability. I guess it's well-hidden then. Don't worry, once you know where it is, it has a way of jumping out at you. We'll park here."

He hopped off his bike, and rested it against the tunnel wall on the right-hand side. I followed. As I got closer to the wall, a passageway opened in the rock face. By the time I stood beside Gelden, it was glaringly obvious.

"This'll take us through to the last Transpoint."

"I was there once, after I quit an assignment."

"Well, no one will recognise you now."

"Right." I glanced at my pink hands and the purple colith that peaked out from under the edge of my cuff. "Sometimes I still manage to forget." *And then it's like seeing myself for the first time all over again.* "Where do we come out? It was just a small shack of a depot, if I remember correctly."

"There's a shop beside a local café that's used for storage. The tunnel connects to a small room, not much bigger than a broom closet – I think they used to use it for interrogating transit thieves. Now a *danger* sign hangs off the door leading to the hall."

I climbed chiselled rock steps as I followed Gelden up. They were nothing like the well-formed steps the Dakturians made back in the aerial caves, or even in the Temple in the Ancient City – but that didn't matter.

A flood of images bombarded my mind. I wavered, and clutched at the rock beneath my fingers. I forced the next rational thought out past my lips.

"Who's guarding the passage?"

He stopped climbing – not because he noticed the change in my voice, but to unlatch the wooden trapdoor above his head.

"The old guy who runs the place."

"How do we know he can be trusted?"

Canned light crept down the tunnel shaft. I looked up and blinked.

"Because he's one of us."

Chapter Twenty-two
Waiting Game

Bazdin

I sloshed the water around in the tiny cut-rock sink before splashing it on my face. In the time-worn mirror above I watched as the water drew lines from the blue of my scalp, down to my chin. Dark rings stared back at me from around tired eyes. I clutched the sides of the basin, staring at my reflection.

"Eight days." Droplets flew from my lips, spotting the tarnished mirror.

I shook my head like the caged animal I'd become. I lay back down on my cot, and stared at the bugs walking across the eight-by-eight patch of ceiling above me.

A knock echoed off the stone walls of the windowless room. Gerrund walked in.

"It's time." He tossed a blindfold onto my stomach. "Put that on."

I sat up and did as I was told. *I'm going to see Tami again.* I had to remember that every time they treated me like a prisoner.

"How long this time?" My voice racked out from unused vocal cords.

"One hour."

What felt like an infinite amount of time later, nausea spiked in my head and stomach as we ascended a set of stairs. A heady burst of dried grasses and crisp evening air assaulted my lax senses. Gerrund guided me with a hand on my elbow. I bumped my shins on a rail of some sort. He pushed my head down, and helped me climb into the back seat of a rider. Four doors slammed shut. Gerrund settled beside me.

"Why do I have to wait? It's not as if I'll remember where we are."

"You might. Can't risk it. You're lucky you're *not* staying. What you already know can cause damage enough. Aelonia never should have made this deal."

"I gave her no choice – just as you're giving me no choice. I believe in the Cause. I don't know why you won't trust me."

"It's too convenient, kid. We'll get you on your way, and by the time you come back, it won't matter what you do or don't know. Here." A small package dropped on my lap. "Eat up. This'll be the last fresh meal you'll get for a while. Deserts travel is not for the faint of heart – or stomach." *Tami... I'm coming.*

We slowed to a stop. My stomach was better for the transition from the rider to lidez, but the dinner I ate wasn't sitting right – probably just nerves. We stopped twice more to let on passengers. Of the last two people to board the transport, I recognised the woman's voice – *Aelonia*.

At least I wasn't being brought to some kind of *body disposal site* for people who knew too much – not that I ever thought that was a possibility, but being trapped in a rock prison for a week made the mental wheels turn faster than ever and spin off down crazy paths. Then again, that's what Ali claimed the Kronik would do to me if I'd stayed and hadn't shut up.

"We're here," Gerrund said, standing up as the other bodies exited the vehicle. I yanked the blindfold off. Gerrund's blazing blue hair disappeared in front of the seat by the door as he disembarked.

We were stopped in the middle of a dusty road surrounded by grain fields. I looked out the front windshield. The face in the rear-view mirror startled me.

"Out ya get, boy."

I scrambled from the seat and out the double doors that creaked shut behind me. A side hatch dropped open as a cacophony of voices lashed my ears. No one had said hardly anything on the ride.

The Beta Sun's fading light flared orange across my vision as it hung low in the sky. I filled my lungs with the fresh air and relished in the breeze as it swept across my skin.

"Give us a hand," called a voice. I walked over to the group and helped lower a small three-wheeled vehicle to the ground. Gerrund slammed the hatch shut with a clang. I glanced up and caught Aelonia's gaze.

She nodded at me.

"Bazdin, you'll want to be a part of this. If anything should happen to your Guide, you'll need to know how to operate the D.V." She turned to a blond man standing next to her. "Gel, let's set up over there. Mardel, ask the Guides to follow us in two minutes." Her copper hair bounced as she jogged along beside the D.V. with Gel. A tall Jeridan woman of black skin and yellow coliths, wearing a flowing shawl of some kind, stood surrounded by a number of people wearing light grey robes. One wore tan fatigues, high boots, and a neck scarf. He carried a large backpack.

A similar back pack landed at my feet.

"You might want to change while Ali and Gelden set up," the soldier, named Mardel, said.

"Where exactly?"

"You don't have many options or much time. I'd sneak behind the lidez, if I were you." Then he turned and joined the woman and her entourage.

I grabbed the pack – it was heavier than it looked – and shuffled to the other side of the lidez. Inside were tall boots, a couple of bandanas, a change of clothes, an extra sweater, some kind of face mask, and ration packs – lots of ration packs. I slipped out of my black pants and navy shirt – clearly they were the wrong colour for Desert travel.

Mardel called out, "Okay. Let's head over. Aelonia's ready now."

I skirted the front of the lidez, and followed the group to the D.V. Nothing but tall dry grasses, and a couple of lakes could be seen for miles around. It definitely felt like the edge of nowhere, but likely this was where it all started for Tamaine.

Aelonia stood by the handlebars on one side of the vehicle, and the guy, Gelden, stood on the opposite side by the double-wide back tires.

"We're losing light, so I'm only going through this once. Laiviis, I want you to operate the D.V. as I describe the various functions. You and Bazdin can review at your first rest-stop. Bazdin?"

"Yeah?"

"Move closer."

"Right."

I shuffled from the back of the semi-circular crowd to the front. I bumped the tall woman's elbow. Her bodyguard cuffed me on the side of my head.

"Watch what you're doing," he said. The older woman just smiled demurely, her focus never leaving Ali.

"Okay, this is the battery box. It'll charge automatically during the day, using the array that unfolds from this section here." Ali said, as Laiviis unfolded the array and affixed it to the top of the battery box. It made the D.V. look like it had a bird's tail.

"This is the charge metre." Laiviis didn't know where to look, so blondie pointed it out on the rear of the battery box. "If the battery drains quickly, or you come across an area of interference, use the pedals to move it like a bicycle."

She detailed every working inch of the Desert Vehicle. If Laiviis didn't have something to open, point to or turn on, then he repeated back what Ali said. Then the blond guy, Gelden, got on the thing and waited for Laiviis to instruct him on the steps to take for driving it.

The Lead Guide hopped on the back and the two men drove off toward the nearest lake on the only stretch of dirt road out here. In the distance they switched places and Laiviis drove the D.V. back. When he pulled up, he didn't even try to hide the grin plastered over his face. Some of the other Guides laughed.

I looked at Ali. She inclined her head for me to join her off to the side.

"I trust him, Bazdin. He'll take you to Tamaine — safely. I've pushed him harder than the others. Let him enjoy this moment. It's what he's trained for. I know what it's like. I felt that same exuberance when I finally passed my probation with the CTF."

"You were with the CTF?"

A shadow of regret crossed her face; whether it was from missing her old job or worrying about telling me, I couldn't say. I decided to ignore it.

"If you say so. How long will it take to reach Tami?"

"Approximately three night's travel. I see Mardel gave you your pack. Listen to Laiviis carefully about how to survive out there. As much as you need to get to Tamaine, I need for this mission to proceed *without* error. Your timeline forced our hand on an issue still being debated and now my loyalty is under suspicion. You owe me."

"I have no intention of dying out there. I'll be the good student — that's a role I'm familiar with anyway. What does Laiviis have in his pack? I've got only clothing and food in mine."

"He has everything else. He's trained to carry three-times the load you're capable of."

"But his pack is the same size as mine."

"You've got *all* the food. So, don't get lost. You might want to put the sweater on before you leave. It gets cold fast out there once Beta completely sets."

I crouched down to undo the top of the pack. Ali knelt beside me, using her body to block sightlines. She pointed to two pockets I hadn't looked in yet.

"I know your determination will bring you to Tamaine no matter the cost, so I've included two special items in your pack."

I looked up. Our eyes locked for what seemed like forever – or maybe time slowed in that moment, it was hard to tell.

"It has to do with the Cause and the Spoken Truth doesn't it?"

She nodded. "Gerrund will have my head if he finds out I gave them to you and not Laiviis. Laiviis knows they're in your pack and he's ready to return with what we need. But, if he fails, I'll need you to carry this out. Do you understand?"

"Aelonia, you're talking in riddles. What's the plan?"

I caught sight of the tall, older woman and her guards moving towards us.

"The back flap on your pack holds a sweater-like bag. The Chronicles will need to be placed inside it." My eyes widened. "Yes. But they are a unique design – an orb. It won't be easy to handle but one person can do it. Also, you'll find a camera wrapped in a pair of gloves, and extra bandanas in this pocket." She pointed. "Either you or Laiviis will need to take pictures of both the Ancient City, and the Great City. When Laiviis comes back, he'll bring these with him. It's of utmost importance that this happens, or things could get complicated for the Cause. Do you understand?"

"Yes."

She slipped something down the side of my boot, then cocked her head sideways and looked me over. Gingerly, she held my chin and turned my head from side to side studying me. This woman couldn't have been more than a year older than me, but somehow it felt as though there was a lifetime between us.

"Did Gerrund treat you well?"

I locked eyes with her a second time. "Well enough," I said, then shrugged. She dropped her hand to the bag. "Like you said – he doesn't trust me."

Ali registered the nearness of the woman, nodded and clapped me on the shoulder as she rose.

"Let's get you on your way then, shall we?"

As we walked over to the returned Laiviis, I pulled the sweater from the pack and slipped it over my head before closing the bag up again. The strange woman with the guards altered course. She shook Gelden's hand after he got off the back of the D.V. I got on in his place. Ali strapped a small pair of kegs to either side of the battery box, which rested immediately behind me.

Laiviis' pack rested in front of him on the D.V., allowing me to grab onto the sides of his robes. My Guide gave a final wave and we were off.

The wind whipped at my hair as we sped into the Greater Expanse past not two, but three lakes. Another three nights and I would be whole again.

Chapter Twenty-three
Upping the Anti

Dezmind

Dearest Ali,

Another five days have scraped my soul with no word from you. I've checked with the delivery service but, after the initial collection of mail, they can't tell me if you're receiving my letters or not.

I have come to understand that you've accepted greater responsibility on behalf of what we're doing – that this new job will keep you away from home for days at a time. I hope that we've simply been missing each other... our letters that is, for there's nothing simple about the way I feel about you. Send word when you can.

Feeling lost without you,

DL

I passed the envelope to the outrider as our paths converged on Seller Street, just off the main road. Today's walk would bring me from the edge of the city core into one of the outlying suburbs where the buildings didn't tower above, sending re-directed sunlight to the avenues below. The agreed upon route would take me past Klax Square.

"What's with the smile?" Dradin, the UG's outrider, asked.

"Just thinking of the first time I met Tay – Ali. We'll be walking past the park today.

Dradin laughed. "I heard about that not long after it happened. Gutsy move if you ask me."

"Nah. Cheeky." I joined him laughing. I handed him one of the pamphlets from my shoulder bag, just as a couple walking their dog approached from a side street.

Show time.

"What they don't tell the public would fill a book – probably more – but what *I* know would cover at least that much. The Kronik have gotten too used to telling half-truths and keeping secrets."

Dradin spoke on cue. "But how do you know? Why should I trust what you have to say any more than the Kronik?"

I smiled at the couple, handed them a pamphlet, and then turned back to Dradin. "I left the Compound for a reason – they weren't just keeping things from the greater public, but from the Society Citizens as well. There were questions I needed answered, and to get those answers, I had to come looking for them myself. Once I breached the wall, there was no turning back. I learned more in one year about what the average citizen faces, than I had in my eighteen years prior. That was over six years ago."

The walkers followed a good five yards behind us. I didn't look over my shoulder, but I could hear the jangle of the small dog's harness. There was no guarantee they were listening to the conversation, but this was how it always began.

I took the path that led straight through Klax Square, not only to allow the dog some space to do its business, but to pull in larger groups – my voice travelled farther in the open spaces of the park.

"What does it matter why you left? What does that have to do with the rest of us?" Dradin asked, flipping through the pamphlet.

"Everything – I just didn't know it at the time. Actually, it wasn't until I travelled into the Deserts in search of the Chronicles that all of the little truths, which really weren't so small, amassed together to reveal just how self-serving the Kronik had become."

Three teens who'd been lounging at a picnic table got up and walked on the grass to the right of the path with us. Then, two older women hovered on the left as I gathered the atoms to my nucleus. Upon leaving the park, the teens walked in front, listening and asking the questions, and everyone else drew closer on the slightly narrower sidewalk.

By the time one of the older women asked, "What did you find on the other side of the Deserts?" our number had grown to almost twenty. The bodies surrounding Dradin and I ate up the remaining empty space, eager to hear my next words.

"Another city."

Several gasps and thoughtful "*mms*" filled the collective space between and above the crowd.

I had learned over the course of these past weeks, not to lead with *aliens*. That threw up walls and slammed doors on ears so fast that I couldn't believe the negativity that came from people.

"You see, the Kahn-lea and I found a very old piece of technology that matched exactly what the Chronicles spoke of – a Generator meant to keep Gamma, our little Zerameteth, functioning properly."

"But why? It's a sun… isn't it?" asked the man with the dog.

"Yes, of course it's a sun. But it's not a natural sun like Alpha and Beta. Gamma was placed in orbit around Xannia thousands of years ago, to affect a change on the planet."

"Do you mean terraforming?" asked a new voice. I turned to hand him a pamphlet.

"Yes. Are you familiar with Professor Denali's theories?"

"That quack scientist who had his license revoked for falsifying findings?"

"That's the one."

"What about him?" a woman asked.

"He was telling the truth. Our world *is* getting warmer – for two reasons: one, the protective layer housing the nucleus of Gamma is degrading, and we're being subjected to harsher gamma rays than we're used to. And two, it was placed in orbit around the equator to do just that – warm things up."

And right on cue, multiple questions came at once.

"Why would the early Xannians want to warm things up?" a teen asked over the din.

I noticed a man in black walk out from between two buildings.

"Did we even have the technology to do something like that?" the female dog walker asked.

Two more men in dark sweats fell into step behind the crowd.

"Are you talking about aliens?"

A loud CRACK exploded. One of the men in black tossed a smoke grenade overhead. The man in front extended a suppression-staff to full length.

"Run!" Dradin yelled. Not for my sake – but for the listeners.

I ducked low out of the thickening smoke that hovered between our waists and heads. Dradin wasn't the only outrider in the group, he was just the only one I was meant to know about. There were always two: the *lead* who spoke with me and the *follow* who blended in with the crowd along the route.

I helped the two older women out of the haze and into a side alley. "Get out of sight, fast," I said. I could see two of the teens lying on the sidewalk holding various body parts, wincing and groaning. Dradin's feet stood toe-to-toe with the man with the staff. Another pair of work boots did the same with another pair of black-clad legs. Two pairs of innocent feet shuffled back from the third attacker.

Don't let the innocent suffer – Taya's voice rang through my conscience. I dove back into the fray, colliding with a man in black.

"Run!" I echoed Dradin's warning.

The innocent took off.

Something heavy connected with the side of my head. The world went black.

My arms and head bumped against someone's back. I convinced my body to stay limp and unresponsive. Another set of footsteps accompanied those of whoever held me. I cracked an eye. Electric fire flashed through my brain. I fought to keep my breathing even. It wasn't working.

I had no idea where I was, except that I was still outside and the man holding me wore black. I shot my knee into his chest. He dropped me, crumbling to all fours. I used the momentum to summersault off his shoulder and run. Each footfall jarred my cranium, sending waves of black or sparks of light across my vision.

Old brick walls scraped my hands. A severely dented metal door slammed open – the crash shattered my senses. Many hands grabbed at my arms, legs and torso before I lost consciousness again.

It was quiet – too quiet. I squinted. Blessed darkness bathed over me, or maybe that was a bad thing.

"I hope for your sake, the words going through your mind right now are, *Gerrund was right*," a voice from the other side of the dark space said.

"No. I was glad I hadn't coloured the inside of my shorts, actually."

"You're such a stubborn ass, you know that?" Gerrund said. I heard him stand up. A switch clicked. I braced for bright light, but a hazy yellow warmed the room. I lay on a cot too short for my height, but at least the pillow was soft… and the right people had me now.

"So I've been told, and by someone far prettier than you." I tried to sit up. The bright lights flashed behind my eyes. Strong hands eased my shoulders back down to the pillow. I relaxed my neck muscles and let my head sink into its soft layers again.

"Lie still or I'll have to wait another two hours to talk to you."

"Fine."

Gerrund pulled a short stool over and sat down near my hip. He leaned forward, resting his elbows on his knees and clasped his hands together.

"Tell me what happened."

"You know what happened."

"No. I don't. Your outriders are in a far worse condition than you are."

"They're not dead?" I sat up again. Thunder joined the fireworks this time. He pushed me back down to the pillow.

"No. But they'll need a paid vacation after this. Now, what the hell happened out there?" he growled.

I sighed. "Probability Factor number four."

"How many were there?"

"Three men in black, twenty-odd civilians."

"Where did it happen?"

"Just beyond the square, before the district changed from mercantile to private housing. How did you find me if the outriders were out of commission? Weren't they back at the attack site?"

"One was there, the other was part way down a service alley sending SOSs over the sub-level coms. The team lit you up and we tracked you down."

"Lit me up?"

"Your clothes are bugged."

"Ah, that explains it."

"Why did you get caught?"

"Excuse me?"

"I said, why did you get caught? Your lead would've told you to run. Why didn't you run?"

I didn't think that deserved a response. I just looked at him.

"I thought so. How are we supposed to pull this off if you refuse to follow protocol? We're propeller-shocked if we don't have you. It's vital to the Cause for you to stay alive and out of their hands."

"You don't need to lecture me."

"Apparently I do."

"I wasn't going to let those people suffer for something I was doing."

"This is war."

"No. This is justice – and the *just* don't let the little guy get trampled, otherwise what are we fighting for?"

"No more walks, Dezmind."

"Fine."

"And no more private meets."

"Not fine."

"Dezmind."

"Gerrund." I kept as even a voice as possible, if only to keep my head from sparking again. "I need to speak with the Sector Magistrates. They have to know about the Chronicles, Gamma and the verrin problem. They need to hear it from me before the Kronik can claim something else is going on, or pretend to solve the problem. You talk about me playing a vital role – then let me play it. This won't work politically if we ostracise the highest form of government in the public sector."

Gerrund scowled and crossed his arms, clearly not happy about the situation.

"You are to be monitored at all times and need to give us full details of each meet. We will shadow you – it's the only way."

"It's the only way to spook them. The Magistrates have their own guard detail and extensive digital security. I have to go in alone."

"I don't *have* to let you do anything."

The look in his eyes said that I could rot in this safe house until they needed me to be their puppet. This was not the man I made plans with six years ago – the man who wanted a better life for *all* citizens… not just the UGC.

Chapter Twenty-four
The Ancient City

Bazdin

The early morning rays from the Alpha sun scorched my skin. No one had thought to pack a hat for me. We were supposed to be travelling at night, per Ali's instructions, but Laiviis pulled rank when he thought he saw a nest of dunes sometime during the twilight hours. Of course, one nest led to another and the next thing I knew, I was suddenly in need of a hat.

The soft sands of the Powder Desert made each footfall feel as if I had ten-pound weights strapped to my ankles. And that was another thing. The D.V. had worked great until we transitioned out of the Valley of the Dunes and into the Power Sands. We made better time pushing the thing by its handles than when we were riding it – and that's saying something.

"Why don't we set up here? I need a break, man."

"Not yet," said Laiviis. "Ali's map shows that the ruins are nearby. We'll rest there."

"I thought she advised you to steer clear of caves and other stuff like that?"

"I've heard the stories – she stayed in the Temple one night. I just have to de-bug the place first. Besides, we need to stop there during the day to complete our mission."

"We can take pictures at night," I said.

"And we will. We'll also get some during the day. Besides, do you really want to go nosing around the bowels of that place to restock on verrin in the dark?"

No. But I didn't give him the satisfaction of saying it out loud. A sharp pain shot up my heel as the blister I'd been forming all morning finally popped.

"Dammit. Let's just drive this thing anyway. My feet are killing me."

"It's faster walking."

"I don't care. I want to be in one piece when I see Tami. This is ridiculous."

"This is reality. Look, Bazdin. You're the one who forced our hand here, so suck it up."

My retort caught in my throat as something solid rose from the earth on the other side of the long dune we travelled on.

"It's about bloody time," I grumbled, spitting accumulated sand out of my mouth.

"Pull up your bandana. You're only making things worse."

My bandana reeked with sweat and hair oil. I'd been using the extras Ali had packed as a head covering in the sun.

"Don't mind me. I'll manage." I didn't need his self-righteous tone. What I needed was sleep.

At the edge of the Ancient City, Laiviis pulled out yet another map. It was surprisingly detailed, considering he'd said Ali hadn't been here long.

"This causeway should lead us to a main spoke we can follow right to the Temple." He stomped his feet. "The ground here is about as stable as it was in the Valley of the Dunes. We can ride in."

"Thank the suns." I climbed on to the Desert Vehicle behind my Guide. He pushed the ignition. Nothing happened. "Great Zita, what is it now?"

Laiviis stood up on the pedals and pushed forward until the gears engaged. "Pocket of charged magnetism, or maybe a static storm blew through this morning leaving residual—"

"Yeah, yeah, yeah. Let's just get this thing moving."

Half an hour later, I hopped off the D.V. to let Laiviis park it by the only building I'd seen that still had a roof. I walked over to the open door. Laiviis' placed a hand on my shoulder stopping me from crossing the threshold.

"De-bugging, remember?" he said.

I stepped back out of his way. He left his pack at my feet by the door and walked in holding a weapon I'd only ever seen on the wire. Two flexible bracings slid over his middle and index finger. Suspended beneath was an oval-shaped tube that extended from his wrist, to just past his fingertips. He let his two fingers hover over the touch-sensitive pads.

I managed a breathy whistle through parched lips. "I thought those were decommissioned?"

"They were. We re-directed a shipment meant for the incinerator."

"Aren't you worried it'll malfunction?"

"Nope. We've got a guy who's good at fixing things."

I rolled my eyes. The PE 22 lit the room with each photon burst. He targeted large white clumps in the upper corners of the Temple. A distinct singed smell hovered in the large room. Laiviis stepped back outside.

"Why don't you grab that camera – we can get some shots while the room airs out a bit."

I knelt down to one side of the door and opened the compartment. "Are you sure that's wise? If a static storm blew through, any residual particles might damage the equipment."

Light brown gloves and a small square of canvas covered the camera. I unfolded it gingerly.

"Yeah, I guess you're right. I'm gonna climb up on the roof to get my bearings. I want to mark the arrow for tonight." He hopped up onto the sill of one of the open windows beside the door and scrambled onto the roof. I was glad. I tucked the camera into my lap and spread open the cloth. Ali had written a message.

Bazdin,

It's imperative that you find more verrin crystals and bring them to the Kahn-lea. There is no verrin in the south lands. None. The engineered supplements in Laiviis' pack are not sufficient. You'll need to dig the crystals out of the fountain by the alter in the Temple. If there's not enough, you'll need to try and reach the underground pipe. Don't do anything stupid.

Ali

I wrapped the camera back up to keep the finer dust particles from gumming up the mechanism; then reached into my boot and fished out the retractable knife she'd slipped me – the real reason my feet were blistering. I pulled up my bandana… oil and sweat were better than the stench Laiviis had left behind.

I went in.

The fountain stood out immediately. I dropped my pack on a bench, about half-way there, before jumping into its large basin. I could easily see inside the triple-orb spout at the top and the chunks clinging to the inside. My fingers were too fat to fit inside with the blade and wiggle the shards out. I looked around the Temple. Nothing there to help. *Wait…*

I jumped down and walked over to the large chair on the altar. A broken chunk of pencil lay at its base. *This'll work.* I hopped back up into the fountain and fished around with the blade and the pencil.

"What are you doing?" Laiviis shouted.

I nearly lost the sliver. He tramped over and huffed at me as I pulled out the long shard.

"What is that? Why do you have a knife?"

"Ali asked me to do something for her. Don't worry about the knife. I'm not going to stab you. Even if I didn't believe in the Cause, I'm not stupid enough to kill the only person who can get me to my fiancée."

He crossed his arms. "Gerrund's not going to like this."

"Then don't tell him." I looked back down the throat of the fountain – the rest of the pieces were too far down. "Since you're here, why don't we check out the underground and top up our verrin before we set camp?"

"I wanted to give this place time to air out and settle. But... all right. Let's do this thing. I'm tired, too. Grab the rope out of my pack. I'm going to get the travel kegs off the D.V."

I jumped down, took apart my bandana hood, and wrapped the concentrated verrin in one of the squares of cloth. Tucking it in the top of my bag, I made sure the fabric inside cradled the delicate piece. I didn't need it turning into powder before we even made it to the Great City. I slid the knife back into my boot... the other one this time.

The rope was in a sub-compartment of Laiviis' bag – his pack was the same size as mine but jammed with all our gear, including the pup tent we usually slept in. The bright blue fibres of the rope had a small, tight weave, but acted like cabling, or so Laiviis had said when I'd quizzed him about the contents of his pack our first night out.

He walked back in carrying the two small travel kegs. After topping up our personal canteens, he walked over behind the large chair.

"Here. Help me with this."

I brought the rope over and left my canteen with his on the bench.

"You grab that handle and I'll get this one. On three... One. Two. Three."

We heaved the rock cover up and out of place. It wasn't so heavy that either one of us couldn't have lifted it alone, it's just that we were both exhausted from the extra-long morning walk.

"I'll climb down first." He slipped into the opening and shimmied down a chiselled rock-ladder. I passed him the kegs and then followed.

An eerie orange glow lit up the chamber. My eyes darted from the strange inverted triangle of in the middle of the plateau, to the rock pipe coming down from the ceiling, to the crazy-high cliff that led to the river of verrin.

"Wow." The word didn't do the view justice, but it was all I had.

"You can say that again. I hope the rope's long enough."

"Here." I handed him the tip of the rope to tie onto the handle of the keg. While he did that, I unravelled the rest of it so it was loose by our feet.

"Okay. Here goes nothing," he said, and chucked it into the air. I wrapped the loose end around my fist. It crashed into the verrin with a satisfying thunk, and slowly sank as it filled. There were still a couple of yards of rope at my feet. *Guess Ali had a good idea how far out it was.*

"Hey. You take it and reel it in. I gotta check something out." I passed him the rope.

"What? Another secret mission?"

"Same one." I walked over to where the ledge met the wall. The end of the pipe extended down on a slope, away from the plateau to a place where, long ago, the river came up to. *There used to be a helluva lot of verrin in here. I wonder what happened?*

There was no way I would reach the end of the pipe, not even with Laiviis' help. But Ali must have known that. *Don't do anything stupid*, her words echoed in my head.

As Laiviis hauled the keg back up to the plateau, I followed the pipe up along the wall to where it disappeared into the ceiling. In a couple of places there was less rock holding the pipe to the wall, almost as if the plumber's chisel slipped or the rock was weaker.

I didn't have a hammer, but I did have a boot. I walked over to one of the thin sections at knee height and kicked. I missed my mark. My other foot shifted under me with the impact. I tried to catch my balance, but my foot slipped over the edge.

"Ah!" I yelled.

A heavy hand anchored itself to my shoulder and pulled me back. I landed on my ass.

"Dammit," I cussed.

"You can say that again. What the hell are you trying to do? Other than get yourself killed." Laiviis pulled the keg up over the ledge and sealed the top.

"I need to break open that pipe. Thought a good swift kick would do it."

"But?"

"But I missed."

It was his turn to roll his eyes at me. I got the head shake, too. I could tell he was itching to tell me what a dumb ass I was being – I was just glad he was too busy with the kegs to bother.

"Find a rock and hit it."

"Yeah. I think I'll do that." There were none, of course. I did manage to break a corner off the inverted pyramid thing and used the heavy chunk as my hammer. It took almost no time to break open the pipe. I shook my head at my idiocy before scraping a couple more chunks of verrin crystal onto another bandana. These ones were shorter and thicker, less likely to shatter or grind themselves into a fine dust.

By the time I'd collected all I could from that section of pipe, Laiviis sealed off the cap of the second keg. Seeing as they were significantly heavier now that they were full, I stood most of the way up on the rock ladder as Laiviis passed them to me to place on the floor above. He'd looped the length of rope loose enough to slide his head and arm through the inner hole and carried it across his shoulder – leaving his hands free for climbing. I scrambled the rest of the way up.

"Laiviis, get your ass up here now!"

"What!" he raced up after me. "Meeka," he swore.

Large, fat white sausage-like creatures crawled out of the strange burnt webbing in the corners of the ceiling. They clung to the wall, leaving trails of phosphorescent ooze behind. Hoards of them slunk across the floor. They all headed in the same direction.

"Are they leaving?" I asked.

"No." He pointed. "Your pack."

"The food," we said together. The floor was nearly full of the soft, spongy-looking creatures. The one thing I remembered from Laiviis' lectures out here was *nothing is safe*. I didn't want to find out what kind of horror these things were, or what they might turn into if they ate our food.

"I'll get the packs and the canteens. Can you handle both kegs?" I asked.

"Yes."

We went to punch each other in the shoulder for luck, and wound up cracking fists instead. You'd think we'd planned it or something. I wanted to laugh, but I was too freaked out. Laiviis grabbed a keg handle in each hand. The muscles in his arms flexed, pressing large veins against his skin. He breathed out three times fast, then sucked in a huge lungful before jumping up onto the throne, over to the table, and onto the front bench on the left side of the room — away from the two packs. I followed, leaping to the right side.

I grabbed the two canteens and his pack from the front bench and nearly dropped it trying to swing it up onto my shoulders. Acting like a pendulum it swung me sideways. I scrambled to stay upright, grabbing at the back of the bench.

The white things noticed me.

Hauling my new bulk up onto the back of the bench, I hurdled to the next one. Launching my body from one back to the next, I didn't dare stop.

I knew my pack was lighter. I grabbed it on my way by, hugging it to my chest. One of the creepers dropped from the bottom of the bag onto my boot. I kicked it off when I hit the floor by the door.

Slamming my ass down on the back of the D.V., Laiviis sped off – the battery now working. What I didn't realise until we stopped a few streets over, was I had another creeper hitching a ride between me and my pack.

Chapter Twenty-five
Spelunking

Taya

"What are you running from?" Gelden's words echoed in my mind. He'd found me sitting alone in the shop this morning, thinking. At least that's what I thought I'd been doing – trying to let go of the D.V. project and ready myself for *cave training* with Gerrund.

I took a sip of my fizzy verrin beverage – *non*-alcoholic this time. He'd lumped everything in together, but more specifically he'd referred to the FOL – Followers of Light.

"You weren't there. You didn't see what happened," I'd said and stormed out. I saw the recognition in his eyes… the incident had been hushed up but, being related to Gerrund, I knew he knew exactly what had happened the day Dezmind left. And yet, he still wanted me to write that damn column. I don't know, maybe there was something to it.

Jak slid into the booth with a rather dark pint of something frothy. My insides jumped a little.

"I didn't think you saw me coming. Heavy thoughts?"

I nodded.

"About your homework, or something else?"

I took another sip of my drink to stall. "I have more on my mind than I'd care to share at the moment."

He nodded back and took a drink. The foam left a moustache on his upper lip, which he licked away. I couldn't help but smile. He must have seen me brooding and bought the beverage just to lighten the mood – he would totally do that.

"So, you're moody today. Anything you do want to share?"

"I'm starting a new job this afternoon."

"And…?"

I frowned, debating how much I was at liberty to reveal. "I've agreed to explore the north caverns. Alone." Going against the very advice I had given my protégé Desert Guides.

His eyes widened. "Well, that *is* big. Are you looking forward to it?"

I appreciated the fact that he didn't ask me how I *felt* about it. He appeared to be taking our last talk seriously.

"I am." But my voice faltered when my mind tried to analyse my split reasoning. Sure, I wanted to help the Cause, help Dez finish this thing, but that wasn't what drove me to put my life on the line... again. Not this time. I had ulterior motives.

"Are you nervous?"

He jolted me from my thoughts. I blinked. I couldn't let him catch me off guard. *Focus Taya.*

"More excited than nervous. Being alone doesn't bother me, at least not down here. I know how to handle myself. Lessons with Gerrund this morning were awkward. He insisted on repeating things I'd already memorised and snapped at me – more than once for no reason."

"And that's what worries you?"

"Part of it. I just keep telling myself he's under a lot of stress, but I can't shake the feeling that he still doesn't trust me after…"

"After what?"

"After I broke protocol on the surface and made a decision that inadvertently benefited my own agenda. Jak, he's different somehow.

I can't explain it, but I swear to you he's not the same man who showed me around after saving me from the Warehouse. I don't know what to make of it. I don't know enough of the *grand plan* to see all the angles, and I don't think I ever will."

"Why is that a problem?"

I stared at him over the rim of my glass. "If I don't know what's going on, I can't prepare myself for what's coming."

"And yet most of the UGC knows considerably less than you and they – including myself – trust Gerrund to handle things."

"Blind trust."

"Not really. He's organised, led, fed, housed and nourished our failing hopes since he was a teenager. He's earned our trust. Have you earned his?"

"I had it by proxy but, as I mentioned, he misconstrued my choices and refuses to listen to reason. I don't know whether to thank him for giving me this chance to work on scouting the north tunnels, or if I should be concerned that he's not *protecting* me the way Dez probably made him promise he would. Part of me feels like he's willing to risk, not only his relationship with Dez, but my life as well – at least based on everything Mardel's told me about tunnel exploration." I shook my head and took a sip of my drink.

"Jak, that doesn't sound like the man you're talking about. I know this job is vital, but it feels more like a test I'm destined to fail than an opportunity to redeem myself."

"You like to be in control."

"Yes." It popped out before I could analyse whether I should've said it or not.

"Don't be afraid to admit what you are, Taya. This actually works in well with today's planned discussion. Do you have your list?"

I nodded.

His eyes glanced down as if he could see my pants pockets through the table top and the hand that should be reaching to retrieve a piece of paper.

"I don't need to write down what I already know. I have a pictographic memory."

"That implies there *was* a list at some point."

I shrugged.

"So tell me, then, who or what has directly influenced your life — made you the woman you are today?"

"My family."

He waited as if expecting more, then prompted, "Lynnia and Matheson?"

"Yes. And the Fyces and the Kronik."

"The Kronik is your family?"

"Don't you think so?" I asked.

He crossed his arms. "Taya, you're blocking again."

I set my glass down on the table and placed my palms flat on its cool surface. "My estranged best friend pointed this out to me. After my second family abandoned me, I chose to seek refuge, and a modicum of control over my life, by going to work in the government mines. Then, I put myself through Contractor Training — an elite government subsidised institution, among other things. I befriended a woman, unknowingly of course, but it still fits, who worked as a Secret Agent for the Kronik and my supposed boyfriend is the son of a Councilman. These people, those establishments, were my family."

And where has that gotten me? Trapped in a giant rock-coffin of someone else's making.

"You sound bitter, and I don't blame you. Dealing with family is never easy. But I have to ask you — do you count yourself in that sub-list somewhere?"

"Myself?"

"Surely you take some responsibility for the choices you've made along the way? That you recognise your place amongst your family?"

"Those *choices* were forced on me by my family. Zaith made it oh, so clear that the only reason I'm still alive is the choices I had to make to survive. And Dez believes that some Oracle could see his destiny and somehow my survival is part of that. By the sounds of things, I wasn't really left with a choice. Fate did what it wanted and I played right into its master plan."

"I didn't think you believed in fate and destiny."

"Jak, I don't know what the Suns to believe in anymore. The Chronicles are real. I exist, even though I shouldn't. And for some inexplicable reason, I find myself in the middle of someone else's war…"

"Just as lost and confused as the day your foster parents stopped loving you?"

Only hot anger kept the tears from falling. I stared through him to Lija, the woman I thought was my mother, holding her arms out and swinging me around laughing; the woman who also fed me table scraps and clothed me in rags because she didn't want me anymore; the woman who named her *real* daughter Jutaya in order to replace me and repair her family; and finally, to the woman I didn't remember at all – except through the eyes of men… to Lynnia Doire, the Talian woman who shouldn't have been able to mate with a Commoner.

We sat that way for a long time. I'm certain he read a lot of what I was going through in my body language, but Jak didn't pry. I had so many unanswered questions and slighted emotions, that I didn't know how to handle it all.

"Taya," he said softly. I shifted my eyes to his, the rest of my body frozen. "I know it looks like every time you open your heart something bad happens, but hiding isn't the answer. There are flesh and blood people who care dearly for you—"

"Save it, Jak. If that were true, I wouldn't have been abandoned time and time again." The old walls shot up around my heart, my mind. "My biological parents cared so much they gave me away. My foster parents cared so much, they left me for dead. My government cared so much, they tried to have me killed – by my best friend, no less! And my boyfriend cares so much that he demands I stay out of his way while he does what's *truly* important – fulfilling his damned destiny. I'm tired, Jak." I flipped my hands over and smacked their backs down on the table, exposing my palms.

"There are people down here who are trying to make me something I'm not because of these stupid scars – scars I got while trying to help people. Who's helping me? Why must I always be set aside for something better?" I stood up, but I dropped my voice since my outburst drew stares from around the bar.

"I'm tired of being someone else's puppet. Maybe Gerrund's right not to trust me. Maybe my choices have been selfish. I don't care anymore." I walked off without looking back, without making plans, and without knowing how he managed to get me so flustered.

I pushed hard against the bike pedals. Gerrund stood with his back to me at the mouth of a cavern that looked like gum had stretched from the bottom to the top of well-hidden teeth. He'd called these thin rock formations *straws*. The sweat from the vigorous ride moistened my brow and the palms of my hands drained out my earlier frustrations.

The stalagmites and stalactites I had to weave around in the explored but unexcavated caves gave a claustrophobic feel compared to the scraped and modernised caves I'd been living in.

I rested the bike next to his, wiped my hands on my grey pants and walked over to stand beside him. A large travel pack sat at his feet just inside the cave. Following his gaze into the dim tunnel, he turned on an electric torch and swept the cavern with its beam.

Here, the rock glistened. There was no trodden path to follow and a lot more rock formations to contend with. While the other tunnels hadn't been scraped, they had been cleared of straws, pearls, helictites – twig-like stalactites and smaller columns that had been made of joined stalagmites and stalactites. They'd been dimly lit by lanterns connected to the main grid, but looked dull and lifeless, as if Mardel's excavation team had drained the natural lustre.

But here, the abundance of formations surrounding me gleamed with otherworldliness. I turned my own torch off. My eyes adjusted to the dimmer light.

"The pack has the supplies we agreed upon. Your first trip will be for two days. If you're not back on time, we'll know you ran into trouble and I'll send a scout team to get you out. We'll discuss your findings and overall progress when you get back."

I don't know why he didn't look at me. Maybe he was thinking of the promise to Dez he was breaking, or of Mardel's concerns about the risks. Then again, he might simply be thinking he really couldn't trust me, and at this point I couldn't deny it.

I handed him my torch. Kneeling down, I searched through every inch of the pack. I had to know exactly where everything was. I slid the tool belt around my hips, zipped everything else back up, and extracted a light-tube from a pocket on the side. I knew he didn't approve of me using the lights, since they couldn't be recharged and would burden me with extra weight, but I had my reasons.

I hitched the pack up over my shoulders and stepped between a pair of soda straws.

"And J.J.," he said. I paused, still looking into the cave. "Don't get yourself killed."

With those final words of wisdom, I heard him grab his bike and ride away. Not exactly the pep talk I expected, but at least he was concerned.

Cracking the light-tube on against my thigh, I stepped into a completely new and awesome world. I held the light up as I walked, it allowed for me to better see where I was headed and absorb some of the beauty that glistened and cascaded around me, while maintaining a lower light level than the electric torches.

I glanced at the digital watch Gerrund had given me while we trained earlier; the display not only told me the time, but gave me my bearings as well. The cool air on my exposed wrist reminded me that I no longer wore my only gift from Dez... but the absence of the ticking watch made every breath easier to take.

Gerrund had demanded I not wear the scarf over my wrist, in case it got caught or snagged and hindered my movements in this new territory. When I'd revealed what lay beneath, he took off his own watch and handed it to me. I accepted it only because I knew it would be the last peace offering from him for a while.

The aquamarine blues and swirls of purple and gold on the moist walls threatened to capture my full attention. I had to watch where I stepped though, and two days, while it sounded like a long time, really wasn't for the distance I needed to cover – the places and the answers I needed to find, not only for Gerrund, but myself.

What happened with Bazdin had rattled me, broken whatever trust Gerrund had given me based on Dez's word... but I couldn't ignore what else happened while I was top-side. In fact, Dez's story from our time in the Deserts, the one about Lady Lynnia being confined for life in a leafy prison... the fact that I'd found Doire, my real father, dead in the Deserts on his way back from having been in the Great City, or at the very least near it – just so that he could be near her... and his family. There were questions I needed answers to, and nothing Jak or Gerrund, or even Dez could say would get me through this.

As my body grew accustomed to the damp chill, my steady pace kept my internal temperature up. I found a mental balance where I could scan and analyse my way, take in the vaulting columns and prismatic colours of the cave, and allow my subconscious time to muse.

My behaviour with Jak this evening surprised me as much as it had him. I'd always had a handle on my emotions, but ever since crossing the Deserts, the regimented control the CTF drilled into me had dissolved.

Suddenly my past, my emotions, were no longer contained and compartmentalised – dismissed as something that had happened once. Now, dealing with the frenzy I faced in the Pit of Chance was a near constant tapping in my brain. I didn't have Dez's solid embrace to keep me from falling to pieces. I didn't have my training to fall back on. I only had a stream of people shredding what little remained of my sanity.

Everyone had their own agenda. It was time I did, too. It was time to take back control of my life.

Gelden's idea for that article had percolated after my talk with Jak. In the intervening hour before meeting Gerrund at the tunnel entrance, I'd poured everything I ever wanted to say to the FOL on to one double-sided piece of paper and sent it with a runner to Gelden. It was time to take back a modicum of control – to tell *my* story and set the record straight.

Chapter Twenty-six
Reclaiming One's Identity

Dezmind

What Gerrund failed to mention was that, after a couple of days, my body would ache even when my head felt better. I sat down in one of two overstuffed reading chairs that dominated my tiny apartment over the Chalklin Pond Restaurant. My joints complained loudly, making Jadis' head rise from the arm of the other chair. She looked at me with her usual disinterest and licked her nose.

I glanced at the clock on the coffee machine in the open-concept kitchen. It was actually a glorified counter with a stove top and sink but no oven. *Good thing the chefs send leftovers home with me every night, or I wouldn't eat half as well as I do.*

I hated waiting. I especially hated waiting in my apartment, but Gerrund spoke with the new head chef who'd refused to let me go anywhere near my office since the ambush.

I did what work I could at my kitchen table, likely reclaimed from the old bistro set belonging to the front patio. The wrought iron patterns and decorative holes made for a terrible work surface.

Thank the Suns I had more books than sense – hard covered relics. Instead of just decorating the already cramped space with another pile, spread out they made a formidable work surface.

And there was the rub – I couldn't risk reaching out to anyone regarding the Cause and the Spoken Truth digitally... too easily traced. So, I had to wait – every day – for the mail carrier to come and go.

I couldn't understand Gerrund's reservations about continuing the social platform of the Cause. Sure, the Rally Walks were clearly hazardous to my health, now that the Kronik's agents were risking public exposure. But trying to stop the political talks? He was losing perspective.

The coup would only work if the general populous agreed that what we were doing was in the best interest for Xannia... for them really. The walks were working, but I couldn't reach as wide an audience with them, which was why the Kronik banned me from speaking on public stages. Still, if I couldn't reach the masses directly, I could at least try to connect with the politicians.

Not that I could ever be sure of anything when dealing with them, but the meeting with the Sector Delegates went at least reasonably well – the Magistrates would be another headache entirely.

A knock at the door startled me. I check my watchcom and realised I'd lost track of time. The fact that Jadis hadn't reacted told me it was the mail delivery. I got up and opened the door.

"Here you are, sir." The tall, lanky lad from the wait staff said, as he handed me a small pile.

I gave him a nod.

"How are you feeling today?"

"Better in some ways, and worse in others," I laughed at the confusion written on his face. "Overall, much better. I should be back to work in another day or two."

He smiled in return, nodded, and then went back downstairs.

I pushed the door shut with my foot as I riffled through the mail, searching for a response from the Magistrate.

"Nothing."

I flopped back down into the chair as something slipped from the pages of the Local Inquisitor. *Probably just an insert Gerrund's people have started including.* A notice on the cover page drew my eye: New Column: *Third Sun's Light, page 2.* I settled back into place, and shook out the small newspaper.

A growl at my knee startled me. I let go of one side of the thin, blue paper and looked at the mountain lynx nudging my leg.

"Well hello, Jadis. Are you hungry?"

She yawned, sat down at my feet and cocked her fuzzy head sideways.

"I wish I knew what you wanted, girl." I cautiously moved my empty hand to scratch her behind the ears. Leaning her heavy body into my legs, she rested her large head on my lap and closed her eyes, purring.

"Well, that's a first."

She pined in her own way for Taya. We both missed her. I couldn't believe she still hadn't sent a return letter. Maybe they're being intercepted? I'd have to ask Gerrund to look into it. I'd been careful not to reveal much about the Cause, and what was said remained informal and coded.

Jadis nudged my knee with her nose – I'd paused in my ministrations. Her newfound companionship was nice. However, it also meant that if I wanted to read the paper, I'd have to do it single-handedly. I re-read the notice and raised an eyebrow. It had to be something related to the Deserts Quest. I balanced the newspaper on the arm of the chair, opened it to page two and read:

Third Sun's Light

I cannot tell you my name, but that doesn't mean you haven't tried to name me. I am not Zimi – Life Giver, or Emvaso-al – Protector of Young, Zerameteth's Child, or even the Child of the Light as so many of you call me.

I am a woman who both does and does not believe.

Taya? It had to be.

It is time you knew my story.

The starburst markings on my hands are not 'gifts' from Zerameteth, nor are they divine markings of any kind. They are scars; scars that hurt and scars that healed – nothing more. While these scars developed from an inability to see others suffer, and an inherent desire to live, no entity from the heavens above or unknown force compelled me to act as I did.

Just as many of you have helped another Xannian, I have too.

No. It's more than that and you know it.

You ask me to lay my scars on the foreheads of your children – I will not claim I can heal an illness or quiet a fevered mind. I have basic emergency medical skills: I can set broken bones, reduce a cut's blood flow, assess a head injury, and help the body heal itself. But I am not a doctor, and I am not a saint.

Maybe not. But you are special, and they can see what I can.

You ask me to pray for lost and ailing family members. Know that the prayers uttered by a non-believer bring nothing but false hope. I am no more special than the Kahn-lea, who are now the true Guardians of the Light – and they are simple people, like you, who believe in a power greater than our understanding. I am a realist.

Ah, but you are no longer blind and that kind of first-hand knowledge is powerful.

I am a woman, an anomaly of genetics, and a person who does believe that we've been lied to. In here, within these lines, these pages and these words, I will bring to light the fears we all face so that we may overcome them together. You have empowered me with your trust, this is all I have to give in return.

The remainder of the article identified several ill or lost souls needing hope, to which Taya asked those who did believe to use the power of their prayers and their faith to help.

Jadis grumbled and snuffled at my immobile hand. My fingers found that spot she favoured as I re-read the article a second time. But she kept nudging and avoiding the scratch, in fact, she nipped one of my fingers with her teeth.

"Hey. What's going on?" I asked her, inspecting my finger. She hadn't broken the skin but it still smarted. She sniffed at the insert that had fallen to the floor. I reached over and picked it up. Turning the small envelope over, my chest ached – and not from my physical injuries.

"Taya."

Jadis lay her paws and head over my left foot. I glanced at the processing date – it had been delayed but only by a few days.

Dez,

You have to stop the madness. Find a way to bring me home or I'll find my own way out.

--

I read it three more times, forcing my brain to look beyond the image of her hand writing and internalise the words themselves.

"Dear Trinity, what I have I done?" My hands trembled. I couldn't look at it, but at the same time I couldn't tear my eyes away from those two simple sentences.

The fear marring her features the day of the incident, when I'd let Gerrund take me away, replayed again and again in my mind.

You have to stop the madness.

My Taya wouldn't have written those words. Something was happening to her – the FOL? The incident amplified? Being cut out of the equation?

"How could I be so stupid?" I cursed.

Jadis sprang up and started pacing the small room. Was my concern for Taya's safety making her stir-crazy? Did I make the wrong choice? Should I have let her come top-side, even if it meant risking her life?

No. This could've worked. *I* blew it.

Other than seeing her at the Consolidating Meeting, we'd had one day together since I'd left.

One day was not enough.

I had to find a way to get back there before she did something she'd regret...

Find a way to bring me home or I'll find my own way out.

A knock at the door made me jump. Jadis gave a long, throaty growl.

"It's okay, girl." I said, but I think it was more to calm my nerves than hers.

She wandered into the small bedroom. *I swear that animal is smarter than some Xannian's I know.* I heard the air cushion groan as she landed on the middle of the bed – her spot. I'd been relegated to either edge. Hurrying to the door, I let the Inquisitor fall to the floor absently bringing the letter with me.

"Yes?" I asked.

The petite, blue-skinned woman on the other side of the door just held up an envelope. I took it, expecting her to leave immediately.

She didn't.

Setting Taya's letter aside on a small table, I ripped the new envelope open and read the letter. I looked up and nodded.

She nodded back and left.

The meet was set.

I shut the door and hurried to change, still clutching the stranger's missive in my hand.

Chapter Twenty-seven
The Great City

Bazdin

L aiviis hit me in the arm and pointed. "There! Did you see it?"

"No. And I already told you, if it's one of the Kahn-lea, they're probably just suspicious."

"I don't buy it." He got quiet for a moment. "Man, that waterfall was something else, but the heat down here is out of touch."

"I thought you were supposed to be a Desert Guide? What's your problem with the heat?" I gingerly peeled my sweat-soaked shirt from my chest, but still winced. The dressing on my stomach had become saturated and stuck to the wound. One minute was all it had taken for that tag-along sausage bug to take advantage of being stuck between my pack and my gut.

What looked like a cave of tall trees ahead promised shade from the direct sunlight. We'd camped at the bottom of the cliff that morning, but neither one of us wanted to wait until Beta went to bed to make the last part of our journey. Besides, we were in the shadow of the cliff or in the caves most of the time anyway, and the heat wasn't an issue – then.

Ever since dusk, the full setting of Alpha and partial setting of Beta, Laiviis jumped at every turn of leaf or unknown crunch. He got on my nerves at the best of times, but this was bloody annoying. Inside the tree line I let the pack slide off my shoulders, and sat down against a giant trunk.

"What are you doing? We're almost there."

"How do you know?" I took a swig from my canteen.

"The map, of course."

"Of course. Why don't you show me? Then maybe I'll consider standing up in less than five minutes."

Laiviis took a half-step back and had that *look* on his face again.

"Then you'd better get comfortable. I haven't trained for this meeka like you."

He dropped his pack the next tree over. "I'll scout out the area. Don't do anything stupid."

"Like what exactly?"

"Fall asleep. It might be some kind of animal stalking us, and I don't need a hysterical fiancée on my hands when I arrive dragging your sorry ass behind."

I leaned my head back and closed my eyes. He made a sound in his throat – I gave a wicked grin as his footsteps left the pebbled path that started not long after a large set of black metal gates.

I opened my eyes. A black man stared back at me from behind the opposite tree.

"Holy Trinity." I scrambled up.

"Peace, Brother." The Jeridan man said. His bright yellow coliths matched the grin on his face. He stepped out from behind the tree, wearing cut off slacks and a short-sleeve T-shirt. The large stick dangling over his back was loaded with silvery fish. "The name's Deltek."

"Bazdin."

"Tamaine's Bazdin?"

"The one and only. Have you been spying on us since the river?"

"No."

"I thought Laiviis was jumpy for no reason."

"Since the falls, yes."

I rolled my eyes.

I heard Laiviis' voice before he stepped from the trees farther up the path. "Hey, Beez," he called, using the pet name to get under my skin. He'd claimed my reaction to what happened after our getaway at the Temple was akin to an adolescent girl's. My screams were entirely justified. "There's a shelter up ah—" He froze.

"Looks like you were right after all, Laiz." I'd reciprocated with an equally childish name to remind him of how he puked after calling *me* a wuss. "Deltek here's been following us since the falls. And why is that, man?"

"I needed to be certain of the two of you. Don't go near that building."

"Why?" Laiviis and I said together.

"It's cursed. Shall we? I'm bringing dinner to the Commons. Join me."

I took another gulp of verrin, then re-shouldered my pack. *Cursed?* Laiviis helped reposition the weight, so I didn't over stretch my arms. He grabbed his bag like it was a damned pack of feathers and we fell into step with Deltek between us.

He rambled on about the canopy of trees being a life-saver down here, what was the best game to hunt, and his favourite flower as dictated by his wife.

"That's all well and good, Deltek, but what's this curse you just mentioned?" I asked.

"I thought you knew?" He stopped, the small building just ahead of us.

"Knew what?" Laiviis asked.

The man ran a hand as black as his closely cropped hair over his head. "The Virus. Didn't Jutaya tell you?"

Laiviis looked confused at first and then pieced something together that I clearly didn't have all the facts about. He sighed. "Oh, that. Yeah, she told us. I take it that's one of the sealed sites not to be disturbed?"

It felt like, in that moment, Deltek should have lowered his head and dug a toe into the path – but he didn't. He looked from Laiviis to me with a steady gaze.

"Too late for that now."

"What do you mean?" Laiviis asked.

"We've had a breach. Everyone's at risk."

"Again, what does that mean?" he asked.

"You're stuck now. Just like us. It's airborne again."

"No. I'll just send Baz with you, and head back by myself without coming any closer."

"If you do that, you risk infecting the folks back home."

"But we haven't been anywhere yet."

"You've been where we've been, and we're probably infected. It's true, you might not be compromised, but do you really want to risk it? Come on. You're here now. Might as well make the best of it. Besides, there's a particular young lady who's been quite dour the past few days… something about having missed a wedding." He gave me a wink.

I nodded.

From what I'd learned about that Virus, Tami was anything but safe here – Jutaya, or Ali, or whoever she was, hadn't told me the whole truth.

"We've got company!" Deltek announced as we approached a hub of action. A series of tables ringed a central fountain which gurgled away. I scanned the faces of the gathering crowd. No Tami, not even her cohort, Jan.

"This is my wife, Lutrice."

I shook her hand. Her eyes widened.

"You're Bazdin, aren't you?" she asked.

I nodded.

She clapped her hands together. "Perfect! Just perfect. Welcome." She reached out and shook Laiviis' hand.

"I'm Laiviis – the Desert Guide assigned to make the first trek out and bring news."

"This is Syvis, he and Lu make sure this place runs smoothly." Deltek continued the introductions.

I shook the big Matin's hand.

"This is Merik—"

A sudden squeal pierced the heavy air.

I dropped the pack and pushed through the crowd. Vaulting over a preparation table, I ignored the rip of pain across my stomach and gathered Tami in my arms. The surrounding applause barely registered, and not because we stood beside the fountain. Her small, perfect hands gripped my sweat-soaked shirt across my back. I ran my hands up the nape of her neck, burying them and my face into her hair.

She slid her chin up my chest to look at me as I moved to rest my forehead against hers. Tears made her pink cheeks glisten.

"Promise me…" My voice husked. "Promise me you'll never leave me again."

She grabbed my face and pulled me down. Our lips found home. Picking her up, I felt her wrap her legs around my waist. I spun her around, relishing the feel of her next to me. I wanted to devour her – re-learn every curve of her body…

Jan coughed.

How did I know? She hadn't made it over to join the group yet, and was the closest person to us. Now was not the time for Tami and me to reconnect. I whispered something half-way coherent about *having an audience.*

She slid down my body to stand on her own two feet. That was a double wince – my gut and my manhood vying for which ached more.

Tami frowned. She knew something wasn't right. I tried to tell her with my eyes that we'd talk later. That seemed to settle her conscience. She gripped my hand and walked with Jan and me over to the others.

"Dinner's almost ready," Lutrice said. "Just let Deltek and I finish up with the fish and we'll dine together and share our stories."

She ushered us over to the community table. Jan brought a pair of jugs over as Merik set the plates and cutlery. They were made of a strange dark metal that reminded me of the buildings surrounding the Common. Laiviis smiled, but sat with a straight back as the Kahn-lea bustled around us.

He studied faces. I was going to ask him about it – I had a feeling it had to do with Deltek's pronouncement about the Virus, but then Tami spoke.

"You came. I can't believe it – you're really here."

I slipped my hand out of her grasp and moved it around her shoulders before twining the fingers of my other hand through hers.

"I've been out of my mind worried. When Dezmind came back alone I was ready to kill him."

"No."

"I didn't. Obviously. He tried to tell me you were fine but I couldn't believe him. Knowing you were out here with a bunch of strangers—"

"I have Jan. We talked about that before I left. Anyway, the Chronicles are real. There's so much to tell you – to show you. But you're here… is it safe to go home again? Jutaya said we couldn't risk it when she left. Maybe the doctors there will be able to come up with a cure?"

I looked into her eyes. The hope that sparkled there was part of what made me love her so much – she always tried to look for the positive in a bad situation… it seemed to be her mantra since the day we met.

Her question had been whispered, but I felt the heavy pause around the table.

"Not yet," I said. "I just got impatient to see you. There's still a lot at stake for the Cause and Dezmind's Spoken Truth. Even if we could be assured that our scientists could cure this thing, there's still the Kronik to deal with. Laiviis'll explain everything about that after dinner."

Her eyes lost focus for a moment. She was such a sensitive soul, I couldn't fathom how she'd managed to survive out here for this long.

Over the course of the next twenty minutes, she and the others at the table spoke of the Generator, the memorial grounds, and the discoveries they'd made while living here. While it all sounded fascinating, what I wondered most about was the one topic not meant for discussion at the table.

The fish were expertly cooked, the water cool and crisp, and the assortment of fruit and vegetables surpassed my expectations. I made a mental note to find Zaith and give her the verrin crystals. The woman was likely too busy to sit down and eat – it's not like she would've been expecting guests anyway.

Lu spoke of her gardens, Syvis described hunting game, and Deltek spoke of fish-whispering and the big-ones that got away. Jan described at length the textile project she and Tami worked on, while Merik talked of their growing library/museum with pride. I had not expected these people to have turned a desolate alien city into a home.

"Wow. That's impressive, Syvis. Do you go hunting every day?" Laiviis asked.

"Most afternoons, some mornings, depending on the prey. If I manage to take down something large, it needs to be bled properly and the meat aged. Merik has passed me a few good hunting books."

Deltek added, "Don't be too impressed, now. What he's not telling you is that Zaith would tell him to get lost at first – preferably as far away as possible from where she was hunting. He was like a giant in a crystal shop: whenever he moved things crashed!" Everyone laughed. Syvis even blushed a bit.

"Speaking of Zaith," Laiviis said. "When do we get to meet her? I noticed we were missing a couple people tonight."

Suddenly everyone managed to stuff a large forkful of food in their mouths. Cutlery clinked and bodies shifted.

Syvis gave a loud sigh, but it was Lu who spoke.

"She and Raylan are *ill*."

Her emphasis on the word ill weighed heavily on every person seated at that long table. She took a sip of her water.

"During a particularly aggressive storm, Raylan broke protocol and entered a sealed dwelling," Syvis explained. *The cursed dome.* "Zaith monitored him closely – closer than any of us – but there's no being careful with this thing. She'd been battling stage one for some time before we even knew – before she even realised," he said.

"She blamed herself for not stopping Ray," Lu said. "She felt she owed it to herself and Jutaya to find a cure – at any cost." The others nodded and shook their heads, alternately agreeing and despairing over this woman's choices.

"I take it she failed," I said evenly.

"No." Merik said.

"Then, I don't understand," Laiviis cut in. "If you know how to stop the Virus why don't you?"

"No one can read the formula."

This time, only the bubbling of the fountain echoed off the nearby buildings as everyone sat silently.

"Holy Trinity!" Tami shouted.

I looked at her.

"Den." She grabbed both my shoulders and shook me. "You took chemistry!"

The Kahn-lea burst into excited babble. Merik banged his cup on the metal table for attention.

"Don't," he warned his group. They sobered fast.

"Don't what?" I asked.

"Don't get your hopes up," he clarified. "How much chemistry do you know?"

"Enough to be able to do my job, but I didn't major in it," I said, and looked at Tami. "I took that job with pharmaceutical regulatory affairs I told you about… wanted to make sure we had money coming in before the wedding."

"So, you're not a doctor?" Lu asked. I shook my head. "Or a scientist?"

"No."

"What does a regulatory affairs person do, then?"

"It's the business side of pharmaceuticals – medicines to be approved for mass use." The way these people looked at me like a gift of the Trinity made my skin crawl. "But I went through for Business Administration – not medicine." Merik was the only one managing to keep a clear head.

"Wait," he advised the others and reminded them. "There are strange symbols we can't decipher and the missing ingredient." He turned to me. "Would you take a look at the journal and see what you can make of it? In the morning, that is? No pressure." *No pressure? Yeah, right.*

"Of course. How can I not?"

Tami pulled me into her little house with a sharp tug. I noticed Jan shake her head and smile as she dragged her sleeping mat over to the library. There was no door, but we were far enough away and the place was dressed with enough shadows to ensure our privacy.

She stripped off her blouse and attacked the buttons on my shirt.

"I don't care if we're not married," she said.

I laughed, "But we are."

"What?" Her fingers paused half-way down. Her eyes locked onto mine.

"I kept hoping you'd make it home in time… I didn't retract the papers."

"So, we got married?"

"Two days ago – officially." A piercing spark from Gamma reflected in her eye. She ripped the rest of my shirt off, making the loss of buttons totally worth it. She pushed me down to the mat. I grimaced as she straddled me. Her fingers deftly found the patch of gauze on my stomach.

"Dear Zola, what happened!" her small digits tried to pry up the large bandage.

"No. Leave it, Tam."

"What happened?" she leaned down and kissed the tender skin pulled taut all around the outside of the dressing.

My back arched. I groaned.

"Am I hurting you?" she pulled back.

"Hell no." I rasped, pulling her down on top of me with a kiss.

Chapter Twenty-eight
I'm Not a Doctor

Bazdin

Tami started walking away even before our lips parted.

"Hey," I said. "You can't take me with you."

"Who says I can't," she laughed. Zola, I missed that sound. But today it was double-edged.

"Merik wants me to look at that stuff. So, unless you want to hang out in the library while we talk shop…"

Her face shone at the mention of me *trying* to help find the cure.

"No, no. I've got clothes to make. I'll leave you to it." She flashed me that same crazed smile she'd used when talking about the Spoken Truth, only this time my intestines knotted up twice as bad. Somehow, I knew I was going to let her down – let them all down.

I walked across the Commons to the library with a roll of gauze, tape, and a long piece of some plant Laiviis picked up in the Deserts. The air was already thick with the signature moist heat of the south, but at least there was a breeze today. The rustle of the leaves high up in the canopy mingled with foreign bird calls and localised activity.

Everyone had a job to do – even Laiviis. Lutrice had convinced him to help transfer Syvis' crude maps of the City to the paper supplies he'd brought along.

"I'd knock if there was a door," I said, entering the spacious dwelling packed with artefacts and thin metal books.

"No need. Come on in." Merik sat behind a large metal desk decorated with a kind of bevelled lattice-work at the front. Numerous items gave the table that scattered-artesian look, but directly centre, extreme organisation ruled. He glanced up from the book lying open in front of him.

"What's with the supplies?" he asked.

"I need a favour before we start. I couldn't ask Tami – it would kill her to see."

"See what?"

I lifted up the front of my shirt to expose the dressing beneath. The large swath of gauze Laiviis had used initially was now tinged pink with dried blood and sweat.

"Things get a little exciting on the trip down?" he asked.

"You could say that."

"What did you have in mind?"

I set the supplies on the corner of his desk and slipped my T-shirt over my head.

"Let me sit in your chair where I can grip the back while you rip off the bandage."

"And underneath?"

"It looks worse than it is. Try not to puke." I snickered. He smiled and moved his chair to the centre of the room. I got into position and used my shirt to wrap my hands together behind the chair-back.

He picked at an edge. The medical tape felt like it fused to my skin. I ground my molars.

"Are you sure you want me to just rip it off? It's not going to tear into your wound is it?"

"Shouldn't. Laiviis made it extra-large."

He nodded. "You'll have to tell me how this happened. I'm collecting tales of the Deserts for my book of poems."

"It's really a story of dual-stupiti – Ahhh!"

He tore the gauze away.

"Ah, ha – wha! Damn, man." I said the last through gritted teeth. Merik just stared at the hole in my stomach. The used bandage fluttered between his finger and thumb. It wasn't actually a hole, but the giant white sausage-creature had certainly intended it to be.

"We figured the lining of the creature's lower body used some kind of acid to breakdown the tissue – to help it eat or digest better. We rinsed it out good but it might need another go… looks worse than it did."

"You should know that the puss and irritated redness around the edges means it's infected. Look, that plant extract is great for surface stuff and preventing scars, but we've got something better." He walked backwards out the door, still looking at my mangled gut.

"I'll get what you need. Let it breathe for a bit." And he was gone.

"Fantastic," I muttered.

The air stung the open wound, but I supposed giving my body time to make a scab was a good way to go… especially since we had a lot of time on our hands all of a sudden – or maybe not, all things considered.

Leaning my head against the high back of the chair I didn't exactly doze, since that would require comfort, but I did let my mind wander. Sleep evaded me last night. Holding Tami again was like a dream I knew would turn into a nightmare. Maybe it already had.

"You still awake?" Merik whispered.

"Yeah." I opened my eyes but looked up at the ceiling.

"This'll hurt."

"Yup. Do it."

"Can I persuade you to move outside?"

I lifted my head up. "Oh. Right."

I grabbed the chair as I sat and kind of waddled through the door. No one else was around – or so I hoped. I plunked myself down again.

"Water first. We'll let you air dry while we look at the journal. Then I'll put the salve on and tape you up again. I highly suggest you spend tomorrow shirtless."

"Sure thing, Doc."

"I'm not a doctor," he said holding a small metal bowl of water and a rag.

"Neither am I."

I left the weight of those words between us until the cold water forced me to cry out. It felt like the better part of the morning passed as the poet tortured me for my own good. But he was right. The wound was infected and this had to be done.

He left me basking in the growing heat of the day far longer than I suspect was necessary – maybe he was hoping for a clearer mind. I was trying to find the right words to let him down easy.

He walked out of the library, grabbed a stool from the closest prep station and sat beside me. Metallic pages clicked as he flipped to a particular place in the journal.

"Let's start here."

I unravelled my hands from behind the chair and brought them around to hold the book. Merik shook my shirt and laid it out nearby.

"What am I looking at?"

"This is where the science starts – not to say that everything up to this point isn't scientific, but it's a list of tried and failed methods and ingredients. The new list of ingredients comes after these, I don't know, equations?"

"I don't understand any of it. It's no language I've ever studied."

"Here." He placed a small paper notebook in my other hand – a cipher of sorts. "The Dakturian alphabet. Above this arrow is NaCl."

The periodic table of elements jumped to the front of my mind. "That's salt."

"Really? I had no idea. I'm familiar with H_2O, so I'm guessing he's getting at saltwater?"

"I suppose. You've read the thing," I said.

"What about this one? Fe?"

"Iron."

"And this one?"

"Magnesium."

It was a list of common elements, all under the saltwater heading: sodium, calcium, magnesium, potassium, chlorine, sulphur and phosphorus; the micronutrients included iodine, iron, zinc, copper, selenium, molybdenum, fluoride, manganese, boron, nickel and cobalt.

I pointed to several notations as I got used to the basic alphabet. "$C_{16}H_{18}N_2O_5S$ - This is a key organic acid found in many pharmaceuticals. This one is more cutting edge, or so the regulatory body says." I couldn't believe how basic this stuff was – well, basic to someone who knew chemistry, that is.

"And this last one?" Merik asked.

I didn't recognise the element. It appeared to have an atomic number and several other identifying factors, but nothing matched the known periodic table or any formula I'd seen before.

"I don't know."

And there it was – the wall I knew we'd slam into eventually.

"Can you guess at anything? It's significance? How it relates to the other elements you identified…"

"Right now, Merik, it's just a bunch of numbers and letters. Do you have a translation of the rest of the book? Maybe something will pop if I can read it myself."

He flipped to the back of the note book. I closed the metal book and started reading.

At the end of a very long hour I had to swallow the hope threatening to suffocate me. I turned to Merik, who skimmed through other books in his collection – close enough to answer any questions, but far enough to give me space to think.

"I think I've found something."

Three hours later, the soles of my feet burned as I stood on a white sandy beach listening to waves crash against rock outcroppings. The blisters on my heels itched and the small particles of sand only made the feeling worse.

Laiviis and the entire Kahn-lea stood with me – those who were still healthy that is. Lutrice passed out one set of diver's goggles for each pair, something they'd apparently brought along with them for travelling in the Deserts. Laiviis and I had used the more inferior carpentry glasses available from the UGC.

Tami was captivated by the shells and quartz-like rocks that made up most of the beach sand.

"How much of the coastline have you mapped?" I asked Syvis.

"Just here. I never thought we'd bother with the place. You're sure this is where the journal said to look?"

"The journal is anything but direct," Merik said. "But considering the new information Bazdin revealed, it only makes sense that the plant described is part of one of the reefs out there."

"But without diving suits we'll be exposed," Jan reasoned. That fact made me nervous, too. Xannian's weren't built to withstand seawater. Small amounts were mostly harmless, but to submerge a body in the stuff was tantamount to suicide.

"Trust me," Merik said. "Zaith looked everywhere – except here." The divided rope they'd used as a safety line to cross the Deserts was modified to work for pairs in the water.

"The searcher will have the mask and your buddy will count your time. Two tugs means come up. One hard yank means trouble," Laiviis instructed.

He'd admitted to never having been underwater before, having lived his whole life underground. But he was the only one of us with tactical training.

"Okay, Syvis, you and I will search the outer reef. The potential current is less likely to pull us off course than anyone else here. Deltek, Lutrice you take the inner left side. Merik, you and Jan the inner right. Tamaine can swap with anyone who feels lightheaded before time is up."

I felt the bandage on my stomach. I wanted to help but if me needing to stay dry meant Tami stayed with me, I was fine with that.

"Remember, it'll look reddish-brown and like a long, scalloped leaf," Merik said, then he looked skyward as if reciting some prayer to the Sun Gods.

Tami and I sat along the tree line next to a travel keg of water and the supply pack as the others waded out along the reef, wearing nothing but their under clothes and shoes. Tamaine shuddered. She looped her arm through mine, drawing close even in the heat of the afternoon.

"They should be fine, Tami. We're taking every possible precaution."

"I know. I just never thought I'd watch anyone willingly walk into the sea."

I knew horror stories of the Nine Seas Massacre played at the edges of her thoughts. None of us escaped that memory – even if it wasn't our own.

As everyone got to their marks along the reef about the same time, Tami counted under her breath.

Ten minutes.

That was their window for today. We'd have to come back tomorrow to search again if it proved too difficult without special gear – gear we desperately needed but didn't have.

"Let's have the ceremony here," I said.

"What?"

I turned to look at her. "It's not that we won't have one when we get back home, but that might not be for, well – I don't know. But I get the impression it'll be a long time. So, let's celebrate with your new friends. Besides, Jan is here so she can help you with the planning again."

Tami launched herself at me so fast I lost my balance and we landed in the grasses just above the beach. Hearing her laughter bubble out like that healed so many wounds.

Ten minutes later, everyone's dive partner resurfaced – or almost everyone. Neither Laiviis nor Syvis could be seen. Tami and I scrambled over to the shoreline. Deltek and Merik linked safety lines as the women walked through the waist deep waters along the top of the reef, before submerging to swim the remaining yards back to shore.

Two more minutes passed.

The guys shivered, rubbing their arms as they patrolled the reef.

"You're going into shock!" I yelled. "Get out of the water!" They waved away my caution.

"Deltek, Merik. Get back here now!" Lu screamed, her usual composure shattered.

Then both men went under at the same time.

Lu shrieked.

The girls wrapped their arms around her. A large burst of bubbles broke the surface of the bright blue water. Four men emerged using each other as support as they waded back to land. The women ran over to meet them. I walked.

"We found it." Syvis said through chattering teeth. The group moved as one toward the keg of water and the shade of the trees.

"Need a knife," Laiviis pushed past blue lips. His red-rimmed eyes looked right at me.

Tami and I pulled cups from the pack and passed out water to everyone. Great gulps filled the wordless space between us. The next round went to rinsing the saltwater off their bodies. Tami helped Syvis and I helped Laiviis.

"You couldn't pull the plant out?" I asked.

He shook his head. His eyes wandered, losing focus. I splashed a cup of water in his face. He blinked and looked at me – eyes clearer than before.

"Do that again—"

"Okay." I splashed him with another cup and laughed as he sputtered, wiping the residual drops over his hair, neck and arms.

"That's not what I meant and you know it, Beez."

"Suck it up, Laiz."

"We need to go back in," Syvis said.

All the joking and bathing stopped.

"We'll wait until tomorrow. Like we planned," Lu said.

A strange darkness shadowed Syvis' eyes. I'd seen that look in the mirror every morning since Dezmind returned without Tami.

"Another thirty hours could cost lives," he said.

"So could another soaking in that ocean. You're not thinking straight," Laiviis said.

"I'll go," I said.

"No." Tami grabbed my arm, spilling a cup of water. "You're injured. You'll end up in a sea-coma from sodium shock." She paused. "I'll go."

"Definitely not," I said, but she was already rubbing the sand from her feet and pulling on one of her boots. I grabbed the other one.

"Den." She used that tone on me. I hated it. I knew I was acting childish, but it was bad enough I might lose her to some alien Virus and now this? "I'll be fine. They can tell me where to look. I'll go straight down, cut the leaves free and come right back up."

I sighed. It was clear someone had to do it and I would be useless helping anyone if I was in a coma.

"Fine. But I'll be your anchor."

"I can do that," Deltek offered.

"No. The water won't reach higher than my hips out there and the swim across to the reef will be short. When we get back I'll wash out the wound and let it air dry on the walk back."

Lu grabbed Deltek's goggles and passed them to Tami as Laiviis detailed where to find the underwater plant. It was quite low, but one good breath to find the right spot and then one return breath should be all she needed to finish the task. He handed her his knife and nodded.

Tami waded into the water. Laiviis walked up beside me but, before he could get a word out, I stole his goggles and plunged in after Tamaine. As I swam the few strides it took to reach the reef, I slipped the goggles over my chin, letting them rest around my neck.

Tami pulled up beside me. We both had small scratches on our hands and knees. The reef was sharp. I hadn't noticed any abrasions on the others but then, I hadn't been looking for them either.

"Over here." She grabbed my hand and we manoeuvred single file along the crest of the reef until a bright orange plant that looked like thick hair signalled we were in the right place. I connected our safety lines. We adjusted our goggles. She shook her head at me when she saw I had a pair.

"I'll be fine." She waved with Laiviis' small knife in her hand, found her mark and dove in. I started counting. A minute and a half later, she resurfaced. Her blonde-tipped black hair floated around her shoulders as she tred water.

"Found it. I'll be right back." She took another breath and dove down.

I kept counting. My side cramped – it felt like miniature spikes poking holes in my stomach. The saltwater had soaked through the dressing. I gritted my teeth and kept counting.

Two minutes later, Tami's pink form broke through the surface of the water. She gasped for air, but held up a handful of long, red leaves. I held my hand down to her. She grabbed it and used it for leverage to walk up to the top of the reef.

"Take these." She shoved the leaves and the knife each into one of my hands and disconnected the safety rope. I opened my mouth to complain, but the bright red welt around her tiny waist said it all. She walked along the reef toward the beach. I knelt to slide the now-closed knife into my boot.

The ground rumbled and shook. An earthquake? We hadn't had one of those in several weeks.

A splash slicked the air.

The Kahn-lea broke out shouting and shrieking.

I looked around.

Tami's arms flailed some yards away; the current pulling her under.

I hesitated...

Shoving the goggles up over my eyes, I dove in. They slammed back down around my neck. I couldn't see anything. My stomach spasmed. I lost my breath. The boots weighed me down as I struggled to breach the surface.

Two sets of hands grabbed hold of my arms. Another pair pried my fist open just as the safety line pulled taut and hauled me out of the water.

Chapter Twenty-nine
No Right Words

Taya

D^{ez,}

The watch you gave me works perfectly fine and yet I find myself losing track of time… I ask myself less and less these days why it is that you're not writing anymore, why it is that you don't seem to have time for me, for us.

Then I hear the voice of reason and it isn't my own, it's yours –

"This is bigger than all of us."

"Sacrifices have to be made."

"Just because I'm not there doesn't mean I'm not thinking about you."

But when those words have to be pulled from an eight-week-old memory, where the sight of you giving up on me – on us – as your reaching hand falls and you let the general walk you farther and farther away from me, those words that once consoled and held a logic I thought I understood, slip away from me.

Where are you?

Why haven't you written?

I need that sense of calm, of home you brought to me even before we knew what we meant to each other...

I've made a decision. I'm going to find that sense of peace again, even if it means doing something I shouldn't.

T

I slipped the letter into an envelope. The alarm in the bedroom beeped. I set the letter on the edge of the breakfast bar, away from the growing disaster of letters from the FOL, and rushed into my room to turn the buzzer off.

Today marked the beginning of my second outing into the caverns. I had convinced Gerrund to give me an additional thirty hours to explore, before needing to check in.

A hard knock sounded.

Mardel.

I grabbed my gear leaning against the back of the couch, and ran for the door.

Chapter Thirty

Secrets

Dezmind

Another cramp pinned my leg to the door of the small rental hover-rider. Thank Zola I sat parked two side streets from the Third Magistrate's municipal building.

I bashed my elbow against the window and dropped the ends of my tie. I opened the pane, rubbed my leg, picked up the ends of the charcoal-flecked black tie – my insurance policy – finished straightening it and felt for the hidden chip within the folds of the knot. I tucked a pamphlet into my inside jacket pocket and got out of the rider.

I hated this suit, but it was the only one I had that went with the tie, hat and sunglasses. I left my briefcase in the rider, even though it would complement the attire better. The pale orange-red button-up shirt was my only pop-of colour. I hated looking washed out, and hoped the splash wouldn't draw any undue attention.

Slipping into the back entrance of the nearest building, I jogged down the metal staircase to the basement. *Third door on the left.* Scanning each door I passed, I looked for the signature scratches, just in case I remembered wrong. They were right where they should be, so I slipped behind the battered door and down another set of steps to the sub-basement.

Luckily, we were still in the hot season and the large pipes and conduit I passed were chill to the touch – in the cool season this place would be a steam bath, and a cesspit of city stench. It wasn't uncommon in these older sectors to find adjoining sub-basements. It saved on building costs, among other things.

The faded yellow stairs appeared without warning as I rushed past. Backtracking a few steps, I went up and punched in my *guest* code. The anti-chamber beyond reminded me of a few spy books I'd read in my youth.

Several lone red dots flickered behind dark reflective panelling. I took off my jacket, set it on a hook that emerged from the wall, and placed my hat, glasses and access card for my rental in an open compartment on the other side of the far wall. A panel slid up revealing two security officers on the other side.

They beckoned.

I walked forward.

The shorter guy pressed something on the wall and returned my things to me. The other guy, around my height, motioned for me to follow him. As we waited at a small bank of elevators down a hall no one used on a regular basis, I put my sunglasses away and placed my hat under my arm. The steel doors opened into a burgundy velvet-lined and tufted box. We stepped in and the gentle sounds of water trickling along a stream filled the room with white noise.

The lift stopped at the top – the twenty-fifth floor. My escort brought me to the reception area, spoke to one of three administrative assistants and then nodded for me to go in. The high ceiling of this floor allowed for two spectacular wooden doors to send a clear message. I pushed one open and walked in. My guard remained outside.

I stepped forward and extended my hand to Magistrate Finwek. Another guard blocked me.

"Arms up please, Mr. Lisle," she said, extending a hand-held NN*EMP*. I obliged but looked at Finwek.

"This isn't necessary. Your men scanned me on the way in."

"You can never be too careful these days," he said, as if everyone who walked through those doors got the same treatment. But today was special... we both knew that. When he finally called off his Danieth guard dog, I straightened my tie and ran my thumb over the brail label on the underside by the knot, activating the small recording device before shaking hands with the man in front of me.

"Come, sit. We have much to discuss," Finwek said.

He led me over to a large sweeping couch, past an oversized desk completely cleared of tablets or e-files. It said something that he brought me to the plush sofa, rather than the imposing meeting table on the opposite side of the room.

I smiled my appreciation. Two glasses of iced verrin rested strategically on the smoky glass-topped table.

We sat.

He sipped.

I didn't.

"If I may?" I indicated my inner pocket.

He nodded and set down his drink.

I passed him the blue walking pamphlet.

He glanced at it as I spoke. "This is the information I've been handing out on my Rally Walks. Nothing in it is inflammatory toward the Kronik, or my race."

"Yes, I see. You offer a lot of speculation and pose some interesting questions." He looked up at me and tossed the booklet onto the table. "But there's nothing in there I haven't already heard."

"I want you to feel comfortable knowing that. It's not my goal to raise an army of Commoners against the Kronik. I want to inform people. To make the government accountable. That's the only way we're going to heal our world."

"Something tells me that you're implying there's more than one wound that needs tending – that this isn't just about stopping the earthquakes and the climate change."

"Nothing is ever simple, Magistrate. And if I could, I'd like to thank you for agreeing to meet with me today. I know how this might look to the wrong set of eyes, and I appreciate your due caution."

"I'm glad you understand. I think it's important to be in the know, and right now it seems like my Sectors Keepers and the average citizen know more than I do. I need you to change that, Mr. Lisle."

"Please, call me Dezmind."

He nodded, then leaned back as if waiting to be entertained. This wasn't a good sign, but I couldn't let that detract from the purpose of my visit.

"Gamma is not a natural solar body."

He crossed his arms.

"It's a nuclear device that's been left degrading in orbit for more than two thousand years."

"Why should I believe you?"

"I'm not asking you to."

He leaned forward, frowning.

"Our satellites gather inexplicable data on every solar system within our reach. For centuries, our scientists have debated what exactly Gamma is because of bizarre celestial phenomena. I *guarantee* that if you're able to acquire un-redacted copies of those records, you will see just how increasingly unstable Gamma has been."

"And how does that help you?"

"Two months ago, the Kahn-lea and I re-initiated a photon particle Generator perfectly aligned to the cresting of Gamma. Since then, the super-quakes have stopped, and the protective membrane around this regenerative nuclear device is starting to heal – that means a noticeable difference in astronomical readings. My physical proof lies hundreds of miles across the barren Deserts in a Great

Alien City – proof that will be brought back here. But until then, I urge you to trust your own judgement and the evidence of your own eyes... You'll find the Kronik have been lying to you."

"And what do you want out of all this, Dezmind? You know you're not the first Xannian to go looking for the truth. The last time this happened you were but a small boy I'd wager."

"Three, actually. Regardless, all I ask is for your neutrality... at the very least. Allow your constituents to continue to learn of the truth just as you are. We both know that the last time a group of radicals tried to change minds by force, they paid the highest price. This is simply about knowing and understanding. Time will take care of the rest."

Finwek leaned his arms over his knees and clasped his hands together.

"It takes time and resources, not to mention a certain covert nature to acquire the proof you say is already available. When the people know the truth, what do you think will happen if not another government sanctioned massacre?"

"If enough people know the truth, the only action the Kronik can take will be to own up to its mistakes, or crumble under the will of the people. If nothing else, the Massacre taught us that much."

"And what do you see rising from the ashes should the Great fall? What will happen to those of us who remain... neutral, as you say? Will we stumble and impale ourselves, too? I need assurances, boy."

As any politician would.

"The only people getting scabbed knees here would be those insisting that secrets and lies prevail. I can assure you that, should you allow the truth to be spoken, you will be honoured."

He stood.

I followed suit, concerned with his abrupt action.

I held out my hand and he grasped it.

"What you speak of is very compelling. I will give it much consideration."

"I appreciate that, Magistrate. Should you feel it warranted, a note to your peers mentioning the constructive nature of our talk would do much to help bring awareness to the Spoken Truth."

His grip tightened along with his smile. The orange-skinned guard stepped forward, reaching for something behind her.

I swallowed.

Had I said too much?

Chapter Thirty-one
Cause & Effect

Taya

Awall of clear crystal icicles reminded me of the falls near Augitmein, the Alien City. They looked alive, just frozen in a nano-second's breath. I kept glancing at the formation as I manoeuvred around columns and various sized stalagmites. I couldn't help but think the water would come rushing down in the next moment. Of course, it didn't.

After sixty-one hours of exploration, well, minus three for sleep, it pained me to compare the sparkle and majesty of these caverns to the empty tunnel I'd helped build shops in only days before. Even the officially explored but unexcavated tunnels lacked the presence of these masterpieces.

But thoughts of construction work only made Gelden and that damned article come to mind. I couldn't tell if writing it had worked, since I was only in town for a day to restock before heading back to the outer tunnels. I'd noticed my mail piling up again and asked Gel to collect it for me while I was working. I think he was just glad I was finally addressing the problem head on – like I should have from the start. The difficulty was that lack of sleep at the time, also meant lack of reasoning. Still, the incident never should have happened. I guess the article was my penance.

I scanned the surrounding cavern with the light-tube. The dance of silver and gold mixed with crimson and jade made me smile. At least I could still appreciate the simple things in life.

I was close. My internal tracker, my gut, had been giving me warnings for the past twenty minutes. Gerrund expected me back on time to check in and go over my findings. His solution to Mardel's concerns for me being out here alone was to schedule regular updates – that way, if I missed one, they knew to send a search team out for me.

It took me two days to get this far but I knew the return trip would be faster. My first time out here told me that much, even in the dark. It was easier to go back over pre-explored ground than it was to learn new terrain. Besides, I wouldn't need to go down the side tunnels that I'd already deemed useless – for both his cause and my own.

Two murky holes opened up before me – branch lines, or so I'd taken to calling them. The tunnel opening on the right stood at twice my height, with only a few columns blocking the way. The opening on the left narrowed and dipped to nearly half my height. A maze of straws and slender columns attempted to block my path.

I knew I should go to the right, but Gerrund be damned – I needed to go left. I was close to solving his surface access problem, but I couldn't afford to complete *that* mission until I finished my own. Between Zaith and Gerrund illuminating the truth of my past, my recent adventures on the surface, and Jak's manipulative mental digging, I could no longer ignore the truth of my past. There were things I needed to know... wrongs to be righted.

Slipping the large pack from my shoulders, I leaned it against the base of several straws and slid past two narrow, glistening columns. I held my last tube-light straight out to my right, illuminating the pale pink and orange straws ahead. I preferred their soft light instead of the cold, piercing rays from the electric torches. It meant I needed to carry more of them with me, since I couldn't recharge them, but the extra weight hadn't been a bother.

Wending around a cluster of pearl-like straws, my canteen snagged and cracked a few. Small rocks pelted me from above as the shattered feature retaliated against the blow.

I shook rock dust off my capped head before gingerly removing the strap from around my neck. I held the canteen away from my body in my left hand and continued through the labyrinth.

The dim light from the tube showed layers of sharp rock-teeth. The ground moulded to small hills at the base of each stalagmite. My ankle rolled. I dropped the light-tube and caught my balance on the side of a stalactite ready to knock me senseless.

I bent down and reached for the light where it had rolled to in the new chamber. *Too far.* But at least it showed a larger space beyond this labyrinth. Sliding between two columns, the wet rock scraped my cheek and crumbled at my chest and rear. My right foot found level ground. I hopped on it to reach the light. My left foot caught at the base of the formation. I slammed down on my hands wrenching my left knee.

"Ahhuhh!" I yelled. My foot jammed in place. Gathering myself up close to the base of the columns, I pushed back.

"Ouch!"

My foot dislodged. Scrambling to hug the nearest column, I leveraged myself back up to ease my leg from the teeth. My left leg dangled at an odd angle. I cursed repeatedly.

I let go of the column to check the damage with my hands through the fabric of my pant and cracked my head on the stone I'd just been hugging.

"Come on!" I shouted, and hopped back to distance myself from the teeth. My heel landed on the round housing of the light tube. The cylinder shifted then smashed. I swung my arms to catch my balance, landing on my left foot which collapsed under me.

I fell back… and back… and back.

My head hit a wall a nano-second before my body plunged into briny water. I swallowed a mouthful and gagged. Hitting bottom, I scooped my right leg under me and shot up out of the liquid gasping and coughing. My lungs ached as I hacked out the liquid death – saltwater.

I opened my eyes once my haggard breaths evened out.

The tube-light was out. I let my eyes adjust to the dark. Unlike the Desert caverns, these caves had no natural source of light – it was darker than twilight. I wiped residual drops from my face. My eyes ached from contact with the saltwater. I felt them dilate but I still couldn't see.

The water soaked me up to my waist, but at least the ground remained level. I felt for the wall I'd connected with on my way down and found it. I traced its slimy side all around until instinct told me I was back where I started.

"A well. Swell." I spit more of the brine from my mouth, then looked straight up. It took longer than I'd hoped, but my eyes did adjust, giving me a vague sense of distance and a ceiling high above pocked with stalactites. The contours were shades of grey and black. Usually I had tonal value from midnight blues and deep purples, too, but not here, not without the light-tubes.

I shivered. I had ten minutes to find a way out. The icy water numbed my wrenched knee. It couldn't stay dislocated or I'd die down here. I shifted around the circumference of the well again, this time feeling with my boot for just the right spot.

Nothing.

I inhaled a raspy breath, coughed, and then circled it again, lifting the boot of my sore leg higher this time.

There it was. A nook big enough to jam the toe of my boot into.

Wedging my foot into the space, I repositioned my knee with my hands and pushed off from the wall.

I shrieked.

But everything was straight again... back where it was supposed to be. I leaned against the wall of the well and wept. This wasn't the first time I had a joint out of socket, but it was the worst.

As the haze in my head cleared and it no longer hurt to breathe, I realised my brain had been working without me – thank Zola. But it meant waiting, patiently, for my shirt to dry. If I was going to get out of here, I'd need to use my back as leverage against a slimy, wet wall – and an equally wet shirt would not provide the friction I'd need.

I only had five minutes left – or did I? I shivered, sure, but I was fairly certain that was from the cold and not sodium-shock. No Xannian could last more than ten minutes in the sea – it was liquid poison.

But I'm not like everyone else. Being half-Talian also meant some small amount of Dakturian DNA resided in my genome. Dezmind had healed from exhaustion and dehydration in record time and I'd never been sick or injured for long... I could only hope that the alien DNA would give me at least an extra ten minutes. I needed every last one to dry out and re-freeze my knee. I couldn't afford to rip a section of my pant leg off to act as a tenser-bandage – it would mean re-submerging myself. I'd have to concentrate on first aid later.

The problem was my Xannian DNA did not go well with the briny water, and I lost track of time. It could have been ten minutes, twenty minutes or two minutes later – all I knew was that I couldn't trust myself anymore. If I wasn't careful, the overload of sodium could cause muscle atrophy or worse – brain damage.

The moment I shifted, spikes of cold attacked my body, the strange stasis now gone. I knocked my bad knee against the wall. Nothing. Had my prayer worked, or was it just dumb-luck?

Regardless, I positioned myself in the middle of the well, lifted my good leg up to the sheer, slimy wall and planted my foot, keeping my leg mostly parallel with the water. I hopped back a bit to straighten out my elevated leg and spread my arms for balance.

Gradually, so as not to disturb the water and splash it up onto the walls, I leaned the back of my neck, and the now mostly-dry shoulders of my shirt, against the far side. Placing my palms against the wall just above my shoulders, as if I were about to do a headstand, I heaved my sore leg from the swill and jammed it against the far wall.

I could already feel my hands slip. The raised portion of the scars on my palms ached in recognition of past abuse. Scuffing my feet a few inches at a time, I did a star-crawl up the well.

Nearly two feet from the top, my knee wobbled and gave out. My hands slipped and scraped against the side. My muscles blazed with anger and overuse and I still didn't have an exit strategy.

I had to keep going – all the way to the top. Locking my bad knee, I shoved my foot against the wall and skimmed up another few inches... and another.

With my pounding head anchored on the rim of the well, I popped my left arm and then shoulder up over the edge before pushing with my right foot, using my last ounce of strength.

Turning like a cat I ended up half-on, half-off the edge of the well lying on my stomach. My body shivered and shook. *I need my pack... my thermal blanket.* I dragged myself away from the hole in the ground. My arm sliced open on a shard of the damaged light-tube.

Without warning, my teeth chattering and mild shivering broke into spasms. My body jolted and pitched without mercy. I bit my tongue and tasted blood. The sodium-shock found and claimed me. Seconds before I blacked out, my hand bumped into something cold but supple... a leather strap... my canteen.

Chapter Thirty-two
Unheard Pleas

Dezmind

*D*earest Ali,

I can't believe it's been twelve days since I last saw you. It breaks my heart that the only letter I've received is a desperate plea for help. Every time I find a moment to get away, business keeps me chained to my desk, to my work — and as much as I know you need me right now, things so much bigger than either of us need tending to.

Know that I have not forgotten or forsaken you. I lie awake at night hearing you chastise me, and wake in the morning with the taste of you on my lips — however brief. It is those moments I cling to, even more so since receiving your letter.

I'm told your new job is fruitful, and your insights are more than helpful with the company. I still worry though — a quick word from you would calm my racing thoughts.

Jadis is still sulking over you being gone. She let me pet her for a while the other day when I read your new column in the paper — it's like she knew some part of you was close to both of us.

Some good news: in the wake of my disastrous Walk, I'm healing well and making new friends. I can't wait to tell you more at the gathering next week… can't wait to see you again — hold you in my arms at our own little after-party… I'll come as soon as I can.

Counting the days,

DL

Chapter Thirty-three
Breaking Point

Taya

My teeth chatter. I can't stop shaking as bucket after bucket of brine water crash over my head – the salt soaks into the slices on my wrists and ankles. His laughter alternates with clapping, all distorted: laugh, clap, clap, laugh, laugh, clap, laugh, clap, clap, clap. His baritone rattles my chest as the claps echo in the concrete and metallic room.

Hot water, cold water, odd tasting water striking me like a whip. A sharp prick on my neck brings waves of dizziness. A light flashes in the dark above in code: Can I trust you?

I shake my head to rid myself of excess water and the haze shrouding my brain.

Then I can't save you.

"No!" I scream. "That's not what I meant!"

Left alone in the cold darkness, the laughter and clapping tick on irregularly. I look at my wrist as a mechanical watch spins its glowing hands around and around. Ticking blends with the clapping and the laughing. I smash my arms against the floor repeatedly.

Just as the sound stops, a hand grabs my shoulder…

I jolted straight up in bed and bashed my head into someone.

"Ouch. Jeeze, Dalla – it's just me."

I opened my eyes. The room tilted, and not from the crack on the head. "What are you? Where am..."

Gelden held one hand over a bloody nose and the other over my wrist on the hand flattened to the bedside table. The glass particles from the broken watch face Dez had given me bit into my palm. My breathing, made irregular from the dream, came in rasps.

I hope that saltwater didn't cause any permanent damage...

Images flashed behind my eyes: waking on the cold ground, shivering but managing to drink from my canteen; nearly impaling myself on stalagmites as I half-staggered, half-crawled back to the explored caverns; fifteen hours of stumbling, blacking out and waking to a pounding head; Mardel carrying me over his shoulder as I begged not to be taken to the hospital – begged him not to tell Gerrund...

"Well it's about time." The man himself stepped out of the shadows from the corner of my bedroom.

"How long?" I croaked.

"Nearly two days. What the hell happened out there?" he snapped.

"Back off, Gerrund," Gel said.

Gerrund crossed his arms.

Gelden let go of my wrist and removed his arm from across my chest. I shifted my palm over a shattered watch casing and sprung clockworks. I remembered placing it on the bedside table for safekeeping until I got back from the tunnel job... and yet I'd still managed to destroy the only gift Dez ever gave me. I brushed the pieces from my hand then flopped back onto my pillow.

"How are you feeling, Dalla?"

"Like pulverised meeka." I shivered and drew my covers up around my chin – after effects of the sodium shock.

"We were worried about you when you were ten hours late."

"When did Mardel find me?"

"Later that night – almost twenty hours after our set meet," Gerrund scoffed. This didn't bode well.

"Gel." I didn't look at him when I spoke. I kept my eyes on Gerrund.

"Yeah?"

"Could you get me some verrin or water – whatever I have in the fridge?"

He sighed. "Yeah. Be right back. I need to clean my nose anyway." I wanted to say sorry, but right then it was the last thing I was feeling. I wanted to rest, to deal with this another day, and tell Gerrund to get the hell out of my apartment – but I couldn't, or he'd never let me finish the job.

Gel left the room.

"I'm nearly there. You can't take me off the job."

"You almost got yourself killed. How would I have explained that to Dezmind?" he growled.

"I don't think he'd give a damn, do you? He's far more interested in helping you conquer the world than he is in romancing me these days."

"You know that's not true. I'm not letting you go back out there."

"Yes, you are." I shoved the covers off and practically sprang out of bed. My sore knee gave out. I staggered, but caught myself before falling into him. My makeshift brace was gone and the swelling was back. They probably didn't even realise anything was wrong. Well, maybe my torn pant leg would've given something away.

"I don't take orders from you, J.J." He pulled something out of his pocket and shook it in my face – the sleeping pills from my pack. "I've known all along that you got the refill. My people talk to me."

I smacked his hand away from my face. "I saw that wacko you call a therapist. I held up my end of the bargain."

"That was for working on the D.V. I'm not going to risk my entire operation on someone I can't trust."

"And why exactly is it that you can't trust me? Is it because I helped Dez find the Chronicles? Got an alien celestial Generator operational to salvage what's left of a dying sun? Risked my life to save your new government figure-head when the present government nearly blew him and your plans up? Found a viable and sustaining way to open a conduit to an alien city that might serve as a new home to your people?"

I threw my hands in the air.

"Come on, Gerrund. I've done nothing but prove myself."

"You don't get it, J.J. You're aggressive, stubborn and narrowminded. You care, but you twist logic to suit your own agenda. You let strangers into my home, cover up ailments, hide your dependency on drugs, and consider yourself better than anyone else down here. So, tell me, exactly which one of those traits says I should trust you? I trusted you because Dez does. I trusted you because you get results. I trusted you because I thought I knew you – but you don't even know yourself, and that makes you dangerous... to yourself, to others, and to this mission."

Dangerous? Does he really believe that? Every single decision I'd made since joining this crazy ride with Dezmind and the Cause jostled forward in my mind.

I staggered back, blinking. How could he not see that I always had the greater good in mind... well, maybe not hiding my nightmares, but I was dealing with it now – or I was before...

I'm so confused. Maybe he's right.

I squeezed my eyes shut and ground my fists against them.

No. I have to focus on this job. This mission. He needs me to finish this – I need to get back out there.

"You didn't need to know about the pills. They were doing their job, which let me do mine. Besides, you've got a deadline to keep."

"I'll extend it."

I stepped closer again to make my point stronger. "Really? That's not the impression I got. The fact that you were willing to side with the Dias proves it. So I got in over my head. If any one of your tunnelling crew had been in my place, they'd still be missing. In fact, they'd be dead."

"What are you talking about?" He crossed his arms.

I probably shouldn't have mentioned that.

"Come on. Out with it."

A shadow hovered just outside the door.

"It was a well, with sheer sides." I pointed at my leg. "My knee got dislocated and I was submerged for nearly twenty minutes." My teeth chattered. I hugged myself and rubbed my arms.

"Good grief, Dalla." Gelden strode in and came around to where Gerrund and I stood nearly nose to nose. "Stop acting like you're invincible."

He guided me back to the bed, handed me the water and pulled up the blanket. I shifted my pillow and leaned my back against the wall – headboards were a luxury down here.

"What are you talking about, twenty minutes? You'd be dead," Gerrund said.

"No. *You'd* be dead. I'm half-Talian, remember? That means there's alien blood running through my veins. You picked me for this job because I can see in the dark, hear things other people can't, stretch my physical limits beyond your comprehension. And I did that. You need that intel before the next Consolidating Meeting – you told me so yourself when you trained me. No one else can do that for you."

Gelden leaned against the wall and rubbed his hands over his face and through his hair. "Why? Why do you insist on doing this? Let him change the timeline and do it himself."

I finally turned to look at Gel. The dark circles under his eyes, the drawn look on his face and his creased brow told me he'd worried over me more than he should have.

"Because I can. Because I need purpose, and right now this is it." I turned back to Gerrund. "Let me finish what I've started."

He stared through me, silent for several breaths.

"On two conditions. One." He slammed the bottle of pills down on the bed-side table. "You go to the hospital and get checked out by a doctor. If you're given a clean bill of health, I'll consider it."

"And two?" I asked even though I knew what was coming.

"You go back to Jak."

I didn't speak, but he must have registered a change in my expression.

"I'll make the next appointment for tomorrow afternoon. That'll give you plenty of time to see a doctor." He walked to the door and addressed Gel, "Make sure she gets there." And he left.

I collapsed onto the bed and crawled back under the covers before taking a sip of water to delay whatever was coming next. A mixing bowl and damp cloth rested on the floor. A folded towel with two distinct knee imprints lay beside it. My eyes shot over to Gelden, still leaning against the door frame.

Question upon question filled my head.

"Thenticia bathed you. She put you in bed, fully dressed, and I stayed the rest of the time." *Not bad for a guy without mental telepathy…*

"Oh, I bet she just loved that assignment." I altered my voice to sound like Gerrund, "Hey, Ticia, get your ass over to the freak's place. She decided to go for a swim in saltwater."

He cracked a smile, but it wasn't one of his shining ones. I patted the bed.

"Take a load off. At least *I* slept."

He dropped down onto the mattress near my feet.

"Thank you," I said.

"For what?"

"For being here. To anyone else, watching over me would've been a chore." I held up a hand to silence him. "I know it and you know it. I don't play well with others." I got him to smile again. The lingering silence forced me to take another sip of water. I shouldn't complain though, every mouthful helped clear my head a little bit more.

He held a fist to his mouth and coughed. "I went through the mail while you were – *resting.*"

I rolled my eyes.

"Actually, it's quite amazing."

"How's that?"

"A number of different citizens are offering to help."

"Help who?"

"Those people you wrote about at the end of your article. These are citizens with knowledge and skills we weren't aware of. Hang on." He popped off the bed, jogged into the kitchen and back with a stack of opened letters.

"This woman has knowledge of herbal medicines that could help reduce the pain that the father wrote to us about his little girl; a young guy who's relatively new down here has news for the old man about his son. Apparently, they worked in the same building before the guy had to disappear."

Gelden passed me the corresponding letters as he gave me the highlights.

"You can use the next article to let everyone know about this and highlight several more cases."

I nodded. The more these people realised that I wasn't the answer to their problems, the better off I'd be.

"Okay. Leave this stuff with me, just there on the bed. I'll put something together in a little while."

"Still tired?"

"Yeah, I guess so."

"When you feel up to it, there are some more letters for you on the breakfast bar."

No more letters.

I gulped the last of the water before relinquishing the glass back to him. "Do you mind?" I wiggled it in the air at him.

"Course not." He reached for the glass. His fingers brushed against mine, distracting me from my next ridiculous comment. Gel left to get me a refill.

I pulled a wrist scarf from the drawer of the night stand. Sliding the shattered pieces of my watch into its lavender folds, I couldn't help but sigh. It was my own fault for not putting it away in the first place. Gerrund's digital watch silently passed the time until Gel returned with a fresh glass of water.

As I walked out of the clinic portion of the hospital the next afternoon, I shoved Gelden in the shoulder to break him of his head-nods. He'd slept on the couch last night, but I was well aware of how uncomfortable that particular piece of furniture could be.

He bumped me back with his shoulder. I handed him the doctor's note to give to Gerrund later.

"Go home and get some sleep," I said.

"Not yet."

"I don't need you following me around town. Go find your bed."

"If I sleep now, I won't sleep tonight. I just have to work through it."

"Not on a construction site, I hope."

"I don't want to end up in traction, Dalla. I just need to keep my mind busy. I'm going to root around for more D.V. parts, and follow up a couple leads on new material sources."

"Make sure you splash some cold water on your face, I don't want you scaring anyone away." I laughed and jumped out of the way of a stray arm punch, then turned to walk backwards in front of him. He shook his head.

"You're amazing, you know that?"

"What are you talking about? Pick up the pace, I have someplace to be."

"Not thirty hours ago you were lying in a coma with a dislocated knee, and now you're bouncing around like you can't burn off enough energy."

"What can I say? I'm resilient. Now, forget about it." I turned mid-step to walk beside him again. "So tell me. How do you go about finding new contacts on the surface when no one up there is supposed to know you're alive?"

He shrugged his shoulders. "If I told you, I'd have to kill you."

"You could try. No one else has figured out how." We laughed again.

I caught a number of bystanders watching me a little too closely. I tightened my hands into fists, crossed my arms and moved over beside Gelden until our shoulders brushed as we walked.

"Everyone down here has a past," he explained. "Not everyone wants to remember it. After the adjustment period, Gerrund gives me the list of newbies and I make house calls."

"What? You just show up on some stranger's door asking for contacts?"

"It's a subtle art, but essentially, yes. I talk to them about making the transition, ask them about their new place, new job, and then explain how we're able to keep the Underground running – through surface contacts and connections. Most people are willing to help. They give me a few names and I see where they lead."

I linked arms with him. He flashed me one of his dazzling smiles, but the joy left his eyes when he noticed where I turned to look back to. A loose crowd had gathered on either side of the street. We'd chosen to walk up the middle, since there was no bike or slider traffic. I might have felt better, but I was in no mood to deal with the FOL.

"Just relax and ignore them."

"I'd like to see how relaxed you are when a hoard of strangers takes to mobbing you on a regular basis. I thought you said these articles would get them to back off."

"No, I said they would help explain your case, since no one knew the truth. You've only done one article, Dalla. Not everyone will've read it, and a lot of people might actually see it as validation for their beliefs."

"Validation?" I stared at him, my nose less than an inch away from his as we walked on. "How could anything I wrote validate having superpowers from a non-existent god?"

"You have superpowers from dead aliens who might as well be gods. What's the difference? I'm sure Magistrate Delenon never thought of himself as anyone particularly special, just a man doing his job. But the people idolised him and, in the Kronik's eyes, that gave him incredible power. Just talk to them already."

"They don't want to hear what I have to say. They've made up their own minds about who I am. I refuse to be—"

"A source of hope?"

I pushed into him. We staggered together slightly.

"A lie," I said.

When Dez and I got separated after the Underground Rally, and he walked off placidly with Gerrund, away from the crowd swarming over me, grabbing at me – being lifted bodily into the air and watching the man I thought I was in love with walk away from me – it broke something inside.

I hadn't cared about the innocent people who struggled to find hope through a damaged woman. The feel of a broken wrist sliding under my scared palm; the spray of blood from a kicked head; the shrieks of those unlucky people who happened to be holding me might not haunt my dreams the way the Warehouse did, but they echoed in my ears whenever I stopped remembering to push them back. No one blamed me outright for the incident, especially considering what I'd recently been saved from... but no one knew how that moment of panic tore at my sanity.

The awful memory faded in the silence between us as the sign for the All Seasons came into view. I slowed down and turned to face him, placing my free hand on his chest. I lost my train of thought as I felt his heartrate increase and his breath slip along my cheek and neck. I placed my lips close to his ear, closing my eyes to regain my bearings.

"If I try to speak to those people and they can't see reason, can't follow logic or common sense, I'll get frustrated and overwhelmed. I don't want to hurt those people." *And I don't want to hurt you.* But I couldn't bring myself to say it.

Pulling away, I backed up a few paces before turning and walking into the din of the gambler's bar.

I didn't buy a drink or meander through the crowd playing the game. Instead, I walked right over to the table that had somehow come to be *our booth*, and plunked myself down in front of Jak. I don't know if I did that because I was still angry with him about our last meeting, because I was angry at Gerrund for making me come back, or at Gelden for making my life a heck of a lot more complicated than it was even two days ago.

"Taya."

"Jak."

The scent of real dark-roasted coffee assaulted my already raw nerves. I watched the mug as it travelled from his lips to the table.

A waitress showed up and placed another one in front of me.

"Trying to bribe me now?" I said.

"More like calming the waters."

"The waters are rapids – swim with caution."

He quirked an eyebrow.

"Yeah, I had a little accident on my last run. Scared a few people who should've known better. Can we get this over with so I can finish the job?" I purposefully did not touch the mug. *Must have cost a week's wages.*

"There's a little more riding on today than you realise, Taya. If I don't sign off on our session, Gerrund grounds you and goes with Plan B. Your hostility is noted, now shelve it so we can talk about what happened."

"Nothing happened. My foot got caught between two rocks, I wrenched my knee trying to get it loose, and I fell backwards into a well. Being that close to the sea, it wasn't surprising the well had saltwater in it. It was an accident. I knew the risks; they knew the risks; now all of a sudden it's like we never had a conversation about what might happen with me exploring on my own."

I have to be careful. If he thinks I'm running my own agenda, he'll never sign off on me returning to the tunnels. I needed answers he couldn't help me find... and I needed them before I drove myself completely insane.

"I wasn't referring to the coma that had all your friends on edge."

"One friend, Jak."

"So I saw." I blushed. There must be security cameras out front or something because there sure weren't any windows. "Something tells me Mardel and Gerrund think differently."

I hadn't thought of Mardel. "Gerrund's not my friend."

"Why do you think that?"

"He doesn't trust me, and I fully reciprocate that feeling."

"Why don't you trust him, Taya?"

I narrowed my eyes. *How much should I say? What can I say... other than it's intuition?*

"We've been through this before, Taya. I'm not going to tell him what you say, so you can stop trying to cleanse the truth."

"Does my gut count for anything? I mean, it's little things mostly. The first time I met Gerrund he acted like my long-lost cousin. There were no apologies for what I'd gone through at the Warehouse – the torture. He never asked me if I said anything about Dezmind or the Cause. He treated me like an equal. He didn't hover over me like I was glass – in fact, he was flirting with the nursing staff when I tried to walk out the door without him." I smiled at the memory.

I'd given him such a hard time, but it was like he knew that was just my way of being worried... of hiding how scared I really was.

"When Dez and I made it back to the Underground after surviving the explosions at the Rally, Gerrund suddenly grew a conscience."

Jak tilted his head to one side.

"Don't even say it, Jak. He parroted everything Dez said. Dez was worried about me and Gerrund solidified that worry by pointing out how me risking my life for Dez, out in public, was a huge tip-off that I was at the very least connected with the Cause, or I literally was Jadis Doire in disguise and that made me a liability top-side. Whereas he told me before I left to help Dez that he intended to work with me to re-train my brain so that I wouldn't act like a CTF agent anymore. Then, I get back and it's all a lost cause – I'm *untrainable*. The CTF's methods couldn't be overcome and therefore I would put Dez and the mission at risk." I gripped the edge of the table as if to shove it, but it was bolted to the rock floor so it wasn't going anywhere.

"Then, he patronises me by inviting me to Consolidating Meetings once a week, but doesn't actually think enough of me to offer me a permanent position on the Committee Body until I raise a stink. I tell you, I was only there at first because he promised Dez he'd look out for me. When I was no longer of *use* to him, other than to placate Dez, he basically ignored me." I could see it in his eyes – Jak thought I was being a spoiled brat.

"Tell me, Jak. How would you feel if one minute you're helping save the world, and the next you're relegated to twiddling your thumbs and running away from people who can't take the hint that you're not a super hero?"

"Have you considered things from Gerrund's perspective?"

"I'm an old friend's daughter who lands in his lap just as he's planning the coup of a lifetime? Yeah. I knew I was excess baggage – in the way."

"Were there other instances your gut spoke to you about Gerrund's behaviour?"

Thankful he'd pulled me back to the matter at hand, I continued, "It seemed that the more I tried to help – with the training schedule for the recruits, the idea for the D.V., reaching out to Bazdin to keep the man from getting killed, and now proving that Mardel was right that it's dangerous for me to explore the tunnels alone – which it isn't half so dangerous as it would be for anyone else down here – it's like I can't do anything right in his eyes.

"I don't know why he isn't hearing my side of things. Lately, he's made assumptions about my abilities and my intentions, without first giving me the benefit of the doubt. He's convinced himself that I can't be trusted, so why should I trust him?"

Why shouldn't I become the person he believes me to be? I couldn't help but think of myself for a change… knowing I was so close to standing face to face with my truth.

"But we've been down this road before, Jak. The reason he's pissed now is I didn't tell him I was having nightmares. But he figured that out on his own anyway and sent me to see you. And guess what? I'm still having them. I thought the point of these sessions was to help me, not dredge up the past and make it worse."

"Have the dreams changed then?"

The echo of Gerrund's coded words – *can I trust you* – and an internal crash of saltwater made me shudder. "Elements of them. But they're basically the same: I'm trapped, being tortured and I can't get free. I can never get free."

"But you did. In real life. Why do you think your subconscious keeps bringing you back there?"

"*I* couldn't get free. That's the problem." I blurted. I didn't even realise I knew the answer. I could tell that any one of his therapist quips made his tongue itch as he licked his lips: *interesting, really, I see, is that so, tell me more…*

"This is why I had you talk to me about who you are and the influences in your life."

"What are you talking about?"

My hands twitched a little closer to the hot mug. The heat would chase away the lingering chill of the sodium-shock. But I just let the radiant liquid warm me from a distance. If I allowed myself to drink it, it would show weakness – and I had to stay strong if I was going to get through this.

"As a child, you fought for control of your life. You made choices, *you* not anyone else, that would not only protect you from getting hurt again but would empower you. You gained wealth and legal solo-status working in the mines. You gained knowledge and physical strength at the CTF. You controlled which contracts to take, until you were forced into a situation – am I right?"

"I had to accept Dezmind's contract or risk my freedom."

"You lost someone very important to you out there, didn't you? A sister of sorts."

I stiffened but nodded. I'd only ever alluded to Zaith's importance in my life, but this man had seen the truth behind my words.

"You also gained someone…"

"Dezmind."

"At what cost, Taya?"

I opened my hands, turned them over and stared at the scars that refused to heal for so long; felt the fear of losing him to the river of verrin; the electricity of his kiss…

"Losing control."

"How do you mean?"

I sighed. "When I… *realised* how I felt for Dez I didn't analyse the consequences, didn't run the numbers or heed the warnings. I just took a blind chance and I've been at someone else's mercy ever since."

"Isn't that the point of a relationship?"

"Sure. Give and take. But it's not Dezmind I'm referring to. It's Gerrund. I agreed to help keep Dez stay safe and be beside him as he figured out the truth of what that Oracle told him, when he was a child. But I'm not doing that, am I?"

"Dezmind and Gerrund think you are – look how far you've come since the day of his leaving… the day of the incident."

I pushed that personal horror back down my throat and into the pit of my stomach. We were not going there.

"No. Dez is afraid to lose me, and Gerrund is afraid to lose Dez."

"Your nightmares are manifestations of your loss of control at the moment you feel it was first taken from you. You don't blame Dezmind because that was your choice. You blame the Kronik and the Secret Agent who stripped you of your ability to choose – the societal manifestation of your *extended family*. You've been betrayed and your psyche is in free-fall."

"Will knowing that stop the nightmares?"

"No."

"Then how am I going to get *cured* so I can go back to work?"

"Why do you want to go back into those caves?"

My heart slammed into my chest. To my ears it was louder than anything else in the room, and I could only hope I hadn't given my secret away.

"I finish what I start."

"Do you?"

My time with the Professor, the Platinum Hall debacle, the architect's accusations all came back to slap me in the face. But he didn't know about those things…

I squinted my eyes at him. "As long as I'm trusted and people don't second-guess me, I do everything within my power to get the job done."

"Touché. I will allow you to finish this job."

Suddenly all the taut strings holding me up like a puppet were cut. My stature didn't change, but Jak smiled – like he saw the difference in my face, could hear it in my breath.

"So, how do I get rid of the nightmares?"

"Keep coming to see me."

"There's got to be something else. You can't be the solution to my problem."

"You're right. I'm not. *You* are. Only by sharing and exploring your feelings will you be able to move forward and conquer the dreams. You need to find someone like Zaith who you feel comfortable talking to."

"Zaith's dead to me."

"Betrayal is never easy to forgive, but without forgiveness it will be difficult to move forward."

Chapter Thirty-four
The Value of Life

Bazdin

I'm telling you, there's no cure." I waved the little metal book in the air between us. Merik grabbed it and flipped through its thin metal pages. The metal book, the metal walls, the metal table I slammed my hands down on, caged me.

"It's right here. This whole section talks about it. We've got everything it lists now," he said.

"You read it *wrong*. I'm going to join the search party." I turned for the door leading to the anti-chamber of the alien building.

"Ray and Zaith are dying."

I spun around. "And what about Tami? Huh? It's been hours! I have to find her."

Merik moved in front of me. "You're more valuable in here than out there."

I shoved him. He staggered back against the main laboratory table.

"She could be lying in a coma on some deserted stretch of beach somewhere!"

"Or she could've been swept out to sea," Merik said. How he could pronounce her death with such cold logic pierced my chest over and over again. "Think about it, Bazdin. If she's dead, there's nothing you can do; if she's unconscious, there's nothing you can do that the others aren't doing already; if she's awake, you'll have wasted precious time for nothing. We need you working on *this*. The cure is important—"

I smashed the scientist's journal down on the recently sanitised table.

"Hey—" Merik said.

"See this marking here, the one you don't have a translation for? It's incredibly similar to the standard symbol for *does not equate* that Xannian mathematicians use. It's right beside the word *cure*. So, where you're reading that there *is* a cure, you should be reading that there's *not* a cure."

"But that doesn't make sense. Why all the equations and notes about healing properties and all those other medical terms?"

"There's a treatment."

"A treatment?"

"A treatment for those infected that works better on stage one symptoms, and hardly at all on stage three. There's a vaccine for those not yet infected and an immunity-booster. Three separate things to attack this Bacteriophage."

"It's not a Virus?"

"Yes and no."

"What is it, and can any of those things you mentioned help us or not?"

"It's a bacterial infection *and* a virus. It's complicated. And of course this stuff can help. Someone could even prevent the damned disease from ever happening again. The point is, I'm not a scientist. I don't manufacture antigens and antibodies. I assess whether or not a drug is safe enough for people to ingest."

"But you understand what's written here. You know the fundamentals of chemistry and that's a heck of a lot more than the rest of us. Zaith risked her life to find a cure. At the very least, we have to try and produce the treatment. If you don't work on this, Tami's risks will have been for nothing – don't do that to her."

I studied the lab for what felt like the tenth time, trying to identify what various instruments were used for and whether certain items, like the centrifuge, still worked. The yawning opening that once held glass, separating a smaller sealed chamber from this one, stood as a reminder of a sacrifice I now had to deal with.

A loud clang shredded the silence. I jumped.

"What was that?" I said.

Merik looked out the window. "Syvis and Deltek just dropped off the basin. They're waving. They're off to relieve Jan and Lu from the search."

"I should be going with them."

"You should be working out how to develop that treatment. Ray and Zaith are nearly in end-stage."

"This won't happen overnight, you know. They might very well die while we're making this stuff."

"That's why we need to start now. We have to give them a chance to live – even if the odds are against us. All the ingredients are in the next room, and we're fully stocked with water. Tell me what to do."

Is it even worth trying? I probably know just enough to get us all killed.

I sighed.

"We need to strip down all the ingredients into various sub-forms to be able to actually make use of them. We have to treat the marrow-weed in two ways: dry it, and boil it through a distiller." I tore my shaking hands through my hair, then flung them out at my side.

The adrenaline coursing through my veins wanted action and so did I... but logic put Merik in the right and yet – the image of Tami's flailing arms disappearing under the water as the current yanked her away from me burned on the inside of my eyelids every time I blinked. I forced my eyes open.

"I'll get you started on that while I figure out how to use this centrifuge. I think there's a manual override from whatever power source the Dakturian's used." I stared at the device, forcing my eyes not to blink, as Merik went to gather supplies.

When he came back with the marrow-weed, he tried to make sense of the heating elements. I pushed myself past the image of Tami's sinking pale pink arm, and walked over to him.

"Here." I pointed. "The metal is reactive. Lay this one over that one and it'll heat up."

He worked on getting everything assembled.

"I'm going to need a sample of Zaith's blood," I said.

"Why?"

"So that I can isolate the viral component of the Bacteriophage that's attacking her white blood cells. When you're done setting up, I'll need you to bring in the fungus, the one with the dark red hat. We'll need to use a specific fermentation process on it before it can be purified to a crystalline bi-product. The antibiotic it will produce is needed for both the vaccine and the treatment."

Merik continued working on setting up the tubes and vials for the various stages of the distillation. I grabbed a syringe from the cabinet on the far wall and went to meet the woman who had me chained to a laboratory while my wife lay dying somewhere.

* * *

Zaith

He didn't notice that my left eye wasn't closed all the way. It had been a fact of life as soon as stage two hit. I couldn't say exactly how long he'd been standing there, but I was aware of him from the moment he leaned against the inner door of my hut.

"I assume you're Bazdin?" I rasped.

He jumped. His eyes cleared as they focused *on* me instead of *through* me.

"Yes."

"Are you working on the cure?"

He sighed. "I'm working on a lot of things, none of which is a cure." He stepped into the room. "I need a sample of your blood for the antigen."

"The what?" I forced both dry eyes open and licked my parched lips. He must have noticed the effort; the next moment he held a glass of verrin-tinged water to my mouth. I took a few sips, then rolled my arm over to expose the veins.

"Tell me about this non-cure you're working on." I coughed.

He cleaned a spot on my arm away from one of the dried patches of skin, tapped for a vein, and slipped the needle into my greying flesh.

"The vaccine requires a less-potent version of the virus that's assaulting your system. Since it attacks your white blood cells, the ones that help build up your immunity, I'll get plenty of what I need from this small sample. I just have to do a bit of work on it before it can be used as part of the vaccine."

"Isn't that like a cure?"

"No. A cure would be me giving you something and you getting better, never having to deal with the illness again. A vaccine is preventative. Those of us who aren't affected yet can build up immunity, so that we won't get sick. The Dakturian scientist had no unaffected people to try this on, you know. It's all based on theory and previous trial and error. Basically, it's his best guess." The hard edge in his voice spoke volumes.

"Better than nothing." I paused. "How are you holding up?"

"What do you mean?" All emotion fled his face and his stance went rigid.

"I heard what happened."

My words continued to float in the air between us, making it heavier and somehow more difficult to breathe. I coughed again.

"I'm doing what's necessary – or so I've been told." He gave a brief nod to me and left with my tainted blood.

I stared up at the domed metal ceiling. I wasn't on the floor, but I might as well have been since the beds we'd found were only metal frames. There'd been no time for comfort, but at least I wasn't breathing in the dust on a regular basis.

No one would tell me much these days, especially about Ray. The last time Syvis stopped by to check on me, I would've cried had I any moisture to spare. My illness hit him hard – we'd connected under the worst of circumstances and now...

No cure.

I closed my eyes, the left lid not quite making the commitment.

*   *   *

Bazdin

"We found her!" Jantice's yell echoed through the science quarter. I looked at Merik. He monitored the distiller and the microorganism growth container. It was critical we reached maximum yield before the cells died – then it was my turn.

"Go. I know what to do."

I hesitated. "We don't have time to make another batch if you miss it," I said.

"Go already. Then you can get back here faster."

I ran.

The immunity booster could wait... luckily. I ditched my mask in an empty sink, washed my hands, and shut the door behind me – all necessary but time consuming.

The others would be bringing her to the bath basin out back, but from what direction I had no idea.

"Bazdin!" Jan shouted. I turned and caught sight of her at the end of a row of buildings. "This way."

"Is she alive?"

"Yes! Come on."

I caught up with her as we raced through the side streets. The sunlight waned as twilight neared. I stumbled, pitching forward with arms flailing. Catching my balance, I looked up. Syvis careened around the far lane – a body draped over his shoulder. I wanted to grab her from him, but that would just slow everyone down.

"Bazdin. Is the water ready?" Deltek asked, breathless as we ran with Syvis.

"Lu filled it before she went back out," I said, trying not to watch Tami's body bump against Syvis' broad back.

Part of me wanted to know where they found her, if she was hurt, was she breathing all right. But none of that mattered right now.

Syvis slipped her from his shoulder and into the fresh-water bath in the middle of the road behind the laboratory. I held her limp head above the waterline as her hair fanned out on the surface. The image of her treading water in the sea and smiling up at me before diving down, hit me like a smack in the face.

Jan removed Tami's boots. "Men, leave," she said. "When Lu gets back she can help."

"I'm staying," I said.

"Bazdin!" Merik called. "Bazdin!"

"She's alive, Den. Now go save the others."

I didn't move. Tami's face was crazy pale and slack. I lapped water over her temple and along her cheek.

"Bazdin! Bazdin!" Merik yelled.

I kissed Tami's brow and set the back of her head on the bath-rest. Jan unbuttoned Tami's shirt. The smell of sea-salted clothing newly dampened made my head spin.

"Bazdin!"

I ran back to the lab.

Let's finish this.

Chapter Thirty-five

Whose Salvation?

Taya

I swung the pick again and again at the group of rock-straws blocking the last possible tunnel. Chips and shards flew back and smacked me in the face. I spat out rock dust and inhaled the salty air permeating throughout the small chamber.

The rumble from an aftershock dislodged the remaining blockage. I covered my head with my arms, ducking down. The sickly-sweet stench of sweat clung to my clothing – I hadn't brought a change with me this time… I needed room for the other supplies.

I should've been used to the mini-quakes by now. After two days of them, they remained a constant reminder that living underground perhaps wasn't the best solution at this point in our history – but when you've got nowhere else to go…

A dull roar had built steadily from two passages ago. The white noise made it difficult to tell when a tremor threatened. Luckily, each successive one was smaller than the last.

I folded the head of my small pick-axe toward the handle, and slipped it into a separate pouch on my pack. I walked through a shallow saltwater pool and wiped my sleeve over my face. It probably only made things worse, but I had no fresh water to spare to pretty myself up.

This tunnel forced me to hunch over as I walked. The dazzling colours of the larger chambers were replaced with brown, wet walls. If the pools kept up like this, I risked walking around in wet boots – unpleasant on its own, but potentially hazardous to one's health, being saltwater.

Skirting around another well, posing as a puddle, the crash of the surf splintered the monotonous roaring. The dull browns I thought the cavern touted suddenly gleamed red and orange from the starlight filtering in. I jogged up the slight incline to the end of the tunnel.

Dusk dominated an indigo sky. For a moment I allowed myself to read the stars, as tidal shifts and the wind smashed salty waves onto the base of the cliff. If it hadn't been for the solid ground beneath my feet, I would've sworn I floated somewhere between the earth and the stars.

As it was, I wasn't where I was supposed to be, but I *was* right where I was hoping to be – half-way up the Shoris-Mar cliffs edging the Talian Compound. I'd seen the potential in the estimated lines on the map in the Consolidating Meeting room. Without realising it, my subconscious tracked and learned everything there was to know about the tunnels, even before the Dias' opportunity landed in my lap.

Leaning against the curved wall of the tunnel, I stared up at the jagged rock-face. A large section at the top showed no sign of protrusions or divots... only cracks along a sheer surface of blasted rock. The last person here was my supposed soul mate; the person before him, my father. Now it was my turn.

I dropped my pack to the ground and opened the main compartment. Pushing past the grappling gear, I found the spike shoes Mardel loaned me for this trip. Gingerly, I pulled them out and strapped the skeletal spiky-metal grips to the soles of my boots and slid gloves on. They were also Mardel's, but they were made of retractable cloth – they shrunk down to a smaller, portable size when not being worn; one size fits all.

Looping the rope for the grapple and line over my shoulder, I closed my pack and left it a few yards back from the opening. The misty air made rock climbing conditions slick, but there were plenty of great holds all the way up and over to the blasted part of the face. I just had to hone my trajectory to align with the longest and deepest crack in that part of the rock, and I'd be okay.

Anticipation made me shudder and my heartbeat quicken.

I spat more dirty saltwater out of my mouth, took a swig of verrin from my canteen, and tucked it beside my pack before returning to the opening. Gamma was just a blur of pale yellow on the horizon, as lazy wisps of cloud alternately covered and revealed clusters of stars. I mentally mapped out my course, found a solid point of purchase, and launched myself out into the night.

The wind whipped loose strands of my hair from its braid. The varying lengths in my hairdo made taming it difficult these days. The rock glistened under a sheen of sea mist, but the cool vapour refreshed my spirit after sweating for the past three hours in the caves.

My pulse urged me to climb faster, but I let my brain handle the decision making. Like those who'd gone before me, I had no safety net beneath me. The sharp scent of the sea overpowered my sense of smell and the crashing of the waves nullified my extrasensory hearing. My eyes worked well enough, so long as my hair didn't settle across my face, and my legs bore the brunt of the climb.

I paced my movements in time to my breathing. My body tingled, not only in anticipation, but with use. For over two months, my muscles had longed for a proper workout. The sprints to and from the shop had helped reawaken them from disuse, but tonight – tonight my blood sang and my heart beat in time to a long-lost tune.

Within twenty minutes, I attained the mainline that travelled up through the blast zone. Reaching deep into the crevice, I crammed my hands and feet in to gain traction. Inching my way along the crack, I contorted my body into a wedge, moving up mere feet at a time.

I felt a twinge in my knee – the bad one. *Oh, Mother Zola if ever you existed...* The knee twisted and gave out.

My stomach launched into my throat.

I gasped for air, kicking the primary spike on my good foot into the rock face. My shoulders ached. The sound of crashing waves took over the beat of my heart.

With the slight stability the grounded spike offered, I managed to gulp salt-laden spit down my throat and push up to alleviate the pressure on my arms – one of which had also recently been dislocated during my escape from the Warehouse.

I looked up.

Only another fifty yards to the hedgerow. I had to move or my joints would freeze up, but a flash of images overwhelmed me: the Ethics Council chambers sub-basement; Zaith standing on the plateau at the edge of the Deserts releasing that mechanical bird; the woman I thought was my mother slapping me for something Blain had done; older Blain tending to me – not knowing who I was, and another Jutaya emerging from the house...

I bit into my lip and tasted blood. The sharp sting of salty-mist wrenched loose one last memory: the picture of a little girl in her mother's arms with a smudged date and the name Jadis printed on the back.

Like a supernova, something in my chest exploded giving me the energy I needed. Hand over hand, one boot wedged at a time, I scaled the crack up the last of the cliff-face. At the top, I lay on my back in the shrubs, only one row of shrubbery trunks between me and the vacuous surf below.

I stretched out my sore leg and alternately worked my rotator cuffs to keep them loose. I had nothing with me to bind my knee, but that didn't matter – *I made it.* Repelling down would be a breeze. Without warning, that night in the Valley of the Dunes when the

Kahn-lea shared their stories around the fake campfire of light tubes invaded my senses. Every face stared, caught in Dezmind's tale of hope and sacrifice. Until then, I hadn't known why the son of a Councilman would have old calluses marring his hands; I envisioned Dez's own hand-over-hand moment of suspension eight years ago as he dangled from these very nezza bushes – determined to find answers… seeking the truth.

And now it's my turn.

In both Dez's story and my father's, he spoke of night liaisons. I was banking on the pattern since break-and-enter wasn't my style.

Rolling over, I did not follow Dez's lead and act like an animal scuffling around the bushes. I utilised my CTF training and moved within the shadows. My knee twinged with the pressure, but nothing I couldn't handle.

The garden was one giant hedge-maze. Exotic scents attacked my raw olfactory glands as I encountered large flowers blooming at night, and small potent bouquets of tightly wrapped buds clinging to bushes and vines. Every nook had a bench or statue – and every nook was empty.

My hunch was wrong.

I couldn't risk entering the estate, it would have an alarm and be heavily monitored. I couldn't risk extending my exploration time – Gerrund was on a deadline. I couldn't risk coming during the day or even during prime-dusk when only Gamma lighted the sky.

I came all this way for nothing.

Then, a burbling and gurgling alighted on the breeze reminding me of the Common in the Great City. It drew me to the very centre of the labyrinth. With the rushing of the waves no longer a constant, dense white-noise, my hearing attuned to my surroundings.

And there she was.

Her long black hair hung loose down her back, as wisps of locks played with the night's breeze. Her white skin seemed paler even than Dez's. She wore a simple blouse with sheer sleeves that followed graceful arms to clasped hands. The wheelchair hid her lower body, but the large loose pant cuffs by her ankles spoke of understated elegance – the metal restriction cuffs spoke of her garden prison.

I scanned the area: no secondary light sources, no patrollers, no other odd noises… Keeping to the shadows, I walked into the clearing.

The slight whip of my booted feet in the tall grass carried on the breeze.

She looked up.

I stopped walking.

Neither of us said anything.

The bubble of unasked questions that brewed unbidden since the Dias mentioned me working on the tunnelling project grew disproportionate in my mind's eye. Everything I wanted to say just twisted my dry tongue as I stared at the perfection of this woman.

I watched as her eyes assessed everything about me, from the dirt on my face, to the damp locks of my wind-blown hair, to my climbing gear, to the way I held my body to keep the weight off my bad knee.

"I'm not leaving." Only her lips moved, and only enough for me to hear her.

"But Lynnia, I came to—"

"I know why you're here. You need to leave before you're discovered."

I knelt down with a grimace and edged closer to the fountain, staying in the dark paths of its shadow.

"I don't think you understand." My nerves sparked like an electrical fire. My body shook as it had with the sodium-shock. *This isn't how it's supposed to be.* "I'm—"

"Not interested. Now leave."

My old impatience whipped through my body – anger overtaking logic.

"I'm your daughter, Jadis."

She cocked her head to the side. I felt her eyes scour my pink skin, my purple coliths. Emptying my mind, I closed my eyes and sent her a message… *Mother, please…*

"Your cruelty is not amusing."

She was not a telepath. *But maybe she's an empath.*

I moved around to allow Lynnia's outline to shield me from the light. Crouching before her, I held out my rough, callused and scarred hand.

She moved as if to wheel the chair away and expose me – then stopped. With one long delicate finger, she reached out and traced the knotted flesh of my palm. The tip swept across the edges of the star-like pattern – once the weakest skin on my body, now the strongest.

I opened my mind, my emotions – let the flood of questions and the hope surge through my body.

Nothing.

No connection.

I searched her face – a glimmer of recognition flashed… not for a lost daughter, but for a woman who had sacrificed everything and written an article to explain it all.

She refolded her hands in her lap.

"Whoever you are, you must know that now is the wrong time to draw attention to the Cause. While I doubt your mission was sanctioned, I appreciate the effort. I've been anticipating true freedom all my life, but most especially these past twenty years." She paused and bowed her head. "I think I can wait a little longer."

I pulled into the shadows of the garden as she wheeled back toward the main estate.

My heart broke in two.

I collapsed.

Lying on my back looking up at the stars, I couldn't help but wonder why I didn't just let her guards find me. The Kronik's Secret Agents – *He* – would put an end to this misery…

Chapter Thirty-six

Tick-Talk

Gelden

D o you really think it's possible to convert the rovers to hydrogen fuel cells?" Gerry asked.

"I wouldn't be here otherwise. Dalla…" Gerrund looked at me funny. I cleared my throat, "Ehem, *Aelonia* came up with the idea. We've discussed it in passing a few times, but last time she left me with some of her notes on the conversion process. It's…" I let my voice trail off with the echo of a foot scuffing the ground.

Gerrund and I both turned.

Dalla hobbled as she walked. Her copper hair looked grey-brown from tunnel dust and mud. Her attire fared much the same. The recruits dispersed for the night, filtering around her to get to their barracks as she methodically hauled herself up to the central platform where we stood in the training cavern.

"It's done," she said.

"There's a way?" Gerry asked.

"Yes, but it'll need some work."

"Nothing the crew can't handle?"

"Nope. I'll map it out and have the full update for the meeting tomorrow night."

"Can't you give me anything else?"

"No. I hurt. I need a shower and I need my bed." She turned around and hobbled back the way she came. Something in her voice said the hurt went deeper than a stubbed toe, twisted ankle or wrenched knee.

"Let me borrow a slider?" I asked.

"Why?" Gerry questioned.

I hit him in the shoulder. "Look at her. She's exhausted. I'll give her a lift home."

He shrugged his shoulders. "Don't get in over your head, kid. Bring your plans for the retrofit to the Daily tomorrow morning. I'd like Mardel and Ticia to check it out."

I nodded, then hopped down from the platform and raided the storage locker on the other side of the training grounds.

"Going my way?" I quipped. Dalla turned her head as I pulled up beside her on the double-long electric slider just as she entered the main tunnel past the shop.

"That's the worst line I've ever heard. And while I may not be the social type, I'm also certain that's the worst line anyone down here has ever heard. What are you doing, Gel?"

"Attempting to give you a lift home. You look like you need it."

She rubbed her sore leg. "If you insist."

I stopped the motor. She climbed onto the narrow platform and wrapped her arms around my waist. My stupid grin came back. *Thank Zita she's behind me.*

I engaged the motor again and we were off. I wasn't setting any land-speed records but we managed a good clip. Her place wasn't that far, but after a few minutes I felt her upper body lean against my back and her head nestle between my shoulder blades. *It doesn't mean anything. She's just tired.*

"You still awake back there?"

"Unfortunately."

I laughed but caught my breath when she hugged me tighter.

Probably doesn't want to risk falling off.

Pulling up outside of her apartment, I leaned my head back to touch hers.

"We're here."

"Okay."

She didn't move.

Holding the slider steady with one hand, I wrapped my arm around the hands clasped over my stomach and stepped sideways off the platform. Her feet followed since her upper body was attached to mine. Leaning the slider against the wall by the front access door left me manoeuvrable enough to scooch down and lift her up on my back. She switched her hands up to my neck mid-hike.

"What are you…?"

"Where's your key-card, Dalla?"

She slipped it from the side of her pack and handed it to me.

"You're lucky I'm tired, or you'd be on your ass right now." I felt her shudder – not the kind of response I expected to go with her words. She was being stubborn again, hiding something.

At her apartment, I unlocked the door and set her keys by the candy dish in the wall. I carried her to the washroom and sat her on the toilet lid. Her stomach growled.

"I'll make you some dinner while you get cleaned up."

"Gel. Go home. You've done enough." She sat staring at her dirty, stained hands, palms up. I slipped the pack from her shoulders, staggering a little. I hadn't realised just how little she weighed and just how much of what I carried was supplies.

"I doubt you have much in your fridge, but I'll find something," I said.

I put the pack down against the wall near her coat rack, and fetched the mail before shutting the door. Shifting through the envelopes, I noticed one was from the surface. I looked at her breakfast bar – the letters I'd left for her last time lay scattered on the floor under the stools, as if she'd swiped them off the counter in a frenzy and then ignored them. I slid the six, thin envelopes from the FOL into my back pocket, and tossed the one from Dezmind into the mess of personal letters on the floor. I walked into the kitchen to raid her cupboards.

Gerry's words made more sense now. There was more going on here than I realised.

The sound of water hitting rock-slab from above told me Dalla finally managed stage two – getting clean. As nice as it was to feel her arms around me, boy did she stink.

I found some fast-noodles and stale bread in her cupboard. Her fridge was little better, but at least it had enough to make a sweet broth. I toasted the bread and set water on the stove to boil the noodles. I didn't make much of any one thing as she was clearly focused on getting some sleep, and I'd already eaten.

When she turned the shower off, I put her meagre dinner in a bowl, bringing it and a glass of verrin to the table by the couch. As I cleaned up the kitchen, she walked out of the bathroom, towel-drying her hair, and wearing clean night clothes. She went straight for the food, dropping the towel over the end of the couch as she sat. Just below the end of the towel I noticed the brace the clinic had given for her knee. I dried off the pot and set it on the counter.

The slight noise made her jump. She whipped around.

"You're still here?"

"You didn't think I'd make a mess and leave it for you, did you?"

"I thought you'd listen when I told you to go home. I don't know why though, you never have before." She turned back to finish her meal. "This is good. I never would've thought to make a sauce like this."

I walked over and sat next to her on the couch. She wiped the bowl clean with her toast, then stood up and brought them to the kitchen. She still limped. I leaned over and picked up the brace.

"You should put this back on."

She got some ice from the freezer and wrapped it in the cloth I'd used to dry the pot.

"I will."

The loose, fine fabric of her pants contrasted with the tight sleeveless shirt she wore. I didn't care if they were pyjamas or not, I couldn't take my eyes of her. She came back and sat down, elevating her leg using the table. Resting the ice on her knee and her head against the back of the couch, after several minutes I thought she'd fallen asleep again.

"Go home, Gel."

"Why? I know you're beat, but something's wrong."

She hesitated, then said, "Nothing's wrong."

I leaned against the far arm of the couch and watched her. "You're not the only one who can read body language, you know. Between the stuff caked on your body, your stiff limp, and the set of your shoulders and jaw, Gerrund and I both knew something was up."

"At least he had the decency to keep it to himself."

Her lip wavered. She sat up and tossed the ice on the table. I grabbed the brace lying between us before she could, and swung around to kneel on the floor by her leg.

"I'm not an invalid."

"No. You're just proud. Now relax and let me help you." She flopped back against the couch and closed her eyes.

"Fine. I'll sleep here. You can leave when you're done playing nurse-maid."

I gingerly slid the light fabric up along her muscular calf, and over a clearly swollen knee, until her shapely thigh prevented any higher movement. I slipped the padded brace under her leg and over her knee, tightening the adjustable straps snug to allow for minimal motion. As I lowered her pant leg inch by inch, she shuddered.

I looked up.

Two long trails of tears curved over the path of least resistance, highlighting her cheekbones.

"What's wrong?" I asked.

She shook her head.

I sat beside her on the couch and picked up her hands.

"Dalla – what's wrong? What happened out there?"

"Can't tell you," she whispered.

"Sure you can."

She shook her head again – eyes still closed. "Gerrund wouldn't approve... I– I–" The sobs vaulted out of her. I drew her in close and wrapped my arms around her trembling frame.

*   *   *

Dezmind

The overhead lights of the main tunnel flickered and faded, leaving only the occasional street lamp to light my way. The last meeting with Magistrate Ignezzi had gone on far later than I'd anticipated. Regardless, I promised Taya in my letter that I'd meet her as soon as I could, and that meant finding my way back to the Underground tonight instead of in the morning.

Walking up to her building, I pulled the spare key-card from my inner jacket pocket. Heading through the front foyer I checked the mailbox, just in case she hadn't with her tunnel expeditions of late. Nothing there.

Must've picked it up earlier.

I walked down the lower hall toward the central staircase before heading up to the second floor. My footsteps echoed in the narrow stairwell. At the top, I held the hallway door as it closed, since the other time I stopped by after resurfacing it had slammed shut behind me.

An odd half-basket hung from the front of her door. I didn't bother knocking in case she'd only just fallen asleep. Gerrund had mentioned she'd been having problems lately, and I didn't want to mess her up again. I slid the key-card in, but it registered as already being unlocked.

So, she did get my letter. She knows I'm coming. I smiled, imagining her passed out on the couch waiting for me.

I slipped in. As I walked backwards to close the door, I slowly turned and looked up into the lamp-lit room.

I stopped.

A man's blond head and broad shoulders rested against the corner of the couch. Curled in his arms, with one leg under her and one leg stretched to the table, was Taya.

My body went hot then cold in a matter of seconds. My synapses fired at random, leaving bright patches of light flickering in my vision. I alternately gripped and shook out my hands.

I don't understand...

A pile of unopened envelopes littered the floor by the breakfast bar. I walked over and looked down. *My letters... what– what's going on?*

Then it hit me. Her desperate plea, me getting side-tracked again and again with work.

"I'm too late." I whispered.

I looked back at the couch; at the look of contentment on her face as she slept – no sign of the nightmares Gerrund warned me of. No sign of the woman I knew.

I walked over, dropped my spare keys next to hers, and shut the door behind me. I'd left my people at eighteen years of age determined to find my Soul Mate, only to ignore her in her most dire moments to fulfil a prophesy that might never come to pass.

I'd assumed too much.

Chapter Thirty-seven
Till Death do us Part

Bazdin

The flames flickered and danced in the half-light of Beta, making it appear as if the world was on fire. Lutrice raised the torch and her open palm to the sky, chanting to the old gods. I forced myself to stand tall. With the final ringing tone, she spoke to those assembled.

"It is with deep sadness we mourn the passing of our late sister. Though our time with her was short, her inner strength and unfailing dedication will live on in our stories and our hearts."

I stiffened as she stepped forward and lit the pyre. The slow, controlled burn drew steam from the fresh leaves and the scent of acrid death from dried twigs and branches. It coiled around the lifeless, travel-weary body, across old and new scars contrasting against the simple wrappings as they maintained her modesty in death.

I trembled.

Tami squeezed my hand and leaned against my arm.

The night birds cawed and called as Beta, too, was laid to rest. I hadn't known this woman, and yet the power of her memory gave weight and substance to the air. The treatment hadn't worked on her failing end-stage organs.

The man with the dark-green skin and silver coliths stood with his arms crossed, scowling into the growing fire. After five days of the treatment, he'd been well enough to leave his hovel and celebrate mine and Tami's union. It was hard to believe that was only this morning.

As we each took a moment to step forward and say a silent prayer for Zaith Beji, everyone but Syvis gradually left the clearing framed by the spired City gates. He took responsibility for her safe passing, and would remain long into the night until nothing remained but ash and bone. I stepped forward.

I'm sorry.

I shook my head. There were no words I could express on behalf of this martyr to whatever gods she may or may not have worshiped. As I stepped back and Tami moved forward, I noticed Syvis caress a metal cylinder etched in Dakturian script. It brought me no pleasure to be able to read the alien writing, for the high price of that knowledge.

The wind pipe read:

Zaith Beji,
Beloved and Loved
Always

Tami took my hand. We turned and walked away, still wearing our marital garland and the long, light silky shirts she and Jan had woven on alien technology. Only now, we bore the scribings of marriage on the inside index finger of our left hands. Merik had done the honour of inking our names together in the final binding tattoo of our promise.

I looked down at the top of Tami's unusually dark hair, her slight frame and her pert little nose… It was our turn to operate the generator, but Deltek and Lutrice gifted us the night off to spend it with each other. I would hold this woman close to me, of that I had no doubt. But tonight, would be a night for unshed tears.

I snapped a picture of everyone seated around the breakfast table, the one empty spot a ghostly reminder of last night's impromptu ceremony. A faint memory of the needle tattooing my skin the morning before lingered. So much had happened to get to this moment. I sat down and the morning meeting began.

"I'd like to thank Laiviis for his help operating the generator last night," Lu said. "I hope the pictures turn out well."

"I've no doubt they will. I'd like to head back today, rather than wait the full ten days for the vaccine to cycle through. Raylan is responding well to the treatment and, even if the vaccine doesn't take, I have pictures of the formula and the Dakturian alphabet; I'm certain the doctors in the Underground will be able to get it right."

"I still don't think we should risk infecting anyone back home, Laiviis," Lu responded. "If this breaks out before your General is ready to put plans for the coup into play, you might just decimate his forces – then what chance will all those people have? What chance will *we* have for going home? We'll be shot on sight; not just for our knowledge of this place and the Chronicles, but because of the threat we'll pose to the population."

Laiviis looked at me with desperation in his eyes. He'd been here more than a week longer than anticipated. As fascinating as this place was, I could tell he fought with himself over duty and homesickness. He'd grown up in the Underground and planned on remaining even after Gerrund's war – or anti-war – movement. I had not been prepared for that news. Ali or Jutaya, whoever she was, had mentioned something was in the works, but I had no idea they were so close to pulling it off. Still, I could help the guy out.

"The antigen for the treatment is the same one we used for the vaccine. Ray?" I looked at the man sitting awkwardly at the end of the long table. "How do you feel?"

"Fine."

I fought with myself not to roll my eyes. Lu closed hers so she wouldn't have to hide it. I smiled. The dynamics of the group had changed dramatically the healthier Ray got.

"Could you expand on that? How were you compared to how you are now?" I asked.

"I was weak. I'd fought the damn thing off for as long as possible, but I couldn't even stand by myself at the end. Now, I don't ache. I can walk without getting winded, the scabs are healing, and I can eat again."

"My estimate of ten days was exactly that – a conservative guess. Who knew it would actually work, especially on a man in end-stage? Yet, Ray is doing just fine. I don't think we need to worry about Laiviis spreading the Bacteriophage."

"You said to me once that you're not a doctor," Merik spoke up.

The table went silent. I wasn't sure what he was getting at. He'd been there. He helped me create the treatment, the vaccine…

"And neither are you, and yet, because you refused to let me give up, Ray is alive. I think the proof is in the product – we've got a handle on things now. We should let him bring back the photos and the Chronicles. Ali– I mean… Jutaya told me how important it was for these things to be ready as proof for the masses. If this coup is really going to happen, and soon, then I think we need to support it the best way we can. If the General manages to take over the capital building, and institute a new government, he needs to have everything in place."

"Tell us again why we all can't go back with you? The UGC, the Underground Community you spoke of last night, why can't they take us in? When Jutaya told us we couldn't go home, she didn't know about that place, right?" Deltek asked.

"No. As far as I'm aware she came to us after a team rescued her from the Kronik's agents. But that doesn't change the fact that the Kronik have spies watching for a large group of people coming home from a mission they claim is a farce.

"While we're fairly certain our efforts to get out here will go undetected, you need to remember that we took all precautions: we didn't all exit the UGC at the same Junction Point and the lidez driver we hired for the trip to the Expanse was a solid supporter of the Cause. He has family in the Underground and a vested interest in seeing them walk free again." Laiviis paused and stroked his chin. "Even if I could bring you back with me, I wouldn't be able to."

"Why not?" Deltek asked.

"Your presence here is vital to keeping Gamma healthy. Jutaya knew that, which is why she returned alone. You know that. I couldn't leave one person behind because you need two people to operate the Generator. I couldn't leave two people behind because they'd exhaust themselves trying to keep up with the schedule you've set. If I ask four of you to stay behind, how do I decide which half of you get to come back with me?

"Besides, I've been trained for a two-person mission. We're not supposed to bring groups across the Deserts until after the coup. We'll continue to make regular trips out here with two guides alternating, but that's just to make sure you have everything you need and you're getting news to and from your loved ones. I'm not Jutaya, though one day I might call myself skilled enough to handle that big a risk – that many lives."

Lu made eye contact with everyone around the table, including Ray. Her ability to read these people said much. Her ability to trust them with this decision said even more.

"All right then, Laiviis, if bringing the photos and the Chronicles back is of such importance, and Ray is feeling as good as he is, then it only makes sense that you leave as soon as you can. If this General of yours is our only hope of returning to our homes and some semblance of the lives we used to live, then whatever small amount of risk there is with the Bacteriophage is acceptable." Heads nodded all around. Tami squeezed my hand, pleased that things were moving forward. I kissed her forehead, then turned to Laiviis.

"Be sure to wrap that camera up good. Don't want a sand or electrical storm destroying what's on it." I said.

He glared at me through a smile. "Don't worry about it, Beez, I got this." He took a look around as the groups' breakfasts dwindled. "Oh, I will need several supplies restocked before I leave."

"Of course." Lu said. "I guess we need to start opening up the City too... now that we've been vaccinated." She paused, then turned to me. "The Bacteriophage shouldn't affect us, right? We can safely work toward restoring the entire City?"

I nodded.

"I'll make sure the General knows the UGC need to be vaccinated, especially the other Guides. Like Bazdin said, a doctor at our hospital will double-check his work. We'll also need a steady supply of ingredients. I'll bring back what I can, seeing as how the batch Beez made won't last the trip."

"Are we sure that opening up sealed buildings is safe?" Jan asked. "Won't we be putting ourselves at greater risk by letting out a more concentrated version of the Virus – uh Bacteriophage?"

"No. I it won't be any different than what you've already been vaccinated for," I said. "But that doesn't mean that the bacteria harbouring the virus won't mutate slightly, and maybe make you sick. But you have the immunity-booster to help with that. As long as you're able to fight off the bacteria, your systems won't be compromised."

Merik chimed in, "That's what happened to the Dakturians – the Virus got to them after their immune systems had been severely weakened; the attack on their remaining white blood cells made them an easy target. By the time they figured out it was a Bacteriophage, and not just a Virus, it was too late. We're ahead of the game now."

I watched as Lu, Deltek and Syvis looked skyward mumbling – a prayer to thank the Trinity no doubt. At this point, I was inclined to join them. It was a miracle we managed what we did.

Later that morning as I filled the second mini-keg with water from the central fountain and shaved a few pieces of verrin crystal into each keg, Laiviis stood by a large boulder near the edge of the Common with two very full packs for the journey back. Merik walked out of the library with the large orb resting in the modified sweater-holder Ali had sent along with me.

It was a small group that gathered this time. Tami and Jan were working on making more fabric, while Syvis and Ray hunted to replenish the community supplies now leaving with Laiviis. I set the kegs down by the packs just as Deltek clapped Laiviis on the shoulder.

"Looks like I'll have to make the trip out to the plateau with you," he said, laughing and gesturing at the supplies surrounding him.

"That won't be necessary," Merik said as he joined the group. "I'm going with him."

"Since when did you become an intrepid south-land Guide?" asked Deltek.

"No. You don't understand." He set the orb down and shouldered the pack I had brought. "I'm going back with Laiviis." Everyone started talking at once – clearly no one had been made aware of his plans, not even Laiviis.

"I don't understand," Lu said. "We need you here."

"No, you don't. The library is coming along great with everyone's help. Bazdin can take over giving lessons in reading Dakturian, and he can do much more for the community than I ever did."

"You're wrong. Your music and stories have helped keep us sane out here, and without your library initiative we never would've learned there was a possible cure in the first place," she said.

"Not only should Laiviis have help with all this stuff and not cross the Deserts alone, I have a dying request to fulfil."

Zaith's burning pyre filled my mind along with the image of Syvis holding her memorial pipe, yet to be added to the haunting song under the protection of the Canopy Goddess.

That shut everyone up.

He looked at Laiviis. "I won't be a burden. I've already crossed it once with this crew. Should be relatively easy going back, eh? So long as we don't run into any Desert creatures along the way."

I rubbed my gut. A rough wide scar was all that remained of my creature catastrophe.

"Relatively easy, yes. We'll need to stop at the Ancient City for a round of photos Baz didn't get the first time through, and figure out how to gain access to the temple without waking up any more giant cannibalistic larvae, but otherwise I'm grateful for the help." His smile came easier now. Perhaps he'd dreaded returning alone.

With several more hugs and well-wishes, Merik slung the large orb containing the Chronicles around his neck and arm, allowing them to rest on his stomach as he walked. The slight man disappeared under his burden and then laughed.

"I guess we'll have to take turns with this thing."

"Don't worry, the D.V. will take care of it most of the time," Laiviis said. The two men waved and walked toward the outskirts of the Great City, and back to a world I no longer needed.

Chapter Thirty-eight
Waking Nightmare

Taya

I let the dark envelope me like the suffocating Desert sands. My cloak wrapped me in shadow, better even than the absence of light from the central source high above in the caverns. Absently, I flipped the spare key-card over and over within the folds of fabric surrounding me. The pleasant feeling of waking in Gelden's arms this morning waged war with the sudden appearance of Dez's key.

I broke all the rules standing down the street from the side entrance of the Inquisitor. For an hour, I stood watching as the first four members entered at their designated times – all within the past twenty minutes. Four of us yet remained but my time was up.

Clearly, he was due after my arrival.

Slipping in through the metal door, the musty smell of damp paper mixed with bitter printer's ink made me cringe. Tonight, the odour seemed more offensive than usual. I made my way up to the second floor with my standard quiet steps, but I was in no mood to play *spy*. I walked right up to Mardel.

"Sweet-nello." I said. The man liked his deserts.

He jumped a little. "J.J.? No tricks? You okay?"

"Well enough. Mind if I wait over here?"

He frowned. "You need to go right in. What's going on?"

"I need to speak with him."

"He's been in town all day, you could've…"

I held my chin a little higher, challenging him to finish his thought.

"You'll have to wait until after. We're having a full house tonight, so don't be surprised if Gerrund has you back on that stool again."

I nodded and entered the hall leading to the meeting room. Inside, Gerrund paced from one wall to the other between the table and the large tunnel map. Randek shuffled through piles of notes, one of which contained the detailed map I'd dropped off personally at Gerrund's apartment that afternoon. But neither he nor Dezmind were there at the time.

Ticia eyed me critically as I hung up my cloak – she might have seen me outside, but right then I couldn't have cared less. Gerrund turned to tell me something but I was already sitting down in my old corner, warming the cushion on my stool. Instead, he nodded and went back to pacing.

The Dias whisked through the door next. That meant Dez was likely escorting our guest and had been legitimately busy all afternoon, preparing for the man's arrival. Still, I knew he was avoiding me. I leaned back into the corner and crossed my arms. I let my left leg remain straight, to ease the chafing of the brace.

The Dias glowed with self-satisfaction and pride. Tonight, would be the first official step toward retribution for all those who died in the Massacre – for her family.

The door opened and Mardel entered with a grand sweep of his arm. Gerrund stopped pacing and the others stood up – not for Dez, no… for the guest of honour; their contact on the *inside*.

The man's stocky build and the way he held himself made him look taller than he really was, as evidenced when Dez walked in behind him. He remained impassive even as he shook hands with Gerrund and the Dias. I rose quietly as Gerrund situated himself at the head of the table. Randek stood to his right across from Hevex, then in left and right pairs along the table were Dias Betauni and Dez, Thenticia and Mardel, and then the informant at the bottom with his back to me.

"Welcome, my brothers and sisters of the Cause. May the hands of our forefathers of the dawning of the Age of Migration guide our hearts this night." He clasped his hands together and then nodded at the newcomer. "Let the Consolidating Body acknowledge Yezzen Dendridge."

"Here," we said as one.

The man never wavered; his body un-acknowledging… it wasn't his real name. *No surprise there.*

Everyone sat.

Gerrund sent the four stacks of notes around the table. Mardel kept a second set and slipped them over to me as everyone resettled.

"As our esteemed guest is incredibly busy and working on a short time-frame I'd like to jump ahead of our customary reports and get right down to business." Head nods and muttered approvals launched us into the business of the night.

"The first order should be with you then, Dezmind. How are things progressing on your front?" Gerrund sat down.

Dez didn't stand. Mardel tried to lean back to allow me a clear view, but Yezzen remained impassive, in the way, and unaware of the turmoil roiling in my brain.

"While the *Walks* were an effective alternative strategy, we've decided to stop them since the attack last week." *Attack!* I bit my lip before I said it out loud.

"This can actually be seen as a positive development overall: the Kronik is clearly worried about the impact I'm having and is getting reckless. Now, we have proof on our side which shows how desperate they are to keep secrets hidden. Word will spread with my absence."

I knew better than to try and mentally reach out to him while he was in the middle of an important update, but with the attack and walking in on a misunderstanding last night – I had to reach him.

I closed my eyes and emptied my thoughts of everything except him. I pushed out, searching for his usually open link... but there was nothing. I could sense him, but all doors were shut. *Is this what it was like when he tried to reach out to me in the Deserts?*

I opened my eyes and, staring at him, pushed again. He coughed. "Excuse me."

And that was it.

"As I was saying, I've met with two of the Magistrates, but the third is too scared to even arrange a clandestine meet as the others have. That doesn't mean we're not getting through. While the other two won't support us outright, they won't stand in our way either, and they're willing to communicate with number three regarding this decision."

"How is having them remain neutral going to help?" Ticia asked.

"They're not supporting the Kronik either. They're being cautious, based on what happened to Magistrate Delenon. I'm positive that, should we prevail, we'll have their support."

"I hear a *but* in there somewhere," Gerrund said.

"I had to assure them the new regime would reflect a balanced society."

"We've never stated otherwise."

"They're unaware of our transitioning methods and I couldn't speak outright of our plans to neutral parties. They'll be looking for a significant gesture – one we hadn't considered. We'll need to integrate them into the new structure somehow, even if it's only on a temporary basis until their time in local power is over. I have the recordings of each meeting to ensure their co-operation, but I don't think it'll be necessary to play that card."

"I see. I'm sure we can work something out."

"We should have it in the structure before the next phase, otherwise we risk putting it off until it decides to bite us in the ass."

Gerrund's cross expression, and lips drawn into a tight line, showed he had much to say about being told how to run his rebellion.

Surprisingly, he nodded then looked at me.

"Aleonia, the tunnel report."

Hearing that name thrust my mind back into the game. I stood up and walked to the front. Gerrund swung his chair over beside Randek to give me the floor.

"We have a penetration point." I grabbed the stick leaning in the corner, and hit the map on the wall inside the Compound.

Approving nods, nasal and throat sounds encouraged me to continue. Yezzen said nothing but his eyes glistened, watching me attentively.

"There's a cistern below a fountain in the middle of a large courtyard outside what I can only assume is the Capital Building." I looked directly at Dez. He looked at Gerrund and nodded.

"That's right. My father used to bring me there. Other than the building itself, there's not much around to use as fortification from an attack. It's parkland."

"Access to the cistern is tight, as is the adjoining tunnel I found – only one or two soldiers could fit through at a time, and I would highly suggest one at a time to allow each person free range of movement should they need it."

Gerrund and a few of the others jotted down notes.

I pointed to a new area sketched onto the map. "Mardel is organising a sweeper-team to make sure this passage is clear enough to act as a sufficient access point. Once empty, the route will take no more than a few hours to traverse." I set the stick down and returned to my spot.

"Mardel?" Gerrund prompted, sliding back to the head of the oval table.

"Based on Ali's extensive notes on each chamber and tunnel sequence, I can give a good estimate of three days for readiness – non-stop. We'll all need at least a day off before final phase can begin."

Gerrund looked at Yezzen. "Will Council be in session in five days?"

A nod.

"Can you make sure to cancel any major school trips or tours – anything that might bring innocent civilians into the fray?"

Another nod.

"What can you tell us of the Kronik's defensive stance? Troop numbers? Standard guard stations? The current level of alert?"

The man cleared his throat and leaned forward ever so slightly. I tried directing my thoughts to Dez again – I was not part of these matters. In fact, if this insider was leaving early, he'd be taking Dezmind with him as an escort back out of the Underground. I had to break through –

"The Kronik remain weary and suspicious, but have not increased their numbers beyond my last estimates."

My heart jolted. A shudder chattered my teeth – I clamped my jaw shut tight as *His* voice shredded every nerve and last link to sanity.

"As the Council are completely unaware of the Underground tunnels, your advantage remains solid. And I'm still hearing plans about reinforcing their ground in the sectors surrounding the Compound, effectively dispersing their forces. I have no definitive troop numbers to offer you, only a simple warning that most of their soldiers are either directly or indirectly involved with the CTF and their training practices – so any one person is likely to be three-times more capable than your volunteers."

Part of my brain heard the lies, but the other part desperately closed down every access point into and out of my mind.

Breathe, breathe... come on Taya, don't forget to breathe. I couldn't afford to pass out, to cough, draw any sort of attention my way.

As my eyes glazed over, my only consolation was Dezmind's startled stare attempting to penetrate my frozen mind.

The sharp sting across my face registered somewhere very far away. Another hand searched to find a pulse at my neck. The cold floor made me shiver.

Cold floor? How did I get down here? I fainted!

"No!" the word tore from my throat. I scrambled back, striking with one arm then another, impacting soft flesh and jarring bone. When they weren't trapped, my feet defended me.

"Ali. Ali!" Voices tried to confuse me. I whipped my head forward and connected with a nose.

"J.J.!" They tried again. I moved to swing around, but my arms were crossed over the front of my body, hands held behind my back. Pressure on my legs meant they were useless.

Taya… a distant voice echoed at the back of my mind – soothing yet frightened at the same time. I searched for that voice...

"Jutaya!" The smack to the other cheek made my eye explode – or so it felt. I took in a breath and screamed at the top of my lungs.

Rough hands held my face. Fingers pried open my closed lids.

Taya… it came again, but fainter – I couldn't even be certain it was there. It had to be there. I reached out with my mind to grasp something, anything… but he was gone.

"Dalla…" a whisper by my ear. I stopped struggling. A cool forehead touched mine. A long slender nose and blond hair came into focus without the aid of prying fingers.

Gelden? Impossible.

"Dalla…" a second time.

"Gel?"

"Release her," he said, louder.

Muffled voices argued. The weight lifted; my hands dropped down and that gentle man gathered me into his arms.

"I don't understand…" I whispered back.

I sipped a glass of verrin at the table. Gelden's strong hands ensconced my shoulders as Gerrund paced, and Mardel sat across from me, holding my gaze. The others were gone. At the very least, I'd learned that Ticia had been ordered to bring Gel here. The number of people who knew I was broken kept growing. I sighed.

"You're certain?" Gerrund asked again.

I nearly spat the verrin at him, but I realised the full extent of the situation and swallowed instead.

"Without a doubt." I said, setting down the glass. "You're sure he was long gone before I fainted?"

"A good ten minutes."

I nodded. My shoulders slumped, more noticeably so with the added weight of Gelden's hands. I patted one and looked up at him.

"It's okay. Thank you – I mean that." Then I looked over at his uncle, still pacing in front of the map, his vivid blue hair nearly stood on end with the number of times he'd run both hands through it at once. "We have some important things to discuss."

"If you're sure," Gelden said.

I nodded.

"I'll wait with the others, outside." He gripped my shoulders lightly in goodbye, then turned and walked out the door.

For a moment no one spoke. I felt I had to state the obvious.

"He's a double-agent and a Special one at that."

"What do we do?" Gerrund addressed Mardel. "He knows everything. We can't trust anything he's given us."

I didn't understand it either.

"Without a doubt, he would've recognised my voice. He never said much before I spoke, and then he didn't even attempt to disguise his voice. Either he was banking on me going comatose or he's purposefully making us second-guess his intentions – do you trust the crazy woman you rescued, or do you trust the turn-coat who's fed you intel this entire time? He's using this situation to put us off kilter – make us back off," I said.

Gerrund scowled.

Mardel leaned back in his chair. "You said it. He knows everything. That means, along with tonight's key intelligence, he and the Kronik have every avenue of this coup covered. He's ending it now before there's any bloodshed. And so should we. They'll have every angle covered."

"We can't give up now. We have to go through with it. They know where we are and they'll find a way to destroy us before we can ever get this far again." Gerrund sucked in a deep breath. "No. We stick to the plan."

Mardel stood up so fast he knocked his chair over. "That's insane. Listen to yourself, Gerrund. You'll be sentencing every one of us to death. At least if we wait, we can fall back—"

"Back to what, exactly? Back to hiding in other people's basements?"

"There is the Great City," I said. They both turned to stare at me. "But I agree with Gerrund. Not for his emotional assessment," I said to Mardel. "But for a logical one."

"What are you talking about, Ali? There's nothing logical about getting slaughtered."

"We need to do both suggestions at the same time."

"Explain yourself," Gerrund said with a mixture of anger and hope in his tone.

"By keeping to your pre-arranged plans, we're calling their bluff. If we back out now, and I'm wrong about him knowing who I am, at the very least they're set to attack us down here where there are too many innocents to defend. They'll strike when we least expect it, before we can come up with an adequate Plan B. Now, he said he couldn't give us an exact number of troops. He tried to intimidate us by making reference to the quality of the soldiers they already have. He's not concerned, but he is. We need to take advantage of that and twist it against him – against them."

Gerrund sat on the edge of the table. Mardel leaned forward on both hands.

I hesitated. They had to know I was being serious.

"We use the CTF against them."

They looked at each other, conferring silently. A nod, a shake, an eyebrow raised, pursed lips… it went on.

"How's that possible?" Mardel asked.

"It might not be, but I have two thoughts on the matter," I said.

"And?" prompted Gerrund. The pain and desire fought for dominance in his eyes. The scary-Gerrund won.

"I'm not without my own contacts. If you'd let me… if you'd *trust* me… I can reach out. If that doesn't work, we can play dress up and you could give the trainees over to me for a few days. Regardless, the timeline stays the same."

"You can't just reach out to anyone and everyone, Ali." Mardel said. "If we do this, you've got one shot and you'll need to make it your best mark." He looked to Gerrund. "I don't want to run and hide. I also don't want to sentence the UGC to extinction. We need to reassess our tactical position and build a backup plan."

Gerrund nodded and stood up. "Bring the others back in, Mardel. And tell my nephew to go home." He looked at me, his eyes still wild.

I was not supposed to be in the middle of things and yet here I was – right where no one wanted me.

I had to nod.

Chapter Thirty-nine
Fight Club

Taya

The whine of the frothing machine always made my teeth ache. At the corner of Grender and Thilik Avenue, in the middle of the business district, Nite/Life Café stayed open thirty hours a day, every day of the week, injecting some form of caffeine into the masses. At 4:00 p.m. I had enough room to move without elbowing someone in the head, but little else. This was the third of five possible locations for an exchange.

I knew better than to stand at the front door and gawk, so I chose as direct a path as possible to the order counter. Surprisingly, only two people stood ahead of me. I glanced through the drink selections lit up on the computerised screen above the prep station. I'd been here before, but only with clients, and not often enough to memorise the sub-level multi-optioned menu.

"What'll it be, miss?" The barista asked.

"Just a small berry iced sour-twist." I paid with my own credit for a change. Working on the D.V. and as a high-risk Tunnel Explorer brought me more than a month's usual wages. I absently brushed at the shadow of the stain still marring my white dress.

I'd thrown it on the floor and kicked it under the bed after my last surfacing. The problem was, I needed to look very unlike myself again with no time to order new *dress-up* clothes. Dish detergent took most of the grime out, but I could still see an off-white water mark yellowing at the edges.

I scanned the open seating area, pretending to look for a place to sit. What I found was my mark. Extracting a city map from the soft brown leather shoulder bag Magda lent me, I grabbed my drink and meandered through the busy bodies to a standing-only table.

Setting down my glass, I turned to the window table beside me and dropped my map between two men in tight short-sleeved T-shirts. One guy ignored me, the Transactionist, and the other guy looked straight at me with a cocky smile, the Conversationalist.

"Hey there, sorry to bother you. I'm new in town and I'm trying to find Klax Square, but I'm not entirely sure where I am right now. Can you help me?" I set a dakor down on the table beneath the map, close to the Transactionist.

"Sure thing." He reached his bronzed arm over the edge of the map and tapped the spot where the café was situated. Seeing his perfect Matin skin and deep red coliths so close to my pink arm sent a jolt of jealousy from my stomach up to my throat. "And here's the Square. If you're going to the sports day, I'd suggest you change in the public rest rooms on this side of the park first."

I smiled back at him, lifted the map to close it while turning my back and my bag on the Transactionist.

"I can't thank you enough. Is there a section for spectators to sit?"

"I believe the benches are for the athletes, so if you're not prepared to participate, you might not be able to see the games."

I nodded. "Okay, thanks."

I turned back to the tall table and finished my drink. I carefully folded the map smaller to look at the area he'd pointed to – keeping up the charade. Five minutes later, I left and headed for the Square.

These things had to be done right or I'd never be welcomed back to the Club. It had been nearly a year since I was last in attendance, but they didn't know that – they'd never seen me in this skin before, and there were rules.

At the park, two blocks down, I sat alone on a bench with the three suns blazing overhead and took a moment to just breathe. Cave living wasn't high on my list of preferences. I slipped off my flats and let my feet and ankles properly worship the long grasses. I'd felt the nudge on my bag in the Café – the barest of pressures actually – so I knew it was in there somewhere.

Sliding the generous satchel onto my lap I searched every fold and compartment it housed. A thin metal tab dropped onto my palm. Placing it between my stomach and Magda's bag I looked it over:

FC
897 Jilwin Court
Door #6 Dusk

Laughter rose from down the hill where the fun day was taking place. When I heard the news from the wire blasting at the repair shop/Junction Point, I figured the monthly event would be the perfect cover story to engage the Conversationalist. It hadn't been what I wanted to hear, but I'd expected it. Bottom line, I needed to change. The meet wasn't for another six hours, but I knew how I wanted to spend the intervening time.

The smell of roast ganoo hit me like a sucker-punch. Images of threatening Dez and his wait staff all those months ago clashed with the kindly face of Werks, the man I'd killed our first night in the Deserts. The Chalklin Pond Restaurant had a new head chef, one carefully vetted by the primary patronage – the very man I was here to see.

The maître d', dressed in a charcoal-grey button-up T-shirt, crimson vest and black slacks bustled over to meet me. The absence of the matching red neck-scarf worn by the wait staff gave a simple air of importance to the man. However, he did carry a red folded table napkin in his front pocket. Another series of images hit me: the crimson handkerchief in the assassin's pocket, a flash of scarlet on a bolder in an alien forest, and that same cloth bathing Dez's dehydrated brow.

Maybe this was a mistake.

"Table for one?"

"I'm here to see Mr. Lisle." My voice wasn't nearly as steady as it should have been.

"Mr. Lisle is out conducting business at the moment."

"Could you seat me in his office to wait for him?"

The middle-aged man blinked a few times and didn't respond right away.

"That would not be wise as he is expected to be gone until close. Perhaps a message would suffice?"

I breathed deeply before replying. "Just tell him Ali stopped by while she was in town." The man quirked an eyebrow at the mention of my *nom de plume* – he knew who I was or at least suspected. I gave a quick smile, then turned and left.

Without thinking, I circled to the back of the building. I was half-way up the fire escape when logic finally caught up with me.

What are you doing?

I'm going to wait for him.

What if someone sees you?

It's a back alley, no one's here.

What if there's an alarm?

He never mentioned one.

What if Jadis doesn't remember you?

Like a jagged blade shredding my heart, the truth of the matter struck home. If she didn't remember me she might attack; she might be capable of holding a grudge and rip me to shreds even if she did remember me.

Do I leave?

No. I have to know.

I leapt up the remaining rungs to a small platform by the window. I had nothing on me for picking locks, and my CTF weapons had been confiscated by the Agent when I was captured. What I did have was the metal chip for the Club. Sliding it from an inner pocket of the handbag I rested on my knees level with the mechanism. I inserted the chip between the sill and the frame, looking to disengage the magnetic locking field.

A soft bump rattled the glass.

I looked up.

Jadis.

The lynx's large wet nose smeared the window. Her tongue licked out twice before she bumped her forehead into the glass.

She remembers!

The lock accepted the chip in place of the lower sill bar. I shoved the window up and scrambled over the ledge. Jadis leapt up. For a nano-second her teeth flashed. I swallowed noisily as we crashed to the bare floor and I was covered in kisses.

For five and a half hours we reconnected as I stretched-out my body and muscles while waiting for Dezmind to come home. He never did – was probably on some kind of back-pedalling mission alerting his contacts of the breach.

Jadis followed me around the apartment. It was smaller than the one Gerrund had given me, and yet the sunlight streaming in through the windows made it seem so much bigger, so much more inviting.

I ran my fingers over the small counter in the kitchen, touched the coffee maker and the lone mug standing ready to be filled. Jadis nearly tripped me, winding through my legs as I walked over to the old hard cover books spread out across the decorative metal bistro table. I let the tips of my fingers trace embossed titles I'd never read.

Lingering in the doorway to his bedroom I didn't let myself enter. Here his musky scent overpowered my senses. I closed my eyes as I clung to the door frame, imagining him walking through the front door and... *and what?* Chastise me for being in the arms of another man? Rave about the chances I was taking being seen here? Ignore me and walking back out again?

Shaking the negative thoughts from my head, I opened my eyes. Still, a part of me felt whole again after so many months away. I didn't need my two-storey house in the city to be home – what I needed was the most important facet of that physical location... my true family.

I grabbed a well-read copy of the Local Inquisitor from a small table between the two chairs. There was a large space at the bottom of an article, my article. Pulling a pen from Magda's bag, I wrote him a note and left the newspaper open on the chair. Jadis nudged the back of my knee with her nose. I knelt down and buried my face in her fur.

In the quarter-light of Gamma, between two large warehouses in the assembly district, I slid my chip into the reader by the side door marked with the number six. Taking in the thin metal, digitally encoded with the pass key, the lock on the door disengaged.

I opened it and went in.

A steep set of stairs led down into the basement of the building. The air oozed the scent of engine grease and stripping agents. At the landing, a large Glaaon man dressed in a tight black tank imprinted with the dark red capital letters 'FC' stood with his thick arms crossed, eyeing my compact form and tightly woven hair. I handed him the bag containing my money and the white dress. In the other hand I gave him thirty dakors and my shoes. He placed the satchel in an open cubby in the wall on the left.

I held up my arms and he patted down the first outfit I ever wore as Aelonia Trellice – the black jumpsuit. Had it been any other colour, blood stains from the last time I'd ripped open my hands would have riddled the fabric. In a way, it was perfect for tonight. He stepped aside and I walked down the hall in my bare feet.

When it came to calling in favours with contacts at the CTF, realistically my options were limited. My first thought had been *Mamma* Niless, but she'd been with the company for so long, even if she did see me as a daughter, she'd never help a criminal. Then there was my science professor, Gellik. He would understand the significance and importance of what Gamma really was, and likely twist himself into knots trying to help me, but in reality he had no solid connections. That left only one man; the walking contradiction in my life prior to being assigned the Deserts job.

Jezetek.

The one roadblock in my plan just happened to be a major one – he was a contracted Justice. He'd taken an oath to uphold the law and, if nothing else, he was a man of his word.

The muffled sounds of yelling and shouting blasted my senses as I crossed the force field between the hall and the Inner Sanctum. Tall, taut, black fabric walls shielded the spectators from the access point. Two females flashed by in the centre of the painted circle before me; one jab-kicked repeatedly as the other blocked – bare feet and bare hands trading blows off bloodied arms and legs.

Sliding around the last black frame, three feet from the edge of the ring, I found a spot to stand. A large list of names spanned a portion of painted concrete wall. I read through who had fought and won so far and who had yet to be challenged.

Tek's fighting name was still listed.

This was my blind punch; unregulated fighting was illegal. When Tek's first undercover assignment brought him into this world he had to disguise himself. It wasn't unheard of, but it was rare enough that it drew attention – that meant proving himself fast. He'd brought me in as a new fighter, as Taya Fyce, to cause a distraction which allowed him to catch his mark without being made. Apparently, he'd taken to the Club and its ideals – it was an outlet that vastly improved his relationships with women. I still didn't understand that connection.

A small Nirian man of dark grey skin and jade coliths tapped my elbow.

"Name?"

"Aleonia Trellice."

He slipped away and, moments later, as the current fight ended with the red-head collapsing, my name went up on the board with a star beside it. Another rule of the Club: all newbies must fight.

More large men in tight black tanks helped the women from the ring. Informally, credit changed hands. Initially, the betting had gotten out of hand and a known gambling master moved in on the scene – one the Justices had been trying to catch for years. Tek now had him locked-down in prison. It was a warning to both organised crime and the participants of the Club – keep it simple or end up behind an energy screen.

A roar went up from the crowd as the next challenger entered the ring. His black, full skin-mask showed only his eyes, nose and mouth before ending just above his collar bones. Two gold bolts of lightning identified the location of his ears and matched his sleek S-shaped body coliths. His broad, bare green chest and tight shorts were mandatory attire for male fighters, but on him, it just looked like he was showing off.

I stepped into the ring.

An even bigger roar reverberated in the close space. I'd broken a rule – no mixed matches.

It was clear from the look in his eyes, the tilt of his head, and his over-the-top stance that Tek didn't recognise his good buddy, Taya. And that's why I had to be here – to be the one to fight him. He'd never take Ali's word, so I had to show him who I really was.

The small Nirian walked into the ring. I knelt down on one knee to speak with him as angry shouts mixed with rallying cries of support.

"I know the rules, Game Master." I hoped giving him his honorific would help show I wasn't completely ignorant. "But I fear I might kill another woman in the ring." I placed my mouth close to his ear and spoke the truth. "I'm CTF trained. I am not a spy – I've recently gone Underground, and I desperately need a release." I pulled back and waited, head bowed.

The crowd hushed when a ruling didn't come immediately. He moved to the centre of the painted circle.

I stood up.

Tek didn't move a muscle.

The Game Master held his arms up in a V, then clapped his hands together.

"It's a match," his deep, throaty voice boomed.

The crowd's silence broke with wild acclamations until Tek and I took starter's stance. Only the clink of dakors and dreseks filled the air.

It was like being back in Master Ulozo's Level 7 sparring ring all over again – I had no idea what to expect, and I was sorely underprepared.

I jumped as his leg swung out, right into a palm punch. I landed on my back near the edge of the circle, head ringing, face on fire. He dove after me, but the bulk of his muscles slowed him. I rolled clear and kicked his right kidney. The force launched me back up onto my feet.

Up he came, barely winded. I feinted a round house, switching my feet to a reverse scissor kick in mid-air. My bare heel connected with the side of his lower neck. He grabbed my ankle and arced my momentum over his shoulder to slam me back down onto the floor. My molars jarred as my body vibrated from the impact on the concrete.

Using his leverage, he twisted my leg, moving to sit on my stomach. I curled my body, looping my arms around his calves and linking my hands. He stumbled away from me, releasing my ankle. I deked in, punching him in the face and kicking him in the chest on the back spin. His fist connected with my nose as he staggered back. Blood sprayed across the ring.

I backed up, wiping the gush of red on my arms to make them slippery. Then, I did a very 'Taya' thing – I gave him a genuine smile.

He blinked, just as two dark semi-circles cupped the insides of his eyes.

Before he had a chance to recover, I gave him my signature move. I got in close to kick at his knees. He jumped back, just enough to allow me time to spring onto my hands and helio my legs. Each foot connected with his jaw as I latched my legs around his neck on the return spin. I swung my body close to his, wrapping my arms around his calves for a second time.

Before I could trip him, he flipped back into an arch with his body – I knew this was coming. Releasing his legs and mine, I crunched up to straddle his stomach. My body remembered the first time we ever fought like this. The connection sizzled through my veins and suddenly I was seventeen again.

I felt him shift beneath me, as if sharing the same memory. Blinking out of it, I squeezed his sides with my thighs just long enough to make him collapse. Shooting my legs to either side into elevated splits, he landed on his back and not on me – a lesson learned from early days.

He sat up, grabbed me around the waist and squeezed. Spots flashed in front of my eyes.

No! I have to win. It's the only way.

Launching my head back into his, I cracked his nose and felt a rush of liquid warmth down the back of my neck. He fell back, still holding me tight. I laid the back of my head next to his on the floor, and kicked my legs up breaking free into a backwards roll. His arms fell to either side of his body. I lay on my stomach behind him, my chin next to his ear...

"My match, Tek." And I kissed the side of his temple leaving a smeared bloody lip print behind.

I pulled my submerged head from the sink full of cold water and flipped my freshly rinsed hair up in the air.

"Hey," he said. "I don't need another bath."

I gave him my cockiest smile as I turned to dry myself under the full-body air dryer in the re-coup room. I was still fully clothed, but decidedly less bloody. I didn't wait for my hair to fully dry, but stepped out from under the vent and gave Tek a hug.

"What are you doing here, Taya? What's with the disguise?"

"It's a long story, just promise not to arrest me."

"That bad?"

"Oh, yeah. Meet me out front. We need to go someplace where we can talk without being overheard." I patted his cheek and returned to the roaring crowd.

Even as I felt the undisputed pressure of a royal black eye, and the fact that it hurt to breathe through my nose, the number of slaps on my back as I made my way over to the entrance stung more than any of my injuries – not that I could show that. The gatekeeper gave me an appraising once over, lingering on my now loose hair, then handed me my shoes and bag with a smile. Apparently, he'd won some money on me. I nodded my thanks and left.

"Took you long enough," Tek said from beside the door. I jumped, then punched him in the shoulder – hard. He no longer wore his own disguise, and was adequately dressed for a night on the town.

"Damn you. Why do you get to take the hidden exit?"

"I didn't leave anything with Grumble."

"Grumble?"

"A kindly nickname." He gave a wicked smile. "Come on. There's a club just down the street where we can talk."

"Not like this one I hope."

"No. Louder, more music and something stiff to drink."

"Been a while since you were beaten by a woman?"

"Just over a year in fact." He slipped his arm around mine and steered me over to Club Daze.

"I'm not vibin' the name of this place."

"It's legit – barely. But it's what you asked for."

We walked in. Between the fake fog, throbbing dance music, and din of conversation, he was mostly right. What he'd failed to mention was that Club Daze was a make-out joint.

"You're insane!" I yelled.

"What?"

He'd heard me – that devious grin said it all. I shook my head, turned and walked right back out the door. He followed.

"Come on, Taya. It's perfect. No one's going to hear anything."

"I'm not one of your throw-always, Tek."

"I know. We're here to talk."

"I have someone in my life now."

The fiendish grin disappeared, and the man I'd become friends with in my final years at the CTF stood there.

"We're not kids anymore." I glanced around to make sure we were still alone. "I'm a fugitive on the run from the government because of what I am."

He took a step closer. What could have been menacing was actually something else entirely. "What are you?"

"Half-Talian."

"No meeka, really? That explains a heck of a lot." He reached out and touched a sore spot on my jaw.

I wasn't doing this. Not here. We weren't these people any more. I stepped back, but yanked his arm nearly out of its socket for him to follow me.

"I think there's a rental place just up the street. Grab us a rider and we can drive around the city." I walked beside him, holding his hand. "What I need is my good buddy – the guy who swapped strategic notes with me in code and kicked my ass in the ring in order to set my head on straight. I'm desperate, Tek."

Chapter Forty
Letter Speak

Dezmind

Leaning one hand and the full weight of my body against the door, I breathed in the latent scent of roast ganoo as I fumbled to lift the latch covering the thumb plate. Jamming the appendage onto the reader I rested my head against my arm.

It beeped twice.

I wiped my sweaty hand against my pant leg; *guess I'll need to get these cleaned before my next meeting*, then tried the print scanner again.

One beep. The lock disengaged and I stumbled into my apartment well after sundown. I'd reached out to every contact I had inside the Compound walls and some incredibly shady characters outside of them, searching for information on the double agent – what little surfaced supported Taya's claims – he was not who he said he was. I'd wasted a day confirming what Taya already knew, just to satisfy Gerrund.

Shuffling over to the bedroom door, Jadis wrapped herself around my legs nearly toppling me over, then sat blocking my way.

"What is it? Are you thirsty? Do you want to go out?"

She just cocked her head to one side and looked at me. I tried to move past her. What I really wanted was to collapse after the day's scouring and endless clandestine meetings.

She growled.

I staggered back.

She moved forward, then sat down in front of me again.

I rubbed my hands over my face and that's when I noticed it – just the hint of spring morning scent after a light rain hung in the air.

Jadis curled around my legs again, then walked over to my reading chair. I followed her, more awake than I had been for the past five hours. She lay down in front of the chair. In the dim glow from the wall-floor lighting I saw a familiar newspaper lying open on the cushion... not where I'd placed it last.

Snatching it up, I turned on the kitchen light and leaned back against the sink to read.

Dez,

I stopped by, but you were out. I didn't want to leave things unsettled between us in case those big plans don't work out. Gel's just a friend – the only person down here who gives a damn about my well-being, except for maybe Mardel. He was there for me time and again when I turned looking for you... and now I'm here and you're still gone. I know that things won't be the same tomorrow or the next day, no matter what happens. Just know that I never stopped loving you.

T

My legs gave out on me. I landed hard on the tile floor, jarring my molars. *She's going to fight.* I don't know why I knew she planned to be in the one place she was never meant to go... but I'd messed up again – avoiding her after seeing them together...

All of it innocent.

How could I be expected to rule the nation, if I couldn't even be there for the one person who really mattered?

I never made it to bed that night. Some time shortly after dawn I awoke on the kitchen floor rumpled and tear-stained, and totally unprepared for my destiny.

Chapter Forty-one
Homecoming

Taya

That tingly feeling of dread at the nape of my neck struck just as I showed my special recruits one final series of close-combative manoeuvres. It's not that it directly bothered me, it's just that it happened so often over the past two days I'd grown weary of it.

"Now, find someone you haven't sparred with in a while. Make sure they're not a close friend. You've got fifteen minutes to practice before we head out."

I looked over my shoulder at the planning platform. Gerrund leaned against one of the smaller tables with his arms crossed, scowling at me and my fifty troops. His attitude in light of the bad situation we found ourselves in, was far from constructive. *And he could just shove his need to be the man-at-the-top where the suns don't shine.*

The morning I'd returned from the surface still played out in my waking mind, analysing my choices and his, but it was a fruitless exercise in diplomacy doomed from the start…

I had arrived to give my report at the Daily, which couldn't have been avoided since the intel was of paramount importance – but that meant Mardel and Ticia got everything first hand and *that* was bad.

Mardel had run down the few steps of the platform to meet me. The swelling on my face, especially around my nose between my eyes made it hard to see.

I waved off his concern as we walked over to the planning table together. My body ached like it hadn't since I was a rookie at the CTF – Tek and I hadn't exactly pulled our punches in the ring.

"Looks like things didn't go so well," Ticia said. It was a difficult emotion to place as she both gloated at my supposed failure, and sounded down-hearted that there might be no plan for moving forward.

"Actually, it couldn't have gone better," I said, which of course was a blatant lie.

"He'll help us then?" Mardel asked.

I nodded but pursed my lips. Gerrund noticed.

"What's the catch?" he asked.

I wasn't in the mood to play his games.

"Why don't we start with what he's gonna do for us, and we can come back to that," I rushed on, not waiting for Gerrund to reply – my first mistake. "He can guarantee ten CTF trained soldiers – men and women he already knows support the Cause. He will quietly inquire into the stance of another twenty in the next two days. I promised we'd send a runner to a pre-arranged location to exchange the information."

"*A* runner?" Gerrund said, gleaning the gist of the catch faster than I'd intended.

I nodded, ignoring his tone for the sake of my update – my second mistake.

"We spent most of the night strategising and looking at how to regain the upper hand, considering what the insider knows and our understanding of the Kronik's forces."

"Let me get this straight; you discussed secret battle tactics regarding the coup with a man none of us have ever met?" Gerrund demanded.

I never wanted to be neck deep in this aspect of the Cause. Battle did not wet my pallet as it did many CTF graduates, but that didn't mean I hadn't learned my lessons well.

"For Trinity's sake, Gerrund, no. I did exactly what I told you I was going to do. I met with my *trusted* CTF liaison and worked out a way for the Cause to complete its mission. If I came back empty handed with only a small number of confirmed soldiers for aid, we'd be arguing various plans of attack until we missed our window of opportunity."

That was my third mistake – saying *we*.

He grabbed me by the throat and pushed me back against the railing.

Self-preservation kicked in. I felt the anger flash in my eyes as I grabbed his wrist and–

"J.J. No!" Mardel yelled.

I didn't snap his wrist, but I did kick him in the shins.

Mardel and Ticia worked at prying Gerrund's hand off my neck.

I gasped. My larynx strained to open as I fought to get air to my lungs. Bright spots flashed in my head for the second time in less than thirty hours. I should've broken his wrist anyway. To meeka if he couldn't fight. I'd put my ass on the line for the Cause.

Mardel wrenched Gerrund back. Ticia caught me before I fell. I shook her off me with a feral snarl. Air filled my lungs, searing my throat on the way down. I held onto to the railing with one hand, my head with the other and coughed.

"Stand down, Gerrund." Mardel pushed his superior back to the other side of the table, keeping his and Gerrund's eyes locked and off me. Ticia tried to help me down from the platform to leave.

"No, Ticia. I'll be finishing this briefing."

"You're just asking for more trouble," she said.

And that was when I walked headlong into my fourth mistake. At the table I massaged my throat. Ticia stayed by my side; Mardel stayed by Gerrund.

"The plan we devised is this: instead of a single assault from below, we split the forces. The Kronik won't be able to have all of their soldiers down in the tunnels – they *will* have reinforcements above when we break through. The original distraction you had planned actually becomes the main body of the force. We overload their check points and guard stations from key Junctions surrounding the Compound *and* we send our guys out in two waves top-side."

"Why two?" Mardel asked.

"We don't want to reveal all our resources at once, nor do we want a back-log of troops standing around not doing anything except acting as targets for any possible snipers – especially around the Compound wall by the main gates. When the first wave tires, the second wave goes in fresh to fight those über-trained soldiers the informant warned us about. We beat them down with our numbers going in, falling back and exchanging fighters between the two waves as many times as necessary to overpower them and breach the wall."

"And in the tunnels?" Ticia asked.

"I train the best of the best, your top fifty troops, for close-quarter combat with CTF counter techniques. It's important for them to be able to anticipate what the enemy will do, has been trained to do, so that they can keep the upper hand. There's a particular narrowing of the tunnel just before it reaches the cistern. If we can bottle-neck their guys in that space, and only let a few through at a time, we can pick them off easier."

"But," Gerrund said.

I sighed. "But Tek won't commit himself and his connections to someone *he's* never met. His terms are to have me continue as liaison and to lead the head group in the tunnels to the designated meeting chamber." Surprisingly, no one said anything – which was worse than I expected.

"If he only has the ten soldiers, all ten will meet with us in the tunnels. If he gets more troops, the extra will be included in the first wave surface attacks to meet with each leader at the various Junction

Points. That way, it'll be like having a secret weapon in each pack who can not only fight, but better assess opponents of similar skill and help with battle strategy."

The silent explosions assaulting Gerrund's brain showed only in the discolouration of his face and the flicker of his eyelids. He held his jaw tight and the table even tighter.

"Look," I said. "I know it's not ideal. I never asked to be a part of the fight. This isn't my war, it's yours. However, you've got the power troops you wanted, you've got the element of surprise back even as you call the Kronik's bluff, and you get to keep your timeline with only slight modifications to the original plan. We did what we could to blend the best of everything and *help*."

"And the best of everything always seems to come right back to you," Gerrund said with a tight jaw. Again, he didn't believe me. He didn't want to admit that he was the reason we were in this position. If he hadn't been so eager to find a Kronik insider, if he'd done a thorough background check – heck if he'd just spoken with his moles on the team who saved me, a double-agent wouldn't have walked off with all our secrets.

His need to correct the mistakes of the Resistance had taken precedence over the safety of his people. The closer we came to fighting this battle, the more single-minded he became; and as always, it was left to me to point out the obvious…

Gerrund hadn't stopped grinding those teeth or ripping my atoms to shreds since that morning, and that scared me. His silent seething only echoed my earlier concern that he wasn't the same man who rescued me… I knew Tek and I had effectively hi-jacked Gerrund's war, but couldn't he see that discovering the informant was better than leading the recruits to slaughter? It had taken him two days to realise that dealing with the Guides *my* way was more sound than having a group of over-enthusiastic innocents go traipsing around the Deserts in large groups. I could only hope that two days would be enough for him to see sense this time.

"All right!" I shouted to my pack. "Gear up and line up. It's time to go." The men and women of my elite class learned fast and trained hard, but now I needed them in the battle environment fighting the enemy – me.

A rumble and roar of voices echoed down the tunnel adjoining the training grounds to the main cavern. Even Gerrund turned to watch as two men were carried in on a wave of hands and shoulders up to the platform. I was going to keep my distance, let Gerrund be the big boss man, but then I saw Laiviis and who he had with him.

Merik.

I gave the signal for the troops to stay in formation, not that they could've gone out the tunnel without causing a war in the first place. Turning, I ran over to the platform but stayed well-back from Gerrund. Laiviis and Merik were set on their feet and they walked up to the man in charge.

Merik got the head-to-toe from the leader of the Underground. The poet bowed his head respectfully then turned and gave me a huge smile. Gerrund's back stiffened. My being here was only going to cause problems. It was time to leave. I'd have to catch up with the men later.

As I backed down the rear of the platform, Merik's face fell in concern. I shook my head and tapped the digital watch on my wrist before circling my finger around the band. He understood and nodded, returning his full attention to Gerrund.

I changed my orders for the pack to stand single-file and then led them out past the crowd gathered to hear the homecoming speech.

My ears rang from the shots fired during our last exercise in the tunnels. We hadn't gone anywhere near the battle zone, but I had taken my troops to a good place to learn the realities of close-quarter fighting. The object had been to show them how to prevent a blood bath and fight with their guns as an extension of their bodies in tight spaces.

The nurse at the clinic sanitised the various scrapes I'd received on the left side of my face while I held an ice pack to my already sore right cheek bone. One officer truly got the better of me during the one-to-one fight as the enemy and clobbered me with the butt of his gun. I'd congratulated him of course, but that didn't make it hurt any less.

The soldiers were being given tomorrow off to visit with friends and family – to try to de-stress a little before zero hour the following morning. I didn't agree with it, but then I was CTF trained and these were volunteers putting their lives on the line for something they believed in. Mardel had emphasised that the need to protect their loved ones would be even greater after a positive reminder of what they were fighting for. I had to go top-side anyway tomorrow for my final meet with Tek to discuss numbers and access points.

"Are you still wearing your brace?" the nurse asked. I nodded. With everything that had been going on in the past few days, I couldn't afford to go lame. "Here's a couple extra-strength pain meds. They'll help you sleep tonight."

"No, thanks. I'll be fine."

"Take them. You'd be surprised just how much your body can complain when you finally allow yourself to stop moving." I nodded, pocketed the small vial, thanked her, and left the clinic portion of the hospital.

I thought of tomorrow's rendezvous with Tek and wondered if I'd have time to stop by the restaurant... I hadn't seen or spoken to Dez since the Consolidating Meeting. There were still things that needed to be said– but... no. I'd left a note last time I was top-side. I could only imagine he'd found it by now, as long as he hadn't recycled it first. He'd be busy elsewhere today just as he had been then. I'd just be a distraction. Now was not the time for reconciliation – it was time for war.

"Dalla!" Gelden called as I approached my apartment building. He jogged over to meet me.

I waved, but there was no lustre or gusto – my muscles were already stiffening and ached like nobody's business. When he got closer, he swore.

"What in Zola's name have you done to yourself?" He took my face in his strong, yet gentle hands and ran his thumbs over the bridge of my nose and along my cheek bones – one even brushed my bottom lip.

My stomached flipped and my head spun. I was in no condition to ward off his charm… his kindness. And yet, whenever I needed some*one* he was always there.

I took his hands from my face and held them loosely between us.

"I'm fine. I was *the enemy* today with my troops. A few of them got the better of me." And then there was the Fight Club, but he didn't need to know about that. I shook my head before I realised what I was doing.

"What's wrong?"

"Nothing. Why are you here?"

"Your friend Merik is looking for you. I said I'd get word to you. He's staying at the barracks until he can be assigned a place. Come on." He tugged me forward, but I held back.

"No. Not tonight. Maybe tomorrow before I head out to a meeting."

"Oh, of course. You're exhausted," he said and walked me over to the door of my building. While it was true I was tired, I knew that wasn't the real reason for my hesitation. The look in Merik's eyes earlier today spoke of despair and grief, even if he had smiled at me. Whatever he needed to tell me I didn't need to know right now – I didn't want to know right now.

I turned and reached into my pocket for my key-card. My fingers slipped from Gelden's grasp as his hand suddenly slid up my arm. I turned back and into his embrace.

"The suspense is killing me," he whispered. "I might never see you again. I have to know…" He gently angled my chin up, caressing my lips with a kiss, sharing half a breath between us before pulling me closer. Our mouths collided and our tongues danced as I gave myself over to him – for just a moment.

We parted.

I rested my forehead on his shoulder, still clinging to his sturdy frame. He bent his cheek to the top of my head and we stood there just holding one another for several heartbeats.

I don't know what it was with the men in my life: Tek had missed an early opportunity, Dez had kept me in the dark, Gel was too late... and I knew he felt it, too.

The spark wasn't there, but neither was Dez and that's what hurt the most.

Chapter Forty-two
Uprising

Taya

I hit the off button on the alarm before it sounded, and collapsed back down. The sheets crinkled with papers read and reread a thousand times, up until three hours ago. But even then, sleep only toyed with me: pulling at my aching limbs, hiding behind a throbbing headache, and leaving me in a haze between two worlds – unconscious bliss and a reality where my battered body fared better than my shattered heart.

For the first time in my life, I didn't get out of bed on time.

I knew very well what day it was, what job was mine in the grand scheme of changing the world, but at that moment I couldn't care less. I fingered the edge of one of Dez's letters. Yet, even as the words flitted through my mind, Gelden's kiss and the returned key-card decimated the hope and the longing etched into every page strewn about my bed.

Five days ago, I'd found the letters Gelden had left behind after taking everything the FOL had sent me. I'd been so mad and frustrated and confused I'd just shoved them off the counter to get them out of my sight.

He's been trying to reach me all this time and I was the one to blame – if I'd only searched through the FOL mail and not given up on him like I thought he had with me…

The pain in my chest flared as my heart constricted and my lungs refused to let me breathe. I picked up the one letter not written by him, but to him… the one I never mailed – and re-read it for the tenth time:

The watch you gave me works perfectly fine and yet I find myself losing track of time… I ask myself less and less these days why it is that you're not writing anymore, why it is that you don't seem to have time for us. Then I hear the voice of reason and it isn't my own, it's yours –

"This is bigger than all of us."

"Sacrifices have to be made."

"Just because I'm not there doesn't mean I'm not thinking about you."

But when those words have to be pulled from an eight-week-old memory where the sight of you giving up on me – on us – as your reaching hand falls and you let the general walk you farther and farther away from me, those words that once consoled and held a logic I thought I understood slip away from me.

Where are you?

Why haven't you written?

I need that sense of calm, of home you brought to me even before we knew what we meant to each other…

I've made a decision. I'm going to find that sense of peace again, even if it means doing something I shouldn't.

T

But finding my mother, my *real* mother hadn't solved anything – hadn't answered the questions still fighting each other in my brain…

Who can I trust? Who are my family? Why did you leave me? Do you still love me?

Only now, those questions have Dez in mind instead of Lynnia.

Tek wanted the woman I used to be; Gelden wanted the woman he thought I was; but I wanted neither of them in that way, and yet the man I loved thought I'd stopped writing to him, thought I'd blocked him out of my head, and thought I'd left him for another man... even as he wrote to me faithfully through it all.

I don't know how long I lay there. I suppose I could've looked at the alarm, but that would have required my eyes adjusting to see the numbers. My internal clock wasn't panicking, so neither was I.

I felt each letter and knew what was written on it just by the texture of the page, the rip of an edge, or the fold of a corner.

How am I supposed to go into battle knowing there's nothing for me at the end of it all?

At the nudge in my gut, I rolled over and clamoured from my bed. It didn't matter that his words fell to the floor or stuck to my pant legs. I stripped down and searched for something I could be buried in, should it come to that.

The walk over to the training cavern left me cold. I didn't bring my cloak because soldiers don't go into battle looking like a debutant. I also didn't bother layering up as everything said about the *heat* of battle was true... including the temperature.

I laughed without mirth.

Everything I knew about the heat of battle was from books and sparring exercises. Xannia wasn't at war, and yet we had a military and highly trained soldiers, courtesy of the CTF and whatever other hidden institutions the Kronik had developed. We were a peaceful nation at war with ourselves – just over twenty years ago we had the Nine Seas Massacre and who knows what opposing forces were at play before that to warrant such precautionary measures.

Regardless, the Kronik knew it would happen again.

At the training site, I did not join the others on the platform. I knew my job and would liaise as necessary to keep things on track. I stood off to one side with my hands in my pockets shivering. A cloak landed over my shoulders. I turned and looked into a pair of haunted eyes.

Merik. I'd half-heartedly intended to find him yesterday, but between meeting with Tek and last-minute preparations I'd allowed time to get away from me. I could read him like a book and I knew that whatever he had to tell me was nothing I wanted to hear.

I nodded my thanks.

He and I both knew he shouldn't be here, but I guessed that staying in the barracks made it difficult to get caught up on events.

He pointed at the finger-shaped bruises on my neck, the brownish-yellow bruising below my eyes and over the bridge of my nose.

"Are you all right?"

"Sure. Just the hazards of doing business."

"Is it true then?" he asked.

"That we're staging a coup? Going into battle? Starting another Massacre?" I held a shallow breath. "Yes."

"I never thought it possible – I mean, after the last attempt…"

"Would you have come back if you'd known?"

We watched as the various troop divisions organised themselves. My fifty were easy to spot. The other hundred and fifty blurred into one large force.

"Yes. You know me… a new story means new poetry. Speaking of stories, have you heard?"

"Probably not. I've been busy."

"Of course." He got quiet.

I look over at him again.

"Ray reactivated the alien Virus."

I swore under my breath.

"But Bazdin helped us develop a vaccine and a treatment – it was a miracle he came to us when he did."

Miracle or not, between the look on his face and the tone of his voice I knew there was more. The part I didn't want to hear.

"Who?" I asked.

"Who what?"

"Who died? Ray?"

"No. His immune system was strong enough to hold out until the treatment was ready."

"So, who then?"

"Zaith."

My body flashed hot then cold, back and forth, but my cheeks burned steady. I sloughed off Merik's cloak and tossed it to him as I left to join my pack.

The woman who'd been my life mentor, my best friend, and ultimately my intended killer was dead. Emotional scars tore open with every step, even as I mentally struggled to sew them back up… bury them along with every other hurt this world had given me. But the wounds festered.

Eking my head up through the rough hole at Piller's Park, I flashed the code on the electric torch as I clung to a makeshift ladder. The black of twilight dominated the sky as the light pollution from the city extinguished the stars.

A return code drew closer until Tek crawled into view with his team. The extra fifteen soldiers he'd confirmed with me yesterday were already dispersed to meet up with Underground Forces at the pre-arranged Junction Points.

"What's wrong, Taya? Are we compromised?" He sent the signal to halt even as he tracked the beam over my face.

My ears were an extension of the fire trapped within me. "No. Bring them," I said, and then slid down the sides of the rope ladder, bypassing the loose rungs. Mardel stepped away from the bottom, then resumed his support position once I was out of the way.

Four women and six men, not including Tek, slid down after me. I could see the apprehension stitched across Mardel's face – those were CTF soldiers – *friendly enemies*. I knew a few of them from my time at the Facility, but most were older than Tek and likely recommended by other operatives. Even I didn't know where their true loyalties lay.

I introduced Tek to Mardel, then we did a formal rollcall for the new soldiers. It was highly unlikely any one of them would mistake a UG Forceman with a Kronik Soldier, but it might happen the other way around and that wouldn't be good. In addition to their name and rank I asked that each soldier on Tek's team reveal something personal about themselves. I'd learned during my time down here that something sentimental was more likely to be remembered than a mere statistic.

"Fren, CTF contracted Justice – five years, favourite flower the Golden Hunter."

"Grinder, CTF trained Finder – twenty years, pet dog named Spitball."

"Rillix, CTF contracted Justice – three years, everyone's nightmare of a best friend."

I stopped listening after that. The way he joked made me want to punch him. I gave myself a mental slap. Merik's news had done more than wake me up this morning – it had given me an anger I could cloak the sorrow with.

After the introductions, we marched on to the ensnarement site. The bulk of our troops fit easily into the expansive cavern that lay just before the narrow tunnel into the cistern. Mardel would lead five of our guys, and five of Tek's through to breach the Compound, then act as a lure and draw the Kronik's forces back through the narrow tunnel. It was important for the UGF to be seen top-side and not the CTF soldiers – this had to be a surprise to work.

Just as Alpha split the divide between night and dawn, the rebels breached the Compound.

A spray of bullets hit the wall by my head. I ducked. The shots fired from the tunnel *behind* us. The entire rear flank dropped like dolls in the eerie glow of the light-tubes surrounding the cavern.

"Incoming!" I yelled, with soldier after soldier taking up the cry. Tek and one of his crew chucked flash grenades down the now-clogged exit tunnel, as a path opened wide before its mouth. The eight casualties were dragged to the outer edge of the chamber as the Cause fought on two fronts, now caught in the middle.

Tek and the other soldiers brought the fight into the open space of the cavern, letting in only twenty or so Kronik Forces. A small contingent of UGF blocked the opening as the role of firearm changed to club.

My goal had been to stay quiet and out of the way – let Tek and Mardel handle the operation. I was just a liaison after all, and still fighting fatigue as well as muscle exhaustion. However, inaction was no longer an option.

Knowing I'd be useless fighting one-on-one, I tag-teamed and kept mobile. Moving in concentric circles through the chamber, I struck out at the Kronik Forces while they fought against Underground Forcemen. Connecting with legs, necks and lower backbones to induce temporary paralysis, I gave the UGF the upper hand as I wove through the carnage.

Smoke bombs landed in the main chamber, cutting off the soldiers' sight. But not mine. I coughed in the thick air. The KF breached our back door a second time.

The remaining twelve fighters wore infrared detectors. They were little more than shadows with my Talian gift, but I was the only UGF un-afflicted – we had no contingency plan for this. The light-tubes gave off a useless glow. Man after man went down; they cut our remaining forces in half.

I had to get rid of the smoke.

But how?

I looked at my moist surroundings still glinting through the haze. A part of my brain extracted a container experiment from one of Gellik's science classes.

I knew what to do.

I grabbed one of the spent smoke bomb canisters. Whipping out my knife, I deked behind a series of columns along one edge of the chamber wall and pried the device open.

Cries of surprise and anguished yells ripped at my oversensitive hearing. Using the light from my digital watch, I found a deep blue vein in the rock wall. Dropping down to diminish my size, and maybe even look like a crumpled body, I chipped away at the silicate to reveal its more densely packed interior. As I scraped powdered fragments into the base of the ball-like canister, small sparks lit like lightning bugs when the knife connected. *Not good.*

In the five desperate minutes it took to gather enough powder, the sounds of fighting lessened. Logic told me Tek and his men were all that remained of our troops. Under these conditions, the recruits were grossly disadvantaged.

I forced the capsule back together.

A hand grabbed my braid, hauling me up. I smashed into the columns behind me smacking my head. That same hand gripped my tender throat, suspending me off the ground. I forced my eyes to focus.

Him.

My brain screamed, slamming metal doors and smashing clocks that ticked out of time. My body went on auto-pilot. I slashed at his arm with my open blade. He dropped me. Sucking in stagnant and spent air, I gripped the metal canister in my fist and punched him in the face. He countered, walloping me in the stomach. I lurched, doubled over, smashing him in the gut with my shoulder, and then pulling up and slamming his head into my knee.

I had the blade in my hand.

My blood demanded retribution.

Anger writhed under my skin, forcing me to fight this man to his death – logic screamed, *he's just a distraction!*

I couldn't let that happen.

Diving between his legs I sliced the tendons at the back of each calf dropping my blade and stealing his Whipstaff before he collapsed. I smashed my bad knee, and bit my lip through to stop the scream from giving away my position.

Spitting out blood, I tumbled into the fray. A boot kicked my head. I scrambled over a dead body. Someone stepped on my side. Another body fell on top of me. A spiked boot sliced my forearm.

I screamed.

It echoed throughout the cavern and yet, out of nowhere Mardel cleared the attackers from around me. I spat blood again and at least one tooth. Crawling into the middle of the chamber, I hobbled from my knees up to my feet. I re-set the charge sequence for a two-second dispersal, pre-impact. I did this with my eyes closed – channelling my spatial memory training.

In Mardel's absence, Tek drew up with me back to back.

"We're out numbered. We need to level the playing field," he rasped.

"Here." I placed the grenade in his hand. My arms were jelly and I couldn't see straight. "Throw it at the ceiling as hard as you can."

"That's a long way up."

"Do it!"

He leaned into me and launched the bomb. I fell to my knees, using gravity's momentum to help raise my arms above my head. I heard the capsule explode. I fired a high-yield electrified ion wave into the cloud of silicate powder.

"Jump!" I yelled.

He jumped.

The metallic particles in the silicate fractured the burst, electrifying everything. The charge bounced back using me as a grounding rod. I dropped to the floor.

It began to rain.

I felt Tek's hesitation to leave me, but the moist air cleared the smoke and he did what he should – struck down the enemy.

I closed my eyes.

I heard and felt what remained of Tek's team, the UGF, and even the KF bring the last dredges of the fight toward the cistern. I knew my guys would pacify those who remained and then go topside to join the external forces in the takeover.

We still have a chance.

My head throbbed, my body ached, and my breathing rasped shallow – but I was alive. I lay there for what felt like an eternity.

My thoughts couldn't latch on to anything concrete, but I refused to allow myself the luxury of going unconscious. Not until I knew for sure…

I heard a sliding, an almost grinding sound. It wasn't footsteps but it was movement.

Movement… survivors?

Someone needed my help, might be bleeding out…

I rolled onto my back and used my stomach muscles to lift me instead of my arms, which remained wrapped around my abdomen. Footsteps echoed from down the cistern tunnel. I had to get to the survivor. It might be the enemy coming. I looked over toward the scrabbling sound.

It was *Him.*

He stood there on his knees, flayed calves leaking blood behind him. He raised his Clinex at me.

He shot.

"Taya!" Tek yelled from the tunnel.

The high-yield plasma blast slammed into my chest just as *His* head exploded.

Chapter Forty-three
The Spoken Truth

Tek

She collided with the ground, spasming in short bursts. Swinging my gun across my back, I ran over fallen bodies, comrades and enemy alike, to reach her. I pulled her tongue from her mouth to make sure she didn't swallow it.

The shaking stopped.

Sliding her close over the rain dampened ground, I scooped her up in my arms and positioned her over my shoulder. I'd lost nearly half my team down here, but I wasn't going to lose *her*.

I couldn't back-track down the safer tunnels to the extraction point, Taya needed medical attention now – and not just the hack stuff they gave us for emergency training. The fastest route lay on the surface.

Crouching low in the smaller adjoining tunnel, the metallic stench of blood rose from piles of dead soldiers – mostly theirs. At the breach, I laid her down and crawled through to the cistern, then turned and dragged her in after me. Her eyelids twitched. I couldn't be sure that meant she was alive or the plasma charge hadn't fully dissipated yet.

"Why do you do this?" I said to her, lifting her into my arms again and angling my body to raise her up through the grates surrounding the fountain above. I pushed her limp body through the opening, then scrambled up.

Dead bodies littered the once pristine park as the Alpha sun rose ever higher to awaken the day. I said a silent prayer to the Gods, and forced myself to move away from the remnants of the top-side battle.

The streets were nearly silent here. It was early enough that none of the citizens would be out, and late enough that the battle had shifted to the interior of the Capital Building. The Kronik and the Council would pose no problem for our remaining troops.

My head kept throwing the rules of engagement at me; my instructors' voices drilling protocol and demanding that I leave her, like I'd left the other fallen, and join the survivors – finish what I started.

But that was impossible.

Taya was impossible to live with, and to live without. It didn't help that she was the only friend I had who really knew me… I was being selfish, but on the other hand, other, more than capable men, knew perfectly well what they were doing in this battle-turned-siege. And so did I.

Except that I didn't. I'd never been inside the Compound before. All I knew was the main gate was down-hill, and relatively close to the Capital Building. Gunfire ricocheted off concrete somewhere to my left. Bodies lying in the street became a maze of dead flesh – some not so dead, but not as important as the woman I carried.

Houses were distant. The buildings in this neighbourhood were vacant, mercantile and unhelpful. Street signs meant nothing to me as I scanned their words. Instead I listened for Taya's breath… shallow as it was. As long as I heard it I could keep moving, keep hoping. I turned down another road, and there it was.

The main gate to the Compound, made of heavy wrought iron and steel, was flanked by ten UGF. Behind me, Alpha's light stabbed them in the eyes. Ten guns raised at the sound of my tramping run.

"Halt!" one called.

I slowed, but didn't stop. We hadn't arranged for this kind of contingency.

Bullets ricocheted off the street in front of me.

I swore, then yelled, "Hey! I need to get her to the hospital."

"Don't move. Who are you? Who's she?"

"I'm on your side. She's..." *Taya* was on the tip of my tongue but that wasn't right – another name, the one from the Club came out instead. "Aelonia Trellice."

Eight guns lowered. One each to the far left and right remained trained on us.

"Turn around. Show us." The same voice spoke.

I turned around, but it wasn't her head they raised, it was her hands...

"It's her! Emvaso-al!"

"Zimi!" two others cried.

Suddenly hands turned me around. Voices urged me on.

"Hurry," the main guy yelled. "Don't let her die."

A cross between joy and fear speared my heart – they knew her all right, and she meant just as much, if not more, to them.

I raced to the nearest residence beyond the barrier of the Compound and hotwired a high-end hover rider. There was no time left.

*   *   *

Dezmind

The heavily perfumed scent of disinfectant hung in the air like a warning. It was well after twilight. I knew I shouldn't be here, but I had to see her. Ten days they'd told me – she'd been in a plasma induced coma for nearly two weeks with no sign of breaking free.

My footsteps echoed down the dimly lit hall as the night nurses bowed their heads when I passed. Everyone knew who I was now. Even then, it hadn't taken much to slip past the guards at the Capital Building and skirt around Gerrund's blockade at the main gate. But they didn't know the Compound the same way I did. I suppose it was just as likely that any of the Kronik's forces still unaccounted for could escape the same way.

I'll have to advise Gerrund of that. It just means this'll be my only chance to visit her.

A man sat slumped in a chair outside the last doorway on the left – a blond man with broad shoulders. The image of Taya sleeping peacefully next to him made me stop.

Maybe I shouldn't have come.

But the desperation of her telepathic fingerprint two weeks ago at the Consolidating Meeting, and the note she'd left me five days before the coup, told me things weren't so black and white. I stepped around the man's legs and turned into the room.

The faint beep of the heart monitor sounded louder than it really was in the silence of the room... of the entire hospital for that matter. But that wasn't the first thing I noticed; a large man with dark green skin and gold coliths sat straight up with his arms crossed in the far corner of the room. His knees were at perfect ninety-degree angles, directly above a pair of CTF issued combat boots.

I choked back a yell.

That's when I noticed his eyes were closed and he wore the amber armband of the UGF.

Must be Tek – Taya's surface contact.

Still, even asleep he appeared to be protecting her. I shook my head. I don't know why it had never occurred to me that there might be other men in her life... she was always so independent. Tek's breathing came deep and even. My sudden appearance hadn't alerted him – the man was likely exhausted from working all day, only to watch over Taya at night... *Taya.*

I finally allowed myself to turn and look at her. Fear, anger, and anguish ripped a chasm in my chest as the beat of my heart exploded in my ears at the sight of her. Her eyes appeared sunken from the dark circles – a combination of bruising and fatigue. A thick strip of medical tape spanned the bridge of her nose; her forehead and cheek lacerations remained red around the stitching, but the worst was the cut below her lower lip that broke the tender contour of her mouth. Dark sutures and residual swelling gave it an angry, accusatory look.

My body trembled. I fell to my knees by her bedside, pulling at my hair with both hands. A shockwave of emotion rippled out from my core. I looked up. Her eyelids shuddered. I reached out to touch her face, her forehead, but left my hand hovering over the uneven pink layer of her painted disguise. This close, I could see the patches of pale, bronzed skin around her hairline, and glimpsed a fraction of the woman I'd fallen in love with.

I drew my arm away and instead rested my cheek on the palm of her open hand lying on the sheets covering her, almost as high as those of a death pyre. The feel of her scarred skin burned hot against my face as tears squeezed free from the corner of my eye, and onto her lifeless palm.

I don't know how long I stayed that way, except that light peaked under the blinds of her window.

A nurse came in and whispered, "Oh."

I stood as she turned to leave and gave her a sad smile. She slipped around the corner into the hall again. I heard her footsteps stop next to the door.

My time was up. Removing a nondescript envelope from my shirt pocket, I tucked it under the hand lying across Taya's stomach, then turned and left.

*   *   *

Taya

As I stood at the nurses' station resting the bulk of my battered body on my good leg, I clutched a stylus in one hand and the only thing of importance from my stay at the hospital in the other – a simple envelope.

"Please, Miss Taya, I urge you to reconsider," The petite Balanis girl said as she waved a doctor over, who walked with another patient farther down the hall.

"No," I said, and signed myself out on my own recognisance and left the building. Being stuck in a coma for ten days was not my idea of survival. Maybe it was the alien DNA, or just my stubborn nature, but I happened to be one of those patients who got snippets of everything going on around me in a weird, waking dream-like state.

The beep of the heart monitor had annoyed me most, luckily it never triggered a nightmare. My brain never felt connected to my body, unless they were injecting something into my IV, but that wasn't the most disturbing thing; Tek never mentioned it, but I know he, Gelden and Merik were my only visitors save one – one time, late at night and well after hours.

None of my protectors were around today to give me a ride to the Rally – mainly because I'd promised them I'd stay put while they attended the biggest event since the Nine Seas Massacre.

And that's exactly where *I* intended to be.

I had no credit of any kind on me, since I hadn't brought any to the gun-show the day of the coup. As it was, my bloodied combat gear was gone, and in its place I found an outfit Gelden was fond of seeing me in. Luckily, the sleeveless cream-coloured blouse and tan pants were suitable attire for such a momentous occasion. Still, even though I couldn't pay for a ride, I hailed a public car just outside the hospital.

I leaned my forearms on the open window frame of the passenger's side of the hover-rider, and clasped my hands together.

"Where you headed?" the driver asked.

"The Rally."

"I'll get'cha as close as I can, but you'll still have to walk a ways. Hop in."

"I won't be able to pay you," I said, and then opened my hands to reveal my palms. "Will that be a problem?" It was a long shot, but there was a chance that he'd read my article in the Inquisitor, or heard about me through word of mouth, since Merik told me of my newly earned 'war hero' status.

His eyes widened. He looked from me to the hospital and back again, then nodded vigorously. I got in the rider.

The walk to the main stage, just inside the gates of the Compound, took nearly half an hour. Making my way through the packed bodies brought back memories of my frantic dash to warn Dez at that fateful Rally all those months ago. It felt like a lifetime. This time I wasn't here to warn him of impending danger, I was here to celebrate this victory with him.

By the time I limped up the back portion of the outdoor stage to the cloth wings, I was just hoping to catch him before he addressed the crowd.

No one stopped me; somehow they all knew who I was, even without looking at my hands. Still, I wasn't fast enough.

The masses swarming by the Compound gate, in front of the makeshift stage, roared to life as Dezmind walked out. I looked around to see if Gerrund was here for this momentous occasion, but I didn't see him. Then again, he still had an entire society of fugitives to oversee, and a hoard of faithful Kronik Agents to keep pacified.

The only reason I came, that I stood back stage in the wings four days before my official release, was the letter I'd clutched in my hands the morning I woke up – the one currently folded and resting in my back pocket. It held no apologies or accusations; it held no sentimental pleadings or empty phrases; what it did hold was a promise and hope.

The doctors tried to keep me for another nine days after waking, but today, day five of being alive again, was Dezmind's Inaugural Address as Kronik. While it was true the doctors told me I suffered some brain damage, I hadn't noticed anything not working right, except for my leg. I was told *that* should heal in time, but for now I walked with a limp in public, and with a cane in private. I knew I would feel the same today as I would four days from now, so why wait?

I opened my mind and, keeping up my end of the deal, brushed Dezmind's consciousness with my own. I felt him smile, at *me* not them.

You made it, he said in my mind, as his body waved to the cheering people standing both inside and outside the wall.

Wouldn't have missed it for the world, I thought back.

Glancing over his shoulder, he instinctively found me. For that brief nano-second, everything we meant to each other passed in that simple look. He smiled brighter than I'd ever seen as a jolt of lightning zapped my heart.

Clearly, I wasn't here in any kind of official capacity, but the importance of my being here today, and that brief look, told me we were still connected. Something had happened to us out in the Deserts, something I don't think I could ever explain, but the person Tek, Merik and even Gelden knew, was not the same woman who stood here today.

"Welcome, everyone," Dezmind said to the crowd, his voice reaching beyond this street to the next and the next, rebounding off the various news vehicles surrounding the court, taking in this momentous event. The signage for Network News Now drew my eye like a bad accident – I wanted to look away, but I couldn't. That was one wound still too fresh to touch.

Dez's voice brought me back.

"Today I'm here to make you a promise. The sacrifices made by all citizens, whether fourteen days ago, twenty-two years ago, or this morning will not be forgotten. We are family, brothers and sisters too long separated by secrets, lies, and hidden agendas. Today, more so than two weeks ago, marks the beginning of a solidarity only made stronger through hope, patience, and understanding. We are healing deep wounds and that will take time."

And that's when I knew I was exactly where I was meant to be. Maybe it was fate or destiny marking the path for me, or maybe it was just a girl making the only choices she could in the world she'd been given.

This all might have started with Dez searching for his Soul Mate, but I think the Followers of Light had it right all along... *Perhaps I am the Child of the Zerameteth* – its creators were a part of my blood, and yet so were the people of Xannia; and like our anomalous sun, I was a product of my creators, a balanced Xannian of common and Talian blood; a *guardian* and not a body*guard*. Dez brought the people hope, but my path has always been to make sure the innocent were kept safe – we'd need each other's strengths in order to heal this nation.

A small commotion behind me reached my ears. I knew it was being handled by Dez's security, but the woman's voice made me turn.

"You don't understand; I was invited. Here, scan my credentials and you'll see." Her long dark hair covered her face as she reached for the card in her belt-pack. Her pale, pearl-white skin gave off a healthier glow than it had the last time I saw her.

She glanced up.

Our eyes connected.

I knew she knew me.

It didn't matter that the dark roots of my hair showed, or that patches of bronze broke through the palest of fake pink skin, and my natural red coliths fought for dominance over the inked purple making me a visual anomaly...

My mother shoved the card into one guard's hands, and pushed away from the other. I scrambled down the steps just as she climbed them. We connected, all arms and feet, falling on our asses laughing and crying.

"Oh, my sweet child," she whispered into the hair above my ear. I hugged her tighter. Nothing I could've said would have changed the past. Yet, in that simple embrace I felt her sorrow and forgave her and my father... Something I hadn't realised was within me to do.

As I looked over her shoulder, at the guard holding her credentials, I knew, without a doubt, that Dez had done this – had seen to her release at some point in the last fourteen days along with trying to bring a sense of organisation to the chaos of a new government, a new Kronik, and a new era.

"I ask now for a moment of silence for all those lost on both sides. Without their sacrifices, today wouldn't have been possible, and tomorrow wouldn't hold the hope of a reunited nation."

And all those present: Commoner, Talian, CTF Contractor, and average person alike paid their respects for the dead – the first act of a nation uniting.

If you enjoyed reading *Cadence of Consequences*, please consider leaving a review at your favourite online resource.

About the Author

Growing up in Ontario, Canada, M.J. was the only child of a single mom. M.J.'s passion for the arts ignited at a young age as she wrote adventure stories and read them aloud to close family and friends. The dramatic arts became a focus in high school as an aid to understanding character motivation in her writing. Majoring in Theatre Production at York University, with a minor in English, she went on to teach in both the elementary and high school divisions.

M.J. currently lives with her husband and young son. She keeps busy these days with her emerging authors' website Infinite Pathways, attending book fairs, and conferences as well as holding writing workshops and helping run the WCYR – Writers' Community of York Region.

Connect with M.J. online:

Author Website – www.mjmoores.com
Facebook – www.facebook.com/AuthorMJMoores
Twitter – www.twitter.com/AuthorMJMoores

www.ingramcontent.com/pod-product-compliance
Lightning Source LLC
Chambersburg PA
CBHW050026030726
47506CB00001B/138